TEMPTED BY HER FAKE FIANCÉ

KATE HARDY

UNBUTTONING THE TUSCAN TYCOON

MICHELLE DOUGLAS

MILLS & BOON

First published in Great Britain 2023
by Mills & Boon, an imprint of HarperCollins*Publishers* Ltd,
1 London Bridge Street, London, SE1 9GF

www.harpercollins.co.uk

HarperCollins*Publishers*
Macken House, 39/40 Mayor Street Upper,
Dublin 1, D01 C9W8, Ireland

Tempted by Her Fake Fiancé © 2023 Pamela Brooks

Unbuttoning the Tuscan Tycoon © 2023 Michelle Douglas

ISBN: 978-0-263-30638-5

02/23

This book is produced from independently certified FSC™ paper
to ensure responsible forest management.
For more information visit: www.harpercollins.co.uk/green.

Printed and Bound in Spain using 100% Renewable Electricity
at CPI Black Print, Barcelona

TEMPTED BY HER FAKE FIANCÉ

KATE HARDY

MILLS & BOON

To my family, friends, readers and editors
who've been with me on the journey to my 100th M&B.

Thank you. I couldn't have done it without you! Xx

CHAPTER ONE

'ELLE, YOU'RE GOOD with shoestring budgets,' Rav said. 'I've got a project I want you to handle.'

Even though Elle had a ridiculous workload at the moment—because she'd been pushing herself harder ever since the head of the agency had announced a restructure that would mean a new senior account manager, a job she really wanted—she smiled at her boss. 'Sure. Do we have a brief and a pitch meeting scheduled?'

'Not *quite*,' Rav said. 'The client's already seen your work and liked it. He happened to be in London this morning, so he wanted to meet you and talk over the brief for the marketing campaign himself.'

'That's fine.' If she worked through lunch—*again*—she'd be able to juggle her deadlines; Elle was pretty sure she could carve out enough time to get herself up to speed on the client's current marketing and his competitors before the meeting. 'What time's he coming in?'

Rav coughed. 'He's waiting in the meeting room, right now.'

Oh. So she wasn't even going to have time to check out the client's website, let alone come up with any ideas. 'Just as well I can think on my feet,' she said dryly.

'It's a skill we're looking for in the new senior account manager,' Rav said.

Her heart skipped a beat. Was her boss hinting…?

'Hugo's delighted with what you've been doing lately,' Rav said. Hugo, the head of the agency, was notoriously difficult to please. He could spot the most minor fault at a thousand paces, and his door-slamming abilities were legendary. 'We were talking about the restructure yesterday, and whether we should recruit internally or externally. We're both of the same mind. Get this campaign going viral, Elle,' Rav added, 'and the senior account manager job's yours.'

That wasn't a hint: it was explicit. All the hours she'd put in were finally going to pay off, provided she got the campaign to go viral; and Elle intended to pull out all the stops to make absolutely sure it did. 'Thank you, Rav,' she said quietly.

'I'll take you in to meet the client,' Rav said.

But no introductions were necessary.

The second Elle walked into the room, she recognised the man sitting at the table. Charlie Webb's stunning blue eyes were unmistakable: the colour, she thought, of the bluebells in the wood at the edge of her family farm. Despite the fact that he was wearing a business suit, he looked more like the presenter of a TV nature programme, with his dark hair brushed back from his forehead. The tan he'd got from working outside really suited him, and she'd just bet that the expensive material of his suit hid some serious muscles.

She damped down the little frisson of attraction that bubbled through her. Charlie Webb was completely off limits. Apart from the fact that he was her dad's business partner, when they'd last met she'd sobbed her heart out on Charlie's shoulder. Prom night, ten years ago, had possibly been the worst episode in her time at high school.

Not that it was relevant now. She'd moved on from the

unhappy, bullied teenager she'd been back then, reinventing herself as hotshot marketer Elle Newton. She fitted in with her colleagues, the way she'd never been able to fit in at school, and she knew she was good at what she did.

'Good morning, Charlie,' she said brightly.

'Hello, Ellie,' he said.

Of course he'd use her old name. Her parents did, too, though she didn't quite have the heart to correct them: because that would lead to too many questions she didn't want to answer. Instead, she gave him a polite smile. 'Actually, nowadays I go by Elle.'

'You two know each other?' Rav asked, looking surprised.

For a moment, adrenaline pumped through Elle's veins. How much was Charlie going to divulge? The last thing she wanted was her life in London colliding with her old, hated life in Norfolk.

'Yes. Ellie—Elle,' Charlie corrected himself, 'was in the same year at school as my little sister.'

Elle had to stop herself from physically sagging with relief, but inwardly she still felt like a half-set jelly. This was too close for comfort. She didn't want her boss to see the vulnerable girl she'd once been; she needed him to keep seeing her as she was now. Confident and capable. The woman who'd make a great senior account manager.

Rav looked delighted. 'As I don't need to introduce you, I'll leave you to it.'

Elle waited until Rav had closed the door behind him. 'Rav said you wanted us to work on a marketing campaign for you, because you've seen my work and liked it.' But why on earth would Bluebell Farm need a London marketing agency's help? Had Charlie got another job and left her parents in the lurch? She took a breath. Jumping to conclusions would be the quickest way to lose this brief—and her promotion. 'I assume,' she said, careful to sound neutral rather than judgmental, 'that you're leaving the farm and you're here for something to do with a new venture?'

'No,' he said. 'I'm here for Bluebell Farm.'

She sat down, frowning. 'Sorry, Charlie, but I don't quite understand.'

'I've managed the farm for the last two years,' Charlie said.

'I know.' And she still felt guilty about it. The job she knew her dad had always wanted her to do: take over Bluebell Farm and manage it until she was ready to hand it over to the next generation. A job she couldn't bear even to think about, much less actually do. She knew her dad had reached the age when the super-early mornings were getting a bit too much for him: the endless grind of milking twice a day, making sure there was clean water in the troughs, feeding the cows, checking the fences, keeping a check on the herd's health, mucking out in winter when the cows were sleeping in the barn overnight, worrying about the weather and how it would affect the grain crops…

She also knew that two years ago she should've offered to give up her life in London and go home: but she simply couldn't force the words out of her mouth. As a child, she'd loved the farm; as a teen, she'd grown to hate it. Her association with the farm had made her life at high school utterly miserable. The popular crowd had called her 'Smelly Ellie' from her first day at high school, claiming that she smelled of cows—even though she knew she didn't, because she'd always showered after milking and before she went to school, and she also used copious amounts of body spray to mask any lingering bovine residue. The bullies had gleefully homed in on her insecurity; it was made worse by the fact that 'new' in the local accent was pronounced 'noo', and it was an easy step from there to 'moo'.

Smelly Ellie Moo-ton. Hurgh, hurgh, hurgh. They'd been so pleased by their wit. *Got a face on her like sour milk, geddit?*

Even the ones who weren't part of the popular set had joined in, grateful that they weren't the ones on the receiving end of the constant teasing and sniping. It hadn't helped that Elle had been plump as a teenager, despite the physical work she did on the farm; if they weren't calling her *Moo-ton* it was *Heifer.*

She'd vowed not to set foot in the place any more often than she had to, once she'd escaped to London. At eighteen, she'd reinvented herself as Elle Newton, worked hard at university, made her mark with internships during the university holidays, and ended up with a glittering career in a high-profile industry. She loved London, she loved her job, and she loved her life here. And she'd been really relieved two years ago when her dad had suggested hiring Charlie—who'd just finished his MSc, after doing a project on the farm—as his new farm manager.

'Do Mum and Dad know you're here?' she asked.

'Of course. We've been talking about the marketing for the farm, and they agreed you were the obvious choice for the job.'

And that was the bit that really flummoxed her. 'Charlie, I really don't get it. Why does Bluebell Farm need a London marketing agency?'

'Because we're moving things forward.' He paused. 'As you'd have seen for yourself, if you ever came back to the farm.'

He'd hit the bullseye of her guilt. Not that she was going to let him know it. 'My life's in London, now, not West Byfield.' The back of beyond: a small market town in Norfolk where everyone knew everything about everyone else, mobile phone coverage was still spotty, broadband speeds meant you were two seconds behind everyone else on a video-call, and there were four buses a day to Norwich and none at all on Sundays. If she went back now, it'd be like being in the same glass box as her teen years, unable to join in and knowing that everyone was mocking her.

Absolutely no way.

Even though Charlie was being a bit judgemental right now—a far cry from the nice guy who'd rescued her, that horrible night—having a fight with him wasn't going to help this project. She'd worked hard for a promotion; this project was going to clinch it for her, and she had no intention of losing out. Which meant being her professional self and unruffling his feathers, rather than escalating the argument. She gave him her best professional smile and said, 'Tell me about the project.'

'We're rewilding the farm,' he said.

'Dad said you've switched from dairy farming to raising rare breeds.'

'There's no money in dairy farming,' Charlie said. 'It's at the point where it costs more to produce the milk than the customer pays for it. A developer offered to buy your dad out, last year, but he refused.'

That was something her dad hadn't mentioned to her, but Elle pushed down the sting of hurt. She could hardly complain about being shut out from anything farm-related when she'd been the one to walk away. 'Accepting an offer like that would've meant he could retire,' she said.

'What, and see a massive housing estate built on the land his family had farmed for generations?' Charlie asked, his tone deceptively mild.

If he could play the guilt card, so could she. 'It could've been affordable housing for local people,' she countered.

Charlie shook his head. 'That's not what those developers were about. And their plans were the complete opposite of what we're doing.'

'So there's money in rare breeds?'

'It's important,' he said.

In other words, there wasn't any money in rare breeds, either.

She knew Charlie had bought into the farm a few months ago; was his money financing the rewilding and keeping the farm afloat? she wondered. And what would happen to Bluebell Farm when his money ran out?

'Conservation saves species from extinction and preserves heritage,' he said.

'What sort of species?' she asked.

'We have a small herd of British White cows, a small flock of Norfolk Horn sheep, a flock of Norfolk Grey chickens and a couple of goats,' he said. 'We might be getting a Suffolk Punch and a donkey, in a couple of weeks.'

Donkeys definitely weren't rare breeds. 'Surely farming rare breeds is an expensive hobby rather than a money-making business,' she said.

'Not necessarily. This is where you come in,' he said. 'We want to raise the profile of the rare breeds and the rewilding project. The farm also needs to support itself a bit better, so we also need to raise awareness of what we offer.'

'Which is?'

'School visits, a farm café and shop, guided nature walks, a few relevant classes—we have an art teacher and a photography teacher, and a woman who runs spinning classes.'

For a mad moment, Elle had a vision of a barn full of exercise cycles, with an instructor at the front encouraging clients to pedal harder. But of *course* Charlie meant spinning as in wool, not spinning as in one of her usual gym classes. 'Right,' she said.

'We have holiday accommodation,' he said, 'and people can choose to help with the rewilding project and the animals, or just use it as a base for exploring the area.'

'You've converted some of the barns for the accommodation?' she asked.

'No. There are the two farm cottages—I live in the third—plus I bought three shepherd's huts. Purpose-built luxury boutique huts with a comfortable bed, a decent shower and a kitchen, and a private space for sitting out with a wood-fired hot tub. They're available for stays of two nights or more.'

No more large dairy herd. No more living in muddy wellies and sludge-coloured boiler suits. No more harvesting at all hours in the summer when the weather was right and the corn was ripe; Elle remembered taking dinner out to her dad in a box because he refused to come indoors until the light was too poor for him to work. It was how things had been for her entire life, and she couldn't quite get her head round the idea of the farm being so different, now.

'Got it,' she fibbed. 'So it's education and rewilding plus glamping and the shop and café, basically.'

'We're also planning to start hosting weddings; we've already got the licence, so we were thinking of holding the ceremony itself at one end of the largest barn, and the wedding breakfast and dancing at the other end.'

'Four different audiences, then. OK.'

Charlie looked at the woman who was sitting opposite him, taking notes. She wasn't the Ellie Newton he'd known ten years ago. The shy girl who kept herself to herself at school because the popular kids jeered at her; the teenager who'd sobbed on his shoulder when she'd literally run into him and he'd taken her to one side, thinking how easily it could've been his sister fleeing from the prom in tears. She'd even changed her name to Elle—sophisticated and glamorous, to match the way she looked. Though he couldn't think of her as anyone other than Ellie.

Right now, she looked like all the women in his old life: wearing a smart office dress, high heels, and with her long dark hair shot through with chestnut highlights. Her nails were perfectly manicured, her make-up flawless—and the bright red lipstick she wore made him very aware of the curve of her mouth. For a mad second, he found himself wondering what it would be like to feel that mouth against his own, sweet and teasing and utterly seductive...

But that wasn't going to happen.

Apart from the fact he wasn't in the market for any kind of relationship—it would still feel like a betrayal of Jess—this meeting was all about business.

Elle Newton had won awards for her work; he knew she'd do an excellent job at raising the farm's profile. Particularly because she'd have a personal stake in it, with Bluebell Farm being her family's business. Or, rather, since he'd bought into it six months ago, almost *half* her family's business.

'I only knew about this meeting about three minutes before I walked in the door,' she said, 'so unfortunately I haven't had time to look at the farm's website or look at what your competitors are doing, and that means I'm working blind. Usually clients book a meeting in advance, giving us a brief, so we can at least do some preliminary work.'

He noted the rebuke, even though it had been polite. 'I happened to be in London for the weekend—a former colleague's retirement do,' he said. 'And it occurred to me that I could drop in this morning and see if Hugo could squeeze me in. If it hadn't been possible, I would've sent in a brief and booked a meeting later.'

Her eyes narrowed. 'Hang on. You're on first-name terms with the head of the agency?'

'He used to play golf with my old boss. I've met him a few times at various functions,' Charlie said.

'So does he know that you work with my dad?'

Charlie didn't understand the momentary expression of wariness on her face, even though it was quickly hidden. 'I wasn't explicit about the connection. I said I'd seen your work and liked it, and I thought you'd be the right one to handle the project.'

'Right.' She was definitely in cool mode now, and Charlie didn't have a clue what he'd done or said to upset her.

'Let's start from the basics. Does Bluebell Farm actually have a website?' she asked.

'Yes.'

'And people can book the accommodation through it?'

'No. They phone us,' he said.

She made a note. 'What about the café and farm shop? Can people book a table through the website, or buy things online?'

'We don't do bookings and we don't have an online shop,' he said. 'We book the school visits in advance, but again they phone us to arrange it.'

'How about a blog? Or any kind of social media?'

'There isn't really any time to handle that,' he said.

'OK. So it sounds as if we're looking at a website re-vamp and a media plan,' she said. 'Social media, article placement, advertising—'

'We don't have a huge budget,' he cut in.

'I was hardly going to suggest a campaign with prime-time TV,' she said, rolling her eyes. 'Actually, now you've mentioned the budget: why didn't Mum and Dad ask me to do this for them in my spare time? They must know I would have done it for them for nothing rather than them having to pay London agency fees.'

He lifted one shoulder. 'Maybe they thought you'd be too busy.'

Her eyes narrowed. 'I'm never too busy for my parents.'

But she never came back to West Byfield. He'd noticed that, over the last two and a half years. Mike and Angie always visited their daughter in London rather than the other way round. They came back bubbling about what a lovely time they'd spent with her, the way she'd surprised them with a show or dinner out and made a huge fuss of them: but it was very obvious to him that Ellie Newton was avoiding Bluebell Farm. He knew that she'd been unhappy in West Byfield, as a teen, but surely she'd moved on from that misery over the last ten years?

'Besides, this isn't about your parents. This is part of my investment,' he said. 'I assume you know I have a forty per cent stake in the farm.'

'Dad mentioned it, yes.'

Was she angry, relieved, or worried about it? He didn't have a clue. She was all cool professionalism, betraying no trace of her feelings. That felt strange; he was used to being able to read people well. Elle Newton was an enigma. She intrigued him, and that made him antsy. He didn't want to feel that spark of interest in anyone.

'We were talking about what you expect from the agency,' she continued. 'Word-of-mouth customer referrals are the best kind, but you need to support that. You need people to know where you are and what you can offer them. That means sending press releases to targeted media about weddings, holidays and ecology; and making sure you have a solid website, so if customers leave a review on any of the tourist websites, then other potential customers can click on the link and take a look at what you're offering.'

'Which is where you come in.'

She nodded. 'I'll need to do a SWOT analysis and look at your USPs—that's jargon for looking at what you're good at and how to maximise it, what you need to improve, what your competition is doing and the differences between that and what you offer. Give me the rest of the day to have a look at where you are now and where you need to be, then maybe we can set up a video-call meeting tomorrow for me to grill you about the rest of it.'

'It's probably easier,' he said, knowing perfectly well that he was practically lobbing a grenade at her, 'if you come back to the farm to see it for yourself.'

Go back to the farm.

It was the last thing Elle wanted to do.

On the other hand, if she refused, it meant that someone else would take over the project, and she didn't want that either. It shocked her to realise that she actually felt protective about the farm; or maybe it was her parents she felt protective about. Even if whoever handled the project in her agency dealt with Charlie, she didn't want anyone else dealing with her parents and maybe judging them the way that the cool kids at school had judged her.

And if her colleagues found out about her background...

It wasn't that she was ashamed of where she came from; it was more that she hated the way other people reacted to it. It hadn't been just the popular kids at school who'd given her a hard time about the farm; her boyfriends at university had behaved in pretty much the same way, once she'd taken them back to West Byfield. OK, so she had rubbish taste in men—what had happened with Damien Price at prom should've warned her about that—but it had squashed

her heart a little bit flatter every time she brought someone to the farm to meet her parents, and they dumped her
shortly afterwards. *'It's not you, it's me...'* She'd heard it
too many times, and she'd known it hadn't been the truth.
It had been Bluebell Farm. Her boyfriends had been put
off by the cows and the mud and the shabbiness.

She didn't want any of it affecting her life in London
now; but she didn't want to let her parents down, either.
There had to be a middle way.

'I'm really not sure I can spare the time to come to
Norfolk,' she said. 'It'd be much quicker to do it all by
video call.'

'I'm sure your boss would let you have a few days,'
Charlie said. 'Maybe even a couple of weeks, so you can
wrap it all up on site.'

'A couple of weeks?' She winced inwardly, hearing the
squeak of panic in her voice. 'Sorry. That's completely
out of the question. And I never spend two whole weeks
doing a client visit—even if they have a massive budget.'

'You said you would've done it for nothing, in your
spare time,' Charlie said. 'Can I be cheeky and ask if you
could maybe take some holiday?'

A working holiday in the place she'd been desperate to
escape from ten years ago?

It was very far from Elle's idea of fun. She had no problems with the concept of a working holiday; it was the destination that rattled her.

'You could stay in one of the shepherd's huts and experience things on the farm, the way our visitors would.
It would give you the perfect insight,' he said.

Back to Bluebell Farm.

It felt as if someone had just draped a blanket of lead
round her shoulders: all the misery of her teenage years,
solidified and weighing her down again.

'I do have other clients. Not to mention deadlines,' she said.

'Your mum said you haven't taken any time off in six months. I'm surprised the HR department hasn't been on your case about it,' he said.

Was this an oblique way of telling her that she needed to go back for a different reason—perhaps that one of her parents was seriously ill but hadn't told her because they didn't want her to worry? 'Are Mum and Dad all right?' she asked. 'There isn't something they're...' Anxiety made her spine prickle and she dragged in a breath. 'Something they're not telling me?'

'They're fine. Why would you...?' He frowned, then grimaced. 'Sorry. I didn't mean to scare you, or make you think there was an ulterior motive for asking you to come back. Your parents are both fine. It's just that I think you'll get a better feel for what we're doing if you come and see it for yourself.'

It was true. With any other client, she'd do a site visit, because it meant she'd come in as a fresh pair of eyes and be able to see things that maybe the client took for granted or hadn't really thought about.

But this was Bluebell Farm. Her unhappy place. Something she'd rather do at a distance.

'I'll need to ask my boss,' she said. She was pretty sure she could couch the request in a way that would make him say no. 'If I can't take the time off, then we'll have to do a video conference instead.'

He frowned. 'I can't take you on a live video tour of the farm.'

She knew why. 'Because of all the Wi-Fi dead spots.'

'But that's part of the charm for people who want to have a complete break.' He smiled. 'Spotty mobile phone coverage means you might as well switch off your phone completely.'

'That's meant to be a selling point?' she scoffed. 'A deal-breaker, more like, in today's world.'

'It's definitely a selling point,' he said. He looked at her. 'Ellie, the farm needs help. It needs you. Your mum and dad need you.'

'That,' she said, 'is emotional blackmail. If you were talking to anyone else in the agency, you wouldn't be saying it.'

'No. But we want you to handle the project,' he said. 'You're good at this. Your mum's got a photograph on the mantelpiece of you accepting your last award, right next to your graduation photo.'

'More emotional blackmail,' she said, folding her arms.

'OK, I get that you don't want to come back to the farm,' he said. 'But we still need help. If you'd rather not do it, then OK: we'll just have to find someone else. You were the first choice because of your parents, and because their share of the farm will be yours one day—I think you ought to have some input into what we're doing, rather than leave it to someone else.'

'I'm not part of the business, and I'll support my parents' choices,' she said, narrowing her eyes at him.

Why had Charlie Webb had to walk into her agency and turn her life upside down?

If she agreed to help, she'd hate every minute she spent at the farm. If she refused to do it, she'd feel as if she was letting her parents down. Whatever she did, she lost.

There wasn't a middle way. She'd have to choose the lesser of two evils. 'If I can get the time off,' she said, 'I'll do it.'

'Great.' He looked pleased. 'I can give you a lift back today.'

'Hang on. I can't just drop everything,' she said. 'I have

commitments and there are things I'll need to move. Let me talk to my boss, and I'll call you later.'

'All right.' He handed her a business card. 'If I'm in a dead spot, my phone will go through to voicemail. Leave me a message and I'll call you back.'

'I'll look over the website later today,' she said, 'and I'll have a list of questions and suggestions.'

'Great.' He stood up and held out his hand. 'Thanks for your time, Ellie. *Elle*,' he corrected himself swiftly.

Shaking his hand was meant to feel like a normal business gesture, but Elle's skin tingled where it touched his. She didn't dare look him in the eye, in case he guessed.

Charlie Webb was her client, she reminded herself. Blurring the boundaries of that relationship would affect her job, and that in turn would mean she'd miss out on the promotion she'd worked so hard for. Not going to happen. Even if that hadn't been a barrier, she wasn't looking for a relationship. She'd given up on trying to find Mr Right and she was totally focused on her career.

'Nice to see you again, Charlie,' she said, giving him her most professional smile.

Once she'd shown him out to Reception, Elle took a quick break to video-call her mum and check that her parents really were on board with what Charlie was doing with the farm. A phone call wasn't good enough; she needed to look into her mum's eyes and be sure that Angie Newton was telling her the truth. 'He's not pushing you into things, Mum, is he?'

'No, love. Actually, his energy's refreshing,' Angie said. 'I was a bit surprised when he, of all people, suggested we start doing weddings, but he's got a point. This is a beautiful part of the world to be married in. And if people want to marry in the local church, he's planning to offer a horse and carriage to transport the bride and groom between here and the church.'

'What do you mean, you were surprised when he suggested weddings?' Elle asked.

'I thought you knew.'

Elle frowned. 'Knew what?'

Angie looked awkward. 'Oh, love. I don't want to gossip. Maybe you should ask him.'

This sounded like something important. 'Mum, please, just tell me,' Elle said. 'I know you're not a gossip and you know I'm not, either. This sounds like something I need to be aware of, so I don't accidentally put my foot in it.'

'His wife was killed in an accident, hit by a car.'

God, he was young to be a widower, Elle thought. Thirty-one: only three years older than herself. 'That's tough. Poor Charlie.'

'He couldn't bear to stay in London after she died. That's why he gave up his job in the City and went to do his Masters in Environmental Studies, and he ended up doing his final project here. Your dad liked his ideas, and that's why he offered Charlie a job to manage the farm and do the rewilding.'

And Charlie's successful career in the City would've given him the cash to buy that chunky share of the farm a few months ago, Elle thought. 'When did she die?'

'Five years ago,' Angie said. 'He's barely dated since. I know Barb—' his mother, and one of Angie's friends even though she'd moved away '—worries herself sick about him.'

Elle took the rest of the comment as read: Angie was just as worried about her singleton daughter. 'Thanks for telling me, Mum. I'll tread carefully.'

'You're really coming back to the farm?' Angie's face brightened.

'If I can get my boss to agree, I'll stay for a few days,' Elle said. 'To sort out everything for the media project.'

'I can't wait to see you, love.'

Guilt flooded through Elle. She loved her parents dearly, and she knew that a thrice-weekly video call and the treats she sent them really weren't enough. But forcing herself to go back to the farm was like taking off a plaster very, very slowly. 'And you, Mum. I'd better go. But I just wanted to be sure you and Dad weren't being steamrollered before I started putting things in place at this end.'

'Charlie's a nice boy,' Angie said. 'He's kind.'

Yeah. But Elle couldn't tell her mother how she already knew that. It would involve explanations that would hurt her parents, and that wasn't fair. 'I'll see you soon. Love you.'

She went to see Rav and closed his office door behind her. 'Can we have a confidential word, please?' she asked.

'Of course.' Rav looked concerned. 'Is something wrong?'

She took a deep breath. 'In the interests of full disclosure—and also in strictest confidence—I need to tell you that Bluebell Farm belongs to my parents as well as to Charlie Webb.'

'Your parents?' He blinked. 'So you already know all about what they want?'

'No.' At his surprised stare, she hedged, 'It's...complicated.'

'Is it a problem?'

It could be. But Rav had asked her to do the project, and been explicit about promoting her if she did a good job. She'd make sure it didn't become a problem. 'No. I was just a bit surprised, because I didn't realise they were changing things quite so much, to the point where they do actually need a marketing plan.' She didn't want to bring up all the mud and the manure. Or her own ambivalence towards the farm. 'They want me to go and stay for a few days. I know a site visit wouldn't normally take more than a day, and I know this is ridiculously short notice, but...' She bit her lip. 'Would it be possible for me to go tomorrow, and take a few days' holiday to do it?'

'In other words, you're planning to work through your holiday to keep their budget low? HR would have my head on a platter for even entertaining the idea,' Rav said, shaking his head.

'Two weeks. One day as work, the rest as holiday,' Elle said.

'When you'll still be working.'

She squirmed. 'Look, I don't want anyone else to do it, because this is my family we're talking about and I want to support them. As long as that's not a problem for you?'

'If anything,' Rav said, 'it means you've got an even stronger motivation to make this campaign succeed.'

'I do. And it's a shoestring budget, so I think this is the best solution,' she said. 'This is my family, so I admit I plan to do some of the work in my own time. But, as far as HR is concerned, I'm on holiday.'

'And you think that's acceptable, not having a proper break?' Rav asked dryly.

'We all have to put in extra hours sometimes, to make things work,' she said. 'I wouldn't do it for any other client. This is my family. You'd do the same, wouldn't you, if it was your family's business?'

Rav looked at her for a long, long moment. 'Yes. I know where you're coming from.'

'Good. There shouldn't be a problem on any of my projects. I'm up to date with everything, and all the dates, deadlines and details for the next steps are in my project plans.'

'I wouldn't expect anything else from the queen of critical path analysis.' Rav inclined his head. 'All right. I'll let HR know. Actually, they did bring your name up this morning as someone who hasn't taken time off for a while and they're a bit antsy about it, so I'm sure we can live with the short notice of your "holiday". Though I do expect you to take a bit of a break while you're away.'

'I will. There won't be any commuting, for a start.' She gave him what she hoped was a winning smile.

He rolled his eyes. 'Go and hand over your projects, then do whatever you need to make that campaign go viral. But I meant it about a break. I want you refreshed when you come back to London, not worn out.'

'Thanks, Rav.'

Elle messaged her parents to say that she'd be at the farm in the morning, and Charlie to say that she'd be getting the seven a.m. train from Liverpool Street to Norwich tomorrow and then grabbing a taxi; then she spent the rest of the day sorting out last-minute issues and handing over her projects to colleagues. Back at her flat, she cancelled her next two weeks of classes at the gym and booked her train ticket, rang her best friend to let her know what was going on and that she needed to cancel drinks and their film night for the next two Thursdays, then settled down to look through Bluebell Farm's website and social media accounts.

Home-made websites could be charming; Bluebell Farm's wasn't. It was muddled and didn't give anywhere near enough information. No wonder the farm wasn't paying for itself.

Well, that was where she came in.

Elle had just finished some notes and was starting to look up farm holidays and weddings, when her phone beeped with a couple of texts. The first was from Charlie, to say he'd meet her at the station. The second was from her dad, to say he was delighted that she was coming to help.

She tried to brush off the flurry of guilt. Right now, she still wasn't entirely sure that this was the best idea. She was filled with a mixture of trepidation at going back to the place where she'd been so unhappy, worry about setting up expectations with her parents that she'd never be able to fulfil, and very muddled-up feelings about Charlie Webb—who'd definitely got hotter over the past ten years. She'd noticed how many women walking through Reception had given him a second look. If she hadn't known him, she would've given him a second look, herself: probably a third.

But his past would put another barrier between them; her mum had said that he wasn't dating, so clearly he wasn't ready to move on after his wife's tragic death. This was going to be strictly business. She'd do the job as professionally as she could, and then she'd come back to London. Get her promotion. And then she could settle down to the lovely, full life she'd worked for—far away from Bluebell Farm.

CHAPTER TWO

CHARLIE HAD COMPLETELY miscalculated how long it would take him to drive through rush-hour traffic. He rarely came into the city, and he hadn't even considered how many sets of roadworks and diversions there might be on the arterial roads. Add frustrated commuters trying to get to work on time, people on e-scooters weaving rashly in and out of the traffic and even driving the wrong way down the road...

At least his car had hands-free connection to his phone, so he was able to text Ellie and let her know he'd be a bit late picking her up at the train station.

Ellie Newton.

Funny how the ends of his fingers were tingling with adrenaline at the idea of seeing her again.

Ten years ago, he'd seen her practically as a child. Eighteen, the same age as his little sister. Completely off limits. Now, she was all grown up. The prodigal daughter, coming home. Except she'd made it clear that she didn't want to be there. He was pretty sure there wasn't a rift between Ellie and her parents; he ate dinner with Mike and Angie in their kitchen, a couple of times a week, and he knew from chatting with them that she called them often and sent them little surprises. So what kept her away from them?

He knew why he avoided his own parents and was glad they'd moved away to be nearer his sister; he loved them, but he simply couldn't cope with their pity and their attempts at finding someone to take Jess's place in his life. He avoided his in-laws and Jess's friends because he couldn't handle the weight of their grief on top of his own; and his friends and former colleagues just didn't know what to say to him, so the gaps between phone calls and promises to meet up soon had grown longer and longer, until eventually he couldn't remember the last time he'd even spoken to one of them, let alone seen them. The only one of his family who didn't make him feel worse, or try to set him up with 'someone suitable who'll heal your heart again', was his little sister, Jo—and he was pretty sure that was only because right now she was busy with a toddler and a new baby.

Mike and Angie Newton had given him space to grieve and space to breathe. Working on Bluebell Farm, both during his MSc project and since they'd offered him a job afterwards, had gone a long way to mending the broken bits inside him. He couldn't understand why Ellie didn't want to be here, with a family who loved her. London was glittery and busy and noisy, yes, but after Jess's death he'd found his life there shallow and empty. It wasn't a boy-friend keeping Ellie in London, either, because Charlie had picked up from several conversations that Angie and Mike worried she'd never settle down.

Ellie the enigma.

He wanted to know what made her tick.

Though he had a feeling that she might have as many barriers around her as he did.

She was waiting for him at the station entrance, concentrating on her phone; he pressed the button to lower the passenger window and called her name.

She looked up and smiled, and it felt as if all the breath had just gone out of his lungs. Dressed much more casually than yesterday, in jeans, a pale yellow T-shirt, canvas shoes and no make-up, she was absolutely gorgeous.

'Thanks for picking me up, Charlie,' she said, putting her case in the back and then climbing into the passenger seat.

'You're welcome. Sorry I'm a bit late.'

'It's OK. It gave me time to grab another coffee.' She fastened her seatbelt. 'I assume this is yours, rather than the farm's?'

He'd swapped his BMW for the Range Rover when he'd accepted the job as farm manager, having spent the previous six months suffering the suspension of Mike Newton's ancient pick-up truck on the rutted farm tracks. 'Yes, though your parents are both insured on it. Assuming you drive, I can add you to the insurance while you're here.'

'Thanks, but I'll borrow Mum's car,' she said. 'I don't fancy parking something this big.'

'I see you're wearing sensible clothes.' The words blurted out before he could stop them. Thank God he hadn't said something stupid about how the denim suited her curves. Even though it did.

She rolled her eyes. 'It'd be a bit stupid to wear a dry-clean-only dress or high heels on a working farm—and obviously I'll change into wellies when I'm at the farm, because I don't want to have to stick these shoes in the washing machine every day.'

'Sorry. I didn't mean...' He shook his head. 'Sorry.'

'I know. I didn't mean to snap, either. I'm just a bit...' She tailed off.

He glanced quickly at her. 'Anxious about going back to the farm?'

'It's been a while,' she said.

Since before he'd started his project at the farm. At least

three years, by his reckoning. 'What happened? Did you fall out with your parents?'

'No. And I don't have a problem with you managing the farm or buying into the business either, before you ask,' she said. 'I know Dad always hoped I'd take over from him, but we all knew it was never going to happen. I'm just not a country girl at heart. I love London. I love the glitz and the glamour and the lights and the noise, and that's where I want to live. I know Dad was disappointed, but we've made our peace with it over the years.'

'But you're still antsy about going back.'

She blew out a breath. 'Yes.'

'Why?'

She grimaced. 'You know why I hate it in West Byfield. It's a small town where everyone's way too interested in everyone else's business. If you don't fit in with everyone's expectations, you're an outsider.'

'Is this about what happened on prom night?' he asked, remembering how she'd cried on his shoulder.

'When I found out that everyone except me knew that Damien Price had only asked me as his date because he thought I'd be so grateful that I'd give him any sexual favour he asked? No.' She grimaced. 'It started years and years before then. High school was a total nightmare.' She shook her head. 'Sorry. Ignore what I just said. It's a hangover from…a long time ago. I'm over it.'

It didn't sound like it to him.

'Want to talk about it?' He kept his voice gentle.

'No.'

He didn't say anything, and eventually the weight of the silence seemed to grow too much for her. She sighed. 'Infant and junior school were fine. It was high school that…' She broke off and swallowed hard. 'It was nothing physical, no hitting me or stealing my bag or tipping my lunch on the floor—but that old thing about "sticks and stones may break my bones but names will never hurt me" just isn't true. The name-calling makes you feel a little bit less valid, every single time. And every day I had to psych myself up a little bit more, so I could walk in with my head held high and pretend I couldn't hear what they were saying about me.'

He ached for her; at the same time, he admired how she hadn't let the bullies' behaviour crush her spirit completely.

'And oh, dear God, when my periods started… I was terrified I'd leak or something and it would give them even more ammunition.' She grimaced. 'The name-calling changed the way I saw myself. I wasn't Eleanor Newton any more, the girl whose family had farmed this land for generations and who used to find the first bluebells every spring and bring some in for the whole class to enjoy. I was Smelly Ellie Moo-ton, who smelled of cows or sour milk. Even though I was pretty sure I didn't smell, it made me paranoid. I bought the strongest-smelling body spray I could find, but that was so obvious and it made the teasing worse. And if they weren't claiming I smelled, they'd call me "heifer" because I wasn't stick-thin, like the popular girls.' She blew out a breath. 'Sometimes I wonder how the hell I made it out of high school without developing an eating disorder.'

'I'm sorry you had to go through that,' he said. 'Kids can be vile.'

'In a pack, definitely. On their own, with no chance of anybody seeing them talking to me and then picking on them, too, some of them weren't so bad.'

'Didn't you tell your parents?' he asked. 'They must've noticed you were miserable.'

'Yes and no,' she said. 'I did tell them, and they went up to school to have a word with the teachers—but that just made things worse. It kind of upped the challenge—to get at me in a way where they couldn't be caught doing it.'

'And you didn't want your parents to go to the school again, in case it made it worse still?' he guessed.

'Partly,' she said. 'But also Mum was under a lot of pressure at the time. Grandad died when I was still in junior school, and then Gran got dementia. Mum and Dad didn't want her to go into a home, so Mum looked after her. I could see how worn down my mum was getting, and I didn't want to add to her burden. I guess I wanted to protect her and not let her know how bad things were for me. And Dad was working all hours, so he was too tired to notice much when he got in. I couldn't dump it all on them.'

'I had no idea,' he said.

'Why would you? You were three years above me at school and, although your sister wasn't one of the bullies, she wasn't a friend either. I didn't really have friends at high school.' She shrugged. 'In a way, it did me a favour. I used to go to the library at lunchtime so I could get away from them. I lost myself in books. I discovered really wonderful poetry—and Shakespeare. That made school bearable, and it meant I didn't have to make Mum's life even harder.' Her smile faded. 'Though, deep down, it didn't stop me wanting to be accepted for myself.'

'You're accepted for yourself now,' he said.

She shook her head. 'In London, yes. In West Byfield, the memories come back. That's why I hate being called Ellie. It rhymes with "smelly". And I'm not that person. I never was.'

'Maybe,' he said carefully, 'you could look at it a different way. It's a pet version of your name, and it's a pretty one. People don't call you Ellie because they're trying to make you feel bad—Eleanor or even Elle sounds a bit formal and distant, so calling you Ellie is their way of showing they want to feel close to you.'

She didn't look convinced.

'But I get where you're coming from, and I'll try to remember to call you Elle, in future,' he said.

'I appreciate that,' she said.

And oh, the bravery in her smile. He knew exactly how that felt. He'd pasted the same expression on his own face every time someone asked him how he was. Lied through his teeth, because how could you tell someone that you felt like a paper husk and the better part of you had been ripped out and buried in your wife's grave?

'I'm trusting you not to say anything to Mum and Dad about what I just told you,' she added. 'I don't want them made to feel guilty about something that wasn't their fault.'

'Of course.' Clearly Ellie—*Elle*—was deeply protective about her parents.

All the same, he couldn't quite drop the subject. 'But you're successful now. A first-class degree, an amazing job. Why didn't you come back to rub it in the bullies' faces?'

'If I was the CEO of a billion-pound company, I'd still be Smelly Ellie or Heifer to them,' she said. 'And I know it's their problem, not mine, but...' She sighed again. 'Actually, it wasn't just people at school. Every boyfriend I brought home from university and beyond dumped me within a week of visiting Bluebell Farm. They couldn't cope with the reality of life in the country—that a dairy farm doesn't mean scones out of the oven every five minutes and roses round the door, it means crazily early mornings and mucking out the byre.'

'It sounds as if you dated the wrong kind of man,' he said.

'I'm very, very good at finding Mr Wrong,' she said.

'Which is why I've given up dating and I'm concentrating on my career.'

Was this Elle's way of making sure he didn't get the wrong idea and think she was interested in him? Charlie pushed aside the thought that he might be interested in her. He'd tried dating once or twice, since Jess's death, but it had never felt right. And it would be way, way too complicated if he got involved with Elle.

'Speaking of which,' she said, 'I wanted to use the travel time to talk to you about the farm's website. I looked at it last night and it's marginally worse than having no website at all.'

'We don't have time to do an all-singing, all-dancing thing,' he said. 'I can't spend an hour a day updating a website.'

'You don't have to,' she said. 'But you do need to organise it better. A website needs to be easy for the customer to find what they want, and easy for you to update. At the moment, the farm's website doesn't work hard enough. You need a calendar and a booking system for the accommodation, at the very least. Not to mention much better pictures and customer testimonials.'

'Flashy booking systems are expensive. People call us if they want to book,' he said.

'You said that yesterday. And is the landline diverted to a mobile when nobody's there to answer it?' she asked, her tone slightly caustic. 'Are you available at, say, nine p.m. when people are browsing their holiday options post-dinner and want to book?'

He sighed. 'It goes to an answering machine, out of office hours. Or they can email us.'

'Meanwhile, the customer gets fed up waiting for an answer and books elsewhere,' she said. 'And you're definitely missing an opportunity with the farm shop and café.

You need a sample menu and possibly a booking system, and consider letting people order stock online. I'll have a word with someone about the logistics of online merch—you might need to start off with just mailing the non-perishable goods first.'

'And who's going to deal with that?'

'I'll tell you when I've had a chat to the farm shop and café staff,' she said. 'Because we need their input, too. Obviously I'm not going to give you a hard time about not having any wedding stuff on there, because that's a new thing. We need to think about how you handle it. And, on the education side, you need to list the courses you run. What you've got at the moment is a bit vague.'

'People—'

'—ring you to book. Yeah, yeah.' She shook her head. 'Thirty years ago, that would've been fine. Now, it's nowhere near enough. Again, you need a minimum of photographs and customer testimonials, so people can see what they're getting for their money and hear how much other people enjoyed it.'

'Anything else?' he asked, very slightly nettled by the criticisms, even though he knew she had made some valid points. He couldn't help thinking that, if she'd ignored her past and come back to the farm earlier, she would've seen all this for herself and done something about it. Though at the same time he knew he was being unfair. She'd tried to cope with the bullying and protect her parents from the extra stress when her grandmother was ill—and that was a big ask of a teenager. In her shoes, would his little sister have coped any better? And Elle had done well for herself at work. She hadn't let the bullies of her teenage years wreck her confidence in what she did; though he rather thought they might have trashed her confidence in who she was.

'How often do you update the farm blog?' she asked.

'It's done on a need-to-post basis.' He couldn't remember the last time he'd updated it.

'If you want people to follow it and spread the word about the farm, you need to set up a regular schedule. It doesn't have to be every day. If readers know you post something, say, every Monday and every Friday, they'll come and look at the blog on Mondays and Fridays, expecting to see a new post. If you just post at random times, they're less likely to find something new whenever they click on the blog, and they'll soon stop bothering to come back.'

'Right.'

'Don't get huffy with me,' she warned. 'You're the one who asked me to look at it and make suggestions. I wouldn't be doing my job properly if I patted you on the head and told you what a good boy you are, when actually it's terrible and a twelve-year-old could do a better job.'

'You really don't mince your words, do you?' he asked. 'Would you say all this to your parents?'

'I might be a bit gentler with them,' she conceded. 'But you're the farm manager, and you're the one who's briefing the agency. This is under your remit. Dad, bless him, wouldn't know one end of a computer from another. He rings me to talk him through sorting out his mobile phone when he gets in a muddle. If it was a cow, he'd know everything there was to know about it. But a phone or a computer...' She chuckled. 'Dad's never going to be a silver surfer. I couldn't see any links on the website, but I'm assuming you do have proper social media?'

'There's a Facebook page,' he said.

'Which gets updated how often?'

'Occasionally,' he muttered. When he had the time and

the inclination: and no doubt she'd say the same about that as she had about the blog.

'What about Instagram? Twitter?'

'There isn't time. Ellie—*Elle*,' he corrected himself swiftly, 'our focus is on the farm and the conservation side of things, not social media.'

'You can do both,' she said. 'Once it's set up, I can look after it remotely and I can schedule posts in advance for you. I'll tell you what I need and when, and I'll chase you if you don't deliver.'

'You're scary,' he said.

'I'm good at my job. Just as I assume you're good at yours, or Dad wouldn't have appointed you as the farm manager or let you buy into the farm,' she pointed out.

'Thank you. I think,' he said. Though, given the organisational skills and clear-sightedness she'd just demonstrated, he was pretty sure Elle would've made an excellent farm manager. She just hadn't wanted to do it.

'Talk me through the farm,' she said.

'I think it'd be easier to show you when we get there, and then you can ask the questions that occur to you as we go round.'

'Good point.' She made a note. 'We'll do that bit later. So we have the glamping. I'll take a proper look round the shepherd's huts and the farm cottages when we're between visitors, but I want to know about the rest of it.'

'Is this an official briefing meeting?' he asked.

'It's information-gathering for me,' Elle said. 'You know all this stuff, so you're perfectly capable of driving and talking at the same time.

'Got it,' he said.

Charlie had worked in banking, a fast-paced industry where wasted time definitely cost money. Surely he realised it was the same in any industry? Or did he have rose-tinted glasses about farming? she wondered.

She gave him a sideways glance. In Ray-Bans, faded jeans and an equally faded blue T-shirt, he looked a lot more down to earth than he had at the agency in his sharp suit. A lot more approachable. *Touchable.*

And there were a million reasons why she wasn't going to go there.

'The website could work a lot harder for you. It needs to be easy for the customer to use and easy for you to update,' she said. Before she could start fixing it, she needed to work out a brief. To do that, she needed to know more about the farm. And she hadn't missed the irony that she ought to know an awful lot more about her family business, the place where she'd grown up, than she actually did. 'What brings in the biggest income stream?'

'Glamping, followed by the courses,' he said. 'Obviously when the wedding stuff starts, that's potentially a bigger income stream.'

'Got it. Start with the glamping,' she said. 'What exactly does Bluebell Farm offer glampers?'

'Self-catering accommodation for people who want a proper rural experience and to work on the farm,' he said.

Which she knew meant more than just chilling out in a luxury shepherd's hut. He'd mentioned earlier that some of them helped with the rewilding. 'And what can they actually do on the farm? I know you said you'd show me, but what does the rewilding actually mean?'

'Restoring the bigger natural processes and minimising human intervention,' he said. 'It's everything from repairing fencing through to planting new bits of hedges; and from clearing brambles in the wood so the bluebells have space to grow through to working with the livestock.'

She coughed. 'Are you seriously telling me you're trying to sell shovelling manure out of the barns as a *holiday*? That's going way beyond "where there's muck, there's brass".'

'If you live in the city, you work in an office and you never see the stars at night, then staying somewhere you can actually see the skies and working on the farm is so completely different from your usual life that it's a holiday,' he said.

It was a fair point. Wasn't that why she'd chosen her own career? She'd wanted something glamorous and sharp that was the polar opposite of her lifestyle growing up. Though she still found it hard to believe that anyone would want to muck out the cattle for fun.

'Working on the land—and with the livestock—reconnects people to nature,' he said.

OK. She got that side of it. Giving people the chance to feel they were making a difference and helping to save the planet. 'I assume you're looking at organic certification?'

'It goes with the territory of rewilding,' he said dryly.

'OK. What else do they get, apart from accommodation and work? Do you feed them?'

'They get breakfast and lunch included at the farm café,' he said, 'and their evenings are their own. We don't do evening meals, but we've negotiated a discount for our holidaymakers at the Red Lion if they don't want to cook for themselves.'

The nearest pub in West Byfield. 'Good.' She made more notes. 'The food at the café: are the ingredients local?'

'As far as possible,' he said. 'Everything in the farm shop's produced locally, from the jams to the chocolates to the ice cream. A local bakery supplies our bread, every day your mum or Lisa who runs the café makes the cakes, and the cheese is mostly our own.'

'Which means lower food miles. Good. That's all stuff I can work with, and the photo opportunities are perfect,' she said. 'What do you sell in the farm shop, apart from food?'

'Local wine, local beer, and local handicrafts. Rosie in the village takes our wool after shearing and spins it. She runs a course here on spinning, for those who are interested.'

'Spinning,' she said, taking a note. That definitely offered photo opportunities. From farm to wear: cute lambs, sheep being shorn, the fleeces, someone spinning the wool, and someone wearing hand-knitted products.

They'd need a few photoshoots; but they might be able to save money on the budget if she could use local people as models. And Charlie Webb would make the perfect model for a high-end hand-knitted sweater. Could she talk him into it?

'What other courses do you run?'

'How to make artisanal dairy products—using milk from the rare breed cattle and sheep—plus photography, art and guided nature walks.'

'What sort of nature?'

'Wildflowers, trees, birds and insects,' he said. 'We tailor it to the group's knowledge.'

'And who runs them?'

'Your dad and I do the nature walks,' he said. 'Your mum runs the dairy stuff, and a local artist runs the art and photography courses.'

Perhaps she could do a deal with the artist for artwork and photography, if Charlie didn't already have what she needed. 'Good.' She thought about what she'd expect to buy from a farm shop. 'Do you sell any toiletries?'

'Yes. They're locally made, too. We include travel-sized ones as part of the welcome basket for the holiday lets.'

'Good.' She made more notes. 'So do you run events at

the café? Say, a knitting morning, or crafting-and-coffee sessions, or toddler group?'

'No.'

'That's something to think about,' she said. 'You said earlier about the farm being part of the community. Maybe it's worth looking at what else is offered in West Byfield and when the café's less busy times are, and see if we can fill some gaps.' She paused. 'Would you have time to run me through a nature walk and a typical day in the life of one of the holidaymakers?'

'Are you offering to clean out the byre or milk the cows?'

'I've done my share of that already, over the years,' she said. Then she took a deep breath. 'But it wouldn't hurt to refresh my memory.' Despite the fact she hated the idea of being dragged back to the past.

He pulled into the long driveway that led to the farm.

'We'll continue this later,' she said. 'I need to see Mum and Dad, first, but perhaps you can show me round and we can have a working lunch or something to brainstorm a few ideas.'

'Fine by me,' he said as he parked outside the farmhouse. 'I'll bring your case in.'

She smiled. 'Thanks, but it's not that heavy—and, even if it was, remember I grew up lugging hay bales around.' At his raised eyebrow, she said, 'And I do weights at the gym twice a week. Respectable ones.'

'That's me told,' he said, smiling back and following her into the farm kitchen.

'Ellie! It's so good to have you home,' Angie said, wrapping her daughter in a bear hug. 'I've got the kettle on. I'm running a course at ten, so I can't stay, and your dad's with the rewilding visitors, but—'

'Mum, it's fine,' Elle cut in, returning the hug. 'I'll see

you later and we'll have a proper catch up. Charlie's going to take me round the farm, and I'm going to ask him so many questions he'll be bored with the sound of my voice.'

'That's pretty much what I hired you for,' he said dryly.

'Yes. Though, as I said to you in London, I would've done this for nothing, if Mum and Dad had asked,' she said, hammering home the point.

'But you're so busy in London,' Angie said.

Guilt seared her. 'I'm never too busy for you and Dad, Mum, and I'm sorry if I've made you feel that way,' she said, hugging her mum. 'Go and teach your students. And I'll cook dinner tonight.'

'I've already prepped lasagne—a veggie one for you, and an ordinary one for your dad and me. They just need forty minutes in the oven,' Angie said.

Elle's favourite dinner, as a teenager; she blinked away the threatening tears. 'Well, I'll make the garlic bread and put the salad together, as well as heating the lasagne.'

'Charlie, you will eat with us tonight, won't you?' Angie asked. 'There's plenty.'

'Surely you'll want to have Elle to yourself?' Charlie asked.

'There's always a place at our table for you. You're practically family,' Angie said.

Elle noticed the hopeful look in her mum's eyes and sighed inwardly. Please don't say her mum was planning to try to set her up with Charlie. Apart from the fact that her mum had given Elle had the impression that Charlie still wasn't over his wife's death—otherwise he wouldn't still be single—she and Charlie weren't right for each other. They wanted different things.

Guilt flooded through her again. She knew how much her mum wanted grandchildren; she'd seen the wistfulness on her mum's face when Angie had spoken about a friend's new grandchild. This was just another way Elle was letting her parents down. Not taking over the farm, not producing the next generation to hand it on to...

She shook herself. 'I'll make coffee, and then we'll get cracking on the farm tour,' she said. 'See you later, Mum. Love you.'

Once Angie had left and Elle had made the coffee, she turned to Charlie. 'I'm sorry about that. If you'd rather not eat with us tonight, I'll make an excuse for you.'

'It's fine. You and I have a working relationship,' Charlie said. 'We might end up being friends, but that's about it.'

'I'm glad we're agreed.'

'If it helps,' Charlie said, 'my mum's the same. She thinks I...' He stopped.

'Should've done all your grieving by now?' Elle asked.

'Ah. So you know,' he said, bracing himself for the usual pity.

'Mum told me. Not to gossip, but to warn me so I didn't put my foot in it. I made her tell me when she said she wasn't sure if you were really OK with the wedding idea.' She looked at him. 'The way I see it, everyone handles the tough stuff in their own way. You'll move on when you're ready. And, in the meantime, I'm guessing you're sick to the back teeth of everyone thinking of you as "poor Charlie".'

'I am,' he admitted.

'The nearest I've been in your shoes was losing my grandparents, but losing the person you chose as your life partner must be a lot tougher. And that's meant to be sympathy, not pity,' she added.

'Thank you,' Charlie said.

'For business purposes,' Elle said, 'I'm going to ask you

the difficult question. Are you really OK about setting up hosting weddings?'

'Yes,' Charlie said. 'For business purposes, I can tell you that I had a happy marriage. I loved Jess and she loved me.' Funny, he could say her name in front of Elle without the usual tight band round his chest. Maybe because Elle had already been so honest with him about her own situation. 'We had a ten-year plan. Work hard, earn a pile of cash—she was a corporate lawyer, so we were both on good money—and then move out of London, find a place in the country and settle down. Kids, horses, dogs, maybe a few other animals. But then she was cycling to work when a guy paying too much attention to his phone clipped her in his car. She came off her bike and hit her head in the wrong place. And she never woke up again.'

'That's tough,' Elle said. Though he was relieved to see sympathy rather than pity in her face.

'We were getting there. We'd even talked about starting our plan a bit early—we were both fed up with working stupid hours and not seeing enough of each other. And then it was too late.'

'Is that why you did your Masters?' Elle asked.

He nodded. 'I still wanted the life we'd planned. And I couldn't bear being in London any more, without her. It felt stifling. I couldn't breathe. And people never stopped talking; it was endless noise, endless traffic, endless mobile phones. I needed wide skies and rolling countryside. Your dad agreed to let me do my final project here because he'd been thinking about changing the farm's focus—just so you know, I haven't pushed him into doing any of the rewilding.'

'I know,' she said. 'Apart from the fact that I checked with my mum, I know that Dad wanted to turn the farm organic years ago and sort out the hedgerows. But it takes time and money.'

'Yeah.' He looked at her. 'Thanks for not wrapping me in cotton wool.'

'No problem. Thanks for not minding that my mum had an unsubtle moment,' she said.

Charlie realised that he actually liked this woman. He'd assumed that by never coming back to Bluebell Farm she'd become a hard-hearted city girl; but that wasn't who she was. Elle Newton was clear-sighted and honest, and he liked that. He liked *her*.

'And obviously,' she said, 'I'll keep what you've told me to myself.'

Just as she'd asked him to keep the stuff about the bullying and her awful boyfriends to himself. 'Thank you,' he said. 'We're officially the keepers of each other's secrets.'

'Good. Now, let's go and look at the farm.'

'I should probably warn you that we had a few April showers last night,' he said.

She looked at her canvas shoes. 'I'd better raid the boot room,' she said, and disappeared from the kitchen. She came back a couple of minutes later wearing green wellies.

'Do you tell the holidaymakers to bring wellies with them?' she asked.

'Yes. I did suggest hiring them, but your mum said that was ick.'

She laughed. 'It's *very* ick. There's a big difference between hiring out bowling shoes you can sanitise easily, and wellies.' She paused. 'Though you could stock them in the farm shop; or, if the shoe shop's still in town, do a deal with them so the holidaymakers get a special offer.'

He loved the way she could make those business connections so easily. Hiring her to do the farm's marketing had definitely been the right decision. 'I'll add it to my list,' he said.

'I'll leave it on the master list, for now,' she said. 'We can divvy things up later.'

Focused, bright and organised. The more Charlie got to know Elle, the more he appreciated her. 'Done. I'll grab my wellies from the car, and we'll start with the cows,' he said.

CHAPTER THREE

WALKING THROUGH THE farm again felt odd. When Elle had last been here, the farm had been half arable and half dairy. There definitely hadn't been a car park; from the looks of the gravelled area filled with cars and the full bike racks at one side, her mum had quite a few students in her class, there were holidaymakers staying, and yet more people were visiting the shop or the café.

Making mental notes, she followed Charlie to the field where the cows were grazing. It was a much, much smaller herd than the one she remembered; a different breed, too. It was familiar, yet at the same time unfamiliar, and Elle found it slightly unsettling.

'These are the British Whites,' he said. 'They're all named after berries.' He introduced her to the two nearest ones. 'This is Elderberry, and this is Juniper.'

Cows.

Smelly Ellie Moo-ton.

But her father had always been really scrupulous about the hygiene of his cows. Until the teasing had started at high school, Elle had loved their cows, too. She'd thought of them as almost like oversized dogs—she remembered them lowing when they saw her, just as a dog would woof softly and wag its tail in greeting, and they'd loved being petted and scratched behind an ear, just like her dad's yellow Labradors.

'They're so pretty.' Their coats were white and they had black noses, black ears and feet; some had a dusting of black spots on their legs. 'Seriously, Charlie, they're really photogenic. Why on earth aren't you using them as poster girls for the farm?' she asked.

'I guess,' he said dryly, 'that'll be your decision.'

'No. It'll be my recommendation, which is a different thing altogether,' she said. 'So they're dairy rather than beef?'

'They were dairy cattle until the middle of the last century. Nowadays, they're seen more as a beef breed, but we're keeping our girls as dairy and to build up the breed,' he said.

'Got it. Hello, you beautiful pair.' She petted them, scratched them behind the ears, and the cows rubbed their faces against her.

'I thought a day in the life of a cow would make a good piece on the website,' she said. 'I'm assuming that the guests like to learn or watch second milking?'

'Yes.'

'Then I'd like to film you milking the cows.' She smiled. 'Do you sing to them?' Her dad had always sung to his cows during milking.

'Ye-es. Though my singing is a long way from being rock star standard.'

He'd definitely look like a rock star, if he was wearing tight jeans and a white shirt. Sexy as hell. The thought made her feel hot all over, and she really needed to get a grip. Charlie could well end up being the face of the farm, and having the hots for him wasn't going to help her do the job properly. 'It doesn't need to be good. We want this to be real. So guests feel comfortable.'

'OK,' he said.

Juniper nudged Charlie with her nose.

He groaned. 'You're worse than a Labrador, Juni. You know I've got cow cake in my pocket, don't you?'

The cow lowed softly and he took a piece of cow cake from his pocket, holding his palm flat so she could take it from him.

Elle couldn't resist filming him on her phone; and she was rewarded big time when Juniper licked his face.

'I had a calf who used to do that, when I was little,' she said.

'Yeah, our girls are all big on kissing,' he said with a grin.

Big on kissing.

An image slid into her head: Charlie Webb, kissing her, his mouth warm and sweet and tempting…

No.

Absolutely not.

'It's good for exfoliation,' she said instead. *Stop thinking about kissing.* 'I'm thinking about how we can save on the budget. Would you be up for being the face of the farm?'

'Me?' He looked surprised.

'Dad might contribute some words, but wouldn't be comfortable working with a photographer—even if I'm the one taking the shots,' she said.

'So you're not saying you think I'm vain?'

It took her a moment to realise that he was teasing her. She smiled. 'Not when you're happy to let a cow kiss you.'

'I used to be vain,' he said. 'In London. Designer suits, silk ties, handmade shoes.'

'You worked in the City.' She shrugged. 'If you didn't dress the part, you'd be marked down, regardless of your ability.'

'I've realised that since being here. I breathe differently,' he said.

She did, too—but not deep and relaxing, the way he meant. Here, she was on edge and her breathing was shallow.

Not that she wanted to think about that. 'You're beautiful, Juniper,' she said, petting the cow. Then she turned back to Charlie. 'So will you do it?'

He took a deep breath. 'OK.'

'Thank you.' She smiled. 'Obviously I grew up with commercial dairy farming, so my experience is different. Tell me more about a day in the life of a cow.'

'Milking,' he said, 'with a bit of singing. Then it's out to pasture. You might want to film them going through the gate, because they practically kick up their heels with joy at feeling grass under their feet again.'

'Dancing through the fields. I forgot they did that,' Elle said.

'We've got toys for them as well,' he said. 'They like playing with balls.'

'The cows play football?' That would be fantastic. 'I need to film that.'

'They like cow brushes, too.'

'Cow brushes?' It wasn't something she remembered from her years on the farm.

'A rotating bristle brush they can scratch themselves against,' he explained. 'It helps improve their blood circulation and keeps them clean and calm, plus there's less chance of them damaging their skin than if they rub against a tree or a fence.'

'Rotating bristles. So it's something like a car wash brush?'

'Yes.'

She grinned. 'This is all stuff that would be so brilliant

for the website. I definitely want to film a football session. That's the sort of thing that's likely to go viral and get you the sort of attention you need.' She looked at him. 'In the interests of transparency, I want the campaign to go viral for two reasons. Most importantly, I want the farm to be a success; but also I'm in line for a promotion. My boss told me that if this campaign does well, the promotion's a definite. Doing well means going viral.'

'Thank you for your honesty,' he said. 'But it's good to know you want the farm to do well, too.'

'So what's next in the life of a cow?'

'The calves go out with their mums. Then it's milking in the afternoon, and we let them stay out overnight when it's warm enough and bring them into the barn when it's not.'

'What happens to the milk?'

'We use it here in your mum's classes, in the café, and for making cheese, butter and yoghurt for the shop.'

She made notes on her phone. 'Perfect. Can we see the calves now?'

'Sure. Actually, they need to come back to their mums, so you can help with that.'

'Bring it on,' she said.

She clearly liked the animals, Charlie thought; at least the bullies hadn't ruined that side of the farm for her. And she looked entranced when he took her to the calves' pen.

'They're beyond cute,' she said, and took a few shots on her phone.

'How old are they?'

'Two weeks. All girls.'

'So they're still feeding from their mums.'

He nodded. 'We put them in here during milking, and let them back in the fields with their mums afterwards.

We need to do their bedding, which as you probably remember is shaking straw over the top.'

'Do you still do the knee test?' she asked.

He looked at her in surprise.

'If you kneel on the straw and your knees are still dry,
then you know it's thick enough for the calves,' she said.
'Or didn't anyone teach you that?'

For someone who insisted that she belonged in the city,
Charlie thought, Elle Newton still had a lot of the country
in her. 'No, actually,' he said. 'Thank you for that.'

She made a fuss of the calves as she helped spread
the fresh wheat straw in the pen, and laughed when they
sucked her fingers. 'You're gorgeous girls, aren't you?' she
crooned to them. 'What are their names?'

'Bilberry, Cranberry and Loganberry,' he said.

'Beautiful,' she said, and snapped some more pics of
them.

The reunion with their mums was touching, too, after
they'd walked the calves through to the field on a halter
and leading rein, and she took more pictures.

The sheep were next.

'Norfolk Horns,' he said, indicating the horned sheep
with black faces and legs and white coats.

'I see they've been sheared,' she said. 'And we have a
couple of lambs.'

'Those ewes over there are Portia and Helena,' he said,
'and Portia's twins are Viola and Sebastian.'

'One female, one male?' She took a snap of them and
looked at him, her eyes glittering with amusement. '*Please*
tell me your oldest ewe is called Cleopatra and the ram's
Antony.'

'Yes. It was your mum's idea,' he said. Of course Elle
would've worked out immediately that they'd named the
sheep after Shakespeare characters. She had an English de-

gree. 'Your dad wanted to call them after famous Barbaras, but we got a bit stuck after Barbra Streisand and Barbara Windsor. That's when your mum suggested Shakespeare.'

'Shakespearean sheep,' she said. 'When I was in sixth form, Mum took me to see this fabulous production of *The Winter's Tale* where they had half the cast dressed as sheep, singing Beyoncé's "Single Ladies".' She grinned, and sang the chorus as 'snippy-snip'. 'There's your new shearing song.'

'Maybe,' he said. He really liked this side of Elle. Relaxed and teasing; clever, yet not arrogant with it. 'We could put Shakespeare quotes on the sheep page, maybe.' He looked at her. 'My A levels were geared to a degree in Economics, so I don't really know much about Shakespeare. Are there quotes about sheep?'

'There are definitely quotes about sheep,' she said. 'I'll dredge them out later.'

When he took her to see the chickens, she gave him a sidelong glance. 'Not fifty of them, then?'

'No. Though their names are shades of grey,' he said, picking up her teasing reference. 'Over there you've got Charcoal, Slate, Pearl, Pewter and Steel. The rooster's called Carbon.'

'They're really pretty, too, with those bright red combs and the silver hackles overlaying the black feathers.' She indicated the feathers round their neck. 'In the sunlight, there's almost a green sheen to the black—like one of those glossy beetles.'

'They're nice hens,' he said. 'They're good-tempered, a bit on the chatty side, and they lay well.'

'Chatty?' she asked.

'They know their names. Rattle a bucket of poultry pellets, and they'll come and tell you they're hungry.'

'Now that's a video for the farm's socials,' she said.

They stood and watched the hens scratching.

'They're free range, then?' she asked.

He nodded. 'They sleep in the hen house at night, but their field's fenced off to keep the foxes out during the day. We use their eggs in the café, in the cakes and the quiches and the breakfasts.'

She took some more notes, as well as photographs.

And she seemed just as entranced by the three hives set next to the wildflower meadow.

'We manage the hedgerows for the wildlife,' he said, 'so there's a high proportion of hawthorn, blackthorn and bramble. The bees like the flowers we have here and seem very settled—and you really should taste the honey.'

Taste.

Definitely a word he should've avoided, because now he was thinking about how Elle Newton might taste: how soft and sweet her lips would be against his. He shook himself. 'I can send you my pictures of the wildflower meadow from last year, but this year's looks a bit sparse while it's at this stage.'

'Last year's pics would be great,' she said. 'And perhaps you can do me some notes on how honey's produced, plus ideas of what's interesting to see and how easy it'd be to photograph. For the honey itself, I can come up with some styling ideas.'

She was definitely in business mode, and her energy and enthusiasm were both infectious.

'I'll do that this evening,' he promised.

She glanced over towards the woodland. 'As it's the end of April, I assume we still have a few bluebells about?'

'Are you thinking about a picture for the website?' he asked.

'Several.' She smiled at him.

Again, her smile made his blood tingle. Charlie knew he

was going to have to be careful. He didn't want to risk getting close to someone again and losing them. It had taken him a long while to climb out of the black hole after Jess had died and, even though his head knew it was highly unlikely he'd lose someone else in the same way, he wasn't sure he could persuade his heart to take that risk.

Bluebells, he reminded himself. This was all about the bluebells. The farm. The marketing.

She took a few snaps. 'I'd forgotten just how pretty the woods are at this time of year,' she said.

'The bluebell carpet looked better than this, last week,' he told her.

'This is good enough for my purposes, though if you have photographs I could potentially use that'd be great. And we should encourage visitors to take photographs of the farm and post them—it'll build a bit more on their relationship with us. Maybe the picture of the month could win a goodie basket or something as well as having the photo showcased.' She took some close-up shots as well. 'It's a shame we don't still have a farm dog. One of Dad's Labradors would've looked seriously pretty, sitting among these.' She looked up from where she'd crouched by a clump of bluebells to take a close-up shot. 'I don't suppose you have a friend with a well-trained dog who'd pose for us?'

'No,' he said, 'and I'd be wary about having any dogs around here during lambing.'

'Good point—even if the dogs were well trained, if they're not used to livestock it might be tricky,' she said, standing up.

They walked further into the wood, and her hand accidentally brushed against his. Charlie's skin tingled where it touched hers, and he had to force himself not to grab her hand and cling to her as if he were drowning.

Elle Newton was the first woman he'd really been aware

of since he'd lost Jess. For a mad moment, he imagined himself walking hand in hand with her in the wood. What would it be like to kiss her, with the subtle green scent of bluebells in the air, the blue haze of the flowers stretching as far as the eye could see and the birds singing their heads off in the ancient woodlands?

Though he knew things didn't stand a chance of working out between them. They wanted completely opposite things from life; it was crazy to let himself feel like this about someone he knew was so incompatible. He needed to get his common sense back and stop thinking about kissing Elle.

'You know,' she said, 'this would be the perfect place for a proposal.'

'A proposal?' Dear God, he hoped he hadn't mumbled out loud any of those mixed-up thoughts whirling through his head.

'We need a narrative for the wedding side of things,' she said. 'A couple falling in love. A proposal. A party. The wedding itself—or at least a mock-up of one. I assume you're going to show me the barn now?'

'Yes.'

She took his hand and squeezed it gently before releasing it. 'Charlie, are you sure you're really OK with this? It's not stamping on a sore spot? Because I don't want you ending up hurt by the marketing ideas.'

For a moment, his heart was so full of memories and longing and loss that he couldn't speak.

'Charlie?'

He resisted the urge to cradle his hand as if it had been burned. And why did the sound of his name on Elle's lips make his knees feel as if they'd turned to jelly?

'I'm fine,' he fibbed. Yes, it would be like pressing on a bruise; but he wanted the farm to be a success. This was all part of learning to move on. 'Let's go and look at the wedding barn.'

He took her over to the old hay barn, which had been re-roofed and re-floored during the early spring, and new windows let in light all down one side to highlight the gorgeous brickwork and the beams in the ceiling.

'This space is incredible,' she said. 'When I was small, the barn was always full of hay bales. I've never seen it empty like this, before. I had no idea it was this huge.'

'It's big enough to have the wedding ceremony at one end, the wedding breakfast at the other, and then move the chairs from the wedding to the side to give the dance floor,' he said.

'It's perfect,' she said. 'Not just for weddings. You could hire it out for corporate events, too. And maybe for performances—acting troupes, a local Battle of the Bands, that sort of thing. With pop-up food and drink stalls, if we didn't want to use the farm café.'

'Maybe,' he said, pleased that she could see the opportunities in the space.

She walked round it, looking up at the rafters and taking a couple of shots, then at the floor. 'So you opted for wood flooring rather than stone?'

'I talked to your parents about using Norfolk pamments,' he said, referring to the traditional clay tiles of the area, 'but I thought wood would be more practical.'

'Absolutely. It's a smoother surface, so it's less likely that a bride would trip; though, if you had gone for pamments, I would've recommended a carpet for the aisle,' she said. 'I can see this full of fairy lights and woven garlands, and then petals scattered at the sides of the aisle. It'd be magical.'

His own wedding had been very different. He and Jess had got married in Chelsea Old Church, followed by a reception in the Petyt Hall, with its rich deep red walls and beautiful furniture. Photographs in the gardens, drinks on the terrace. All very London and swish.

Jess would have loved it here, though. Knowing her, she would've spent half her week as a wedding planner and the other half doing *pro bono* legal work, a couple of spaniels curled at her feet when she was at her desk. She would've been a pillar of the local toddler group, then joined the PTA when they moved up to infant school, and...

'Charlie?'

'Sorry. Miles away.' And all the might-have-been had brought back the melancholy. 'What did you say?'

'I asked you to sing me something so I can check out the acoustics.'

Every time he thought he had a handle on who Elle was, she surprised him. Jolted him out of his rut. 'What do you want me to sing?' he asked, feeling slow-witted.

'You sing to the cows when you're milking. Sing me something you'd sing to them.'

'Apart from the fact you're not a cow—'

She laughed. 'Are you quite sure about that?'

He couldn't help laughing back.

What was it about this woman that she could melt the shadows away with a single smile?

'I already warned you, I'm not rock-star standard,' he said.

'You don't have to be. Just enough to give me an idea.' She smiled. 'Or I'll sing and you can do the harmonies, if you like. Dad and I always used to sing Oasis songs when I helped him with the milking.' She started singing 'Wonderwall'.

Elle had a lovely voice, but the words were bittersweet. Had the fire in his heart gone out completely when Jess died? Or was the fire still there, just waiting to be fanned back into life?

She nudged him when she got to the chorus, and he joined in, their voices echoing through the barn.

It felt as if he was actually singing it to her, rather than with her; and it unnerved him slightly. Of course nothing was going to happen between them. This was a job. For both of them. But he couldn't shake the feeling that there was something else there. All he had to do was reach out...

'Yeah, that'll do. The acoustics are great,' she said. 'We can definitely offer this space for performances—music, plays, whatever.' She glanced at her watch. 'I know it's a tiny bit early for lunch, but I had breakfast at a truly ridiculous hour this morning. Have you got time for lunch in the farm café? Or, if you're busy, I'll introduce myself to the team and have a poke about in the shop.'

'I do have some stuff I need to sort out,' he said, knowing that he was being a bit of a coward but wanting to let his common sense straighten his head out again.

'Then I'll let you get on. Actually, I'd like to use the time to have a chat with the team about how things work at the moment, and what ideas they might have for change. And then I'd like to put some initial thoughts together that we can discuss with Mum and Dad over dinner tonight.'

Elle Newton was absolutely driven, he thought. The pace of London suited her.

Yet the farm suited her, too. The way she'd looked when she'd made a fuss of the cows, and that wistful expression on her face in the bluebell woods...

'By the way, I recommend the Brie and chutney toastie,' he said.

'What, a farmer not offering a fry-up or a bacon sandwich?' she asked lightly.

'Afraid not. I'm vegetarian,' he said. 'I have been, ever

since I started working here. If someone offered me a steak or a roast beef dinner, now, I'd think of the girls.' He shook his head, grimacing. 'I just couldn't. I'm fine about other people eating meat—it's their choice—but I choose not to, and I'd expect them to respect my choices in the same way I respect theirs.'

'I get that,' she said. 'I'm veggie, too. For the same reason. It made things…interesting, at school.'

'They gave you a hard time for not eating meat?'

She lifted a shoulder. 'It marked me out as different. Though, when one of them tried to force-feed me a ham sandwich, I was sick over him. They never did it again after that.'

'That's disgusting—them, not you,' he said, angry on her behalf. 'I hope you told a teacher.'

'No point. The ringleader smelled of sick all day, and I think it took a while to get the stench out of his shoes. That was enough revenge for me. Yeah, there was a bit more name-calling, oinking followed by vomiting noises, but it's over now,' she said.

'Are you OK?' He reached out and squeezed her shoulder briefly.

'I'm fine. But thank you for being nice about it. I'd better go and chat with the team before the lunchtime rush.'

'Ask for Lisa. She's in charge,' he said as she walked to the door.

Had Elle felt that weird pull of attraction, too, he wondered, and was she using work as an excuse to put some space between them the same way that he was? Though he didn't want to think about that and where it might lead. Better to focus on work, too. And he liked the fact she'd talked about listening to the team's ideas; it was a good sign that she planned to collaborate rather than impose her ideas on them.

* * *

In the cafe, Elle introduced herself to Lisa.

'Ellie Newton. I haven't seen you since I was a dinner lady and you were knee-high to a grasshopper,' Lisa said. 'Welcome home.'

'Thank you,' Elle said. 'Though it's a flying visit. I'm working with Charlie on the marketing for the farm. And if there's any chance you can join me for a quick chat, coffee and one of the Brie toasties Charlie just recommended...'

'The Brie's really good,' Lisa said. 'Your mum makes it. Let's get us both a toastie and a coffee so you can taste for yourself.'

The Brie and chutney in her toastie—which were both produced on the farm—were fantastic, as was the coffee. Lisa had cut a small sliver of the three cakes on offer that day so Elle could taste them all.

'This is every bit as good as the stuff I buy from the deli round the corner from my office in London,' Elle said. 'The presentation's fabulous. I'd love to be able to take shots of all our dishes, and possibly their ingredients as they're being made, so we can showcase the fact that we're offering really local food with very few food miles. That's a big selling point on the eco front.' She turned to the next page in her notebook. 'Would it make your life easier or harder if people could book tables on the website? Or is there something else that would be useful?'

By the end of her conversation with Lisa, she'd learned that the café tended to be busy at lunchtime but was quiet between ten and eleven-thirty, and again after four. The room in the barn complex that was used for classes between half-past nine and half-past two would be free for children's parties from four, which would fit in with school times. And between them the café crew had suggested holding stitching or knitting and coffee groups, toddler story time and a silver surfer session, as well as the children's parties based on the activities that the farm offered for younger school classes.

'The library used to run story time and a drop-in silver surfer café, but their opening hours are down to two mornings and one afternoon a week and they just don't have time to run everything, now,' Lisa said. 'There's a playgroup in the village, but it doesn't help new mums with babies and toddlers.'

Elle finished making notes and closed her notebook. 'I'm going to check out what else is on offer at the village hall, and I think you're right: we might be able to fill some gaps in the community,' she said. 'Though when I come up with a potential plan I'm going to run it by you all before I put it in an official report, to make sure you're happy with what I'm suggesting, and I'll have a second look at anything you think needs tweaking.'

'That sounds great. It's good to see you back, Ellie,' Lisa said.

Elle flinched inwardly at the name, but couldn't be mean-spirited enough to correct her to Elle.

'Your mum and dad are so proud of you, but they really miss you.' Lisa gave a rueful smile. 'I know just how they feel. My Mandy's up in Leeds now and, although she video-calls me every week and I read a bedtime story to my grandson, it's not the same as being there by Jack's bedside and getting a hug before he goes to sleep.'

'I'm only back in West Byfield for a little while, Lisa,' Elle warned gently. 'I love Mum and Dad, but London's my home now.'

Lisa gave her a sad nod. 'You never want to stand in your children's way, but sometimes it's so hard. You just want to hold them close again, but you know you can't because you'll have to drive for hours first.'

'Yeah.' Elle had a lump in her throat. Were her parents as sad as Lisa because she'd chosen to live so far away from them? But it was the farm that had driven her away, not them. And, now she was back, her feelings towards the farm were starting to shift again. Charlie had shown her the place in a new light, and she didn't quite know what to think any more.

When she'd finished at the café, she took a look round the shop. As Charlie had told her, they sold produce both from the farm and from local suppliers. The labels were handwritten, but Elle could see opportunities for branding and cross-selling through the website.

There were framed photographs and paintings on the wall, with a discreet price tag to show which ones were for sale. Elle checked her notes and the framed artwork was indeed by Frieda, the artist who ran photography and art classes here, as were the beautiful greetings cards. There were handmade toiletries, ceramics, glassware, and jewellery so pretty that she ended up buying three pairs of earrings, two for herself and one to send to her best friend.

She took a note of the artist's website and phone number, then headed back to the farmhouse. A quick call netted her a meeting later that afternoon with Frieda, and she texted Charlie.

Seeing Frieda this afternoon to brief her on ideas for logo. Let me know if you want to be at the meeting.

And then she settled down to look at what was on offer in West Byfield, and what sort of things their competitors were offering in different parts of the country.

By the time she'd sketched out a list of potential events they could offer and what she wanted to do with the website, it was time to meet Frieda; Charlie had texted back to say that he was sure she knew what she was doing. In some ways, she was pleased that he had so much faith in her; yet part of her was disappointed that he wouldn't be joining her.

Which was ridiculous.

Charlie was her client. Her parents' business partner. That made a line she shouldn't cross.

Frieda turned out to be beautifully receptive to Elle's suggestions and made some excellent ones of her own. Back at the farm, she put dinner on and changed; when her parents came in, she poured them both a glass of wine.

'Welcome home, love.' Mike hugged his daughter fiercely.

'It's good to be back,' Elle said; and, to her surprise, she actually meant it. 'Charlie should be here in a few minutes. And we have a *lot* to talk about.'

CHAPTER FOUR

CHARLIE HAD EATEN dinner with Angie and Mike plenty of times over the last three years. He enjoyed their company.

But tonight was different.

Elle would be there, too.

OK, so she'd said it would be a business meeting, and they'd be talking about her ideas for the farm's marketing plans. But it didn't feel like a business meeting. It felt like a date.

And that in turn made him feel guilty.

This wasn't meant to be about feeling really attracted to someone for the first time in years; it was meant to be about making the rewilding project a success.

All the same, he couldn't stop thinking about Elle, and it felt like a betrayal of Jess.

As he scrubbed himself in the shower, he could almost hear Jess talking to him. *You can't be on your own for ever, Charlie. You need to meet someone. You've got so much love to give. And you need someone to love you back.*

Maybe he did. Maybe his family and his friends were right: it had been five years, now, and it was time to move on with his life. He'd done the first part of his ten-year plan early, moving out of London and buying into a farm where he had space and animals and could make a real difference to the area. But maybe he was using the rewilding project to distract himself from the fact that he didn't know how to move forward with the emotional side of his life.

He definitely couldn't face the idea of signing up for online dating.

Being set up by well-meaning family and friends had also felt wrong. Even though the women had been nice, they hadn't been Jess and his heart hadn't been in it.

He'd leave it for now. Concentrate on getting the farm sorted. And hopefully that would keep his head occupied enough that he wouldn't let himself get distracted by Elle. By the way her dark eyes sparkled when she was interested in something, by the curve of her mouth, by...

'Focus,' he told himself, and turned the temperature of the shower savagely downwards. He changed into something a little smarter than the jeans and T-shirt he usually wore, then made sure he was at the farmhouse at seven on the dot—not eager and early, yet not trying-too-hard-to-be-casual late.

'Hi.' Elle opened the door and smiled at him.

She'd changed, too. Black trousers, a pretty top, and barely-there make-up. A little more formal than his own work clothes, yet more casual than London office dress; she was good at judging the tone, he thought. He found himself wondering what that soft pink lipstick might taste like, and slammed the brakes on. This evening wasn't meant to have anything to do with kissing Elle Newton.

'My contribution,' he said, handing her a bottle of wine and the locally made chocolates that he'd picked up earlier from the farm shop.

'Thank you. The chocolates will be perfect with coffee,' she said, and stood to the side. 'Come in.'

Why was his heart suddenly beating erratically, just because she'd smiled at him? For pity's sake. He was thirty-one, not fifteen. Getting a grip on himself—just—he followed her into the kitchen.

'We're eating in the dining room tonight,' she said, and ushered him through.

He was used to eating in the farmhouse kitchen with Mike and Angie and whoever happened to be around. This felt way more formal, particularly as she'd set the table with a pristine white tablecloth, silver and crystal.

'Take a seat,' she said. 'I'll bring everything in.'

'Can I help?' he asked.

'Nope. Sit,' she insisted.

He greeted Mike and Angie, accepted a glass of red wine from Mike, and sat down.

She served everything up. 'I'm going to let you eat before we do the business stuff,' she said. 'You can't make decisions on an empty stomach.'

The lasagne—like Elle, he chose the vegetarian option—was wonderful. And he enjoyed the conversation, too. It showed him a different side of Elle, one where she teased her dad about being a dinosaur and swapped recipe suggestions with her mum.

She'd fit perfectly into his family. His mum, dad and sister would love her.

The thought took his breath away. They weren't even dating casually, much less in a place to think about a long-term relationship. He didn't understand where these feelings were coming from: just that they seemed to be bubbling up under the barriers he'd put round his heart, and there didn't seem to be anything he could do to stop them.

'We'll have a break before pudding,' she said. 'This is where you're all going to be working.' She grinned. 'You won't exactly be singing for your supper—especially as you're the one who actually cooked it, Mum, and all I did was heat it through and put together the salad and the garlic bread—but I want the three of you sitting opposite me where you can see the screen of my laptop.'

'This is the first time we've ever seen you do anything—well, to do with your work,' Mike said. 'It feels a bit...' He wrinkled his nose. 'Strange.'

'Doing it this way means no wasted paper with me scribbling things on a display pad, plus I can't draw a straight line with a ruler,' she said with a smile. 'Righty. We've got six different things your customers want to know about. The first is general information about the farm and the rewilding. The second is the accommodation and the third is the courses—both of them need a proper online booking system and calendar, which the office can sort out for me. Then there's the farm shop, which needs an online shopping cart; the café, which needs a sample menu and an online booking system; and finally the wedding and function room, which is the one where the customer fills in a very simple online form with their basic requirements and you call them back.'

'That's an awful lot of work,' Angie said.

'And I have specialists back in the office who can sort out the forms, the systems and the shopping cart for us,' she said. 'I've talked to Frieda about doing us a logo, so basically people see it and think of us straight away. It'll tie in everything from the labels in the farm shop to the menus in the café, from the wedding brochure to the accommodation brochure, plus the website and the blog and the newsletter.'

She was animated and all lit up, clearly pleased with the work she'd done so far on the project, and her enthusiasm was infectious. Charlie liked the fact she didn't spin everything out. Short, sweet and very much to the point.

'I've been chatting to the team at the café,' Elle said. 'They'd like an online booking system for lunches and maybe for afternoon tea, which I can sort out via the website. And they've got some good ideas about how they can use the quieter times more effectively: if we hold a few more classes before lunch, people will have coffee beforehand and maybe stay for lunch as well. And we could host children's parties after school.'

'How would the parties work?' Charlie asked.

'We'd have one person from the café team in charge, but also make sure there were enough parents attending the party to keep all the children safe. We'd set up in the room we use for classes, so it doesn't matter if it's raining—or we could even use the wedding barn, because that would give them plenty of room. We can run party games in the room, and have a table with a birthday tea at one end,' she said. 'The team suggested we could offer a birthday cake for an extra charge—a hedgehog cake with the "spines" made out of chocolate buttons, perhaps. Lisa's already been looking up templates for a lamb, a tractor and a squirrel. We can also offer goodie bags as an extra—a pencil, a notebook, an animal mask, a packet of seeds, that sort of thing. We were thinking we could do some of the things we already offer on infant school visits: pond dipping, bug hunts, planting a sunflower or something and feeding the chickens or the lambs. And we'd have some indoor games, too: pass the parcel, pin the tail on the lamb—except we'd use magnets on a board rather than something with a pin, so it'd be safer for little ones.'

'I like that idea,' Angie said. 'It's got a lovely community feel about it.'

'That's what the café team thinks, too. I've been looking at what other rare breeds places do. We could consider offering yearly animal adoptions,' Elle said, 'and give the adopter an official Bluebell Farm adoption certificate, a photo of the animal they've adopted, a quarterly newsletter and a voucher for a drink and a piece of cake in our café on their birthday.'

'That sounds doable,' Mike said.

'And we could offer mail order from the shop, or even click-and-collect,' Elle added. 'One of the team at the agency can set up the computer side of it, and we can take advice about the packaging side—perishable foods, ambient groceries and then the non-food items.'

She'd really thought about this, and Charlie was impressed by the fact that she'd got the café team on board before they even considered making changes to the website.

'It sounds as if you've really been busy,' Mike said.

She smiled. 'I haven't finished, yet, Dad. I think it's worthwhile doing a survey to see what people in the area would like us to provide. Lisa said that since the library opens fewer days a week, there aren't as many facilities available for young parents or retired people. We can fill the gap. I've had a look at what other farms in other parts of the country do, and there are some really good courses that mix nature and art—things that I think would work well with what we're doing here. Plant-dyeing yarn would fit in well with the spinning classes and possibly a knitting or stitching club. And there's print making with cyanotypes.'

'Cyanotypes?' Angie asked.

Elle took her phone from her pocket, tapped into the internet and handed it to her mother. 'It's an early form of photo printing, using the power of the sun plus an iron and salt solution. So kids could do it as well as adults. We're looking to attract families as well as couples, right?'

'Right,' Charlie said.

'This is something I would've loved to do as a kid. Or even now. I love the deep blue of the background. The leaves and the flowers look almost like ghosts on the page. I think people will sign up for this in droves, Mum.'

Angie handed the phone to Mike, who peered at it and passed it to Charlie.

'We can use things from the farm to make the pictures—everything from curly ferns through to cow parsley and feathers. The longer you leave the project, the better the detail is. And people on the course can make a print and a couple of cards to take home,' Elle continued. 'Actually, I mentioned it to Frieda, this afternoon, when I briefed her on the farm logo, and she's very happy to run a course.'

'That sounds a great idea,' Charlie said.

'Good.' Elle smiled at him, and again he felt that weird squeezing around the area of his heart. He didn't understand why she was affecting him like this, and it made him antsy.

'Given that we're all about sustainability, I was thinking that we could offer willow weaving classes,' Elle continued. 'There are loads of things we could do. Hearts for Valentine's Day, or to decorate summer solar-powered string lights. Garden trugs, decorations for Christmas, or a willow Christmas tree which can be decorated with ivy and lights for the holidays, and could be used outdoors in the spring and summer to support climbing plants in the garden. Not to mention we could weave the stuff ourselves for the wedding barn: willow hearts for the walls, willow pyramids we can festoon with fairy lights, and a willow arch for the "altar" that we can decorate with flowers. And we can cross-sell everything.'

She ticked off the items on her fingers as she spoke; Charlie could see how she could've persuaded her clients to try something new. Her energy was irresistible, and she was fizzing with ideas: but she was also very aware of the practical side of things and how they'd fit in to the farm's current offerings.

'It all sounds wonderful,' Angie said. She bit her lip. 'But it also sounds like an awful lot of extra work, love.'

'It's not as much work as it sounds, once everything's set up,' Elle said. 'We can keep the newsletter simple and structured: a calendar showing what activities are available for booking this month, and a couple of paragraphs and pictures showing what's happening on the farm this month. You can talk about any new arrivals, or something you've changed or discovered.'

'The thing is, love, we can't afford to employ anyone new to handle this sort of stuff,' Mike warned gently.

'You don't have to employ anyone,' Elle said. 'I can do the newsletter and updates for you in London, in my spare time—not as part of the agency, but as your daughter doing her bit for the family business. You tell me about it, I'll write it up, and then when you've approved the copy and sent me photos, I can put everything up for you on the blog and send the newsletter to your mailing list.'

'I think it sounds a great idea,' Charlie said. 'And I'm happy to liaise with you to do the newsletter and blog.' That would take the burden off Mike and Angie's shoulders.

The brilliant smile she gave him made him feel warm all over.

'I'll do what I can to set everything up while I'm here, for a soft launch,' she said.

'Soft launch?' Mike asked.

'Making a couple of little changes every day, rather than setting it all up and then transferring it over all at once. Word of mouth will get people looking at the farm's website and social media every day. And I'll do the maintenance in London so you don't have to worry about it.'

'I can help with the videos and pictures,' Charlie said.

'Thank you. I think we can start with the things that you're so used to, you take them a bit for granted, but potential visitors would love—things like cows grazing in the field, lambs skipping about, someone bottle-feeding an early lamb where you can see its little tail whizzing round. And people have no idea how loud a sheep sounds when it baas, or that a lamb sounds so much higher-pitched than its mum,' she said.

'Newborn calves would be good, too—when they're still wobbly on their legs and their mum's licking them clean.' Charlie grinned. 'Watching lambs learning to jump is fun, too. That's one of the things that really caught my eye when I was doing my course.'

She made notes. 'And the cows playing football. I am *so* having a video of that on our blog. I've got the caption already.' She raised her eyebrows. 'Moo-ve over, Cristiano Ronaldo.'

Everyone groaned, and she laughed.

'Is it worth filming the chickens?' Charlie asked.

'When they're scratching in the fields? Definitely,' she said. 'And you told me they're chatty. I want to film them chatting to you. Plus we need to borrow some children to play "hunt the egg" and show us what they find. I'll style the eggs for some still shots, too, depending on what colour they are.'

'They're all tinted—that's brown, to you,' he said.

She tipped her head slightly to one side. How cute she looked, he thought. 'Explain tinted.'

'It means the eggs are light brown on the outside, and white inside the shell. It's all because of the pigment protoporphyrin, and when it's deposited on the shell during the laying process,' he explained.

Her dark eyes glittered with interest. 'I had no idea

about that sort of thing. It might make a good blog post. Can you give me some facts and figures?'

'Sure. It takes twenty-six hours for an egg to pass through a hen's oviduct, and it takes twenty of those hours for the shell to be produced,' he said, blurting out the first couple of facts that came to mind.

'That's amazing. I had no idea. Can you let me have some more like that, so I can do a "top ten things you didn't know about eggs" post?' she asked.

'Sure,' he said. 'I'll email you later tonight.'

'Great.' She looked pleased. 'I thought we could also cover special days—not just Valentine's Day and Christmas, but things like World Bee Day. We can have videos of the bees in the hive, stills of the wildflower meadow, and maybe put up some ideas of what people can do to help bring bees into their gardens.'

'I've got some notes on bees,' he said. 'I'll dig them out.'

'That'd be brilliant. Thank you, Charlie.'

And again she gave him that heart-squeezing smile, before clearing the table and bringing in a large glass dish which looked as if it contained a rhubarb fool, decorated with little slices of rhubarb. It had the perfect blend of tartness and creaminess, but there was something he couldn't quite work out. Elle had clearly read his expression, because she said, 'I used Greek yoghurt rather than cream, and there's a tiny bit of orange juice and grated orange rind in with the rhubarb.'

'It's lovely,' he said.

She shrugged. 'It's simple and quick. Plus I love rhubarb, so I raided Mum's patch.'

Elle Newton was incredibly capable, he thought. She'd clearly been really busy working on the marketing ideas for the farm, yet she'd produced an excellent pudding as well—food that was good enough to be on the menu of the farm café.

After the pudding, she brought in a platter of cheese and crackers. 'These are all from the farm shop—though I want to actually do one of your cheese-making courses, Mum, so I can take photos and write it up so people realise how awesome it is.'

Though she hadn't just dumped the cheese on a plate and the crackers in a dish; she'd styled it as a proper platter, with tiny bunches of grapes and sticks of celery heart with the fronded leaves still on them, and the crackers were arranged beautifully. Charlie would just bet she'd taken photographs, too, planning to use them to showcase the farm shop's produce. Yet, at the same time, it felt as if she was making a real fuss of her parents and of him, making everything look nice so they'd feel special.

How did she do that, combining her work and her personal life so everything was multi-tasked but didn't feel fake? It made him realise that his own attempts on the farm website really were as hopeless as she'd pronounced them, and he shouldn't have been offended at her bluntness. His own work had been plodding and pedestrian, and Elle would make it sparkle.

'We've pretty much covered everything except the wedding stuff,' she said. 'Until we actually have some weddings whose photos we can use, we'll need a narrative.'

'What sort of narrative?' Charlie asked.

'Show the romantic side of the farm. Watching the sun set over the fields, cuddling new lambs, walking among the bluebells and the wildflower meadow—that sort of thing.'

He knew she was talking about business, but somehow it felt as if those words were purely for him. A personal offer. It was scary and exhilarating all at the same time: as if life was suddenly opening up again in front of him.

They spent the rest of dinner batting ideas around, drinking coffee and eating the chocolates he'd brought, and by the end of the evening Elle's parents had overcome their reluctance to change things and were definitely on board with what she wanted to do to the website.

'Let me do the washing up before I go home,' he said when he helped her take the coffee mugs back into the kitchen.

'No. You have to be up early tomorrow for milking. I'll sort it,' she said firmly.

'My parents brought me up the same way yours brought you up,' he reminded her. 'If I'd cooked, you would've insisted on doing the washing up.'

She spread her hands. 'You've already done your bit. You helped convince Mum and Dad. Besides, the cows won't be happy with me if I make you late for milking. Anyway, I want to talk to you tomorrow about the wedding stuff. Run something by you before I suggest it to Mum and Dad.' She paused. 'Maybe I could do the milking with you tomorrow? At least, I'll bring coffee and talk your ear off, and maybe take a couple of pics for the website.'

Multi-tasking again.

Even though Charlie was enjoying working with Elle, and he liked milking the cows, if he was honest with himself he had to admit they weren't the things he was looking forward to most, tomorrow.

What he really wanted was to spend time with her. For the sparkle she brought to rub off on his life.

'I start milking at half-past six,' he warned.

'I'll be there. The byre, yes?'

'Yes.'

Her dark eyes were huge. For a moment, Charlie wondered if she was going to lean in and kiss his cheek. He realised that he was even swaying slightly forward, inviting her to do it. He'd only had one glass of wine, so he couldn't blame his behaviour on that—or even on a sugar rush from the chocolate. It was all Elle, making him feel a little bit wobbly.

Get a grip, he told himself, and straightened up again. 'See you tomorrow. Thank you for dinner.' His mouth clearly wasn't on track with the programme, because he found himself adding, 'Maybe I can cook dinner for you.'

Noooo. Why had he suggested that? It was practically inviting her on a date.

'And we can brainstorm a bit more of the website,' he added hastily, to make it seem more like work.

'I'd like that.'

Did she have any idea what was going on in his head? Was the same thing going on in hers? He didn't dare meet her eyes properly, and he knew he was being an utter coward. 'Goodnight,' he said, and made a hasty retreat.

Back at his cottage, Charlie looked up the social media links Elle had sent him, using the passwords she'd given him for the accounts she'd set up for the farm. The first picture on *@bluebellfarmnorfolk* was one of the bluebells shimmering in the wood, with a comment about how the farm had got its name. There was a picture of the farmhouse, one of Elderberry eating hay with her head framed in the hay rack, and the three calves, captioned *#moobellfarm*; the chickens, captioned *#notquite50shades* *#norfolkgrey*; and Portia with Viola and Sebastian, the lambs skipping along beside their mother.

All things he loved; but Elle made him see them with new eyes. The sharpness of the detail. The single bluebell, its narrow bell-shaped flowers bending the stem into a graceful curve, the richness.

Her post was practically a love letter to the farm.

OK, so her job was to sell things—and she'd definitely

picked up on the farm's big selling points—but surely it wasn't all surface? Surely she felt a connection to the farm?

Yet he knew why she'd hated it so much here. Ten years ago, he'd had a distraught teenager sobbing on his shoulder after prom about how she didn't fit in with the rest of the school; she'd fled prom when she'd overheard Damien Price saying he'd only asked her to go with him because Smelly Ellie Moo-ton would be so grateful to have a date for prom that she'd definitely have sex with him and... She'd stopped then, clearly not wanting to repeat what Damien had suggested, and instead mumbled that he thought she'd do anything he asked her to. Charlie had a pretty good idea what the guy had suggested.

And then, she'd continued, he'd tell his friends all the details of exactly what she'd done with him, and the whole town would know and despise her. And everyone was laughing at her anyway, because they were all just seeing a heifer in a fancy dress...

Charlie had wanted to find Damien Price, pin him to a wall and make him take on board the fact that you never, *ever* treated a date like that; but he knew that wouldn't help Elle, right then. So instead he'd told her that she was worth far, far more than a selfish loser like Damien. He'd told her to ignore the small minds of the town, and that she could be whoever she wanted to be. The best judge of who she was was *herself* and nobody else.

Clearly she'd taken his words to heart, because she'd gone to university and she'd blossomed; she'd carved out a good career.

And now Elle was back in West Byfield. She'd changed the way she looked, turned herself from scruffy farm girl to elegant city businesswoman; though that was purely surface and Charlie really didn't care about that. The woman he was getting to know was bright, independent and strong, and he really liked her.

He looked further back in her social media feeds. She posted all about the perfect London life: fabulous food, cocktails and stylish coffee bars. There were shots of Elle next to posters for theatre performances and gigs, either on her own or as part of a crowd. He saw what appeared to be a couple of boyfriends in the pictures, even tagged *#Londondate* and *#romance*, but the men seemed to be identikit city types. The type of man he'd been, when he'd been married to Jess, he thought wryly. But none of them had seemed to last for more than a couple of dates. Elle herself had said they dumped her as soon as they saw where she came from.

Even more interestingly, not everything Elle posted was about the glamour of the city. She'd snapped patches of green in London, too, and there were vases of flowers. Perhaps he should've taken her flowers tonight after all, because she clearly loved them.

Maybe she'd join him tomorrow on the nature walk, and he could find out a bit more about what made her tick.

CHAPTER FIVE

IF ANYONE HAD told Elle back in London that a boiler suit and green wellies could look sexy, she would never have believed them. Seeing Charlie Webb in the milking parlour was a revelation. In a boiler suit and wellies, he looked utterly gorgeous.

Or was she just confusing herself and starting to believe the narrative she was creating in her head for the farm?

She'd brought two travel mugs of coffee—remembering from the previous evening that he took his coffee black—and handed one to him.

'Thanks,' he said.

He'd already brought the cows in, and Juniper was tied to the hitching post.

'Can I film some of this for the farm website?' she asked.

'Sure. What do you need me to do?'

'Telling me what you're doing as you're doing it, basically. Introduce me to the cow. Pretend you're talking to people who've never met a cow but might fancy a weekend in the country.'

He looked awkward. 'All right.'

She raised her camera. 'Ready?' At his nod, she started to film.

'Our girls all like us to sing ballads while we milk

them. This is Juniper, one of our British White cows, and she likes the kind of songs my parents grew up with.' He broke into 'Hey Jude', changing the name from Jude to Juniper, and Elle grinned, enjoying the wordplay. She filmed a verse and chorus, then stopped the video and put her phone back in her pocket.

He stopped singing and frowned. 'Was my voice that bad?'

She smiled. 'No, but I don't need the entire song. I'll be cutting small clips together to make a single short film. Now talk me through milking.'

She filmed more clips, paying attention to his hands and how he handled the cow. She'd forgotten the scent of warm milk with its faintly grassy tang.

Finally, he finished milking the cow, wiped her teats with dip, made a fuss of her and unhitched her.

'Have you finished filming now?' he asked, looking slightly pained. 'I thought we were going to have the conversation we didn't have last night?'

There was a weird tingling in the ends of Elle's fingers as she looked at Charlie. The conversation they hadn't had. The moment when she'd felt he was leaning slightly towards her, and every nerve in her body had screamed at her to lean right back towards him and touch her mouth to his…

'Uh—yes. The conversation,' she said.

'So what did you want to run by me?' Charlie asked.

'The wedding stuff.' She looked awkward. 'I know this is a big ask, so I didn't want to bring it up in front of Mum and Dad—but you said you'd be the face of the farm.'

'Ye-es.' He'd already agreed that. Why was she repeating herself?

She took a deep breath. 'Could you be our groom, too, until we get a real one?'

'A fake bridegroom?' That was a horrible idea.

His distaste must've shown in his face, because she said hastily, 'Fake's probably the wrong word. What I mean is, would you act as the groom in our narrative?'

His head was spinning. 'I…'

'Don't worry. I thought it was an ask too far,' she said. 'I was hoping we would save on the budget. If you'd do it, we wouldn't have to pay models or agency fees, but maybe I can call in a favour from someone.'

Her expression said it was pretty unlikely. And he'd rather the money for the marketing campaign was spent on something more urgent, like building the booking system and shopping cart. 'What would it involve?'

'We'd be cross-selling everything, showing that the farm's the background to every bit of a romance. The story is that a couple stay on the farm in the accommodation, and watch the sunset together or the sunrise.' She spread her hands. 'Maybe both. A romantic dinner, a stroll in the woods or through the wildflower meadow, an afternoon cuddling newborn lambs. Then a proposal—I was thinking at the beach, to give people an idea of the wonderful bits of the countryside nearby. And we can have the barn all dressed up for a small intimate wedding.'

'And who would be the bride?'

'Me,' she said.

Elle, acting as his girlfriend and then his bride. His heart started to thud. Maybe this would put an extra barrier between them, making her safe to be around. And maybe it was what he needed: pretending to date, as the next step to actually dating. Finally moving on.

It wouldn't be putting his past in a box—he'd always

love Jess—but maybe it might be the catalyst he needed. 'Who's going to take the photographs?' he asked.

'Of us? We are. Selfies,' she explained. 'I want to keep an intimate feel.'

Intimate. Now there was a word that made him feel completely flustered.

'So our dinner tonight will be a date,' she said, ruffling his peace of mind even further. 'As far as the website is concerned, I mean. Both of us dressed glamorously.' She narrowed her eyes at him. 'The suit you wore in London will do very nicely.'

'Are you telling me you brought glamorous clothes with you?'

'No,' she said, 'but there are these special things you might have heard of. They're called shops.'

He couldn't remember the last time someone had teased him. And it felt amazingly good. He grinned. 'I'm not sure that West Byfield is up to London fashion standards.'

'I'm not going shopping in West Byfield. Now, is your kitchen tidy, or can we use one of the shepherd's huts?'

His place wasn't untidy, but it wasn't glamorous, either. It was just a place to lay his head.

'Shepherd's hut, I think. Check with your mum.'

'Will do.' She smiled at him. 'Right. That's me going on a prop hunt.'

'I've got a nature walk this afternoon, if you wanted to come along,' he said. Because of course she needed to experience it. It had absolutely nothing to do with him wanting her company.

'What time?'

'Half-past three.'

'I'll be there,' she promised. 'It's an hour and a half, right?' At his nod, she said, 'Which gives me enough time to change and cook dinner. Any food dislikes or allergies I need to know about?'

'You already know I'm vegetarian. Nothing else.'

'Good. I'll go and talk to Mum about schedules, and then do my props run.'

'Have fun,' he said. 'See you at half-past three by the café.'

'Perfect,' she said.

And funny how her smile felt as if it lit up the whole world—including the darkest corners of his heart that had been hidden for years.

Elle checked with her mum which shepherd's hut she could use, then borrowed her car and drove into Norwich. She'd made a list on her phone of the clothes that would work in the different scenarios, and it didn't take her long to find what she wanted. She spent a bit more time working on the farm's media plan, including several press releases and the media she wanted to target; and then it was time to meet Charlie and the nature walkers.

He was in the courtyard with six people, whom she assumed were all guests staying in the holiday accommodation. There were two couples of around their own age—she winced inwardly, wondering if that would remind Charlie of himself and Jess—and an older couple who were holding hands. The older couple that Charlie and Jess hadn't had the chance to become.

'Hello, Elle,' Charlie said with a broad smile, and introduced her to their guests. 'Elle grew up here,' he said, 'so although I'm leading the walk I'm pretty sure she'll chip in and correct me from time to time.'

'Think of me as one of the guests. I'm revamping the farm's website,' she explained to the walkers, 'so I'm reviewing what we offer.' She grinned. 'And if you'd like to mark Charlie out of ten at the end, I'm all ears.'

He coughed and gave her a pained look, before saying, 'You really don't have to mark me.'

'I was teasing about that,' she agreed, 'but, seriously, if there's anything you would've liked to see more or less of, please let me know. We want everyone to really enjoy their stay here and get the most out of their time on the farm.'

Clearly she'd said the right thing, this time, because Charlie gave her a warm smile of approval. Except her libido interpreted it rather differently, and her knees felt as if they were buckling.

Somehow she managed to keep herself upright, and she strolled along behind the group as Charlie led them through the meadows, telling them about the cows and the sheep and the chickens, and how they were rewilding the farm. He really knew his stuff; he was able to answer every single question, and he couched it in terms that everyone could understand.

Everyone gave a delighted gasp when they saw the bluebells. 'It's a proper carpet,' one of the younger women said.

'We're getting near the end of the season now, but they've been here a very long time,' Elle said. 'Having this many bluebells in one place is a sign of ancient woodland—it shows that the wood dates back at least four hundred years. I remember coming here with my mum and my gran when I was a toddler, and it was like a sea of flowers.'

Charlie made the group stop and listen in the middle of the woods, and taught them how to distinguish between several different birdcalls. Elle had never been any good at distinguishing them, but Charlie's words helped her to isolate some of the calls and hear them clearly. He obviously loved this part of country life and looked delighted to share it with others and help them feel the magic, too.

'What's the one that sounds like a rattle?' one of the others asked.

'That,' Charlie said, 'is a magpie who's a bit annoyed about something and making his displeasure known.' He rolled his eyes. 'There's one nesting in the tree outside my bedroom window who likes to wake me at four in the morning using that exact call.'

'It'd drive me *mad*,' one of the younger men said.

'It gets me up in time for milking,' Charlie said. 'But, yes, I admit, if it's not my turn for milking, I can't help wishing it nested on the other side of the wood, so I could get a couple more hours of sleep!'

When they reached the wildflower meadow, Elle couldn't resist asking everyone to name as many of the flowers as they could before she filled in the gaps.

'You know so much about the flowers. Are you a plant specialist?' the older man asked.

'Most of it is stuff my gran taught me when I was very small,' Elle said. 'I used to love walking by the hedgerows with her and seeing all the different flowers.' She'd forgotten how much she loved it; today had scrubbed away some of the stains of the bullying and let her see the farm for what it really was rather than the place that had haunted her.

After Charlie had introduced the walkers to the cattle and let them pet the cows, and they'd answered all the questions, they took their guests back to the café.

'I thought we made a good team on the walk,' he said, when the guests had gone. 'Me on the birdsong and you on the flowers.'

'It worked well,' she agreed. 'And I think our guests had a good time and learned a lot. Is that usually how it goes?'

'I try to tailor the talks to whatever they're interested in,' he said. 'But you had them in the palm of your hand with all the flower stuff. You taught me a lot, too—I had no idea about some of the things you were telling them. Soapwort actually being used as soap, and called Bouncing Bet because it looks like a laundrymaid at work.'

'I admit I learned that when I was working on a detergent campaign, but I've always liked flowers,' she said. 'Actually, my guilty pleasure is to go to the flower market at Columbia Road every week and treat myself to a bunch of something gorgeous.' She shrugged. 'Which I guess is better for me than chocolate.' She glanced at her watch. 'See you at six-thirty in Hut Two. Which needs a proper name,' she said. 'We'll brainstorm it.'

'It's a date,' he said. And then his eyes widened. 'Not a *date* date,' he said, sounding awkward.

'Of course not. It's an acting date,' she said. 'For the farm.'

'For the farm.'

And it stung a bit that he sounded so grateful. What would be so bad about actually dating her for herself? Or maybe she was overreacting, because West Byfield still made her feel antsy. Charlie had helped remind her of the times when she'd been happy here, milking with her dad and looking at the wildflowers with her mum and her gran; but the misery of her high school years still echoed in her head. 'See you later,' she said coolly.

What had just happened? Charlie wondered. Elle had been perfectly friendly during the nature walk; she was a natural, responding to the walkers and judging the right amount of detail to keep them interested. They'd agreed to meet this evening, as planned, to start the marketing campaign. He couldn't think what on earth he'd said to upset her. Unless, maybe, she'd realised that he was protesting a bit too much about tonight not being a date. That she'd guessed he was attracted to her, and she didn't feel the same way about him.

He raked a hand through his hair. Or maybe he was overcomplicating things and she hadn't been cool towards him at all; maybe it was simply that he felt guilty for being attracted to her. Survivor guilt, perhaps. He knew Jess wouldn't have wanted him to mourn her for ever, but it just seemed so unfair that she'd never had the chance to live their dreams.

He didn't have any answers, but at least he could distract himself by going to check the fences around the livestock. And he'd need to be back at his cottage in time to scrub up properly for his 'date' with Elle.

Elle walked back to the farmhouse via the bluebell woods, so she could gather a small posy for the table. Once she'd showered and changed and put together a box of the ingredients she needed, she headed for Hut Two.

She sorted out the main dish first, and popped it into the oven, before setting up the hut for filming. A bit of raffia tied round the neck of a jam jar made it look rustic and chic, once the bluebells were in water. She set the table outside with a plain tablecloth and a candle as well as the bluebells, then went back into the shepherd's hut and prepped the starter and the pudding.

As the minutes ticked by, anticipation started to fizz in her veins. Even though she knew this was just for the farm's website, and they'd agreed it was an acting date rather than a proper date, it *felt* as if she were cooking for her new man. And she hadn't felt like this about a real date in years; she'd dated so many Mr Wrongs that she'd just given up trying to find the right one.

'It's not real. Charlie's your fake boyfriend,' she reminded herself. 'Fake fiancé-to-be.'

But maybe feeling as if it was real would make the photos more convincing. And they needed their potential brides and grooms to see the romance, didn't they?

At precisely half-past six, Charlie arrived. He sniffed the air. 'Something smells fabulous.'

'It's very easy,' she said. 'My go-to dinner party menu in London. You can ignore it and leave it to look after itself in the oven.'

'And you look gorgeous,' he said.

'Thank you.' She inclined her head. 'As do you. Can you open this for me?' She retrieved the Prosecco from the fridge. 'Then we can take a selfie at the table.'

He opened the bottle without spilling a drop, and poured two glasses. Elle took various selfies of them holding their glasses together in a toast, then put on a playlist of romantic songs. 'Give me five minutes to mess about in the kitchen,' she said.

And she was glad of the break; Charlie, all scrubbed up and in formal clothes, was breathtaking. She'd wanted the romance to look realistic, yes; but she also needed to flatten some of those little flutters of attraction, because it would be too easy to make a fool of herself.

'That looks sublime,' Charlie said, when Elle brought out two plates of griddled asparagus in melted butter, with half a lemon tied in muslin on the side.

'Very, very early English asparagus that I begged off Lisa,' she said, and took photographs of the plate.

It tasted as good as it looked.

Then she brought out a baked mushroom risotto with chickpeas, teamed with a dish of very garlicky wilted spinach and another of tomatoes roasted on the vine. It was a domestic side of Elle he hadn't expected; from what he remembered, London was all about eating out or takeaways, and there was never enough time to cook properly. Though she had mentioned dinner parties; and he already knew she'd inherited her mother's amazing organisational skills. So maybe she really was the sharp city girl she'd told him she was.

She took more photographs. 'This is going to look great as a collage,' she told him. 'The shepherd's hut lit with fairy lights inside—they were an excellent idea, by the way.'

He smiled in acknowledgement of the compliment.

'The table with the candle and bluebells, framed by the lavender,' she continued, 'the food, and us with glasses of fizz.'

'The perfect romantic evening,' he said.

But the weird thing was, even though he knew this was all for show, it *felt* romantic. Like a proper date.

Elle was still virtually a stranger, and yet on a deeper level Charlie felt that he knew her.

'So what's your five-year plan?' he asked, refilling their glasses.

'Promotion to Senior Account Manager, then head of creative, and then maybe start my own agency,' she said.

'So you wouldn't come back here if your parents want to retire?'

'There's no need. They have a perfectly adequate farm manager,' she said.

'I wasn't fishing for compliments.'

'I know.' She sighed. 'But I don't want Mum and Dad getting their hopes up. I'm not going to come back here with Mr Right and produce the next generation to hand the farm to.'

'You don't want children?'

'It's more that I don't think I'll ever find the Mr Right to have children with. And I'm concentrating on my career,' she said. 'It's not as bad at Bluebell Farm as I remember it being during my teens, I admit. And thank you for reminding me of the bits I'd forgotten I loved about the farm. But nowadays I belong in London.' She paused. 'So what's your five-year plan?'

'The rewilding project,' he said. 'I want to increase the diversity of the flora and fauna. Reverse the decline in numbers of the species we do have.' Which meant living here, not London.

'What about when you've done that?' she asked.

'Consolidation.'

'It's about as far as you can possibly get from the life you had in London,' she mused.

She was right on the nail. 'I needed a change.'

'Would Jess have liked it here?' she asked quietly.

He liked the fact that she didn't shy away from saying his late wife's name. 'Yes. She would've loved the sunrises, being up with the birds in the morning, listening to the skylarks and trying to spot them.'

'Is that what you like, too?' she asked.

'As I said earlier, I can breathe here. I couldn't, in London. Not any more.' He swallowed. 'Not without Jess.'

'It's still hard to cope?' she asked gently.

She was being kind, not prying or smothering him with unwanted pity. 'It's been five years. It's not as raw, not like the early days when I couldn't even get out of bed and I was curled into a ball, sobbing my eyes out.' He looked at her. 'But there are still days where it feels as if the centre's been sucked out of the world. Where I just want to be on my own: me and the fields and the animals and the wide skies. I'll never be able to repay your parents for giving me the space I needed, when I needed it.'

'My parents are great,' she said. 'Which is why I don't want them to know about how bad it was at school, or what really happened at the prom. It wasn't their fault; plus they already had more than enough to handle, with Gran's illness, so I don't want them hurt by finding out about it now and realising I kept it from them.'

That sense of loyalty alone would've drawn him to Elle. Charlie didn't let himself dwell too deeply on what else drew him to her.

'I'm fortunate never to have experienced a loss like yours—I was too small to remember much about Grandad, and when Gran died I was sad but relieved that she wasn't in pain and just *lost*, any more. My mum's parents were older, when they died, and they'd had time to have a good and happy life together,' she said. 'But I can imagine how hard it must be for you, with Jess being so young and all the things you didn't have time to do together.' She reached out and squeezed his hand briefly. 'You were really kind to me, all those years ago. You made everything bearable, that night. So if you ever need a friend, someone who'll listen and not judge, and keep everything you say completely private, I'm here for you.'

She meant it. He could see the sincerity in her expression. 'Thank you.' But if he opened up to her, if he let her close, if he let himself start to feel again…that was a risk he wasn't quite ready to take. 'I was looking through the stuff you've done for the farm on social media,' he said. 'It's amazing.'

'It's a start,' she said. 'I've asked Frieda to use bluebells in the farm logo; I'm hoping she'll come up with a really simple line-drawing that we can use on the labels of everything we produce as well as on the website. Make it recognisable as ours, and tie everything together.'

'Sounds good,' he said. 'I looked at your social media, too. It looks like you have the perfect life in London.'

'The West End, cocktails, afternoon tea. It's pretty

much what people expect to see in my life,' she said with a shrug.

'So it's not real?'

'It is and it isn't,' she said. 'I work hard, but I play hard as well. My socials don't show the admin or the chores, because nobody's interested in that.'

'Aren't they?'

'No,' she said. 'People who come to the Bluebell Farm account won't want to see you wrestling with the accounts, or filing receipts, or ordering cow cake, or even mucking out the byre. They'll want to see the highlights—the bluebells, the newborn lambs and the cows playing football. The stuff that makes them feel all warm and fuzzy.'

'I guess,' he said.

'And, for the record, I love my life in London. Summer evenings with cocktails on a rooftop terrace as you watch the sun set over the Thames, spring when the rain makes Covent Garden glisten and all the wisteria comes out in Chelsea, winter with all the Christmas lights and the sparkly stuff, and autumn when you go to see the deer on a misty morning in Richmond Park and walk under falling leaves on the Embankment.'

Things that sounded delightful; things that Charlie hadn't done with Jess, because he'd been too focused on work and not focused enough on life outside—just as Jess had been. It had taken losing her to make him get a better work-life balance. Or maybe he'd just swapped one workaholic lifestyle for a slightly different but equally intense one. The pictures Elle had just painted in his head made him wonder if he'd see London differently now.

'You're really happy there,' he said.

'I am,' she confirmed.

'Then we'd better make sure this campaign goes viral,

so the farm's a success and you get your dream job,' he said. 'That way, we both win.'

'We both win,' she said, and clinked her glass against his.

Maybe the bubbles had gone to his head, because he held his hand out to her. 'Dance with me?'

Her eyes went wide and her lips parted slightly. Her breathing looked as shallow as his suddenly felt.

'I…' Then she seemed to pull herself together. 'Method acting? You're absolutely right. The best way to write copy about dancing under the stars is to do it first,' she said.

Her words brought his common sense back—but only for as long as it took to stand up and take her into his arms. Then all the sparkly stuff seemed to start up again. Even though the stars weren't out and it wasn't really that dark.

They didn't talk, just danced cheek to cheek. He hadn't danced with anyone since Jess. Yet, although in some ways this should've felt like a betrayal, it felt *right*.

A slow, smoochy dance. Where Elle was close enough that he could smell the vanilla scent of her perfume, a sweetness that undercut her sharp city girl persona. Where her arms were wrapped tightly around his. Where it felt as if his heart was beating time with hers.

His cheek was right next to hers, and her skin felt so soft.

All he had to do was move his head slightly, and the corner of her mouth would be right next to his. And if she turned hers, too, then the angles would be perfect and his mouth would meet hers, and…

A shrill crowing noise split the air, and he pulled back. *Saved by the rooster.*

'I thought roosters only crowed in the morning?' Elle said, looking dazed.

Had she, too, thought about them kissing? He pulled

himself together with an effort. He needed to get them back on a friend-zone footing. Like *now*. 'According to Carbon, any time of day's good for crowing. It's an "all clear" to let the hens know it's safe to forage.' Plus the rooster had just stopped Charlie making what could've been the worst mistake ever. 'And he's a pretty good dancer, too.'

'He dances?'

'Flutters his feathers, struts his stuff and circles the hen until she says yes.'

She grinned. 'I've seen Carlos Acosta dance "Little Red Rooster" on stage when I was in the front row, so I completely get that. Total stage presence.'

'Carbon has that. Stag presence, perhaps,' he added, hoping that the terrible pun would lighten things up again. He didn't want to think about strutting his own stuff.

She laughed. 'I'm going to make a note of that. And I want a vi—'

'—deo for the farm website,' he finished. 'Got it.'

Carbon was still crowing.

'Not quite the romantic birdsong I would've liked to film,' she said.

'There's always the nightingales,' he said, before he could stop himself.

That made her look at him. 'We have nightingales?'

'They arrived a couple of weeks ago.'

'Can you show me where to find them so I can film them singing?'

'They do actually sing in the day as well as the night, you know,' he said.

'A nightingale,' she pointed out, 'ought to be filmed at night, to live up to its name. And, actually, it'll be wonderful just to have the sounds of the woodland and a dark screen. Something different. Something to make people use a different sense instead of just glancing at it and scrolling on. Something to make people listen and feel.'

'It's probably a stupid question,' he said, 'but I assume that means you want to do the nightingales tonight?'

'Given that I'm back in London in less than a fortnight? Absolutely.'

'You probably already know this,' he said, 'but only unpaired males sing at night. They use their song to attract a mate. Hang on.' He grabbed his phone, searched the internet and found her some audio. 'This is what we'll be listening for.'

'That's lovely, all the whistles and trills and gurgles—and it's really loud,' she said, sounding surprised.

'They're show offs,' he said with a grin.

'Figures that they're male,' she said dryly.

He raised an eyebrow. 'You really have been mixing with Mr Wrong.'

'That wasn't meant to sound bitter. I wouldn't give any of them the power to take the joy away from my life. Plus,' she added, 'someone very wise once told me that the best judge of who I was was me.'

She remembered what he'd said to her, all those years ago? 'I'm glad it helped,' he said, meaning it.

'If it hadn't been for you, that night, making me see that Damien was the problem, not me, I would've gone right back into my shell,' she said. 'But you gave me the confidence to be myself.' She lifted one shoulder in a half-shrug. 'Right now, I'm in a place where I'm content with my life and I'm happy to focus on work. And I think maybe I've tried too hard to look for Mr Right, so I convinced myself that all the Mr Wrongs weren't really as awful as they turned out to be. So I've stopped looking. As far as I'm concerned, it's time for Mr Right to try and find me.'

'Sounds like a plan,' he said. He wasn't Mr Right for

her, was he? Not when they both wanted such different things. Besides, he wasn't looking for another partner. He glanced at his watch. 'We could get changed into something more suitable for woodland, then meet at my cottage at ten.'

'You're on,' she said.

'Actually, I've got a better idea. I'll do the washing up, and bring all your stuff back to you at ten. Then we'll go looking for the nightingale,' he said.

'Are you sure?'

'Definitely.' Because washing up with her would be tricky. The shepherd's hut would make it too intimate: and he'd be very aware that there was a wide bed with soft pillows and fairy lights, only a short distance away...

'Thank you.'

'Take the rest of the bubbles back to your mum and dad,' he said.

'Will do. In the meantime, I'm going to sort out a piece for the website,' she said.

That had been close, Elle thought.

Too close.

She'd almost kissed Charlie. And there was a huge difference between method acting and actually kissing someone for real.

Charlie Webb and his amazing bluebell-coloured eyes could all too easily turn her head, if she let him.

She was still thinking about that kiss as she handed over the Prosecco to her parents. And as she changed out of her little black dress and high heels into jeans and walking boots. And while she was reviewing the snaps she'd taken on her phone.

The shepherd's hut looked idyllic. The food looked fabulous. And she and Charlie looked as if they were a real couple, laughing into the camera.

'Client. Dad's business partner. Still getting over his grief. Wants the complete opposite of what you want in life,' she told herself out loud.

Why didn't any of the barriers feel enough, even when they were layered together? Why was her mouth still tingling at the thought of his lips brushing hers? They'd been dancing cheek to cheek. He'd held her close, and she'd felt his arms tightening round her.

If the rooster hadn't crowed at that exact moment, she was pretty sure they would've ended up kissing.

And who knew where that might have led?

She forced herself to concentrate on the website. But then she went downstairs to get a drink of water, and realised that it was raining.

She sent a text to Charlie.

Assume weather means nightingale off? E

He replied relatively quickly.

If it's stopped raining in half an hour, still on. Wellies rather than walking boots. C

The weather was clearly on her side, because it stopped raining. Just before ten, she pulled on wellington boots and a light raincoat, and then she heard the knock on the kitchen door.

'Perfect timing,' she said when he opened the door.

For a mad moment, she thought he was going to lean forward and kiss her on the cheek. And a very rash part of her would've been tempted to angle her face so his lips touched hers instead of her cheek.

'Thanks for bringing my stuff back,' she said, and put the box on the kitchen countertop.

He handed her a torch and switched on his own. She followed him to the woods, making sure that she stepped where he did—except for the moment when she found herself daydreaming, and then was aware that she was slipping.

'No!' she yelled, dropping her torch and flailing her arms in the air, trying to keep her balance on a surface that slid away from her.

Charlie's reflexes were lightning-quick; he turned round, saw that she was struggling with the edge of the ditch and was about to fall flat into the mud, grabbed her with the hand that wasn't holding the torch and swung her up to safety.

In one way, it was a good thing, because it meant she didn't make a fool of herself or get covered in mud.

In another way, it was very far from being a good thing, because now they were up close and personal again, and the way her torch had fallen meant that its light was shining straight onto them both. Her breathing was all shaky because of his nearness. Because of his clean masculine scent. Because he was looking into her eyes, and his pupils were absolutely huge.

Pupils dilate to let the light in, her common sense said.

They also dilate when your brain gets a good boost of dopamine and oxytocin, her libido pointed out.

Nah, he was just worried that you were going to fall, her common sense countered.

Yeah, but the hormonal stuff only happens when you're really attracted to someone, her libido said, doing the equivalent of breathing on its nails and polishing them. *He likes you. He really, really likes you. And you like him. You wanted to kiss him, earlier. And it looks as if he wants to kiss you...*

His lips were parted.

So were hers.

And he was close, so close. Not invading her space and marking his physical superiority, but as if he couldn't bear to pull himself away from her.

He was definitely looking at her mouth, as if he was wondering what it would feel like against his. She was looking at his mouth, too. And she saw the very moment he moistened his lips. Her own lips were tingling, too. She'd never wanted to kiss anyone so much in her entire life.

This was crazy. She knew that. All the same, she found herself leaning forward. He leaned forward, too. And then his mouth grazed against hers. Once, twice: almost shy, but oh, so sweet. And she was lost; she slid her arms underneath his, drawing him closer. He cupped her cheek with one hand and lowered his mouth to hers again, soft and tender.

All of a sudden, her skin felt too tight. And she was definitely wearing too much. And she didn't care that it was dark and they were in the middle of the woods: all she could focus on was Charlie and the way his mouth moved against hers, teasing and tempting and making her want more.

An owl hooted a warning, long and low, and he pulled back.

Another avian intervention. Did the entire local bird population want to warn them off each other, or something?

'Sorry. I...' His words trailed off.

She shook her head. She wasn't sorry, and she didn't want him to regret it, either. 'Not your fault,' she said. 'It's the adrenaline from nearly falling flat on my face and you rescuing me. It didn't mean anything.'

'No, of course.'

Elle was lying through her teeth, and she was pretty sure that Charlie was lying through his teeth, too.

That kiss had *meant* something.

But she needed time and space to process it and work out what it had actually meant.

He gave her his torch, then got down into the ditch to rescue hers; he wiped the mud off on his jeans. 'Let's go find that nightingale,' he said.

She walked behind him, hating the sudden awkwardness that had sprung up between them.

Then she heard it.

A sweet, complex song, with short verses and pauses and rippling phrases.

'Is that the nightingale?' she asked.

'No. It's a robin,' he said.

'I want to film this anyway,' she said. 'It's lovely. And so loud.'

'Robins *are* loud,' he said, but he stood still so she could film the song without the sound of his footsteps trampling through it.

'Done,' she said, when she'd tapped the screen to stop recording.

They walked a bit further, and he stopped.

'Listen,' he whispered.

She couldn't hear it at first, but then she did: a bubbling exuberance, whistling phrases and warbling, even louder than the robin. She recorded a minute of the song, then just listened, transfixed, until the song faded. It was an incredibly beautiful moment, one she wouldn't have wanted to share with anyone else. And it would be very foolish to wish that Charlie was standing behind her, with his arms wrapped round her and his cheek pressed against hers, as they listened to the nightingale singing. It wasn't going to happen.

'"And as it gets dark loud nightingales/ In bushes/ Pipe, as they can when April wears,/ As if all Time were theirs,"' she whispered.

'That's lovely,' he said. 'Poetry, I'm guessing, though I don't know it.'

'It's Thomas Hardy. *Proud Songsters*,' she said. 'It's not the most famous nightingale poem—that'd be Keats or Milton—but it's one of my favourites.'

'I'll look it up,' he said. 'Unless you know the whole thing by heart.'

She wasn't going to stand here quoting her favourite poems. Because it was a short skip from Hardy to Shakespeare and Donne; and she could just imagine Charlie reading her favourite Donne poem to her, his voice low and sensual, undressing her with the poet's words and making her very hot and bothered indeed...

'Look it up,' she said. And her voice *would* have to croak, she thought crossly. She didn't want him thinking that that kiss had thrown her. Particularly because it had. She couldn't remember the last time she'd felt this flustered.

The nightingale started up again, to her relief, and they listened for a while longer. And she made very, very sure she didn't sway towards Charlie, much as she was tempted.

'You've got milking tomorrow,' she said when the nightingale stopped singing. 'I'd better let you get back.'

'I'll see you back to the farmhouse,' he said.

Given that it was dark and she'd already nearly fallen flat on her face, she wasn't going to protest that she could find her way perfectly well by herself. 'Thank you,' she said.

* * *

Charlie didn't trust himself to speak on the way back out of the woods. That kiss had shaken him, and he didn't want to say anything stupid. 'If we're quiet on the way back, we might catch more nightingales or robins singing.'

'Good idea,' she said, to his relief.

Though silence didn't actually help. It gave him room to think. To brood about the way he'd kissed Eleanor Newton—and the way she'd kissed him back. The way his skin had felt as if little currents of electricity were running across it. The sweetness of her mouth, her initially shy response, and then the way she'd held him, drawn him close.

He hadn't kissed anyone like that for a long, long time.

What the hell had possessed him?

Elle was the first woman he'd really kissed since Jess. Not that he was beating himself up for being unfaithful; Jess had been gone for five years now, and if he was honest with himself he was lonely. Bone-deep lonely. And he'd chosen this job in part because he could work hard enough to be so physically tired at the end of the day that he didn't have the energy to think.

Jess wouldn't have wanted him to be on his own—just as he would've wanted her to find someone else to love and cherish her, if he'd been the one who'd died. But, at the same time, the idea terrified him: what if he let Elle close?

He knew she didn't want to stay here in Norfolk, and he didn't want to go back to his old life in London. There wasn't any workable compromise, here. One of them would have to give up their life to accommodate the other, and that just wasn't fair—on either of them.

By the time they got back to the farmhouse, he felt prickly and out of sorts. So his tone was a bit gruffer than it should've been when he muttered, 'Good night, Elle.'

'Good night. And thank you for taking me to the night-ingales,' she said politely.

She sounded cool and confident and perfectly normal. That kiss clearly hadn't scrambled her brains, the way it had scrambled his. He was the problem here, not her. He shoved his hands in his pockets and hunched his shoulders. 'You're welcome.' And please don't let her ask him in for a coffee or whatever. He didn't think he could face her in a really bright light, particularly as he thought she might be rather good at reading people and seeing what they'd rather keep hidden. 'I'd better go,' he said. 'Milking.'

'Of course.'

He waited until she'd closed the door behind her—he wasn't *that* rude—and then headed back to his own cottage.

A shower didn't help, because he found himself daydreaming about taking a shower with her.

A mug of coffee didn't help, because he thought about having coffee with Elle.

He didn't have a dog to talk to, either. One day he would, but right now he didn't have time to train a pup and it wasn't fair to bring a rescue dog who might not be used to livestock onto the farm.

He didn't have anything.

Thoroughly out of sorts, he went to bed. Though he spent a good half-hour tossing and turning and bashing his pillow, and trying to stop thinking about Elle. And, when sleep finally claimed him, he dreamed of kissing her all over again…

CHAPTER SIX

FACT: ELLE HAD liked Charlie kissing her.

Fact: she'd liked kissing him back, too.

Fact: in a little over a week's time, they'd be a hundred or so miles apart, for the rest of their lives. So it would be utterly, *utterly* stupid to let herself dream about him. Wouldn't it?

It didn't help that she spent Thursday morning helping her mum prepare one of the shepherd's huts for new guests. She kept thinking of the meal she'd shared with Charlie in the hut next door, their slow dance and near-kiss, and then the actual kiss in the woods—a real bone-melting kiss.

For pity's sake. What was wrong with her? She was meant to be focusing on her job and getting that promotion, not dreaming about yet another Mr Wrong. The only way that she and Charlie were going to be together would be on the pictures for the farm website.

'Love?'

Elle's face heated as she realised her mum was talking to her. 'Sorry. Miles away. What did you say?'

'I was asking what you thought of the huts.'

'They're lovely,' Elle said, meaning it. 'Though I think they need names.' She and Charlie had been supposed to brainstorm some names yesterday, but dancing with him had swept it completely out of her head. 'Maybe after flowers? Say, one of them could be Primrose, and all the colour accents could be primrose?'

'That's a great idea,' Angie said. 'I'll have to get wooden plaques made with the names painted on them.'

'The gardens round the huts look nice, too. All the lavender—it'll smell gorgeous for the whole summer,' Elle said. 'And those woven willow fencing panels are great.'

'We wanted to give people a bit of privacy, but we didn't want to use brick walls,' Angie explained.

'Where did you get the panels? I could maybe ask the people who make them to come and give willow weaving classes.'

'I'll find their name for you. They're not far from here—about ten miles.' Angie gave her a sidelong look. 'Charlie could probably give you a lift, if you want to pop over and see them.'

'He won't have the time,' Elle said. 'It's a busy time of year with the animals. I'll just borrow your car, if you don't mind.'

'It's lovely that you're working with him,' Angie said.

Uh-oh. Her mum sounded so hopeful. And Elle was pretty sure she knew where this was leading. Right now, she'd better be cruel to be kind. 'Mum, right now Charlie and I are colleagues. We're becoming friends,' she said. 'But it's never going to be any more than that.' Even though part of her secretly hoped that might change. 'And I'll be back in London at the end of next week.'

'I had hoped,' Angie began, and then she wrinkled her nose. 'Sorry. I'm not trying to manage your life. It's just… I miss you, Ellie. And having you home—it makes the place feel as if the heart's back in it.'

Elle hugged her mother. 'I love you and Dad, Mum. I really do. I'm honestly not trying to avoid you. But my life is in London. It's where I fit.'

'You could fit here,' Angie said. 'Look at all the work you're doing for the farm. There are loads of other local businesses that would love to have your input. You don't have to live in the farmhouse with us; you could have one of the farm cottages, if you'd rather keep your independence.'

'I appreciate the offer, Mum,' Elle said. 'I really appreciate your support, and Dad's. But I'm not staying for ever,' she added, as gently as she could. 'I'm going back to London.'

Her mum was clearly trying to be brave about it, and Elle felt even worse.

'It's not you, Mum. Or Dad. It's me,' she said.

'Is there someone waiting for you in London?'

Elle hugged her again. 'No, Mum. I haven't found the right one, yet.' And she repressed the thought that kissing Charlie, last night, had felt right. Because she and Charlie wanted different things, and there just wasn't room for compromise.

Charlie knew he was going to have to face Elle at some point today—even though it was going to make him squirm. How was he going to manage this? They needed to keep working together; but his feelings towards her weren't colleague-ly. If that was even a word. She put his head in such a spin, he couldn't even find the right words for things.

He needed to get over this, fast, for the farm's sake.

Just as he was chugging down his coffee, ready to go out to collect the cows, his phone beeped with a text.

Elle? His heart leaped.

No, of course not. How ridiculous. It could be anyone at all texting him; though it turned out to be Jo, his little sister, checking in before her early-morning dog-walk.

Something you want to tell us, C?

He frowned and texted back.

Sorry, no idea what you mean.

Her reply was a link to a page on the Bluebell Farm website. He clicked on it and groaned; it was the page Elle had tweaked for the shepherd's hut, complete with a collage of the pictures she'd taken last night: the table set for two, the fairy lights giving the inside of the shepherd's hut a romantic air, the food…and a couple of pictures of them together, laughing and drinking bubbles.

He typed back, to explain.

That's Elle. You must remember Mike and Angie's daughter. She was in your year at school. She's revamping the farm's marketing. We're spending the budget on online booking and shopping, and saving money by being the models ourselves.

There was a pause.

If you say so, bro, but the expressions on your faces…

He typed back.

Hey, just nominate us for an acting award. There's nothing going on!

Except Jo had a point. He and Elle *did* look like a real couple. Like two people getting to know each other, being attracted to each other, having a romantic meal together.

He flicked through the website to see what else Elle had

done. There were a couple of pictures of flowers, with little snippets of facts he hadn't known: the greater stitchwort's seed capsules made a loud popping when they ripened and fired their seeds, and the plant's name came from its use as a herbal remedy for a stitch, the pain in the side people sometimes felt while out running.

She'd posted more pictures of bluebells, too. *Did you know the bluebell's sticky sap was used to bind the pages of books and to glue feathers onto arrows? In Elizabethan times, the bulbs were crushed to make starch for ruffs. And it takes at least five years for a bluebell seed to develop into a bulb.*

Charlie hadn't known any of that, either. So far, so good. From what he could see, the number of likes on the posts was ticking steadily upwards. They were definitely building an audience.

But then he found the nightingale video. She'd edited it down to thirty seconds of gorgeous song and titled it 'A Nightingale Sang in Bluebell Wood'.

Have you ever heard a nightingale sing? #sweetestsong #soromantic Imagine dancing cheek to cheek in the woods, just the two of you and the nightingale singing and the air full of the scent of bluebells. The sweetest song. The sweetest kiss.

He went hot all over. And for a moment he closed his eyes, remembering how it had felt to dance with her. Remembering how it had felt to smell the vanilla scent of her perfume. The warmth of her skin against his. The way she'd held him close. The way he'd pulled her close, later, when he'd rescued her from falling into the ditch. The way they'd looked at each other in the torchlight, and they'd both leaned in as if some kind of magnet had pulled them together. The way her mouth had felt against his, so sweet and enticing, offering and demanding at the same time.

Even thinking about it made him feel dizzy with a mixture of desire and guilt and pure need.

Had Elle seen his expression on the photograph and interpreted it the same way his sister had? And, if so, just what was he going to do?

He still felt fractious and unsettled when he went to milk the cows. Luckily none of the guests had surfaced early enough to help, so he was free to talk over his thoughts with the cows while he was milking.

'I met her ten years ago. I wouldn't have kissed her then. Apart from the fact that I was dating someone else, that night she was vulnerable,' he said to Elderberry.

The cow lowed softly, as if to encourage him to continue.

He carried on milking and talking. 'She was in tears, for pity's sake. I'd never take advantage of a girl in distress. Besides, she was the same age as my little sister. Way too young for me.'

Elderberry mooed, as if to point out that the three-year age gap didn't matter any more, now that he was thirty-one and she was twenty-eight.

'I know the farm needs a shake-up in the marketing. Her ideas are great. But this romantic narrative thing… it's getting too complicated.'

Elderberry swished her tail, as if to say, 'Nonsense.'

'I kissed her last night.' He sighed. 'It wasn't meant to happen. She slipped, and I grabbed her before she fell in the mud, and…it just felt natural for her to be in my arms. Especially because we'd danced together, earlier. And then I kissed her.' He leaned his forehead against Elderberry's flank. 'One kiss wasn't enough. The next thing I knew, she was kissing me back. And it was perfect.'

Elderberry's next moo was very clearly the bovine version of, *So what happened next?*

'An owl hooted. It brought us to our senses. We broke apart, and we both said it was an accident.' He switched buckets. 'Except I wasn't telling the truth. I wanted to kiss her again. I still do. Even though I know it's a bad idea.'

Another swish of her tail.

'It's a *really* bad idea, Elderberry. I'm not going to offer her a fling—that's not who I am. But how can I offer her anything more? She doesn't want to stay here, and I don't want to go to London. There isn't a way to compromise. Besides, she's the daughter of my business partners. I don't want to make things complicated. I *like* living here. I'm happy.'

As he said it, he realised to his surprise that he was.

He missed Jess and he still felt hollow, without her; but working with the animals and the land had helped to heal the rawness of that loss. Now, he could enjoy his daily routine, noticing the changes in the plants and the animals. He could find pleasure in watching a lamb bouncing about in the fields or the cows kicking up their heels as they went into new pasture. He could appreciate the sight of a fairy ring of mushrooms appearing overnight, the sound of rich birdsong heralding the dawn, the scent of woodland flowers as he walked the land, the rich taste of the cheese made on the farm from the cows he'd milked with his own hands.

What was missing was *touch*.

He'd coped without it until Elle had held him close and kissed him back. Her touch had been like water on a parched flower, letting his feelings bloom—and now he wanted more. He wanted *her*.

'I really don't know how to fix this, Elderberry,' he said to the cow as he finished milking her, put the milk out of the way and made a fuss of her.

She licked his face.

'It's not as easy as that,' he said.

She licked him again, her sandpapery tongue telling

him that he was making too big a deal about it and he just needed to talk to Elle.

'It isn't,' he repeated.

Another lick.

'I'll think about it,' he promised.

Somehow he'd find a way to get back on an even keel with Elle—and keep his feelings completely under control. But, until he'd sorted his head out, he thought it might be a good idea to avoid her.

When Elle had finished helping her mum, she visited Rosie on the other side of town and had a wonderful time learning to card and spin wool, as well as making a fuss of Rosie's sheep. And she was delighted when Rosie agreed to run a class on dyeing yarn as well as helping with a weekly craft session in the café.

She checked her emails in the car, and was thrilled to see that Frieda had sent four potential logos. There was one that particularly stood out for her, but this wasn't her decision. She'd need to discuss it with her parents.

And with Charlie.

She sighed. OK, so it had been awkward between them since that kiss. She'd pretty much avoided him this morning, and she was pretty sure that he'd been avoiding her in exactly the same way. But, if she was going to do this job professionally, she needed to move past that kiss and work with Charlie. Particularly as they didn't have much time to get the media stuff up and running.

Maybe the best way forward was to pretend that the kiss hadn't happened. Keep it brisk and businesslike.

She flicked into her messaging app.

Hi. Discussed classes with Rosie and just had logo drafts from Frieda. When are you free to discuss farm website? Thanks, E

Elle had just parked the car back at the farm when her phone pinged with a message.

Free at 3. My kitchen? Will have kettle on. C

She only realised how tense she'd been when she leaned back against the seat. He wasn't going to make it difficult. He, too, was clearly going to pretend that kiss hadn't happened.

Good.

She texted back.

3 works for me.

She called into the café to see her mum and Lisa, and arranged to observe her mum's cheese-making class, the following day; then she mocked up four versions of the home page for the farm's website, using the different logos.

The butterflies in her stomach grew restless again as she walked to Charlie's cottage with her laptop. Would she get away with pretending that kiss hadn't happened, or would he bring it up? And, if he did… What then?

Was he trying to persuade himself that he didn't want to repeat it, the way she was? Did he want her to keep her distance? Or had he found a way where they could compromise?

There was a knock on the kitchen door at exactly three o'clock.

Elle.

Keep it cool and calm, Charlie reminded himself, and went to answer the door.

She was dressed casually, in jeans and a T-shirt and canvas shoes, with a lime-green satchel slung over her shoulder. He wished she'd been wearing her fancy London clothes instead, because the formal dress made her look much less approachable. As it was, he itched to pull her into his arms again and kiss her until they were both dizzy.

Not happening, he reminded himself, and he knew he sounded grumpy when he asked, 'Did you want coffee?' He just hoped she'd put it down to anything but the truth. Anything but the fact that he was crazily attracted to a woman who didn't want the same things out of life that he did and it would never, ever work between them.

She acted as if he'd been perfectly sweet and pleasant towards her. 'Coffee would be lovely, thank you, Charlie.'

Oh, the way his name sounded on her mouth. He wanted to make her groan it in pleasure. To scream it in joy.

He didn't dare close his eyes, because then he'd see the pictures in his head even more clearly. Think of mucking out the byre, he told himself. Think of cleaning things. Think of anything except Eleanor Newton and her lush, perfect Cupid's bow of a mouth.

'Take a seat.' He gestured to the kitchen table and went to make coffee, hoping that the activity would give him the space for his common sense to kick back in.

By the time he brought the two mugs over to the table, she'd taken her laptop out of the satchel and switched it on. 'Frieda's sent me four logos. I've done a mock-up of the new home page, but I wanted to run things by you, first. I've also written a few blog posts, which we can schedule in for the next few weeks.'

'I saw the one on bluebells,' he said. 'I learned a lot—and I like the way you write.'

She went pink. 'Thank you.'

She'd looked as pink as that when the owl had interrupted their kiss. All flushed and dewy and delectable.

Then he realised he'd missed what she'd said. 'Sorry. Could you repeat that, please?'

'We need to talk about tags. What people are likely to search for. Cows, flowers, recipes…'

'Right.'

Where did he sit?

Opposite her felt too intimate.

At right angles to her meant he risked accidentally touching her, which would also be too intimate. Even the thought of her skin brushing against his made his blood feel as if it were fizzing in his veins.

How the hell did he feel so off kilter and out of place in his own home?

And it shook him to realise that, actually, this *was* home. The cottage might not belong to him, but he belonged there.

Completely flustered—and knowing that Elle was the cause of said flusterment—Charlie put the mugs of coffee on the table and took the chair at right angles to hers.

She moved her laptop so he could see the screen. 'These are Frieda's four suggestions.'

Simple, clear lettering—Bluebell Farm—with an equally simple line-drawing of bluebells. He studied them, trying to ignore just how close Elle's hand was to his own. 'I really like this one, where she's turned the F of farm into a bluebell,' he said.

'That's my favourite, too,' she said. 'I think it'd work really well on the website, on leaflets, and on labels. Black lettering, with just the bluebell in blue. As soon as people see that flower, they'll think of us. But,' she added, 'obviously Mum and Dad need to be on board with it.'

'I'm sure they will be.' He could keep himself focused on business. Even if his head was full of pictures of Elle lying on a picnic rug, laughing up at him, with the re-

mains of a punnet of strawberries between them and her
lips stained with strawberry juice as he'd fed them to her
one by one...

'Yup,' he mumbled. Oh, dear God. No, he wasn't func-
tioning as if this was a business meeting. He'd never even
been like this with Jess. What the hell was going on with
his head?

'Rosie's agreed to run a class on dyeing yarn and help
with a knitting hour.' She grinned. 'And I had a go at spinning wool today.'

Wool was a neutral topic. He seized on it gratefully.
'So how did it go?'

'She showed me loads of the different staples—that's
a length of wool, to you, and how long it is differs by the
breed of sheep—and how you card it to make sure all the
fibres go the same way. Actually, she uses a dog comb
because it's easier. And you wouldn't believe how soft
camel hair is.'

'Camel hair?' he repeated. This was surreal.

'People knit with camel hair and goat hair,' Elle said.
'Even dog hair.'

'And that's what you're suggesting people do here?'

Her smile sparkled with mischief. 'That might be a bit
too way out. But I love the idea of people working with
wool from our sheep. I had a go with a drop spindle. It's
amazing to think that for millennia women have taken a
piece of fluffy wool, used a drop spindle to turn it into
yarn, then woven it into cloth,' she said. 'It really connects
you with the past.'

He had a feeling that she was going to write a blog all
about it. A feeling that deepened when she showed him
photos of herself grinning widely as she spun the drop
spindle and the yarn began to form. 'Right.' Focus, for
pity's sake, he told himself. On something other than how

easy it would be to lean over and kiss Elle again. 'So, the spinning: was it easy?'

'No,' she admitted. 'I found it really hard to hold the fleece right and tease it out. But then I had a go on the spinning wheel. And that…' Her smile broadened. 'It's like learning to drive again and having to do several things at once when you've never done one of them before—using the treadle to keep the wheel moving, drawing out the fleece and feeding it into the wheel, keeping the tension even so the spun wool's spaced evenly on the spindle. It's like steering and changing gear and indicating and checking your road position and everything round you all at the same time, for the very first time.'

He had a feeling that he was going to enjoy reading more of her blog posts.

'And then—' she paused dramatically '—there's the niddy-noddy.'

'The *what*?' Surely she'd made that word up?

'Niddy-noddy,' she repeated. 'It's a wooden thing and you wind the wool round it to make a skein.' She pulled up some photos of herself winding wool around a wooden instrument that reminded him a bit of a mug-tree. 'See?'

'You've made the name up, right?'

'No. There are two possible etymologies. I was going to do a poll to see what the most popular one is.'

'And you're going to leave it there?'

'I could,' she teased.

This version of Elle was irresistible. If she carried on like this, he'd need to sit on his hands to stop himself pulling her into his arms. Except that would be too obvious. He crossed his arms, hoping that she would think he was being grumpy rather than realising that he was protecting himself. 'But you're not going to.'

'OK. The first one is that the name comes from the nodding motion made as you wind the wool.'

He'd just bet that the second explanation was better.

'Or,' she said, 'it's because winding the wool into skein was usually done by an elderly granny, known as a "niddy". That, plus the motion of winding the wool... Isn't that *delicious*?'

She was delicious. Her enthusiasm brightened up his day. Unable to say a word, he just nodded.

She laughed. 'Excellent response. Oh, and just so you know, they've been used for centuries. Two niddy-noddies were found in a Viking ship burial of two women in Norway, along with other weaving equipment. There are pictures in medieval manuscripts. And even Leonardo da Vinci painted one in his "Madonna of the Yarnwinder".'

'You're going to write a blog post about a niddy-noddy, aren't you?'

'Along with a video of Rosie demonstrating how to use one,' she said. 'Want to see the skein I made?' She drew a bundle out of her pocket. 'Rosie started me off. That's this bit which is all even and lovely.' She threw one hand out in a 'ta-da' gesture. 'And this bit is mine.'

The yarn was thin and twisted to the point where it curled back over itself in some places, and fluffy with thick blobs in others. It looked utterly hopeless, but he didn't want to squash her enthusiasm. He didn't know what to say.

'I know, I know—I think it's absolutely terrible, too,' she said, still laughing. 'Though Rosie said it was good for a very first attempt, and if I did the full class I'd get the hang of it. But feel how soft the wool is.'

Bad move. It made him think about how soft her skin was. How much he wanted to kiss her...

But they were already in trouble over that. And he needed to tell her about it.

'My sister texted me, this morning,' he said. 'About the post you put up.'

'The bluebells?'

'The shepherd's huts.'

She smiled. 'I was pleased with that. We did a good job between us.'

'Yeah, but Jo thought we were dating.'

She stilled. 'What did you say to her?' Her voice was filled with wariness.

'That she could nominate us for an award.'

'Because we're acting a part,' Elle said. 'Good save.' She drained her mug. 'I'd better let you get on. I'll wash this up first.'

'No need,' he said.

'OK. I'll let you know what Mum and Dad say about the logo.' She gave him a smile he could only describe as tight, and left the kitchen.

What had he said?

He thought about it. Was she upset because Jo had thought they were dating, or because he'd been so quick to refute the suggestion?

Asking her bluntly would open a massive can of worms. He needed to think about a better way of broaching the subject. Particularly as he was still torn over the whole idea of dating again and moving on. He knew it was something he needed to do, but it was so hard.

Charlie was working in the woods, an hour later, when he saw the swans at the pool with their cygnets.

Despite the slight awkwardness between them, he knew Elle wouldn't want to miss this.

He called her. 'Can you spare five minutes—and I mean as in can you come here right this very second?'

'Ye-es. Why?'

'You'll see when you get here. If your phone battery's low, you can use mine.'

'Where exactly are you?' she asked, sounding intrigued.

'By the pond in the woods.' He knew he didn't need to be more specific. She knew the land.

'Be there in five,' she said.

He took some video of the swans and cygnets, just in case they'd gone by the time she arrived; but then he heard someone walking towards him. Funny how he didn't even need to turn round to know it was her rather than someone else; his spine was tingling, his skin felt tight, and his breathing had gone all shallow.

'What was so urg—? Ohh,' she said, seeing the swans.

He loved the way her face lit up with pleasure, her dark eyes shimmering with joy.

'Thank you for sharing this with me,' she said as she flicked into her camera app. 'Aren't they gorgeous?' She filmed the cygnets as they paddled across the lake between their mum at the front of the line and their dad at the rear; the cygnets were peeping madly, as if to say, 'Hurry up, Dad!'

Finally, the swan family came to a stop and climbed out onto the bank of the pool, where they sat in the dappled sunlight.

'That was absolutely amazing,' she said. 'Thank you for sharing it with me.'

'I knew you'd love it as much as I did. Do you miss this side of the farm?' he asked, taking a risk because he thought that bringing up the subject might send her rushing away again.

She lifted one shoulder. 'There are swans in London as well as in the country, you know. Kensington Park, Bushy Park—and there are black swans at St James's Park.'

Of course there were. He'd seen them himself, in the

years when he'd lived in London. But he thought she might be protesting just a little bit too much, and he was glad that—even if she didn't admit it—she was starting to see the good side of the farm again.

'Mum and Dad agreed with you about the logo, by the way, so I've asked Frieda to do me the final artwork. I've touched base with the agency, and the techy team tells me the booking system for accommodation, classes and lunch is ready for testing, but we still need to do a bit of work on packaging and handling the shipping of perishables before we can test the farm shop system.'

'I salute your organisational skills,' he said.

She grinned. 'I'm the scary one in the office—the one who's always talking about critical path analysis.'

'So what else do we need to do on the wedding side?'

'A picture of our couple with a romantic sunset and a romantic sunrise, one or both also being with the wild-flower meadow in the background,' she said.

'Sunset would be better for the meadow. Hang on a second.' He checked the weather forecast. 'Sunrise tomorrow is at half-past five. Are you up for being out in the fields at five o'clock? Because that way we'll get all the gorgeous colours just before the sun comes up.'

'Wide Norfolk skies looking like a watercolour. That's one of the things I miss, in London,' she said.

'It's a—' He stopped himself before the d-word came out of his mouth. 'Plan,' he said instead. 'And now I'd better let you get on.'

'I'll plan the other shots I need,' she said. 'Including video of cows playing football and lambs gambolling, oh and us cuddling lambs.'

'And we need photos of Brick,' he said.

'Brick?'

'The Suffolk Punch who arrives here next week with

Eddie—his best friend's a donkey,' he reminded her. 'If our wedding parties want it, Brick will pull the carriage.'

'What carriage?'

'It's at the local college at the moment. I have a friend who teaches woodwork, and his students—apprentices, really—are restoring it for me,' he said, and flicked into the photos app of his phone. 'This is what it looked like last year.'

'Are you quite sure that's a carriage and not a heap of firewood?' she asked.

He smiled. 'Our apprentices have fixed the wheels, mended the carriage and painted it white, and they're working on the upholstery and the convertible hood. Imagine arriving to your wedding in this, pulled by a Suffolk Punch whose coat has been burnished to a bright sheen and his mane and tail braided.' He showed her the most recent photograph of the carriage.

'That's gorgeous,' she said. 'Can I have more information on the carriage restoration? Because I think this is the sort of thing people would be really interested in. And photographs. Including the apprentices, if they'll sign a release for me. That's really heartwarming. From firewood to…' She looked thoughtful. 'I'll work on the headline for the press release.'

'OK. I'll send them over to you tonight and check with the lecturers. See you tomorrow at five for the sunrise,' he said.

She smiled at him, her expression much warmer and, to his relief, without the wariness she'd exhibited this afternoon. 'See you tomorrow at five, outside your place.'

CHAPTER SEVEN

On Friday, Elle met Charlie at his kitchen door. He had a waterproof rug over one arm and was carrying two travel mugs of coffee, one of which he gave to her.

'Nicely prepared,' she said. 'I didn't even think about coffee; I was focusing on the photographs.'

He laughed. 'Nice pun, Ms Newton.'

'Sadly, it was unintentional.' She laughed back at him.

The sky was still pale blue when they reached the spot Charlie had mentioned yesterday. 'So much for a sky full of colour,' she said, disappointed.

'At least we've got the dawn chorus,' he reminded her.

'So it's worth taking a bit of video as well as stills. Good point,' she said. She took some video of the birds singing, then settled down on the blanket next to him. She shivered. 'It's a bit colder than I expected.'

'Maybe we need to share some body heat.' He shifted closer and put his arm round her. 'Better?'

'Better,' she said, though the warmth blooming through her wasn't just because of his body heat: it was because of him. She knew he was doing this solely because he was a nice guy, and she needed to tamp down the fizzy feelings of pleasure because they weren't a real couple. He was her fake boyfriend, soon to be fake fiancé, and they were doing this simply to help sell the idea of holding a wedding at Bluebell Farm.

The sky gradually turned lilac and the top edge of the sun appeared at the far end of the fields, a deep rich pink in colour.

'That's stunning. What a colour!' She took an array of shots as the sun rose steadily. 'With those wisps of cloud across it, it looks as stripy as Jupiter.'

'It's fantastic,' he agreed. 'Sights like these make it worth getting up earlier than I need to for milking.'

'Do you want me to give you a hand this morning?' she asked.

'If you have time,' he said.

She thoroughly enjoyed helping bring the cows in, then milking them by hand and taking the covered buckets of milk through to the dairy barn next door.

'I'm doing Mum's dairy class today,' she said. 'I could bring the cheese over and make us a pasta dinner.'

'Or we could cook together,' he suggested. 'You bring the pasta or whatever, and I'll sort the pudding and the wine.'

It felt quite like a date, but Charlie had already made it clear he didn't think of her in that way. 'OK. I'll take more pics of a romantic meal, if you don't mind.'

'Just as well my kitchen's tidy,' he grumbled.

'Otherwise I would've made you clean it,' she said.

'So bossy.' He rolled his eyes. 'I thought the client was supposed to be the boss?'

'The client agreed the brief,' she said sweetly, 'so now I'm in charge.'

He laughed. 'Got it. See you later.'

Elle spent the morning doing her mum's class, picked up what she wanted for the rest of the main course from the farm shop, and did some more work on the farm's website before heading over to Charlie's.

'So what are we cooking?' he asked.

'Gnocchi alla Sorrentina,' she said. 'I cooked the potatoes at Mum's, just to save a bit of time.'

'We're making the gnocchi?'

'It's really easy. Potato and flour. My best friend's vegan, so I tend to use olive oil rather than egg. And I'm assuming you don't have a potato ricer, so I've borrowed Mum's.'

'Potato ricer?'

She took the gadget out of her bag and waved it at him. 'You'll enjoy this,' she promised.

And it was immense fun, teaching him how to make gnocchi and how to roll the balls of dough down the tines of a fork to get the little ridges on one side and photographing him doing it. She made the tomato, basil and mozzarella sauce while the gnocchi cooked, then added the gnocchi to the sauce, topped it with more mozzarella and slid it into the oven.

'Twenty minutes. So we have time to clear up first,' she said.

'I feel a bit guilty that I completely cheated with pudding,' he said. 'I bought berries, ice cream and shortbread from the farm shop.'

'No complaints from me,' she said, smiling.

By the time they'd finished clearing up, the gnocchi was ready.

'This is delicious,' he said. 'This is the cheese you made with your mum, this morning?'

'Yes. Mozzarella-style. We've got some Brie maturing as well. I might need you to take photos of the finished product when I'm back in London,' she said.

It was the first time ever that she could remember not

quite looking forward to going back to London. Though that was ridiculous. London was where she belonged, not here.

She pushed the thoughts away and chatted with Charlie over dinner, then curled up in a corner of his sofa with a glass of red wine and music playing in the background.

'I was impressed by the way you could heft a full pail of milk, this morning,' he said.

She rolled her eyes at him. 'I already told you I lift weights in the gym. Fifteen litres of milk is nothing.' She smiled. 'I love the gym. It clears my head after work and lets me wind down. I do classes mainly, with my best friend: Zumba, dance aerobics, and spin, and sometimes Pilates on a Sunday morning.'

'You're not a runner, then?'

She shook her head. 'I loathe steady state cardio, except spin class. My weights routines are all HIIT, because otherwise I get bored.' She looked at him. 'I'm guessing you don't bother with the gym, because you get all the exercise you need on the farm.'

'A lot of walking, a bit of lifting—it's enough to make me hot and sweaty,' he agreed.

She thought of what else would make them hot and sweaty, and her temperature rose a degree.

'Did you go to the gym when you lived in London?' she asked.

'I used to go before work,' he said. 'I did weights, and intervals on the rowing machine.'

'You're not a runner, either, then?'

'No, but I've been thinking lately I'd like a dog to walk around the farm with me,' he admitted.

'The farm doesn't feel quite right without a dog,' she said. 'When we lost our Honey, it was when Gran was really ill, and Dad said it was the wrong time to get a puppy.

And then, later, he said we were all too busy to have time for a pup.' She shrugged. 'I guess he had a point.'

'You miss having a dog?'

'Yes, but it wouldn't be fair to have a dog in London. Not with the hours I work. She'd be left on her own all the time. Not like here, where you could take your dog to work with you.'

'True.' He paused. 'I've been thinking. The last pictures we need to do are dressing the barn for a wedding, and the "engagement". How are we going to manage that?'

'Gran left me her engagement ring. We could use that for the "engagement" pictures.' She looked at him. 'Are you sure you're OK about this?'

'Surprisingly, yes. You've made it feel less…' He shook his head. 'I can't find the right words. Less like being sucked into the middle of a black hole, I guess.'

'I'm glad.'

'I have a day off, tomorrow. It's meant to be sunny, so we could go to the beach, if you like.'

'And make sandcastles—we need to show that the farm is great for families, as well as for romantic breaks. Maybe we could go to Wells-next-the-Sea? I haven't been there since…' She shook her head. 'I can't remember when. But sometimes Dad would bundle us all into the car, including Honey, and we'd walk the whole length of the beach from Wells to Holkham before going back to the café for hot chocolate and some cake.'

'Wells it is,' he said.

It was a perfect day when Charlie drove them to the beach; the sky was the deep blue of early summer with fluffy white clouds scudding across, and it was warm enough not to need a coat.

Elle said, 'It's such a treat to come to the beach. That's

something else I miss in London. I've been to Brighton, but the beach is all pebbly and it's not like having acres of golden sand to walk on.'

Charlie took two bamboo cups out of the back of the car. 'The beach is even more of a treat with coffee.'

People were already seated at the wooden tables outside the beach café with their dogs, enjoying the sunshine; Elle couldn't resist stopping to make a fuss of a golden Labrador pup, and by the time she joined Charlie inside he'd already bought the coffee—and, to her amusement, buckets and spades.

'Seriously? You actually bought buckets and spades?'

'You said you wanted pictures of sandcastles,' he reminded her, 'and if we just use our hands the sandcastles are going to be pretty feeble.'

'You're right. Thank you for remembering.'

He shrugged off the compliment, but he looked faintly pleased.

Even though there were quite a few cars in the car park, the beach was long enough and wide enough for them to have plenty of space.

'When does the tide come back in?' she asked, remembering that the tide rushed in quite quickly on this part of the coast.

'Early evening. We don't have to hurry,' he said.

She rolled up her jeans to her knees and took off her shoes, enjoying the feel of wet sand beneath her feet.

'You're seriously going to paddle in the North Sea when it's only just May?' he asked.

'It's glorious,' she said. 'The rush of the waves as they come tumbling in, and the swishing as the water trickles back out.' She looked pointedly at his feet. 'Or are you too chicken to join me?'

'I'm fine as I am. I'll look after your shoes and your

coffee,' he said, and sat on the sand with his arms wrapped round his knees.

'Your choice,' she said, and went to paddle at the edge of the sea.

This was where her fiancé would play in the waves next to her, scooping her up in his arms and pretending to drop her into the water. Where she'd shriek and he'd laugh and then he'd kiss her...

Except she and Charlie weren't an item.

And maybe this hadn't been a great idea.

If he'd loved going to the beach with Jess, this must be bringing back memories for him—and with memories would come the emptiness of loss.

Guilt flooded through her, and she went back to join him. 'You OK?' she asked.

'Yes. Why?'

'It was your idea to come here,' she said, 'but you're not paddling in the sea and you look as if you're a million miles away, in your head.' She took his hand and squeezed it briefly. 'I'm assuming Jess loved the sea.'

'She did,' he said. 'We honeymooned in St Lucia, and it was amazing—cobalt sea, white sands, and the volcanos rising up. We did a bit of exploring while we were there: hiking through the rainforest, visiting waterfalls, and on one day we actually drove into a volcano and walked round the sulphur pools.' He smiled. 'It takes a while to get the mud off your skin, though. We used to sit and watch the sun setting over the sea every night. And we went during hatchling season, so there was one night when we went to see the turtles. It's humbling, watching hundreds and hundreds of these tiny creatures flippering their way across the sand towards the sea.'

'That sounds amazing,' she said. 'Is that what made

you decide to do your Masters in Environmental Studies, seeing the turtles and the rainforest?'

'It was probably one of the seeds,' he said. 'I just knew I wanted to make a difference. To make the world a better place.'

'And you're doing exactly that,' she said. 'I never knew your Jess, but I'd just bet she's up there right now, beaming down, really proud of you and what you're doing at Bluebell Farm.'

'You might well be right.' He paused. 'Funny, you're the only person I can really talk to about her.'

'Probably because I never knew her,' she said. 'So it's not like it must be with her family and friends, when you'd be trying to spare their feelings or worry that you're trampling over their grief.'

'I appreciate it,' he said, lacing his fingers through hers. 'I appreciate *you*.'

Her skin was tingling where he touched her. 'I appreciate you, too,' she said. More than appreciated him. It would be very easy to let herself fall in love with Charlie Webb. But, with her track record in men, she knew it wouldn't work out. Better to leave things as they were. 'Now I think it's time to regress a quarter of a century and make sandcastles. I challenge you to make a better one than me.' She gently disengaged her fingers from his and set the alarm on her phone. 'We've got ten minutes. Starting...now!'

Armed with a bucket and spade each, they shovelled sand into the buckets to build towers, and dug moats. Charlie didn't start a conversation, clearly concentrating on building his sandcastle; but, to Elle's relief, his expression wasn't quite as bleak as it had been earlier.

'Five minutes to decorate them and fill the moats,' she said when the alarm went off.

When the second alarm went off, she'd just finished making windows in her towers with shells.

'All right. Let judgement commence,' she said. Being rude about his castle was probably the best way to get him to tease her back and finish getting him out of his bleak mood. 'Castle Webb has five towers, because her builder is showing off. It has a moat, but no drawbridge, and no door or windows. Plus I assume that bit of seaweed on a twig is meant to be some kind of pennant?'

'It's *obviously* a pennant,' he said. 'And it looks like a web so it's a visual representation of the name.'

'It doesn't look anything like a web,' she scoffed. 'Any spider making *that* would have to be drunk.'

'Let's have a look at Castle Newton,' he said. 'Four towers, because her builder is being super-traditional and boring. No pennant, so the castle could belong to absolutely anyone.'

'Yeah, but there's a drawbridge over my moat,' she said, indicating the razor clam shells, 'and a doorway, and windows. I win.'

'No way. That's just girly showing-off,' Charlie pronounced.

What could she do but upend the bucket of seawater over him instead of pouring it into her moat?

He stared at her, looking utterly shocked—and then did exactly the same thing to her.

'Sauce for the goose,' he said when she gasped in outrage.

'We don't have geese on the farm—and neither of us would eat the goose, anyway,' she pointed out.

'True,' he admitted. 'Even though you soaked me first, I apologise.'

'You don't look in the slightest bit sorry,' she said.

'Neither do you,' he retorted.

'I'm not. I'm planning a second ambush.'

'You're playing a dangerous game, there,' he said. 'Because I could pick you up, carry you to the sea and drop you in.'

'In which case I'd take your legs out from under you,' she said, 'so you'd end up just as wet. Do you have a change of clothes in the car, or even a towel?'

'Um…no,' he admitted. 'Perhaps we should both call a truce.'

'Admit my shell windows are pretty, first.'

He folded his arms. 'Only if you admit my pennant is genius.'

She beckoned him closer. He bent his head slightly so she could whisper into his ear. 'It's pants.'

'The truce is off,' he said, and to her shock he picked her up.

'No. No. Charlie! You wouldn't!' she shrieked as he strode over to the sea.

'Say it. The pennant is genius,' he demanded.

'It's a bit of seaweed on a twig.' She coughed. 'You say it. The shells are pretty.'

'They *match*. It's meant to be a sandcastle, Elle. You're supposed to use the first shells you find.'

'That's *so* blokey,' she retorted.

He was standing in the sea, now, and the water was up to mid-calf. 'Did I hear the word "genius"?'

'You absolutely did not.' The way he was carrying her meant that she couldn't wrap her legs round him, but she could cling on to his neck. 'Say "pretty shells".'

'Nope.'

'Drop me, and I'll make sure you're soaked,' she warned.

'Am I meant to be scared?'

'Yeah, you are. I'm Elle Newton. Everyone knows I deliver on my promises,' she said.

'You do indeed,' he said.

She'd fantasised about her fake fiancé doing precisely this, but the reality was something else.

Charlie Webb was utterly gorgeous. Those blue, blue eyes that sparkled brighter than the ocean. His hair, still wet from the seawater she'd tipped over his head, was slicked back and starting to curl as it dried, making him look like the Greek god of the sea. She was no lightweight, but he'd carried her down the beach with perfect ease. And his mouth, curved into a teasing smile, was beautiful. She wanted to pull his head down to hers and kiss him until they were both dizzy.

He was staring at her mouth, too, as if he was thinking exactly the same thing. That she was some nymph of the sea, one of the Sirens, and he was a sailor driven to distraction by her song.

Just when she was convinced that he was going to follow through on his threat and drop her into the sea, instead he lowered her safely to the ground.

Her arms were still round his neck, and for the life of her she couldn't let him go. He stared at her, his tongue moistening his lower lip, and her control snapped. She pulled his head down to hers and kissed him. His mouth was warm and sweet, and she wanted more. Pressing closer, she nibbled at his lower lip until he opened his mouth and let her deepen the kiss.

His body was hard and muscular against hers: and the muscles were all from hard work rather than being honed in a gym. Charlie Webb made her head spin. And she'd never wanted anyone so badly in her l—

She pulled away from him and shrieked as cold seawater splashed all over her.

A chocolate Labrador, a tennis ball in his mouth, was

bounding through the shallows and showering them with water.

'Sorry!' the owner called, looking mortified.

'That's OK!' she called back.

It was probably just as well that the cold water had brought them both back to their senses. Who knew what that kiss might have led to?

'I'm sorry. I shouldn't have done that,' she said.

'I shouldn't have kissed you back, either,' he said, flushing scarlet.

'Let's pretend that didn't happen,' she said.

'Except it did,' he said. 'Twice. And I think, if we're both honest, we both want it to happen again.'

All the breath went out of her lungs and she couldn't say a word.

'Elle?'

'Yeah,' she managed eventually. 'It's the same for me.'

'So what are we going to do about it?'

He was braver than her, asking that. So she owed it to him to be honest. 'I'm going back to London in a week. My life's there, not here. And I...' She blew out a breath. 'My relationships have all been disasters. Right from what I thought was a prom date with Damien Price—and of *course* the most popular boy in school didn't want to go to prom with me.'

'The hurt from that night really went deep, didn't it?' Charlie asked.

'I'm not sure what hurt more,' she said. 'The fact that everyone except me knew it was fake, or the fact that Damien thought I'd be so grateful to be asked that I'd do absolutely anything he wanted.'

Charlie threaded his fingers through hers again. 'Damien

Price was an immature, callous little boy. The blame's on him, not you.'

'Is it, though?' she asked. 'Because why do I always pick men who seem perfect, and then when they see where I come from they can't back away fast enough?'

'I'm no psychologist,' he said. 'I can't help you find an answer to that.' He paused. 'But I see where you come from. And it doesn't make me want to run.'

'Because you bought into it. It's your dream,' she said. 'And it's my nightmare.'

'Is it, though?' Charlie asked, echoing her earlier question. 'Because, this last week, I've seen you throw yourself into helping make the farm work.'

'It's my job,' she said, 'and you know I've got a promotion riding on the campaign being a success. Plus it's for my parents. And—' She stopped.

And for him? Charlie wondered. Or for the farm itself? Her drew her hand up to his lips and kissed each knuckle in turn. 'What if,' he said, 'this thing between you and me isn't just... I dunno, propinquity?'

'That's not a farming term. Or a banking one.'

'And that's not an answer,' he retorted. 'I like you, Elle Newton. I like you a lot.'

'And I like you,' she admitted.

'You're the first woman I've kissed—the first woman I've *wanted* to kiss—since Jess.'

'But every time we kiss, we get interrupted. The rooster. The owl. The dog who splashed us just now. Maybe Nature's trying to tell us something. That we shouldn't be together.'

'Running scared, Elle?'

'No—yes.' She wrinkled her nose. 'You asked me once about my five-year plan. I told you what I wanted. Promotion, and then eventually running my own agency. In London.' She looked him straight in the eyes. 'So if this thing between you and me becomes more of a thing—would you be prepared to move back to London to be with me?'

'Would you move back to the farm to be with me?' he countered.

'That's a question, not an answer,' she said. 'Or maybe it *is* an answer. The same as mine. No. I admit, you're right in that it's changed since I was a teenager. But this isn't London. London's what I want.' She brought their joined hands to her mouth and copied his earlier actions, kissing each knuckle in turn. 'I don't think it'd be fair to either of us to have a fling. It'd get messy. We need to agree to be friends, and keep it there.'

'Friends,' he said. 'I'd like us to be more—and I'm not saying that to guilt you into doing what I want. The sensible side of me knows that you're absolutely right.' He wasn't quite ready to relinquish her hand. 'Just for the record, Damien and the rest of the Mr Wrongs were completely clueless. You're special, Elle. And you deserve someone who not only accepts where you come from, but backs you all the way and helps you get your dreams.'

Her gorgeous dark eyes glittered with tears. 'You're special, too, Charlie. And you deserve someone who'll love you and who'll love the farm as much as you do.'

He dropped her hand so he could put his arms round her, then held her close. She was the most stubborn woman he'd ever met. But he'd back off now, for her sake. 'Right, Ms Newton.' He released her and took a step back. 'We're skiving off, and we have a job to do—taking pictures for the farm. Of our fake—*acting*,' he corrected, 'fiancé and fiancée. What did you have in mind?'

'An open ring box on top of a castle,' she said.

'Castle Webb,' he said immediately.

She scoffed. 'Castle Newton's way more photogenic.'

'And it's very girly. Nobody's going to believe that your fiancé made something like that,' he pointed out.

'I suppose you have a point,' she admitted.

'So the narrative is—I built a castle, you went to get water to fill the moat, and came back to find the box on top of the castle?'

'That works,' she said. 'I guess you ought to see the ring.' She took the box from her pocket and opened it. 'It was my grandmother's.'

'It's really pretty,' he said. 'So is this what you'll wear when you eventually get engaged?'

'No,' she said. 'In London, I wear this most days on my right hand.'

'What sort of engagement ring would you like?'

She narrowed her eyes, clearly thinking about it. 'I think one of those *toi-et-moi* rings.'

'You and me,' he translated. 'One stone for you, and one for your fiancé?'

'Yes. A tanzanite, because it's the colour of the blue-bells at home, and a pink sapphire heart.'

He wondered if she'd realised the significance of what she'd just said: she'd described a ring that would be so important to her, and she'd chosen a stone to remind her of where she'd grown up. The place she'd once loved...

She'd said that her life was in London now, but he'd seen her all lit up at the farm when she was with the animals and the flowers and the sunrise. She'd admitted that she didn't hate it here, the way she had as a teen. So maybe he just needed to be patient. Wait for her to see it for herself: to realise that maybe she could learn to love it again. Could learn to love *him*.

She set the open box on the top of his sandcastle, and took a snap.

'There's something missing,' he said.

'What?'

'Water for the moat.' And something else. Which he probably shouldn't do, but it was irresistible. 'Off you go. Two buckets.' He made shooing motions in the direction of the sea

Charlie could've fetched the water himself, Elle thought crossly. On the other hand, maybe he'd done it deliberately to give her some space, because thinking about her grandmother and the bluebell woods had made her all wistful.

When she came back, she saw the words written in the wet sand by the moat. *Marry me?*

For a moment, it felt real. As if he'd actually proposed to her. Wanted to spend his life with her. Wanted to build a future with her.

She couldn't breathe, and her knees had turned to seafoam.

But then a dog barked in the distance, and reality swooped back in. Of course Charlie didn't want to marry her. This was window-dressing for the farm website. Nothing more.

He didn't want her to shriek with excitement, fling her arms round him and say yes.

'Nice touch,' she said. 'And I like the fact you punctuated it properly. A question rather than a demand.' She risked a very quick glance and was relieved to see that she'd struck the right tone.

'I wouldn't have dared to do otherwise,' he said. 'Otherwise you'd have lambasted me about my rubbish grammar and made me write it out correctly a hundred times.'

'I might've let you off with twenty,' she said lightly. 'Can you pour the water in the moat for me? I don't want it to vanish into the sand before I can take the picture. And you need to be on this side so there's no shadow.'

'Sure. I'll count you down. Three, two, one, water,' he said, and poured the first bucket in.

'Perfect,' she said, 'Thank you.' She showed him the snap, the water in the moat glittering in the sunlight almost as much as the ring on top of the castle.

'Our target audience would expect to see the ring on the third finger of your left hand,' he said.

She winced. 'Charlie, I can't ask you to...'

'It's OK. I have good memories of my engagement to Jess,' he said. 'We need these shots for the farm. I can do it if you can.'

She took the box from the sandcastle and handed it to him. He took the ring from the box and slid it onto the ring finger of her left hand, letting her snap a picture as he did so. The second photograph was of his right hand palm-up while her left hand was curled round it, showing off the ring with the sea and the blue sky in the background; and finally they stood with the sea behind them, her right arm wrapped around him and her left hand held out to display the ring, while he took the snap on her phone.

In another life, this could've been real.

And it was oh, so tempting.

But there was too much in the way.

'That should do,' she said. 'I don't know about you, but all that sandcastle-building has made me hungry. I vote we go and get some chips for lunch.'

'Works for me,' he said.

They headed for the pathway back to the town, brushed the sand off their feet and slid their shoes back on, then walked along the raised path with its spectacular views across the marshes. She didn't have a clue what to say, so she used the excuse of concentrating on the scenery and taking more photographs; and Charlie didn't seem to be disposed to make conversation, either.

At the harbour front, she bought them both a box of chips; after liberal use of salt and vinegar, they sat and ate their chips on the harbour wall, closely watched by the seagulls.

'These are good,' Charlie said.

'Very,' she replied.

She was careful to keep smiling, but inside she was full of questions she couldn't answer.

Had she done the wrong thing, telling Charlie they should stick to being friends? Should she have taken a risk? But what if she took the risk and it went wrong?

As if he knew that she needed space, he didn't chatter on the way back to the car, and just put music on the stereo during the drive back to the farm.

She busied herself revising the farm website and added the photos to the farm's social media; and then, to distract herself and clear her head, she went for a walk. But, as she drew closer to the farmhouse after her walk, her phone started to chime with notifications.

Quickly, she checked them, worrying that something night have happened to one of her parents while her phone was out of range.

Her relief at not seeing a message from either of them was short-lived, because the rest of the messages made no sense.

Congratulations!

About time someone swept you off your feet!

And then the kicker, a private message from her boss.

When I asked you to take the campaign viral, I wasn't expecting you to get *engaged* to do it...

Engaged?

Then her knees turned to water as she realised just what a huge mistake she'd made. Instead of posting the photos to the farm's social media, she'd accidentally posted them on her own.

With the hashtags *#soromantic* *#dayattheseaside* *#beautifulnorfolk*, she'd posted a picture of the sandcastle with her grandmother's engagement ring, the one of Charlie slipping the ring onto her finger, and the two of them standing by the sea, showing off the ring.

Oh, no.

This was a disaster.

She was always so meticulous. How had she managed to make such a stupid, elementary error?

Quickly, she logged into her account, deleted the posts and put them where they were supposed to be, on the farm's account: but it was too late. The messages still kept coming in. People she knew had reposted it onto their account, and people they knew had reposted it, and on and on it went...

She sent a quick message back to her boss.

Sea air clearly went to my head—posted shots to wrong account. It's for the farm. We're acting as models to save budget!

She sent the same message to her closest friends, though none of them seemed to believe her. They all wanted to know how and why she'd kept such a gorgeous man under wraps.

And then there was Charlie himself. She really needed to warn him about her mistake. He'd told her about his sister thinking they were dating; this went way, way beyond that.

She sent him a message.

Are you free? Need to talk to you pretty urgently about a tricky situation.

His reply was almost instantaneous.

Come over now.

* * *

When the knock came at his kitchen door, Charlie opened it and handed Elle a glass of wine before she'd even crossed the threshold.

'Thank you, but I think you might want to throw this over me when you find out what I've done,' she said. 'I'm so sorry. Somehow I managed to post the pictures to my own social media instead of the farm's. Everyone I know thinks we're engaged, even though I've told them we're being models for the farm and it's all fake. And it's gone viral.'

'I kind of already know,' he said. 'Jo follows you on social media. She already asked me why I was keeping you a secret.'

'Oh.' Elle grimaced. 'I'll send her a direct message and apologise. I've put a note up about how all this lovely fresh air has turned me into an airhead who posted the wrong photos to the wrong account—my "fiancé" is actually my colleague and we're showcasing the farm, how it's the perfect place to get engaged and then married.' She shook her head. 'I'm so sorry I've been so ditsy. I don't have a clue how it happened. I never usually make this sort of stupid mistake.'

'Don't worry about it,' he said. Though he couldn't help wondering: what would it be like to be with her for real? Instead, he said, 'Actually, it's quite nice to know you're capable of making a mistake. It was beginning to be a bit scary, how perfect you are.'

'Perfect?' She scoffed. 'I'm just me.'

'You're not "just" anything, Elle Newton,' he said.

'Thank you.' Her eyes were wide and earnest. 'Though I wasn't fishing for compliments.'

'I know you weren't.'

She sighed. 'So what do we do now, Mr Fake Fiancé?'

'Carry on with the soft launch, Ms Fake Fiancée,' he said. 'How long until the shopping side is sorted?'

'Not long. Frieda's given me the artwork files I need, so I'm going to sort out the produce labels for the next lot of stock, as well as sorting the website header and making sure it's consistent across all the social media sites.'

'Good.' He paused. 'We might have something else that could go viral this week.'

'What?'

'Mulberry's due to calve any day now.'

'Ohh—you mean we could have a video of a calf taking its first wobbly steps?'

'Yup.'

'I'm in. Even if she goes into labour at ridiculous o'clock in the morning, call me,' she said.

'I will,' he promised. 'I love what you've done with the website so far. The way you've brought in interest. The videos of our bees in the wildflower meadow, and the dawn chorus, and the cows playing football, the lambs skipping about, and that owl swooping just above your head.'

'That last one was more luck than judgement,' she warned.

'But it works. If I didn't live here, I'd want to visit. I'd want to see the lambs waggling their tails like little helicopters, and the calves in your "moo-rning from Bluebell Farm" posts. I can't believe how many people log on to say "moo-rning" back.'

'They've all gone viral,' she said. 'People we don't know are copying and reposting. My boss is really pleased.'

'I'd want to come and try making cheese, have a go at spinning wool, and watch the deer foraging in the fields at dusk. I'd want to try the cake of the week in the café, and use your reference guide to name the flowers and the butterflies I see on my visit, and watch the swans at the pond, and see the damselflies flitting about. What you've done to the website makes this feel a really exciting, happening place.'

'It *is* an exciting, happening place,' she said.

He didn't push her on it, but he was secretly pleased. At last she'd moved past her bad memories of West Byfield and could see the farm for what it was.

'Give it a couple of weeks for the schedule to be firmed up, and all the new sessions the café team suggested will be in place,' she said. 'The toddler group, the knit-and-natter sessions, the silver surfer group, and the coffee-and-crafting club. I think you might need to recruit some extra staff in a couple of months, even if it's for mid-morning to mid-afternoon shifts.'

'Not just that,' he said. 'Our accommodation's fully booked for the summer, and we have a waiting list for that and the courses. And I've had a couple of enquiries about weddings, despite the fact we did it as a soft launch. I've got people wanting to know how big the barn is and if we'll have a wedding fair here.'

'Cake-bakers, florists, dressmakers, balloon suppliers, and the like,' she said. 'It's a really good idea. Hold a wedding fair once every six months. That way you'll get the spring and summer brides at one, and the autumn and winter brides at the other.' She smiled. 'So, despite the mess I made of posting the pictures today, you're happy with the job I'm doing?'

'More than happy,' he said.

'Good.' She finished her glass of wine. 'I think Rav is going to wait for me to come back to London before we have the official chat, but he did say he was pleased with the way this job is going.'

'So you'll get your promotion?'

'Let's just say that next week I think I'll be ticking off the next step in my five-year plan,' she said.

'Congratulations. I'm really pleased for you,' he said.

Though part of him didn't want Elle to leave. He loved working alongside her, and he'd felt more happy and fulfilled than he had for years. He loved being with her.

And he had a horrible idea that it was more than that: was he developing feelings for her? Or was it even more than that? Was he falling in love with her? With the bright, sparkly, confident woman who was full of ideas and saw the joy in things. With the woman who was facing up to her past, owning the misery she'd felt and was moving past it. She didn't have that slightly pinched look in her eyes any more, at the farm. She fitted right in to the community. She was fast becoming the heart of the farm, for him.

But he knew she wanted to go back to London, and he wanted to stay here. There was no middle ground. So, much as he wanted to ask her to move their friendship into a real relationship, he wasn't going to put that pressure on her. He'd let her go, unburdened by guilt at leaving him behind. They'd stay friends.

And he hoped that in London she'd find someone who deserved her: someone who could give her what he couldn't.

CHAPTER EIGHT

ON MONDAY AFTERNOON, Charlie noticed that Mulberry was in the early stages of calving: she was restless, off her food, and there was a dip between the head of her tail and the pin-bones. Her tummy seemed less full, because the calf was moving into the birth canal, and she'd separated herself from the rest of the herd.

He disinfected the calving pen and added plenty of clean bedding, then brought her in to the pen. Then he messaged Elle.

Mulberry likely to calve today. Will keep you posted.

Do you know when?

No. Checking every three hours. She's in the calving pen in the barn.

And at one o'clock in the morning, he knew Mulberry was in labour. He had everything prepared in case she needed him to help her; now it was a waiting game.

One in the morning really wasn't a good time to call someone; but on the other hand Elle had been adamant that she wanted him to let her know, even at ridiculous o'clock.

She answered on the third ring. 'Is Mulberry having her calf?'

'Yes. I'm in the barn with her, if you want to come and join us.'

'On my way,' she said.

She turned up a few minutes later, in jeans and a sweater, which he suspected she might've pulled on over her pyjamas, and wellies. 'I haven't seen a calf born in years. Is this her first one?'

'Yes. I've got gloves and lubricant and equipment in case she needs help.' He looked at her. 'So you know the routine?'

'For an uncomplicated birth, yes. Though I don't remember enough to be much use other than calling the vet for you.' She handed him a travel mug. 'Coffee.'

'Thank you.'

They sat on a bale of straw, giving Mulberry space. The cow was lying down, now, and starting to strain and push.

'I can see two feet,' she said. 'Front feet, so the calf is head-first.'

'Normal presentation. That's good,' he said. He pulled his gloves on. 'As soon as the head's out, I'll give her a little help. I had a good tip from your dad: cross the front legs of the calf and turn it so its backbone is eleven o'clock to its mum's backbone. That prevents the calf's hips getting stuck and saves the mum from a pinched nerve.'

He did exactly as he'd said to her, and the birth was fast after that, with the calf slithering out. He gave Mulberry a drink of lukewarm water, and helped her to her feet.

Mulberry sniffed her calf, her tail swishing, and started to lick the calf.

Elle took a couple of shots, her phone on silent so there wouldn't be any noise to disturb the cow and her new calf. 'I'd forgotten how amazing it is to see a newborn. She's licking the calf to stimulate blood flow and muscle movement, isn't she?'

'And to help it dry off from the amniotic fluid. She'll deliver the placenta in the next three hours and the calf should stand in the next half an hour,' he said.

He checked the calf, then came back to join Elle on the straw bale. 'We have a girl. She looks normal and healthy. I'll give her a temporary neck band to ID her, but I'll fit her ear tag tomorrow.'

This was really special, Elle thought: just Charlie, herself, the cow and her newborn calf in the dimly lit barn. The first moments of new life, in the middle of the night; they didn't need to talk because this was just perfect.

A few minutes later, the calf got to her feet, all wobbly, and Elle took pictures of the calf's first few steps.

'She's gorgeous,' Elle whispered, looking at the pure white calf with her perfect black ears and nose. 'I've never seen such long eyelashes.'

'Yeah, she's a beauty,' Charlie agreed.

Mulberry lowed gently to encourage her calf to stand; she was answered by a high-pitched moo from the calf. Mulberry stood still, letting the calf work out what to do, and finally the calf nuzzled her mum and began to suck, her tail swishing.

'This is amazing,' Elle said softly, taking Charlie's hand and squeezing it briefly. 'Such a privilege.'

'Do you want to name her?' he asked.

'Can I?'

He smiled. 'If you can think up a berry name we haven't used yet.'

'The current calves are Bilberry, Cranberry and Loganberry, right?' she asked.

'Yes.'

She thought about it. 'How about Huckleberry?'

'Huckleberry works for me,' he said, and sang a snatch of 'Moon River'.

She smiled as they leaned on the gate, watching Huckleberry and Mulberry together.

'Let's give them a bit of bonding time,' he said quietly.

She turned to face him, and the next thing she knew he'd pulled her into his arms. Hers wrapped around him, and they were kissing.

Her blood felt as if it was sizzling. She'd never wanted anyone so much in her life.

He broke the kiss and leaned his forehead against hers. 'I know we said we were going to stick to being just friends and colleagues,' he whispered, 'but I want you so badly, Elle. You make me ache. I dream of you. You're in my head, all the time. I can't think straight, any more.'

'Same here,' she whispered back. 'I know it can't be forever, because we want different things, but maybe just for a little while? I think I'd regret it otherwise.' He nodded, as if agreeing that this couldn't last, but they had right now. 'Take me to bed, Charlie.'

'Sure?'

'Very sure,' she said.

It took them a while to get back to his cottage, because they kept having to stop and kiss.

By the time they got there, every nerve end felt as if it was fizzing. He looked just as hot and bothered as she felt.

Both of them kicked off their wellies, and it took him three seconds to strip off his boiler suit. Underneath he was wearing a pair of jeans and nothing else. She sucked in a breath. 'Do you have any idea how hot you look, right now?' An environmental warrior, his muscles toned from hard work and his skin tanned by the sun.

His answer was to kiss her, scoop her up and carry her to his room.

She had no idea which of them took off the other's clothes; she was too swept away with that visceral need for him.

Then, just when he'd laid her back against the pillows, he paused.

Adrenaline fluttered through her. Had he changed his mind? Was he thinking about Jess? 'What's wrong?' she asked, inwardly dreading the answer.

He grimaced, and she braced herself for the worst.

'I hate to tell you this, but I don't have any condoms,' he said.

She almost laughed with relief. He wasn't rejecting her; he was being sensible. 'Neither do I,' she said. 'But I don't want to stop, because right now I want you so much I think I'm going to spontaneously combust.'

'Me, too—but we need to be sensible,' he said.

'We will be.' She kept her gaze firmly fixed on his, and loved the way his eyes darkened when she said, 'Because there are other things we can do that *don't* need a condom.' His eyes darkened further when she moistened her lower lip with the tip of her tongue.

'Oh, God, yes,' he said, and his voice was so raspy and sexy that she went hot all over.

She held out her arms and he kissed her again; and then he kissed his way down her body, exploring her with his hands and his mouth until all she could see were fireworks inside her head. She exchanged touch for touch, kiss for kiss, exploring him in turn and delighting in discovering what made him gasp and what made his body surge. And then, finally, when she'd come apart in his arms, he drew the covers over them, holding her close. Cherishing her.

When she woke, a couple of hours later, Charlie was gone. Assuming he'd gone to check on Mulberry and her new calf, she dressed and headed down to his kitchen. His wellies were gone, so she knew her guess had been right; she made coffee, and took two mugs out to the barn.

Charlie was sitting on the bale of straw next to the pen,

and looked up as she walked in. 'Hey. Sorry to desert you. I was just checking on our girls.'

'That's what I assumed,' she said, handing him a mug. 'How are they?'

'Mulberry's fine. She's delivered the afterbirth and I'm happy she's doing well. I'll do all the registration stuff with your dad later. And thank you for the coffee.'

'Pleasure. How's Huckleberry doing?'

'She's doing great. They're both having a rest on the straw right now.' He glanced at his watch. 'The sun will be up in half an hour. The sky's at its prettiest right now, so it might be a good shot for your blog.'

The last sunrise she'd photographed, he'd put his arms around her to keep her from shivering. This time, his arms were round her because he wanted her close. Just as she wanted him close. And how good it made her feel.

The birds sang their heads off to greet the new day, and the sun rose over the treeline, a big burnt-orange ball in a pale peach sky.

'Hear the skylark?' he asked.

She looked up, trying to see the bird that had soared up to sing in the dawn, the song going on for so much longer than that of the robins and blackbirds: but all she could see was sky, even as she heard the song.

'"And drowned in yonder living blue/The lark becomes a sightless song",' she quoted.

'Is that Shelley?' he asked.

She shook her head. 'Tennyson, *In Memoriam*. Shelley's *To a Skylark* starts "Hail to thee, blithe Spirit!"'

'I'm going to have a lot of reading to do, to keep up with you,' he teased.

'I'll make you a reading list,' she teased back. 'Poetry for farmers.'

'Moo-etry,' he said, riffing on the way the local dialect pronounced 'oh' as 'oo'.

Just like the way the bullies of her teens had changed Newton to Moo-ton. Except that memory didn't hurt any more. Charlie had given her a different perspective on the past. She'd always be grateful to him for that.

Except the farm *was* her past, wasn't it? Her life was in London, now. And she'd be going back to it soon. Leaving him behind.

The problem was, last night had made her feel differently. Raised all sort of questions. Ones she didn't want to tackle right now, when she was still half-asleep; she needed to think about it properly. This was something that needed handling carefully, when her brain was sharp.

Eventually he said, 'Nice as it is, sitting here with you, I'd better get on with the milking, or the cows are going to be so grumpy with me.'

Before she could offer to help, he added, 'And you had a broken night with Huckleberry. Go and get some sleep.'

Huckleberry wasn't the only reason she'd had a broken night.

And right then she felt completely confused about the situation.

Maybe he was right. She needed sleep.

'I'll catch you later,' she said lightly, and headed back to the farmhouse. Her father was in the kitchen, making a pot of tea.

'Mulberry had her calf last night,' she said.

'Charlie texted me. You called her Huckleberry. Good name,' Mike said approvingly. 'It's a magical moment, watching those first wobbly steps, isn't it?'

'Amazing,' she said. 'I took some film. I'm going to put it up on the farm's website today.'

'Get some sleep, first, love. You must be shattered,' he said, patting her shoulder.

Elle gave in and went to bed, but every time she closed her eyes she thought of Charlie. The way he'd touched her, the way he'd made her feel...

She wanted him and she wanted to be with him, but her whole life was in London. Everything she'd worked for. If she gave it all up, it was a huge risk. She'd never managed to pick Mr Right. Would she be setting herself up for heartache all over again?

Falling for her fake fiancé would be the most stupid thing she could do.

Except she had a nasty feeling she'd already done it.

CHAPTER NINE

A POWER NAP HELPED; and then Elle did what she always did when things were going wrong in her personal life. She threw herself into work.

This particular part of the project felt a bit too close to the bone, now, but she'd pretend it was all for someone else. Which it *was*, really: she was showcasing the romantic side of the farm to tempt their future brides and grooms. It wasn't real. She needed to remind herself that it wasn't going to become real, either, and keep her head straight.

Charlie Webb was her parents' business partner and her friend. Nothing more, nothing less.

And she'd be leaving Bluebell Farm at the end of the week.

She sent him a quick text.

Setting up the wedding barn. Still OK to act as groom tomorrow afternoon? Thanks, E

No kiss.

Because this was business.

So it was ridiculous to feel hurt when the reply came back, OK. Let me know timings. C

Also no kiss.

Was that because he, too, saw this as a business communication? Or had he had the space to think about it, and come to the same conclusion that she had: that they'd made a huge mistake in sleeping together?

'Think of Mum and Dad,' she told herself fiercely. 'The farm needs to be a success.' Because, if it wasn't and her parents ran out of money—including Charlie's investment—they'd be forced to sell. Meaning that not only would they lose their dream, they'd lose generations of family history.

So, much as the fake fiancée/wedding business rattled her, she'd simply have to put up with it. For their sakes.

A couple of calls netted her most of the window dressing she needed; she could pick everything up later today, do the shoot with Frieda tomorrow afternoon, and finalise the website details in the evening. She'd take Thursday to wrap things up, and Friday she could be on the train to London.

Back to her proper life.

But first she needed to talk some of it over with her mum and Lisa in the farm shop café.

'So you're planning a fake wedding?' Lisa asked.

'We're doing a mock-up of a wedding venue for publicity photos,' Elle corrected. 'Until we've actually hosted a wedding and the bride and groom have agreed to let us use photos for publicity, we can't show people what sort of thing they can expect. The barn's an amazing space, but potential clients need to see it as it could be.' Elle spread her hands. 'So we're going to photograph the barn set up as a wedding venue. Well, not me—Frieda is. She's a landscape specialist, but she's agreed to take the publicity photos for us.'

'So what are you thinking?' Angie asked.

'We need to show the ceremony area, the wedding breakfast area, and the dance area.' Elle ticked them off on her fingers. 'I've talked to the willow weaving people, and they're going to lend us an arch and a few big willow heart outlines that we can decorate with fairy lights, gauzy fabric and flowers. We can set up an aisle with, say, twenty-four chairs, to give the feel of a small family wedding. And we'll set up a couple of tables with cutlery, glasses, table confetti and flowers. That leaves the dance floor area; I'm hiring some of those big light-up letters to spell out "love", and we'll have the hearts on the wall.'

'What about a cake?' Angie asked. 'You can't have a wedding without a cake.'

'I could go into town and pick up a couple of those ready-iced plain wedding cakes, and we'll add wild flowers or something to dress it up,' Elle said.

'No. We're about doing things locally. I'll make the cake,' Lisa said.

'But you don't have enough time to ice it,' Elle said.

'I don't need to. Naked cakes are trendy,' Lisa said. 'That's what my niece had at her wedding.' She flicked into her phone and showed Elle the photograph. 'It's not formally iced all the way round—it's decorated with a bit of chocolate drip, and then flowers and berries.'

'That'd be brilliant,' Elle said. 'Could you do something like that, ready for tomorrow afternoon?'

'Definitely,' Lisa said. 'And then we can give away free slices in the café—I don't think it's fair to sell it, when we've used it for a prop.'

'And it's also good publicity,' Elle said. 'I can print up some cards to go with them, directing people to the website, and tell them to pass it on to anyone in their family and friends who might be thinking about weddings.'

'We can dress all the chairs for the ceremony with ivory sashes, and maybe have petals and tea-lights on the borders of the aisle,' Angie suggested.

'That'd be wonderful,' Elle said.

'What about the bride and groom?' Angie asked. 'Who are you getting to do that? Models from London?'

'No. We don't have the budget.' Elle took a deep breath. 'Charlie and I are doing it.'

Angie's eyes widened. 'Are you sure? I mean…'

'I asked him last week—and, yes, I was sensitive about how I phrased it—and he agreed,' Elle said.

'What about your dress, Elle?' Angie asked.

'Already sorted,' Elle reassured her. 'I bought it in a charity shop in Norwich last week. There's a short veil and a flower crown, too. Charlie can wear his sharp London suit.'

'Flowers?' Lisa asked.

'I'm keeping it simple.' She smiled. 'The obvious thing would be a posy of bluebells.'

'Scarlett in the shop is really good with displays,' Lisa said. 'She's really creative. And she did the flowers for my niece's wedding. We could ask her to do the flowers.'

'And any other ideas for styling the barn or the tables,' Elle said. 'Can we bring her in now?'

'I'll go and get her,' Lisa said.

When she'd gone, Angie turned to Elle. 'Sitting here, planning a wedding reception with you—I wish we were doing this for real.'

Elle felt the colour sweep into her face. 'I'm sorry. I wanted you involved because the farm's yours. It didn't occur to me that you might…' She blew out a breath. 'I never meant to hurt you, Mum. But I have to be honest with you. I just don't think I'll ever find Mr Right.'

She ignored how she'd felt when Charlie had kissed her. When he'd swept her off her feet and up to his bed. There was too much in the way for it to work between them.

'I don't mean to pressure you, love,' Angie said.

'I know. Love you, Mum.'

'Love you, too.' Angie hugged her. 'And you know your dad and I are so proud of you, don't you?'

Elle's throat was too thick with unshed tears for her to reply. She simply nodded.

Scarlett turned out to be full of great ideas, and between them they came up with the perfect wedding day. Elle spent the rest of the day picking up props, but she had a case of severely cold feet by the end of the day.

How could she get this to work, when there was still unfinished business between her and Charlie? Any awkwardness between them would show in the photographs, and undercut what they were trying to do. She needed to make sure they were on the same page.

She texted him.

Can we talk?

It was a while before he replied, with a cagey When?

Whenever's convenient.

She hoped he'd pick up that she meant as soon as possible.

He typed back.

Free now.

Thanks. Coming over.

But she didn't want to sit in his kitchen and remember the last time she'd been in his cottage.

Maybe we can go for a walk?

Works for me.

So he didn't want to sit in his kitchen with her, either. She wasn't sure whether that was a good thing or not.

Where would they go? Not the bluebell woods, she decided: she'd spend all the time there thinking of that kiss. And the kiss on the beach. And the kiss near newborn Huckleberry. Near the shepherd's huts was also a bad idea, because then she'd think about dancing with him.

'Thanks for making time,' she said when he answered the door. 'I thought we could walk by the wildflower meadow.'

'Good idea,' he said.

She didn't try making small talk. And he waited until they'd reached the wildflower meadows before asking, 'So what did you want to talk about?'

'The shoot tomorrow,' she said. 'If it's awkward between us, it'll show. And then the pictures won't be any use.'

'So we have to discuss the elephant in the room. Not that we're in a room.' He shrugged. 'All right. You go first.'

'I...' Where did she start? 'For the record, I don't just hop into bed with anyone.'

He frowned. 'Of course you don't. I never for a minute thought you were like that.'

'Good.' She huffed out a breath. Why was this so difficult? 'Charlie—I like you. In other circumstances...' But it wasn't going to work, was it? 'Since I've been here, you've made me see that the farm isn't the awful place I built it up to be in my head and I can enjoy it again. I'm grateful that you've shown me I can come back and it's fine. People aren't going to make me feel like an outsider. They don't see me as—well, how I was as a teen.'

'But?'

Either it showed on her face, or he was really perceptive. 'My life's in London,' she said simply. 'My five-year plan's there. I've worked hard for that promotion. I'd intended to go back to a job I really, really want.' She paused. This was where she had to be brave. 'But then there's you. And you're here.' She couldn't read his expression. At all. But if they didn't get this out in the open, it was going to simmer away until it exploded in their faces. 'OK. Cards on table. I'm terrified of saying this. I have no idea what's in your head, and if I say what's in mine there's a chance that it's going to make things even more complicated. And we need that photo shoot tomorrow to be perfect.' She took a deep breath. 'But if I don't say it…things are going to be complicated anyway.'

His eyes narrowed. 'You're the communications expert, Elle. Right now I have no idea where this is going.'

'I'll keep it simple. I'm going back to London on Friday.' The words were stuck in her throat. This could be a disaster. If he said no, this time she'd know that she'd been rejected for who she was, not where she came from. If he said yes, then it might be fabulous at first: but what if he started to resent her for wrecking his own five-year plan? She closed her eyes to stop the words spinning. 'Will you come back to London with me?'

'Come back to London with you,' he repeated.

She couldn't tell a thing from the tone of his voice. But if she opened her eyes and looked at him, she knew she wouldn't have the courage to say the rest of it. 'I know you hate London. I know it's where Jess died. But you taught me that I could move on and love Bluebell Farm again. Maybe I can teach you to move on and love London again. I don't mean forget Jess, I mean be in a place where you can cherish her memory and let yourself love again.'

Elle was a lot braver than he was, Charlie thought. He'd been thinking about this ever since they'd slept together;

even though they'd agreed that it was just a one-off, a moment out of time, it had thrown him into a spin. He liked her—more than liked her—but there was so much in the way.

Yeah. She was right. It was complicated.

With Elle by his side, he thought he could finally move on.

Although he didn't want to go back to his old job, he still had a good network and he was pretty sure he'd be able to find something working with environmentally friendly funds.

But.

Bluebell Farm had changed him.

His heart belonged here, now. He didn't want to go back to London.

'Maybe we can work things out between us,' he said, 'but not in London. I'll be honest with you, too. Looking back, I don't like the person I was, when I lived in London. I've changed, and I don't want to be that person again.'

'So what you're saying is that you'd be with me—but only if I stayed here?' she asked. 'How could that work? Commuting would be terrible: half an hour from here to Norwich, two hours on the train, half an hour on the Tube, and then three hours at the other end of the day. With that sort of travel time factored in, we'd barely see each other.'

'What about working in London during the week and spending your weekends here?' he suggested. 'That way, we'd both get what we wanted.'

She looked thoughtful, then shook her head. 'I'd be trying to split myself between the two parts of my life, and I'd feel that I wasn't giving enough to either of them.'

She didn't want to stay here; so, if he wanted to be with her, he'd have to be the one to move. Go back to London. Back to the daily drag of commuting. Back to working ridiculous hours in a culture that expected him to be seen in the office every possible minute. Back to not being able to breathe. 'I just can't do London,' he said softly. 'Even for you. I'm sorry. I could try, but I already know I'd feel trapped and smothered—even if I had a part-time job in the City and we had an allotment and a huge garden so I could spend half the week outdoors. I'd end up resenting you for making me go back. And if you stayed here for me, you'd end up resenting me because you'd lose all the opportunities you have in London.'

Elle knew he was right. She wouldn't be able to change his mind about London.

But if she stayed here for him… What if he changed his mind about her, too? Then she'd be left with nothing. The risk was terrifying and even the thought of it sent ice slithering through her veins.

She'd secretly hoped that Charlie might be falling for her, the way she'd found herself falling for him; but clearly he wasn't. Or, at least, not enough. Although her feelings about the farm had changed, and she'd found a man who also loved it and didn't think less of her for her background… At the moment, it was hypothetical and they were both assuming he could make space in his life for her. But she knew that losing Jess had hit him hard. If Elle wasn't enough for him to go to London, then who was to say she'd be enough for him here? Pining for him in London when she didn't have to see him was one thing; staying here and seeing him every day, getting more and more miserable, would be even worse.

'There isn't a viable compromise, is there?' she asked.

'I can't see one.' He drew in a breath. 'I'm sorry. You're the one woman I would try it for.'

'But you already know you'd be unhappy.' Because she wasn't enough for him.

'Just as you'd be unhappy here.' He paused. 'As you said, in other circumstances it could've been wonderful between us. But I can't see a compromise that would work for both of us. I don't want you to leave; but I also don't want you to stay here and be unhappy. It's not fair to ask you to give up everything for me.'

She reached out and touched his face. 'I wish things were different. That we could be together in London. But you're right. I don't want you to be here, miles away from me; but I don't want you to be unhappy in London, either.'

'Bottom line: to be fair to both of us, all I can offer you is friendship, Elle,' he said.

Just as he had, the very first time she'd met him and he'd let her sob out her misery onto his shoulder.

'Friends it is,' she said, smiling widely despite the fact that she wanted to curl into a ball and sob her heart out. 'So we're OK for the photo shoot tomorrow?'

'Yeah. We're OK,' he said.

'Great. I have stuff to do,' she said, striving for brightness and breeziness. 'I'll see you tomorrow.'

Wednesday. The wedding day.

Well, the not-wedding day. The acting wedding day. The day when they were mocking up the barn as if there was a wedding, but the wedding wasn't happening.

Weirdly, Charlie found himself as nervous as if it was real. As if his best man was running through the checklist to make sure they hadn't forgotten anything; as if his mum was checking that his buttonhole looked right and his tie was straight; as if his sister was all thrilled that her eighteen-month-old daughter Ivy was going to toddle down the aisle behind Elle as a flower girl.

None of it was happening.

It was just photographs.

He hadn't even been involved in dressing the barn; he'd offered to help, but Elle had sent him a very polite text saying that it was quite all right, thank you, because she, her mum, Lisa and Scarlett had everything under control. All he had to do was turn up for a couple of photographs at three o'clock.

He arrived at five minutes to three, knowing that Elle would be a stickler for time.

And the transformation of the barn was amazing.

She'd said something about borrowing a willow arch; there it was, by a small table, covered in gauzy ivory fabric, greenery and fairy lights.

The limewashed chiavari chairs were set out in two sections with an aisle in between, as if ready for an intimate family wedding, the backs dressed with simple ivory sashes. There were ivory flower petals marking the edges of the aisle, and tiny globe vases filled with more fairy lights.

The centre of the barn was set up for the wedding breakfast: two round tables, with damask tablecloths. The cutlery was gleaming, as were the glasses; there was an ivory enamelled jug in the centre of each table, filled with a delicate spray of wild flowers. Each place was set with a small ivory box, which he assumed were empty and represented the wedding favours; each was tied with a narrow gold ribbon to match the gold hearts of the table confetti, and a single stem of bluebells adorned the boxes.

There was a small table set with a cake; instead of being covered in icing, it was decorated with flowers and berries, and the word 'love' in a fancy script as a cake topper.

At the dance floor end, there were enormous letters made of lights, spelling out the word 'love'; on the walls there were willow hearts, festooned with the same green-ery, gauzy fabric and fairy lights as the bridal arch.

'This is stunning,' he said as Angie came over to him. 'It really looks like…' He dragged in a breath. 'Just wow. You've all worked so hard.'

But where was Elle?

He knew she wasn't there, because even if his back had been turned he would've known where she was. He would've felt her presence.

Hoping he sounded a lot more casual than he felt, he enquired, 'Where's Elle?'

'Gone to change,' Angie said. 'So you like what we've done?'

'It's amazing,' he said.

'A lot of the ideas were Elle's and Scarlett's,' Lisa said, coming over to join them. 'I think we might have our wed-ding co-ordinator role covered.'

Elle? Or Scarlett?

'It's perfect,' he said. 'And I really like that cake.'

'My idea,' Lisa said, and turned slightly pink. 'Though it's not just a prop. We're giving out free slices in the café, afterwards, with a card telling people about the wedding services.'

'It's great,' he said.

'Ah, here's our bride,' Frieda, the photographer, called.

He turned, almost as if he really were waiting for Elle at the altar. She was wearing a simple ivory strapless dress with a beaded bodice, a short veil attached to her hair with a narrow crown of ivory flowers, and she was carrying a sheaf of bluebells.

Was this the wedding of her dreams—the wedding she thought she'd never have?

Charlie couldn't say a word. His tongue was definitely stuck to the roof of his mouth. With superglue.

Every step she took towards him made him ache a little bit more.

He wanted her. Wanted to be with her. Wanted to make his life with her.

But he just couldn't do it in London. Not any more.

'Hi,' she said quietly as she reached him. 'What do you think?'

She was talking about the barn. 'Stunning.' He was talking about her.

'I'd recommend Scarlett as your wedding co-ordinator. She has great ideas.'

He nodded. 'Lisa said.'

'Shall we?'

He'd never seen himself as an actor, but now he would have to act his socks off.

Or maybe he wouldn't. Maybe he just had to imagine that this was real, that Elle had walked down the aisle towards him. That they'd found a workable compromise and today was the first day of the rest of their lives.

So he smiled.

Even when Angie and Lisa set off a dried petal confetti cannon, and Frieda took shot after shot of himself and Elle.

Even when they posed to cut the cake.

Even when Angie, a huge Bryan Adams fan, whipped out her phone and started playing '(Everything I Do) I Do It For You' while he and Elle danced with the letters as a background and Frieda snapped away.

'And that's a wrap,' Frieda said at last. 'I'm going to do a bit of post production at home, Elle, but I'll send you the link to the private files in a couple of hours.'

'That's fabulous, Frieda. Thank you.' Elle stepped away from him. 'Thank you, team. We've done a great job. I'll help clear up, then I'm going back to the farmhouse to finish off putting most of this together, so all I have to do is slot Frieda's photos in.'

'Go now. I'll do the clearing up,' Charlie said, 'because I didn't do anything to help, this morning.'

'Are you sure?' Angie asked.

'I'm sure,' Charlie said.

'I'll save you a slice of cake,' Lisa promised, and patted his shoulder.

It didn't take long to put the cutlery and glasses back in their boxes, fold the tablecloth and the sashes back into their boxes, and sweep up the confetti and stack the chairs and tables.

Charlie was glad he had the afternoon milking to take his mind off things.

And when Elle texted him later, to ask if he wanted to be involved in choosing the photos, he texted back,

That's OK, trust your judgement.

So he wasn't even going to come and help choose the photographs?

Elle stifled the hurt, telling herself to be reasonable about it. It wasn't so surprising, was it? Today must've brought back a million memories of his real wedding—and his loss.

She texted back.

If you want to take a look, here's the link.

And then she got on with choosing the photos with her parents.

Frieda had done a fantastic job. But Elle just hoped that nobody noticed the expression on her face and guessed what she really felt about Charlie Webb, her fake fiancé and her fake bridegroom.

Ten minutes after she'd loaded the last bit of the website, her phone pinged.

Charlie?

Of course not. She damped down the disappointment and opened her boss's note.

Website fabulous. Looking forward to toasting our new senior account manager with champagne on Monday. Congratulations, Elle!

'Was that Charlie?' Mike asked.

'No. My boss. I got the promotion,' she said, and the tears spilled over. She just hoped her parents thought they were tears of joy rather than tears that she was walking away from Charlie. 'So I'll be going back to London for definite on Friday.'

'Elle.' Angie wrapped her arms round her daughter. 'I'll miss you so much. Are you sure you won't stay? You couldn't work remotely for the agency from here?'

'No,' Elle said, as gently as she could. 'But I'll be back soon, Mum.'

'You can't stay until Sunday?' Mike asked.

'I've got tons to do in London before Monday,' she said. 'But it doesn't mean I don't love you. And I promise I will definitely visit more.'

'Then we'll drive you to the station,' Mike said.

Her dad's pick-up might be jolty and a far cry from the comfort of Charlie's Range Rover, but at least she wouldn't have to face Charlie again. Face all the loss.

'Thanks, Dad. I'd better start packing. Love you,' she said.

CHAPTER TEN

GOING BACK TO London on Friday morning was harder than she'd expected. Saying goodbye to the animals was hard. She was almost in tears as she hugged the calves. She made a fuss of the sheep, and gave the hens some mealworms that had them thanking her very vocally and Carbon the rooster doing a dance. She had a last walk by the wildflower meadow and in the woods to say goodbye to the swans.

Last time she'd been here, she couldn't get away quickly enough.

This time—leaving was much harder.

The news had spread quickly, and Elle was shocked by how many visitors she had on Thursday. Rosie, with a pair of the softest gloves knitted from the wool of Bluebell Farm's sheep. Frieda, with a watercolour of the farm. Nicki, from the willow weavers, with a beautiful woven heart. Lisa, with a carrot cake. Scarlett, with a beautifully styled box full of goodies. 'It's from all the café and shop team,' she said, 'but it's also a prototype hamper.' She beamed. 'I'm thinking Christmas. And then we can offer seasonal variations.'

The only person who didn't come to see her was Charlie. She'd thought she might see him while she was saying goodbye to the animals, but he was clearly avoiding her.

She'd texted him, to let him know that she started her new job on Monday and was going back to London on Friday, but his reply had been cool.

Congratulations. I'm pleased for you.

Well, that told her where she stood.

Right at the far edge of the friend zone. Where it was civil, not warm.

And it was only when Elle was on the train back to London on Friday morning that she realised how much she'd secretly been hoping that Charlie would drive to the station, sweep her off her feet before she could go through the barrier to the platform, and tell her that he was only letting her go temporarily and he was going to join her in London.

Friends.

That had been the deal.

So she'd go back to London. Back to her lovely, busy life. And she'd try not to miss him.

Though that was easier said than done. Despite meeting up with friends for lunch and drinks over the weekend to celebrate her new job, and getting back into the routine of gym classes, she found herself feeling lonely.

Everyone celebrated in the office when Rav officially announced her appointment as Senior Account Manager; she'd brought in cakes, fruit and bubbly, and Hugo took her and the senior management team out for an upmarket lunch. Everyone oohed and aahed over the lambs and the calves on the Bluebell Farm website, tried doing their own version of Carbon the rooster's special dance, and came up with terrible puns involving 'moo' that she wrote down for future use.

When a huge bouquet of flowers arrived for her at Reception, she looked at the name on the card and caught her breath.

Charlie.

Did this mean…?

Heart pounding, she read the message.

Congratulations on your promotion—very well deserved. Now go and shine. Best, Charlie

Anyone who didn't know what had happened between them would think this was simply a message from a grateful client. But she knew differently. This was Charlie making it clear that he was staying put and telling her to be happy in London. To shine.

Right.

Shine.

How, when she felt more like a rainy Wednesday afternoon than a Saturday lunchtime with blue skies and a blazing sun?

Flowers had been a good idea, Charlie thought. And that message. Elle would know what he was really saying, telling her to shine. That he wished he could be different, but he couldn't, so he wouldn't hold her back.

The problem was, he missed her.

He missed her helping out with the milking and singing to the cows.

He missed her gleefully telling him random facts she'd found about something on the farm.

He missed her straight talking and her teasing.

And the bed he'd always slept in alone, except for that half a night with her, felt huge and empty. Now, it was nothing more than a place to lay his head.

Without Elle, nothing felt right. Food tasted of nothing. Even the cows noticed, and nudged him and licked his face and lowed softly in his ear as if to tell him to cheer up, it might never happen.

Except it had, and it was his own fault. She'd asked him

to go to London with her. He'd said no. So he'd just have to fake it until life felt back on an even keel again.

'Earth to Elle?'

'Sorry, Marce. Busy day,' Elle said, smiling at her best friend.

Marcie coughed. 'Busy fortnight, more like. You haven't been the same since you've been back in London. And don't try to flannel me that it's because you're busy in your new role. The Elle Newton I know and love is the empress of project management. You're the epitome of the busy woman to ask if you want something done. You *thrive* on it. So what's really wrong?'

Elle bit her lip. 'You mean, who's Mr Wrong, this time?'

'No,' Marcie said. 'Because whenever you get let down by a bloke who was never good enough for you in the first place, you pick yourself up, dust yourself down, and go and find something fun to do. Right now,' she said gently, 'I don't think you're enjoying anything. Not your new job, not the film we saw last night—you were in another world, not paying any attention to it—not dinner out with the girls, and not cocktails the other night. So what's wrong, Elle? And what can I do to help you fix it?'

Elle sighed. 'This is in strictest confidence, right?'

'I'm your best friend. Of *course* it's in strictest confidence,' Marcie said, looking hurt.

'I know that. Sorry. I didn't mean to insult you. I'm all over the place.' Elle sighed again, and told her about Charlie. 'And there's no way of compromising,' she said. 'He doesn't want to be in London.'

'And you told him you don't want to be at Bluebell Farm,' Marcie said, giving her a hug. 'But, the way you've talked to me about the place, I'd say you've fallen back in love with it, as well as with him.'

'I have,' Elle admitted. 'But my job's here. There's no compromise.'

'Isn't there?' Marcie held up her forefinger. 'Firstly, there's this little thing called remote working—you could spend maybe one day a week in London and the rest in Norfolk. If the alternative's not having you at all, I reckon Rav's not going to refuse you.'

'Even with our spotty Wi-Fi?'

'If it's that desperate, go into town to send the emails and do the video calls,' Marcie said, and held up her middle finger to join the first. 'Secondly, you want to set up your own agency, eventually. Who says it can't be at the farm?'

Elle considered it. 'Why didn't Charlie or I think of that?' she asked.

'Because I think you were both too busy falling in love with each other and then panicking your socks off,' Marcie said.

'You're right,' Elle said with a sigh. 'We both panicked and weren't thinking straight.'

'What do you want, Elle?' Marcie asked.

'Everything. I want Charlie, I want to be part of everything that's happening at the farm, I want my parents, I want my friends, I want my job here, I want a Labrador puppy...' Her voice faded. 'But I can't have it all, can I?'

'Not all of the time, no,' Marcie said. 'But you can have all of it, some of the time. Be with the man you love, make your job more flexible, come and party once in a while in London, and invite us all down to cuddle the lambs and eat too much cake.'

'All of it, some of the time,' Elle repeated. Could she?

Marcie nodded. 'Honey, you need to talk to Charlie. Tell him what you told me. But face to face, not on the phone or even in a video call. He needs to look into your eyes so he knows what's in your heart.'

Elle glanced at her watch. 'If I leave in the next thirty minutes, I can get a train back to Norwich and a taxi to the farm. And if Charlie turns me down again…then I'll get the six o'clock train in to Liverpool Street tomorrow morning and just be a tiny bit late for work.'

'And if he doesn't turn you down, I get to be chief bridesmaid and dance under the fairy lights in that amazing barn?' Marcie asked.

Elle grinned. 'You most definitely do.'

'Good. I'm going back to my place. Pack your overnight bag,' Marcie said, and hugged her.

A fortnight without Elle.

It had felt like a year.

Longer than a year.

Charlie closed his eyes. He should've said yes. Then he could've managed here without her, simply counting down the days until Mike and Angie had found his replacement and he could move back to London with Elle. Now, he was counting endless days—and torturing himself with her ElleOfLondon social media accounts. He could've been sharing all those things with her, if he hadn't been so stupid and pushed her away. Cocktails in rooftop bars. Wisteria cascading down Chelsea walls. Geraniums in window-boxes. Swans and deckchairs in Green Park. Coffee in a trendy shop, perfectly styled in a double-walled glass. Street food and dancing on the banks of the Thames.

He didn't want to live in London any more; but he was miserable at Bluebell Farm without her.

And finally he came to the conclusion that it was time to risk his heart again. Home was where Elle was. If he couldn't persuade her to come back to Bluebell Farm, then he'd move to London. Better to be with her, than to be without her.

But how did he persuade her to give him a chance? What would convince her that he meant it?

He could write his feelings on A3 cards and stand at her doorway, playing romantic music on his phone and getting her to read the cards one by one.

He could take her to a small theatre where he'd hired a singer-songwriter to play her a love song on a piano, under a spotlight.

He could sing to her himself—as he'd sort of done during milking. Say, The Beatles' 'Michelle', but switching her name into the song instead.

He could take her to a flashy restaurant to declare himself, or for afternoon tea in the glitziest hotel in London. Whisk her off to Paris, to Rome, to Venice.

But somehow an extravagant gesture didn't feel right. Not when he'd first fallen for a girl in a bluebell wood with a nightingale singing in the background.

Keep it simple, he decided. He went to see her parents and explained to them what he wanted to do, and they gave him their blessing along with her address. Then he caught the train to London. It felt very strange to be back in the city, the place that had held some of his darkest days as well as some of his happiest.

He still hadn't worked out what to say to Elle; but one thing he did know she liked was flowers. At Liverpool Street, he bought an armful of the prettiest flowers at the flower stand, then caught the Tube to the Oval. His heart was racing as he followed the directions on his phone to the mansion block where she lived.

The building was beautiful, a large Edwardian brick-and-slate building with white windows and balconies: exactly the sort of place he could imagine her living.

He pressed the intercom button and waited.

* * *

Elle wasn't expecting visitors. She hadn't made any arrangements to meet anyone, either.

It was probably someone door-knocking for a politician. She thought about ignoring it, but then the buzzer went again.

Whoever it was, they were persistent.

She rolled her eyes. She'd answer with a polite 'thank you, but no', and then get on with her packing. 'Tha—' she began.

'Elle. Can I come in?'

She recognised the voice instantly 'Charlie? What are you doing here?'

'I wanted to see you.'

'I'm on the ground floor. Turn right into the corridor, and I'm the second door on the right.'

Why did Charlie want to see her? And why was he in London, when he'd said he didn't want to be there any more?

When he knocked on the door, she opened it and he thrust a large bunch of flowers into her hands.

'Thank you—they're gorgeous,' she said.

'They're not great, but they're the best I could get at the station,' he said, looking apologetic.

'They're perfect. Even nicer than the ones you sent me last week.' She paused. 'Can I get you a coffee or something?'

'No. I just want to talk.' He gave her a wry smile. 'I don't think I've ever felt so nervous in my life.'

'Nervous?' she echoed, puzzled. Why on earth would Charlie be feeling nervous?

'Because I'm just about to…' He blew out a breath. 'This could be the best thing I've ever done, or the most stupid, and I have no idea which.'

'Come and sit down,' she said, and ushered him into the living room. 'I'll just put these flowers in water.'

The living room was as Charlie expected: pale walls, wooden flooring with a bright rug, a comfortable sofa, an armchair with a reading lamp and a large bookcase stuffed with books. There was a small table with four chairs, which he guessed doubled as her desk as well as her dining table; and prominent on the wall was Frieda's watercolour of Bluebell Farm. On the mantelpiece were framed photos of Elle on her graduation day with her parents, one of her parents at Bluebell Farm, and one of Elle with another woman he guessed might be her best friend.

She came back in. 'Are you sure you don't want anything to drink?'

'I just want to talk.' He shook his head. 'I've been trying to work out the right words, all the way here, and I can't find them. But a flashy gesture doesn't seem right, either. So what I'm saying now is unpolished, but it's honest. Straight from my heart.' He took a deep breath. 'You've been gone for two weeks. It feels like a lifetime. So I'm here to say I'm sorry I pushed you away. I love Bluebell Farm, but I hate being there without you. If being with you means being in London, then—even though I never wanted to come back—it's London all the way. Because you're here, and you're where my heart is.' And then, because he couldn't hold the words back any longer, he blurted out, 'I love you.'

She stared at him. He couldn't read her expression.

Was she pleased, horrified, indifferent?

All his wits seemed to have deserted him.

The time he'd thought crawled so slowly before was now setting a new world slowness record.

Or maybe he'd got this very badly wrong.

'I'm sorry,' he said. 'Now you're back in London, things must seem different. I'll go. Forget we had this conversation, because I don't want you to feel awkward with your parents. I'll make sure I stay out of your way, so it won't be cringey when you come home.' He stood up, ready to walk away and leave her to find what she really wanted from life.

Except she stood up, too. Took his hand. 'You love me. You want to be with me. Even if it means coming back to London,' she repeated.

He couldn't speak, just nodded.

'When you rang my doorbell, I was packing,' she said. 'I was coming back to Bluebell Farm to ask you to be with me. To say I'll come back to Norfolk if that's the only way we can be together.'

'But—what about your job? The one you worked so hard for?'

'It's not enough, if I don't have you,' she said. 'London isn't enough, either. I want you.'

She wanted him.

She'd been coming home to him, just as he'd been trying to come home to her.

It might still be a bit complicated but, together, he knew they'd find a way to work this out.

He wrapped his arms round her and kissed her lingeringly.

'I wasn't looking to fall in love,' he said. 'And opening my heart to love again and risking losing you scares me witless. But then I realised that being without you was way, way worse than living with the fear.' He stroked her face. 'That photo shoot for the wedding—that's when it hit me what I really wanted. You walking down the aisle to me with an armful of bluebells, our closest family and friends there to share the moment. It felt so right. I wanted it to be for real.'

'But you didn't even come over to review the photographs,' she protested.

'Because I was terrified that Frieda's lens might have captured how I really felt about you—and that you didn't feel the same way.' He took out his phone and showed her a photograph. 'Tell me what you see.'

'We're acting out a first dance.' She looked at him. 'I was thinking about the night we danced together outside the shepherd's hut.'

'The night I kissed you for the first time, with the nightingale singing.' He nodded. 'I was remembering that, too. And thinking about how much I wanted to kiss you again, even though I knew you were leaving and it wouldn't be fair of me to hold you back.'

'I wanted to kiss you, too, but you'd told me we could only be friends. I thought it was better to stay in London and be miserable without you, than to see you every day and pine for you.'

'How stupid are we?' he asked. 'There has to be a way to make this work for both of us, Elle. I love you. I want to watch the seasons change at Bluebell Farm with you at my side—but I don't want you to sacrifice your job. I know how hard you've worked for your promotion.'

'My best friend suggested something today,' Elle said. 'Flexible working. Maybe I can work a couple of days a week in London, and the rest of the time in Norfolk.'

'That's it.' He stared at her. 'Why the hell didn't *we* think of that?'

'Because neither of us has been in a good place,' she said. 'You're still healing from losing Jess.'

'I'll always miss her and I'll always love her,' Charlie said. 'But the thing is, love isn't like a cake that gets scoffed and then there's nothing left. It's something that grows and changes. And I'm finally ready to move on—with you.' He paused. 'But what about you and the Mr Wrongs?'

She nodded. 'I was thinking of all the men who'd let me down, and panicking that if things went wrong between us it would make life difficult for Mum and Dad. Using my work as a barrier between us meant that I could be a coward and not have to take the risk. Except I've really missed you, Charlie. And although I love the bright lights and the glitter of London, it's all felt a bit pointless without you. I don't feel connected, the way I used to. I want my job—but I want you more.'

'What if your manager says you need to stay in London?'

'Then we tweak my five-year plan and I set up my own consultancy a little bit early.' She dragged in a breath. 'Which is a bit scary.'

'I've got your back,' he said. 'Whatever support you need, it's yours. Anything from building you the office of your dreams through to helping you stuff promotional goody bags at three in the morning.'

'I'll hold you to that,' she said. 'And I've got your back, too. Everything from teaching you all the wildflower stuff for your nature walks through to bringing your lunch when you're busy foxproofing the hen house.'

'I'll hold you to that,' he echoed.

'And we need a new five-year plan. A joint one.'

'A flexible one,' he added. 'Starting with seeing if your boss agrees to changing the way you work. The main thing is that you're happy.'

'That we're *both* happy,' she corrected.

'And next on the list is to take our time. Much as I'd love to sweep you off your feet, ask you to marry me and then be the first couple married in the barn, that wouldn't be fair. I want you to be sure that life at Bluebell Farm is enough for you,' he said. 'If it's not, we'll do a re-think. We'll tweak things until it works for both of us.'

'That's fair,' she said. 'Though I'm pretty sure my feelings aren't going to change.' She reached up to kiss him. 'I love you too, Charlie. And you've missed the last train back. Can you bear a night in London?'

'With you,' he said, 'I think I can.'

EPILOGUE

Four months later

'I KNOW YOU'RE BUSY, but breakfast is the most important meal of the day,' Charlie said, leaning against the jamb of the door of Elle's office in the farmhouse.

Elle sniffed the air. 'Is that croissants I smell?'

'You'll have to come with me to find out.' He held out a hand. 'Half an hour's break. Most people aren't even at their desk yet.'

'I am, because I'm a morning person,' Elle said. 'Which is just as well, since you're up at mad o'clock to do the milking.'

'Indeed.' He smiled as she saved her file, closed her laptop and went to join him.

'Are Mum and Dad in the kitchen?'

'No idea. We're not eating here.'

She frowned. 'Why didn't you just text me from the cottage and tell me you had croissants?'

'Because we're not eating there, either.' He picked up the wicker basket he'd stashed in the hallway. 'We're eating al fresco.' He stole a kiss. 'I did think about blindfolding you, but I didn't want anyone getting the wrong idea.'

She kissed him back. 'Indeed. So is there any particular reason for breakfast outdoors?'

'I just thought it would be nice.'

She gave him a sidelong look. 'In four months of living with you, I've learned there's always a reason why you do something.'

He just laughed. 'Stop being so suspicious.'

She realised that they were heading towards the wildflower meadow. As they got closer, she saw that he'd set out a table and two chairs. The table was neatly set for two with a damask tablecloth and napkins, plus a milk jug containing a froth of meadowsweet.

'This definitely looks like a special occasion,' she said, letting him seat her.

'It's a Wednesday, the weather's nice, and you're here. That's special enough for me. Can't a man try to do something romantic for his girlfriend, once in a while?' He opened the wicker basket, took out a flask and a stainless steel bottle, and poured them both some coffee, adding milk to hers.

'Thank you.' She smiled. 'Actually, this is lovely. There must be a gazillion birds in that meadow, singing their heads off and scoffing all the seed. Just as I'm going to be scoffing croissants in a moment, right?'

He rolled his eyes and took a dish of butter and a pot of raspberry jam from the basket, swiftly followed by a box containing croissants wrapped in a linen napkin. 'As you demand, princess.'

'And they're still warm. You are a prince among men,' Elle declared.

'No regrets about moving back?' he asked, taking a croissant and buttering it.

'No. I can do most of my job from here, with a Tuesday catch-up in the London office and the occasional client visit. I still get the buzz of London, and I get the cows and the sheep and the chickens and all this gorgeousness six days a week.' She grinned. 'And, best of all, I get to wake up with you every morning—which is worth putting up with the stroppy magpies yelling their heads off.'

'Good,' he said.

'No regrets about asking me to move in with you?' she asked.

'I get to wake up every morning with the woman I love, even though she hogs the duvet and the pillows and she warms her cold feet on me,' he said. 'Nope. No regrets. But I do want to propose...'

Elle's heartbeat bumped up a notch.

'...a tweak to the five-year plan,' he said.

'I'm listening,' she said.

'Four months ago, I did something very stupid. I walked by this meadow, and I told someone to go back to London without me. I propose to change that.'

She frowned. 'We already changed it. You came after me—on exactly the same day I decided to come back for you.'

'The thing with communications specialists is that they never stop talking,' Charlie said. 'Even more than the hens.'

'Oi. That's cheeky,' she protested.

He coughed. 'I was going to wait until the first bluebells, next year. Except I can't. So I'm going to ask you now.' He dropped to one knee beside her. 'Elle Newton, I love you very much. I want to make a family with you, and I want to make that family here, where your ancestors have farmed for decades. Though, if you really want to move back to London,' he added, 'I know now I'll do it for you, because being with you is more important to me than anything else in the world. Will you marry me?'

He took a box from his pocket and opened it. Nestled among the velvet was the *moi-et-toi* ring she'd described to him on the beach, the day that they'd taken the fake engagement pictures for the farm. A narrow band of platinum, with a pink sapphire heart nestled next to a tanzanite, the colour of the bluebells in the wood and of Charlie's eyes.

Charlie paid attention. He noticed. He remembered.

And she knew they were going to have a good and happy life together.

'Charlie Webb, you're the love of my life,' she said. 'Yes, I'll marry you and make a family with you, too. Here. Because you've made this place home for me again.'

He slid the ring onto her finger, and kissed her. 'And in the spring,' he said, 'I want you to walk down the aisle of the barn to me, carrying a posy of bluebells. Except this time it's going to be for real. And for ever.'

'That,' she said, 'sounds perfect.'

* * * * *

UNBUTTONING THE TUSCAN TYCOON

MICHELLE DOUGLAS

MILLS & BOON

With thanks and gratitude to the
Hunter Writers Centre, City of Newcastle,
and the Port Authority of New South Wales for creating
the Nobbys-Whibayganba Lighthouse Arts residency
programme. These studio spaces are such a boon
to local creatives and visitors alike.
It has been an honour to take part in the programme.

PROLOGUE

FRANKIE GLANCED ACROSS the table at Audrey. Nonna's restaurant was hushed in a way it never had been before, the shades at the windows drawn and the door firmly shut. Audrey looked as glum and gutted as she felt. She lit the table's candle, but it did little to dispel the gloom.

She hadn't thought she had any tears left, but her vision blurred. Audrey instantly reached across and covered Frankie's hand. She managed to send her cousin a watery smile. 'I miss her so much.'

After today's reading of the will, the fact they'd never see their beloved nonna again had become all too real.

Audrey's grip tightened, and her chin wobbled. If Audrey started crying, Frankie would start howling and—

'We promised her we'd be strong,' she croaked.

Both women straightened, pushed their shoulders back.

Audrey gestured around. 'I expect they'll sell it.'

Frankie tried to keep her voice level. 'It's no doubt the sensible thing to do.'

The will had held no surprises. Nonna's children—Audrey's father and Frankie's mother—had inherited equal shares of Nonna's estate, with both Audrey and Frankie receiving...

Frankie glanced at the A4 envelopes on the table in front

of them. One of them Audrey's, the other hers. Nonna had left them whatever was in those envelopes.

Neither she nor Audrey had been in any hurry to open them. Audrey gestured. 'Once I open it… It's just… It all seems so final.'

Audrey had the kindest heart on the planet. And the softest. Frankie needed to be strong for her. She needed to be strong for them both.

'She loved us both so much.' Reaching out, she gripped both of Audrey's hands. 'And she'll live on in our hearts forever. One day when we have children, we'll regale them with stories about Nonna and her restaurant, and they'll come to love her too.' For a moment that vision filled her soul.

Audrey's mouth curved into the smile that never failed to lighten Frankie's heart. 'We will.' Pulling in a breath, she nodded. 'It's time.'

With a final squeeze, they released each other's hands and reached for their envelopes.

Frankie pulled forth a letter. With trembling hands, she unfolded it.

My darling Frankie,
You know how much I love you. What you may not realise is how much I worry for you.

She blinked.

Do not become a slave to duty. Do not become a slave to others' expectations. If I had one wish for you, my darling girl, it would be that you have the opportunity to forge your own path—one that will bring you happiness and satisfaction. Life is so much more than work. Do not forget to live, and love, and find joy in your life.

The words speared into the sorest part of her heart.

Frankie, you need a holiday. You need the time to evaluate your life and weigh up all your options.

She didn't have time for a holiday! She didn't…

Will you please do your nonna one final favour and make my wish for you come true? I ask that you spend this summer in Tuscany. You always spoke about doing so as a teenager—your eyes lighting up as you told me in the greatest detail how you planned to work and tour the area, enjoying the sights and the sounds…and the freedom, as you found out about your family who had once come from there.

The sudden memory of those old dreams burned through her. Once they'd made her ache with anticipation and tremble with excitement.

Her heart started to pound. Maybe Nonna was right. Maybe it was time for Frankie to pull her head from the sand and face a few hard facts, make some hard decisions. She swallowed. Decisions that would have a lasting impact on her life.

You stopped talking about it after your father died. Frankie, my dearest girl, you need to start dreaming again. Please, will you do this one thing for me?

Tears blurred her vision. Blinking hard, she returned to the envelope to discover an air ticket to Rome, a modest cheque to cover travelling expenses and a small velvet box. Lifting the lid, she found a silver pendant of a bird in flight—a symbol of freedom. She immediately fastened it about her throat.

When she glanced across at Audrey, she found her cousin staring at an air ticket of her own. Frankie cleared her throat. 'I'm off to Tuscany. You?'

'Lake Como. Wide eyes lifted to hers. 'When are you planning to leave?'

The European summer had already started, but... 'In two weeks.'

Audrey gulped. 'Make it one week and we could travel as far as Rome together.'

She didn't give herself time to think or waver. 'Deal.'

They shook on it.

CHAPTER ONE

FRANKIE PULLED BERTHA, her sky-blue Kombi van, onto the hard shoulder and surveyed the huge wooden sign above a rather imposing set of gates. They were a tasteful combination of stone and wood, giving them an impression of permanence and prosperity. Of wealth.

They were the kind of gates that knew their purpose.

Unlike you.

She wrinkled her nose, tried to blow a raspberry at the needling voice full of censure.

You should be settling on your medical specialty, not gallivanting.

'I'm not gallivanting!'

Three months, that was all she was asking. *Three months.*

On cue, her phone rang. Staring at the name on the screen, she was tempted to ignore it. Guilt got the better of her and at the last moment she pressed it to her ear. 'Mum.'

'Frankie, you know how worried I am about you and—'

'Hi, I'm great! How are you?'

There was a pause at the other end.

'Sorry, Mum, terrible timing. I'll have to call you back.'

Dropping the phone to the seat beside her, she blinked hard. Why couldn't her mother just be happy for her? Why couldn't she tell her to have a lovely holiday? Why—

A fist tightened about her chest squeezing the air from her lungs. Closing her eyes, she concentrated on her breathing.

You have a whole summer in Tuscany.

She didn't need to choose her medical specialty yet. She didn't need to know if medicine was her future. She didn't need to know *anything*.

Opening her eyes, she straightened. She had time. Nonna had made sure of it. And she had no intention of wasting the gift her grandmother had given her. She'd focus on the here and now.

And the here and now were those gates and that sign.

The sign read Vigna di Riposo—Vineyard of Rest— with carved grapevines bracketing the words. Brass plaques on the gates were etched with fat bunches of grapes. It might look fancy, but an unpretentious warmth threaded through it too.

'Right.' She clapped her hands. 'We're going to be chilled and laid-back.' Two words that were completely alien to her, but ones she meant to master over the course of the summer.

Carefree and happy-go-lucky, that was her catchphrase. She was in Tuscany, the beautiful heartland of Italy, and this was dream-come-true stuff. She *would* relax.

Deep inside, a flicker of excitement began to burn. For the next six weeks she'd be based here at this beautiful vineyard. She'd arrived several weeks before the grapes were due to be harvested, but Senor Silva had said that he would find jobs for her to do prior to the picking—odd jobs like preparing the staff quarters for the mass arrival of the seasonal staff. It all sounded gloriously mindless.

She did a happy dance in her seat. She didn't have any other responsibilities, wasn't in charge of making any momentous decisions that would impact other people's lives, wouldn't need to make any split-second decisions that could have life and death consequences. *Perfection!*

In her mind's eye, she saw herself as a puffy dandelion seed head and the image made her feel light and free. All of Tuscany was her playground for the next three months. She *would* make the most of it.

Driving through the gates, she pointed Bertha up the gravelled drive. Topping the rise, her jaw dropped at the vista that spread before her. The view looked as if it'd been pulled from the pages of a guidebook.

In the hollow below sat a low-slung building, built of the local honey-coloured stone and accented with the same dark wood as the gates. It would be the main public building where the wine was sold and tastings took place. In the blinding summer sun, its shady interior promised ease and comfort.

Outbuildings stretched off further to her left, but it was the surrounding countryside that held her spellbound. Spreading down the hillside in front of her and along the valley, and up the slope beyond, grapevines marched in lush greenness beneath a perfect blue sky—green and gold throbbed in the air, and things inside of her that had been knotted too tight, began to loosen.

It was a classic Tuscan landscape—beautifully serene— and a sigh that seemed to last forever eased from her lungs.

Pulling Bertha into the visitors' car park, she gazed her fill, but didn't switch off the engine. This car park wasn't for employees. Signor Silva had told her to follow the road around to where she'd find the staff car park, and the seasonal quarters beyond where she'd be able to set up camp in Bertha.

She snapped a picture to send to Audrey before pushing the van into reverse. At the same moment, a man emerged from the shady interior of the building, and made a bee-line for her.

The precision of his movements, and the alarming amount of ground those long legs covered, had her blinking. But any alarm she might have felt at having perhaps stepped out of line by stopping to admire the area was quickly overridden by a shock of feminine appreciation.

She swallowed, hard, her throat becoming strangely dry. She and Audrey had joked that Italian men were devastatingly handsome, but she hadn't expected to be confronted by the most beautiful man she'd ever seen on the first day of arriving at her new job.

Part-time job.

The reminder of just how much free time was now hers had her lifting her face to the sun and drawing in a breath of fragrant summer air as she waited for the man to reach her.

Raven-dark hair gleamed rich in the early afternoon sun and dark eyes that looked black from this distance connected with hers, sending a crackle of something through her, like an electrical pulse. He looked oddly familiar as if she'd seen him somewhere before. Was he a film star or some kind of celebrity?

At just over six feet, there wasn't an ounce of spare flesh on that lean muscular body. Powerful shoulders tapered to lean hips and long, strong thighs. Maybe he was an athlete? Or a dancer? Her knowledge of either was meagre, though, so it didn't help her identify him. What she did know, was that he moved with an innate grace that had a sigh welling in her chest.

Pick your jaw up off the floor, Frankie.

She managed it just before he reached her door. 'We've been expecting you.'

He spoke perfect English in a thick—and divine—Italian accent, and—

One look at his face told her he wasn't happy about something. She straightened. 'Signor Silva? I'm very excited to be here. I hope I've not stepped on any toes by stopping to admire all of this. It's beautiful. I'll head around to the staff car park now.'

'I will show you the way.'

He strode around the van and leaped into the passenger seat. His scent—all lemon and sage and sunshine—invaded Bertha's interior, pulling oxygen out of Frankie's lungs and replacing it with something that made her head feel light. He pointed the way and, swallowing, she turned Betha in that direction, unable to utter a single sensible syllable. If forced to talk, her words would probably emerge in a gabble of *g* and *b* sounds.

Which wasn't the impression she wanted to make.

Except we're not worrying about any of that at the moment, are we?

That was right! And it wasn't like she wanted to impress the man or anything. His beauty had taken her off guard, that's all. And nobody wanted to look or sound like a fool. Her included. Even with a catchphrase of carefree and happy-go-lucky.

'Not Signor Silva,' he said now in that beautiful accent.

Signor Silva was the vineyard's staff supervisor. He'd said he'd meet her on arrival. She glanced at the man beside her, moistened her lips and swallowed carefully, doing all she could to ensure her voice would work without disgracing her. 'Then…who are you?'

'My name is Dante Alberici.'

Dante…? Summoning the research she'd done on Riposo, she sifted through her mind. Alberici…? 'Oh, my God!' She swung to him. 'You *own* Vigna di Riposo.' And a large portion of real estate in Tuscany too—including prime sites in Florence. The Alberici Corporation was world-renowned, and Dante Alberici a self-made man. 'You're the *big* boss!'

Careful of incoherent g *and* b *sounds.*

'Please do not run into that wine barrel with your van.'

She reefed her gaze back to the front and negotiated the entrance to a car park demarcated on either side with wine barrels. As the car park was hidden behind several outbuildings, it was clearly meant for staff like her.

'They might only be for decorative purposes, but I should like them to remain in one piece, yes? And your van too.'

'Yes, absolutely. That's definitely what we want. No minor prangs happening here or anything of the sort. No indeedy.'

Shut up, Frankie.

Wincing, she concentrated on parking neatly *and* safely. She and Bertha were still getting used to each other and she had no intention of disgracing herself in front of this impossibly perfect man.

'You are surprised to see me.'

It was a statement, not a question, but she figured he still expected an answer. 'I thought you'd delegate staff to a manager or supervisor.'

'Ah, but this project is one that is very dear to my heart. I wish to be involved in all of its aspects.'

Okay. So the harvest meant a lot to him. She switched off Bertha's engine. Was he in the process of making a new wine or—?

Yours is not to reason why.

That was right! Carefree and happy-go-lucky, that was her. She sent him her widest smile. 'That's very admirable.'

'Not admirable, necessary.' He didn't smile back. 'Now come with me.'

Giving her no time to reply, he was out of Bertha and striding towards a side entrance of the main building before she'd even pushed open her door. She had to run to catch up with him.

'There is not much time for you to survey the equipment and give us a list of anything additional you might need, but I do have suppliers on standby.'

Equipment? For the harvest? Surely all she needed was a bucket and gloves. And probably some secateurs or sharp scissors or something. And bug spray. And sunscreen. And as she'd bought those last two with her...

She glanced at him. Noted the way his lips pressed together, the tension in his jaw and shoulders. He was cross. With *her*. And trying not to show it. What on earth had she done to disturb his peace of mind?

Lifting her chin, she loosened hands that had started to clench. She had no intention of letting him disturb her peace. She was going to be Zen. *Very* Zen.

But she wasn't Zen enough to contain a gasp when he led her around a corner and she found herself at the back of the main complex in an amazing dining area. She pulled to a halt. 'That *view*!'

From floor-to-ceiling windows, the undulating valley of lush gold greenness spread before her. The neat rows of grapevines were prolific, rich and somehow soothing. In the middle distance a river sparkled silver, and a line of cypresses stood tall and proud. The sky was a deep true blue with a few well-placed fluffy clouds to highlight the depth of all that blue and green.

Clasping her hands beneath her chin, she moved to the windows until her nose almost touched the glass. *In a few weeks' time she'd be on one of those hillsides, pick-*

ing grapes...part of that landscape. Oh, Nonna, what an adventure.

'You approve, yes?'

'Approve? Signor Alberici, it's *sublime*.'

'You may call me Dante.'

He stared at the view too, and for a brief moment those broad shoulders unhitched. 'It is a very pleasing picture for the eye. I think our diners will be most pleased.'

She pointed. 'The terrace is going to be *the* place to be.'

Tables sat on honey-coloured pavers, and above them a lush green vine wound around a wooden pergola. And spread before them was that view. Dante folded his arms and smiled. Her breath did a funny little one-two in her chest. Talk about a pleasing picture for the eye! He should smile more—a whole lot more.

'Your words are music to my ears.' He clapped his hands and made an abrupt about turn. 'Come with me to survey your domain.'

She pointed back towards the grapevines. Weren't *they* her domain? But he was already striding away, and she had to trot to catch up with him. Perhaps the odd-jobbing started *right now*.

He pushed through a set of swinging doors and then gestured with a flourish. 'No expense has been spared. I am hoping you will work much magic here and give my restaurant a reputation to be proud of.'

Her shoulders inched up towards her ears. Who exactly did he think she was? 'Um… Dante…' Actually, on second thoughts, she doubted he'd invite a lowly grape picker to call him by his first name. 'Signor Alberici, I think there's been some mistake. I—'

That gaze snapped back to hers, dark brows lowering over flashing eyes crackling with tension, and carefree and happy-go-lucky fled. 'We created this kitchen to *your* specifications!' He stabbed a finger in the air. 'What is wrong with it? What fault do you find?'

She held her hands up—conciliatory and mollifying. It had sometimes worked on frantic patients at the hospital. 'The kitchen is absolute perfection. The thing is—'

'We have a problem, Dante!' The kitchen doors swung open as a man with an American accent came tearing through them. 'Eleanora Toussaint has done a bunk. She's just accepted a position with a Michelin-starred restaurant in Tokyo. She flies out there this afternoon.'

'No, she's here! She—'

He swung back to Frankie, who grimaced and shrugged an apology. With a face as dark as the devil's, he swung back to the other man. 'Ring her *now* and tell her I will sue her if she does not show up as arranged.'

'I *could* do that.'

Up close she could see the other man was probably a decade older than Dante.

'Except, as she never actually *signed* the contract, a fact she just pointed out to me, I'm afraid it would be something of an empty threat.'

'Why did you not make sure it was signed!'

'Because you told me you wanted to take care of it *personally* yourself.'

A flurry of rapid-fire Italian left Dante's perfect lips—oaths and curses directed at both himself and Eleanora. He stomped around the kitchen island, waving his arms above his head, as if he couldn't contain his outrage and frustration.

The older man's eyes widened, and Frankie swallowed. She *really* didn't belong here. Time to tiptoe out, find Signor Silva, get her work instructions, and then get her carefree and happy-go-lucky vibe back on. Hopefully they could all just pretend this misunderstanding had never happened and—

She started edging towards the door, but froze when dark eyes fixed on her. 'Who in the blazes are *you*?'

His English was utter perfection when he was in a temper—clearly enunciated and delivered with precision. She managed a weak smile and held out a hand. 'Hi, I'm Frankie Weaver. I'm here to pick grapes.'

He gave her hand a cursory shake, as if the politeness had been bred into him. But the fact that he resented having to be civil was as clear as his English. His brows drew down low over his eyes. 'Why did you not say anything? Why did you not correct my misapprehension?'

The implicit accusation put steel in her spine. 'Because I didn't initially realise you were working under a misapprehension. I only realised it once you showed me the kitchen. I was trying to tell you when Mr…' she gestured towards the other man, 'broke the clearly unwelcome news that the person you thought I was has left you in the lurch.'

Another round of rapid-fire Italian followed—mostly curses. Creative ones too, which in normal circumstances might have made her laugh. But she didn't dare laugh. She—

Why not? *She* hadn't done anything wrong. *Carefree and happy-go-lucky.* When he paused for breath, she said in perfect Italian, 'She indeed sounds like pond scum— some prehistoric slug-like creature that has dragged its sorry butt from the slime and brings with it a prehistoric stench at odds with grapevines and summer. You definitely don't want someone like that in charge of your kitchen.'

He stiffened. 'Are you mocking me, Ms Weaver?'

Oops. Okay, so maybe she hadn't got the tone quite right. She backtracked as fast as she could. 'Nope, absolutely not.'

'You speak Italian?' he snapped out.

'*Si.*'

Elegant nostrils flared. 'I apologise if any of the things I just said were offensive to your ears.'

He dragged a hand through short, thick hair. It was the kind of hair that looked as if it never dared be out of place. It also looked ridiculously soft and—

'I'm Michael Alcott, Dante's personal assistant.'

The other man leaned across, breaking her train of thought. *Mercifully.* She shook the outstretched hand. 'Nice to meet you.'

Michael turned back to Dante. 'I have Donna and Alessio looking for replacements, but it's not going to be possible to acquire a big name by Saturday. We might need to delay the opening.'

Dante snapped up to his full height. 'I refuse to allow that woman to derail my plans. If we delay now, Lorenzo's reputation will be tainted. People will think we are inefficient and unorganised. I refuse to allow such a thing.'

'In that case, Dante, you need to reconsider your decision and take over the chef's role. You have the skills and training.'

Those arms started waving about his head again. 'I need to be front of house! I need to be Lorenzo's eyes and ears, to ensure everything runs smoothly.' He swung to Frankie. 'Tell me you are a chef.'

'I'd…uh…love to—' *liar* '—but I'm lucky to not burn toast.' She shrugged—carefully, she didn't want him misconstruing it as her laughing at him again. 'But if *you* can cook, then you can train anyone to be a halfway decent maître d' before Saturday.'

Halfway decent…

Dante's mouth opened and closed, his hands clenching.

Halfway decent wasn't anywhere *near* good enough. Lorenzo's had to be the best.

His throat thickened. To his eternal regret, he'd not spent as much time at the vineyard during the last three or four summers as he should've. Oh, he knew Lorenzo had been proud of him, proud of all he'd achieved, but he'd also forever been telling Dante he needed to stop and smell the roses too.

His hands clenched. He should've spent more time with his grandfather during these last few years. Now he couldn't and—

Dragging in a breath, he fought for control. What he could do was take one entire summer off from running his business empire, to create a restaurant that would pay worthy tribute to the man who'd made such a difference to his life. It would be his attempt to spend one last summer with his grandfather.

This summer he'd create the restaurant of Lorenzo's dreams. He'd do everything in his power to provide the restaurant with a rock-solid foundation that they could build on. One that would not only ensure its success but set it on the path to become a leading light in culinary circles. His grandfather's name would be celebrated across the land.

Halfway decent? No. *Halfway decent* wasn't anywhere near good enough.

'Look, it's a cinch,' the woman said—what was her name again? Frankie? She strode out into the dining room and, passing by the maître d' stand, mimed picking up two menus. In rather lovely Italian—perfectly understandable, but with an accent he couldn't for the moment place—she said, 'Mr and Mrs Conti, how lovely to see you. Welcome to Lorenzo's.'

The welcome of her smile had him blinking and, in that moment, he could see why he'd mistaken her for Eleanora

Toussaint. Beneath the surface warmth, Frankie had an easy and innate air of command. Like—

He clenched up so hard he started to shake. Like a chef!

Damn Eleanora Toussaint! She might not have signed a physical contract, but she'd verbally agreed to their arrangement. He could still sue her. He might not win, but he had the kind of money to drag out a suit that would tarnish her reputation.

He rubbed a hand over his face. Except he didn't want that kind of publicity for Lorenzo's. Besides, he wasn't a vindictive man. Throwing good money away on an exercise like that was utter foolishness.

He'd allowed emotion to sway him too much already. If this had been any of his other projects, he'd have done everything by the book. Instead, he'd unwisely thrown the rulebook out of the window, so delighted to have captured the attention of such a celebrated chef. He'd congratulated himself prematurely, ignoring the fact she'd delayed signing the contract.

One should not give in to emotion. He'd learned that lesson the hard way. When one allowed emotion to rule them, they risked losing everything. Like his mother had lost everything when his father had left. If she'd been able to view her husband with a clear eye, she might've protected herself from hardship, heartbreak and deprivation. He would not let that happen again—not to him, not to her, not to his sisters. And he would not let it happen to Lorenzo's now either.

'Your table is this way.'

He snapped back, his temples pounding, as Frankie led her hypothetical diners to a table by the window and seated them. Her smile held welcome while her manner exuded poise and confidence. There was something else too, but it eluded him, defying definition.

Whatever it was, it would have customers blooming beneath it like grapes under a warm Tuscan sun.

Although he'd mistaken her for Eleanora, and although he'd been vexed with her late arrival, he'd been relieved when he'd finally come face-to-face with her. Or thought he had. It was odd, but something about Frankie put him at his ease. He felt that he could depend on her.

He frowned. It would be foolishness to trust such an impression. In his experience, that immediate impression of reliability was the province of con men and those with hidden agendas. Except he had an excellent nose for those, and nothing about Frankie rang any alarm bells.

His stomach knotted as he again tried to identify the elusive quality she possessed. Maybe it wasn't a quality but the way she looked. She had an interesting face, attractive rather than beautiful, but it was a face he suspected he could stare at for a very long time without ever tiring of.

He jerked back. *Cavolo.* This woman was an employee. He did not have dalliances with employees. If the elusive quality he was trying to identify was attraction, then he would annihilate it immediately.

As if sensing the weight of his gaze, she glanced up, and he immediately smoothed his face out. She didn't deserve his frustration. The situation he now found himself in was not of her making. However, her suggestion he find another maître d' was not one which interested him. He opened his mouth to tell her where to report to Signor Silva, when she kicked back into action.

'Yes, the seats on the terrace are the best seats in the house on an evening like this, but they're always snapped up well in advance. However, I could get you a reservation out there for a fortnight's time.' She leaned in close to her imaginary couple as if to keep her next words just between them. 'We had a cancellation not five minutes ago.'

He bit back a smile. Clever. Crafty. Yet still charming.

'Why don't you let me know if you're interested when you're leaving. I'll keep it free until then. In the meantime, this table is also among our best and I think you'll agree the view from the window is splendid. The food, I promise, will not disappoint.'

An attractive offer made without any pressure. He couldn't have done better himself. She was charm personified.

She then proceeded to rattle off a hypothetical list of the chef's specials for the evening without a single stutter or hesitation.

Beside him, Michael murmured, 'She's good.' Then his phone rang. 'I need to take this. I'll be in my office if you need me.'

Dante nodded, his attention trained on Frankie, his mind racing. He did have the necessary skills to cook the kind of meals he dreamed of for this restaurant. It would work as a temporary measure until he could find a suitable replacement for Eleanora. It would buy him the time to woo someone with a name that would put Lorenzo's on the map.

'You have worked as a maître d' or restaurant hostess before.'

One slim shoulder lifted. 'My grandmother had an Italian restaurant in an inner-city suburb of Melbourne.'

Melbourne, Australia? *That* was her accent.

'My cousin and I started bussing tables when we were just nine or ten. We loved it.'

He imagined a child version of this woman, lip caught between her teeth as she collected plates, just as it had when she'd parked her van. He could almost see the proud nonna standing nearby, and the restaurant patrons charmed by the enchanting child.

Of course, he expected he imagined for her far lovelier memories than they were in reality, and certainly lovelier than he'd had himself, but the way her lips lifted told him the memory was a fond one, so maybe his imagination wasn't too far wrong.

She shook her head, those blue eyes dancing. Something inside of him tightened before instantly relaxing, but then those eyes met his and everything tightened again twice as hard. His pulse accelerated with a speed that would do an Italian sportscar proud.

'Over the years, our roles there evolved. I was always drawn to front of house—waitressing and hostessing— while Audrey would head straight for the kitchen. Now if Audrey were here, she'd do an admirable job filling in as your temporary chef.'

'Audrey, however, is not here.' Despite the strange constriction in his throat, his voice emerged smoothly enough. 'You are, and it appears that you could do an admirable job as Lorenzo's maître d'.'

She stepped back, her face falling. '*Me*?'

'You just proved—' he waved at the table where she'd seated her hypothetical guests '—how suited you are to the position.' With her warmth and charm, she would be perfect.

He made some calculations, mentally shuffled his plans to fit the new criteria. Frankie had experience plus she'd clearly enjoyed working at her nonna's restaurant. *And* she spoke fluent Italian.

He *would* save Lorenzo's from the disaster of a false start. Failure was not an option. He needed to honour the man who had saved him and his family. He was determined to pay homage where it was due.

He glanced back at Frankie. 'Your grandmother is Italian?'

'Was,' she murmured. 'She recently passed away.'

His heart grew heavy at the sadness in her eyes. He had to fight the urge to pull her into his arms and comfort her as he would one of his sisters. 'I am very sorry for your loss.'

'Thank you.'

But that happy light had bled from her face, and his temples pounded as he belatedly registered her lack of enthusiasm to work in his restaurant. *Why?* She had said she was here to pick grapes, but the job he was offering her was ten times better. 'Is your grief too fresh? Will working in my restaurant make you feel your grandmother's absence more keenly?'

She opened her mouth, then closed it, frowned. 'This trip to Italy…well it's because of my grandmother that I'm here and…' She folded her arms. 'Working as maître d' wasn't part of the plan.'

'What is the plan?' What was she hoping to achieve? If he could help her achieve it, perhaps she would help him in return?

'For the six weeks I'm here at Riposo, I plan to do whatever odd jobs Senor Silva asks of me before the grape-picking starts. In my spare time I'm going to explore the area. After that I mean to travel wherever the mood takes me.'

It took a superhuman effort to stop his lip from curling. Her nonna had left her a legacy and she was squandering it on an extended holiday? 'May I ask how old you are?'

She blinked. 'Twenty-six.'

Bah! She was too old to be squandering her life, and her grandmother's fortune, in such an irresponsible fashion. Irresponsible *and* immature. He'd sworn to avoid such people at all costs.

Her gaze narrowed. 'Why are you looking at me like that?'

But saying as much would not win her cooperation. It

was none of his business what she did with her money. It was none of his business what her grandmother might think of her granddaughter's behaviour. Still, Frankie's nonna had clearly worked hard all of her life. Why hadn't Frankie learned from that example? Why hadn't she—

He pulled in a breath, focussed on the problem at hand. 'It is very important to me that Lorenzo's is a success. I want the restaurant to gain an international reputation for being one of the best restaurants in all of Tuscany. I want people to flock here from far and wide.'

Her nose wrinkled. 'It has to be *the best*?'

Nothing else would do. Lorenzo had thrown Dante, his mother and sisters a lifeline when they'd most needed it. Dante had worked all the hours of the day since to achieve what he had. He would never squander it. He would never stop being grateful for it. And he would pay Lorenzo back the only way he knew how.

'Signor Alberici—'

'Dante,' he said automatically, but then wondered why. He rarely invited employees to refer to him by his first name, unless he worked with them daily like Michael.

She moistened her lips. 'Is it usual for you to personally oversee a project like this?'

'Some projects I decide to oversee myself.'

Her gaze dwelled on his jaw, moved to his throat, and then his shoulders. Her mouth tightened and things inside of him tightened too. Women did not usually look at him like this when appraising him. Women usually found him attractive.

'I hope you don't stress this much about every project or you'll end up with an ulcer.'

What did this woman know about stress? 'My health is none of your concern.' He thrust out his jaw. He knew he must look insufferably haughty, but who did this woman think she was, questioning him like this?

She took a step back. 'No, of course it isn't.'

This was going all wrong! He wanted to win her cooperation, not alienate her. He pulled in a measured breath. 'The loss of Eleanora is a blow. It is going to take time for me to find a suitable replacement. With me working the kitchen and you working front of house, it will give me the breathing space I need to sort things out.'

She waved her hands in front of her face. 'But maître d' *won't* be a hard role to fill.'

Frankie might think it would be easy to train someone for the position, but she was wrong. She had something unique—an air or aura that would be impossible to replicate. Lorenzo's diners would love her. 'Why waste time finding someone else when you have already demonstrated your competence?'

Her continued—and *obvious*—reticence had his temper flaring. 'Have you always been such a restless gadabout?' he demanded, slamming his hands to his hips.

Her eyes widened and she stared at him for several beats, not saying anything. Then she clapped a hand to her mouth, as if to halt a bark of laughter. Those irrepressible eyes danced and he waited rather fatalistically for her to call him stuffy or pompous or something equally unflattering. She didn't. Which was just as well, because if she had, he'd have had to dismiss her. Eventually she just pulled her hand from her mouth and said nothing.

He reached for the threads of his temper. He could order her to take on the role, he was her employer for the next six weeks after all. But ultimatums rarely produced satisfactory results.

'The harvesting of the grapes will not take place for several weeks yet, so why not take this opportunity that presents itself to you? It might not be part of your plan, but it is an exciting and interesting opportunity.'

'The grape picking and odd-jobbing was part-time. I suspect this will be full-time. I'm not interested in working full-time.'

He breathed in through his nose and out through his mouth. 'Lorenzo's is only doing a dinner service. And for the first month we are only open Thursday through Sunday.'

She blinked as if his words had taken the wind out of the sails of her protests.

'As you heard earlier, we open this Saturday night. This week we do have staff training, but again it is only a few hours here and there.'

'You want me to do this instead of the odd-jobbing and grape picking?'

He gave a hard nod. He wanted her focussed wholly on the restaurant. 'What do you say, Frankie, will you be maître d' for a month until I can find a replacement chef? You will earn twice as much money than you would picking grapes. That will ensure you have plenty of money to continue your travels when you leave here—meaning less working and more holiday.'

Perfect lips pursed.

'You are on a working holiday, yes? Consider this one of those unexpected things that happen when one travels overseas—an adventure.'

Her eyes suddenly brightened. 'Can I still camp in Bertha as arranged?'

'Bertha?'

'My van.'

She had named her van? 'All of your former arrangements will stand.'

'Fine.' She rolled her eyes ceilingward. 'You have a deal.'

He tried to not feel affronted at her lack of enthusiasm. There were people who would jump at the opportunity to be front of house at his restaurant.

'You will give me your best work, yes?' His hands slammed to his hips. 'You do not mean to sigh, roll your eyes heavenward and make my patrons feel they are a chore.'

She straightened. 'Of course not. You have my word.'

But what was the word of a restless gadabout worth? He would need to keep a close eye on Frankie Weaver. He refused to let anything else go wrong in the lead up to Lorenzo's opening.

Yes, he'd keep a *very* close eye on Frankie.

CHAPTER TWO

'C, C, F, F, G... C, C, F, F, G...'

Frankie sang the notes over and over, trying to fix them in her mind, while madly strumming on Saffy—her ukulele—and doing all she could to channel the Beatles 'Twist and Shout'. She suspected it sounded better in her head than it did in reality, but what did that matter? She was having *fun*!

Glancing out of Bertha's wide-open back window, she grinned and kicked her heels against the mattress. Look at her lounging on the bed in her sky-blue retro Kombi, with all the splendour of a Tuscan vineyard spread before her, while playing her ukulele. If there was a better picture of holiday indolence, she didn't know what it could be.

Oh, and to make matters even better? Dante had called her a gadabout. *Her?* He thought her an unreliable flake. Nobody had *ever* accused her of that before. She grinned so hard her cheeks started to hurt.

The sudden freedom from having to be responsible and sensible, the freedom from the weight of other people's expectations...the freedom of not being Dr Weaver, made her lift her ukulele in the air in a victory salute.

Unbidden, her father's face rose in her mind. *'Dr Weaver, is this really the best use of your time?'*

Her smile faded and her heart plummeted. For as long

as she could remember, she'd wanted to be a doctor. It had felt like what she was supposed to do with her life. It had felt right.

Until her father had died. And she'd promised to follow in his footsteps.

She stared out at grapevines and golden hills and blue sky. Let out a long breath. The joy had slowly bled from that dream, she now acknowledged. Duty had replaced passion. Now whenever she thought about choosing her medical specialty, it felt like a prison sentence.

You promised!

A lump lodged in her throat. How did she reconcile the promise she'd made with the growing certainty that she wanted to be a mother? She couldn't be the mother she wanted to be *and* be the surgeon her father had been.

She hugged Saffy to her chest. She wanted to be present in her child's life. *Very* present. One day she hoped to be like her nonna—wise, loving…the heart of the family. Giving up that dream would…

Her lungs cramped and her breath came in short sharp gasps.

Don't hyperventilate. Stop thinking about it. Three months.

Grabbing Saffy, she launched into her 'C, C, F, F, G' routine until some of the tightness eased from her and she could breathe again. She huffed out a wry laugh. Maybe one day she'd prescribe the ukulele to her patients.

If you're still a doctor.

Gritting her teeth, she strummed on Saffy for all she was worth.

A shadow passed along the wall of her van and she followed it, waiting to see who would appear, blinking when Dante materialised at Bertha's wide-open back window.

She halted mid strum, considered leaping to her feet—

though, one had to be careful leaping in the close confines of the van—and then remembered he thought her a *'restless gadabout'*, and resisted the urge. For the next three months, she *wanted* to be the person he thought her. She had every intention of channelling that person for all she was worth.

'*Ciao*, Dante.'

'Hello, Frankie.'

They stared at each other for a moment and she registered the shadows in his eyes, the tight set of his shoulders as if he were constantly braced against some vast invisible weight, and bit back a sigh. If ever a person needed a holiday, it was Dante.

He glanced beyond, clearly curious about the van's setup.

'Come around,' she gestured to the sliding door at the side, 'and see it properly.'

He did as she bid. She currently had the sofa folded down as a bed, and lounged on it crosswise with Saffy negligently held between her hands. He took her in with barely a glance, and then gazed at her tiny hotplates and sink. The cupboards above.

'It's cute, isn't it?'

She shuffled down the bed, handed him Saffy, and then demonstrated how the bed folded into a sofa. For some reason it seemed more comfortable to not have a bed in the vicinity when Dante was nearby. She didn't want to give off *those* kinds of casual vibes.

She showed him how the table folded out, before slotting it back into place, and making shooing gestures so she could exit the van without bumping into him.

The van had an awning which she'd pulled out, and beneath it rested two camp chairs and a wooden crate that served as a coffee table. She waved him to one of the seats now. 'Soda?'

He blinked. 'I…'

She took that as a yes, and set two cans of soda on the wooden crate.

He held her ukulele out towards her and a thread of mischief wormed through her. She folded her arms and stared at him. 'You're here to talk about work, right?'

'I am.'

'Even thought I don't officially start work until tomorrow.'

He started to rise. '*Si*, I am impinging on your leisure time.'

'Sit down, Dante. I'm happy to talk work if you humour me.'

'Humour you how?'

She had no idea what devil was prompting her, but it felt carefree and fun, and it wouldn't hurt anyone. 'Dante, meet Saffy.' She gestured to the ukulele he still held. 'Saffy, meet Dante.'

'You name your van Bertha and your ukulele Saffy?'

'It's short for Saffron.' Because Saffy was the hottest of bright oranges. She reached inside the van and pulled out a second ukulele. 'And this is Leilani, the ukulele I've always aspired to play well.' Made from beautiful Hawaiian koa wood, a gorgeous beach scene had been painted onto its surface—a still lagoon and the setting sun framed by a palm tree. 'It's a work of art, don't you think?'

For the first time since she'd met him, his lips twitched with genuine humour. 'It is not exactly what I would call a Raphael or Michelangelo.'

She held Leilani at arm's length and surveyed her. 'No, I believe this is of a school all its own.'

Her nonsense was greeted with a warm chuckle that made her pulse hitch.

'How am I to humour you, Frankie?'

For the briefest of moments her mind flashed to him stretched out naked on the bed behind her. Her tongue stuck to the roof of her mouth. She gulped and coughed and tried to get her mind back on track. Men were strictly off the agenda until she had her life worked out. She wasn't letting any man influence the decisions she had to make this summer.

Ha! As if Dante would be interested in a woman like her anyway. Her sudden awareness was nothing more than a result of his gorgeous Italian accent and the fact that with his whisky and smoke voice Dante could be an audio book narrator. Her imagination had gone into overdrive, that was all. She wasn't in the market for that kind of holiday fun.

Are you sure?

Ignoring that traitorous inner voice, she gestured at Saffy, refusing to notice how gently he clasped the neck of the ukulele. As if it were precious. She could imagine those fingers—

Oh, no you can't!

'Have you ever played the ukulele before?'

One dark eyebrow rose.

That looked like a no then. This close, she could see his eyes were the darkest of browns—like coffee beans—all smoke and spice. 'Well, I'm here to tell you that it's fun—ridiculous fun—to play a ukulele.'

'And this is why you play?'

'Absolutely. I'm going to show you a couple of chords and—'

'Why?'

He didn't ask in a mean or even impatient way. He was simply perplexed.

She lowered Leilani back to her lap and stared at him. 'Don't you ever do things just for fun?'

He shifted. 'Of course.'

She wasn't convinced. Though maybe opening restaurants and making money *was* his idea of fun.

'So…' His brow pleated. 'This is just for fun?'

'Partly.'

'And the other part?'

'We're going to be working together for the next month?'

He nodded, tension vibrating from him.

He *really* needed to relax. She lifted her ukulele 'This will show me if you're easy to work with or not.'

Those brows shot up. 'You think you will be able to tell what kind of employer I'll be by making me learn a few chords on the ukulele?'

'Absolutely. Now ready?'

For the next ten minutes she showed him four chords and then a strum pattern. Once he had the strum pattern mastered, she called out the chord changes, and when he'd found the rhythm, she started singing 'You Are My Sunshine'.

He stumbled in surprise, so she began calling out the chords again, and when she next started singing, he maintained the pace and pattern, even humming along. And when the song came to an end, his lips broke into the largest of smiles.

'*Dio!* I played a song—a whole song!'

She grinned back, wanting to leap to her feet and dance under the awning as energy poured through her. 'See? It's fun!'

He stared at the ukulele in amazement, then Frankie. 'Thank you.'

His simple gratitude made her chest ache. 'You're welcome. Anytime you want another lesson, you know where to find me.'

She took the ukuleles and stowed them back inside Bertha, and the wistful expression in his eyes made her smile. 'One can learn basic ukulele very quickly, and that means you get to noodle around on your own and feel halfway accomplished.'

'*You* are very good,' he observed.

'I'm terrible! But I'm improving every day and I'm having a ball doing it, and that's the main thing. Learning to play is a joy rather than a stress or...' She trailed off with a shrug, taking her seat again. 'So, Dante, it's your turn now. What did you want to talk to me about?'

He immediately sobered. 'I am uneasy. I cannot lie. I sensed your... I won't call it reluctance, but your lack of enthusiasm to act as maître d'.'

When he didn't say more, it was her turn to shift and fidget. 'And you want to assure yourself that I will give you my best work rather than a half-hearted devil-may-care, "Oh, my God, I'm at work and when does my shift end?" kind of attitude.'

His brow pleated. She had an urge to reach across and smooth it out. Or to push a ukulele into his hands again and make him play another song.

'I would like to know why, when you're clearly very good with people, and made such a great case for how well suited you were to such a position, that you would prefer to be picking grapes and doing menial chores than working in a lovely restaurant with happy people and a beautiful view?'

And just like that he got to the heart of the problem. While also making an attractive case for working in the restaurant. He made it sound like a wonderful job rather than an onerous obligation.

It was just… She'd come to Tuscany to avoid responsibility. She was supposed to be relaxing and unwinding and clearing her mind. Not landing herself with the weight of someone else's expectations to be *the best*.

But telling him that would lead to questions, which would mean giving explanations. And that would change his view of her as a *restless gadabout*, and she didn't want that. When people learned she was a doctor, their attitude towards her changed. For the next three months she wanted to be unremarkable and anonymous.

'My vision of a working holiday was picking grapes in golden fields under a warm sun.' She shrugged. 'I was sad to lose that vision.'

'If you wish it, I will ensure you still get the chance to pick grapes. Though I think that maybe you have romanticised this. It is sweaty physical work.'

Which sounded like heaven to her at the moment.

'And are not working holidays about adventure and having new experiences?'

Which had been the only part of his earlier argument that had carried weight with her.

'One day when Lorenzo's is a world-renowned restaurant with a Michelin star and Eleanora is gnashing her teeth that she cannot count it as a feather to put into her cap, you will be able to say that you were the restaurant's very first maître d' and had a hand in making the restaurant what it has become.'

His vision of grandeur made her laugh. 'You like to dream big.'

'It is the only way to dream.'

A position as maître d' wasn't what she'd envisaged when planning her trip, but maybe she was looking at this wrong. She'd been thinking she needed mindless work that would let her mind rest and be free, but new experiences would renew her too, just in a different way.

Maybe this job would help her find the answers she needed too? If not, it *was* only temporary, the work still only part-time. Even if it wasn't all fun and games, at least she wouldn't be working in a hospital in charge of people's lives where a split-second decision could mean the difference between life and death.

She met his gaze, sensed the anxiety eating at him behind those dark eyes. 'Lorenzo's means a lot to you.'

'It does.'

'Who is Lorenzo.'

'My grandfather.'

Oh!

'I wish to honour his memory.'

And just like that, every hard thing inside her melted. 'What a lovely thing to do. When did you lose him?'

'Last summer.'

She missed Nonna every single day. It was clear he missed his grandfather every bit as much.

'Dante, I'm sorry about my lack of enthusiasm. I didn't mean to be rude. You took me by surprise, that's all. I loved the vision I had in my mind and I didn't want to change it, but you're right—there'll be time for picking grapes under a Tuscan sun. I'd be delighted to act as your maître d' until you can find a new chef.'

Some of the tension in his shoulders eased. 'Thank you.' And then the briefest of smiles curved his lips. 'And now I should like to know what it was you learned from teaching me 'You Are My Sunshine' on the ukulele.'

She'd been surprised when he'd submitted to the lesson without argument. She knew it had been motivated by his desire to win her cooperation, but he'd also given it his best. He'd given her what he hoped to get back from her in return—*her* best.

'I learned you're not a tyrant or a despot,' she said. 'I wasn't looking forward to working with someone like that, but thankfully that's not something I need to worry about.'

He started to draw himself up, as if unsure whether to be affronted or not, but a moment later his lips twisted. 'Ah, my temper tantrum in the kitchen, it gave you a bad impression.'

She shrugged. 'I don't like to be yelled at.'

Those eyes widened. 'I was not yelling at you! I would not yell at you!'

'You're yelling now.'

His mouth opened and closed, and then he glared at her. 'I will treat you with respect, Frankie. I treat all my employees with respect.'

'And I'll treat you with respect too, Dante. But if you yell at me, I might just yell back.'

'No yelling!'

'Fine by me!' she shot back at exactly the same volume.

He rose, eyes flashing. 'Thank you for your assurances that you will work hard. You have put my mind at rest.'

'Thank you for playing the ukulele with me.'

He turned to go but swung back. 'You are a most unusual woman.'

She grinned. 'I'm going to take that as a compliment.'

With a huff, he stalked away, and she grabbed Saffy and sent him off with 'You Are My Sunshine' ringing in his ears.

She glanced down when her phone started ringing. Biting back a sigh, she pressed it to her ear and made her voice super cheerful. 'Hi, Mum, did you just get the picture of the glorious view I'm currently enjoying?'

* * *

Dante watched from the door of the kitchen as Frankie put the waitstaff through their paces. He'd personally chosen each and every member of the team. He wanted only the best for Lorenzo's. It was what his grandfather deserved.

But he had to curl a hand around the door to keep from striding through it and taking over from Frankie. Not that he thought she was doing anything wrong. It was just…

This was *his* restaurant and he wanted to run it *his* way.

In a faraway part of his brain, he knew his attitude was ludicrous, not to mention counterproductive. If he attempted to micromanage every tiny detail, he would alienate his staff. He needed to trust them to do the jobs he'd employed them for.

He just hadn't realised it'd be this difficult.

As if sensing him there, Frankie turned, those clear blue eyes spotlighting him. He felt suddenly and uncomfortably seen.

Dio. He was losing his mind. He had to find a way to manage all of his anxiety about the restaurant. He had to find a way to maintain a sense of proportion. Because Frankie was not the kind of woman who could see inside of another's soul. She might be personable and charming, but she had no depth, no direction, none of the things that gave one the ability to see below the surface into other people's hearts.

He swallowed. Frankie was like his father.

He'd seen the heartache his mother had suffered at his father's hands. He wasn't wishing that on himself. He wouldn't wish it on anyone!

One laughed and had fun with the Frankies and Riccardos of the world. They played ukuleles with them, and hired them for temporary positions, which suited their short attention spans and their wanderlust. The one thing they didn't do was try to see more depth and complexity in them than existed.

And yet Frankie's eyes seem to recognise every chafe and worry in his soul.

She waved him over. 'Why don't you join us, Dante?' Then before he could either decline or accept her invitation, she turned back to the waitstaff. 'Everyone, this is Signor Dante Alberici, who owns the vineyard and restaurant.'

She dimpled cheekily as he moved across to where she stood and he wondered if she ever managed to maintain a semblance of seriousness for ten minutes straight.

'Apparently Signor Alberici has a secret passion for cooking, which I confess I'm looking forward to sampling. He's Lorenzo's head chef for the foreseeable future.'

He gave a brief nod. *'Buongiorno.'*

A rush of *buongiornos* were murmured back to him, along with wide-eyed stares. It was clear they hadn't expected to meet the tycoon himself.

He felt suddenly awkward, as if he didn't belong here. *Dio!* Riposo *was* his home. It was the one place where he *did* belong.

'Have you ever waited tables before, Dante?'

Frankie's words hauled him back and he shook his head. 'When I was at university I had part-time jobs in construction—building houses and apartments. I have never worked front of house in a restaurant.'

She blinked, frowned, then shook herself. 'Would you like to give it a try?'

He who *was* a good judge of character and *did* have the ability to see below other people's surfaces, couldn't work out if she wanted him to accept or decline her invitation.

He wavered momentarily. *What would you like to do?* His back straightened. 'Yes, I would like that very much.'

For the next two hours Dante found himself setting tables,

taking mock orders, delivering dishes of pretend food to the tables. Frankie created scenarios, acting the role of the paying customer, and then asking the staff what they would do. 'Could I get a booster seat for my toddler and some crayons for my little girl, so she can draw while we eat our meal.'

Cavolo! He hadn't factored children in at all. This might be a winery, but of course some patrons would have children with them when they came to dine. He made a mental note to research that further.

'A couple arrives and the woman is crying. You've seen the man slap her in the car park. What do you do?'

His every muscle stiffened. He—

'First of all, when they come inside, you point out to the woman where the washroom is, and you send a female member of staff in after her to check if she needs help or needs you to call the police. We have a code word in Australian bars—Angela. If a woman comes up to the bar and asks if Angela is there, it means she needs help. There are usually posters in the women's bathrooms explaining how this works. Sometimes she needs the police to be called, other times she might just need a discreet exit.'

They would do this! They would—

'This is a restaurant, not a nightclub or bar where a woman might be approached by a strange man who frightens her, so a poster like that isn't necessary here. Two things to remember in this situation, though—the first is we're not to play hero. Starting a brawl in the restaurant won't help anyone. Also, the woman may simply tell you to mind your own business, and you need to accept her decision. It is our duty as reasonable human beings to ask the question and offer assistance, nothing more.'

He wanted to rail and rage against this cold-hearted pragmatism. He wanted to tell Frankie that he wouldn't countenance violence against women on his premises. He—

'Now, Lorenzo's is the kind of restaurant where the waitstaff need to familiarise themselves with the menu. And with Dante here, we're lucky enough to have the opportunity to ask him any questions we might have in relation to said menu.'

Nobody opened their mouth to ask him anything. While they'd welcomed him with smiles and he sensed they enjoyed having him work alongside them, he still clearly intimidated them.

Frankie picked up a menu. 'Okay, Dante, my customer is trying to decide between the lamb and the chicken pasta. What advice can I give her?'

He straightened. *Now* he was in his element. 'If she prefers strong savoury flavours she should choose the lamb, while the chicken has a more delicate flavour and a creamier texture which might be more to her liking.'

A waitress turned to him. 'I strongly dislike the taste of mushrooms, but I know many people love them. How would you recommend I describe a dish that includes mushrooms as a main ingredient?'

He couldn't help but smile at her hesitant earnestness. 'By not curling up your nose or looking as if you've sucked on a lemon when you mention the word mushrooms.'

She along with everyone else laughed. He then went on to explain how he would focus on the flavours in the dish that the mushrooms were a vehicle for.

He had several other questions, one related to food intolerances and another about the restaurant's stance on customers who requested changes to a listed dish. He answered them easily, and finished by assuring all of the staff that they were always welcome to seek him out in the kitchen to check if such changes could be accommodated.

Before he was either aware or ready for it, the induction and training session was over. The two hours had flown by! He found, though, that his anxieties had calmed. Instead, of feeling restless and tense, a growing optimism flooded his veins. He could rest easy in the knowledge that his front of house staff *were* friendly, efficient and knew what they were doing.

He pushed his shoulders back. Lorenzo's would be a success, and a fitting tribute to his grandfather for all of his kindness—for picking up the reins of familial duty where his father had not.

Movement from the corner of his eye had him blinking himself back into the present. With easy economical movements, Frankie straightened the menus and placed them in their spot on the maître d' stand. She turned to him with a smile. 'That went well. Wouldn't you agree?'

'*Si*, yes. Thank you for asking me to join you.'

One corner of her mouth lifted. 'Well, we couldn't have you spending the entire time bristling in the doorway and glaring at us as if daring us to make a mistake now, could we?'

'I wasn't—'

'Was too.'

She planted her hands on her hips. Very nice hips. They flared gently from a slender waist. Her fitted button-down blouse hinted at generous curves there as well. His mouth dried. Moistening his lips, he forced his gaze back to her face.

'You were clearly itching to be out here, to reassure yourself the staff were competent and things will be fine on the night.'

She had read him like a book. He had been too transparent. It did not do to wear one's heart on their sleeve. Lorenzo's meant a great deal to him, but it would be foolhardy to advertise that fact so explicitly.

'But now you're happy with your staff. You're no longer so worried. That has to be a good thing.'

'I am very happy with the staff.' It took all his strength not to frown. 'You were very good too.'

'Thank you,' she said just as gravely, though he couldn't help thinking she was laughing at him behind her momentary and uncharacteristically solemn demeanour.

'You remembered everybody's names.' It had amazed him.

'I have a very good memory.' And then she winked, shattering the solemnity. 'It's one of my many talents.'

He didn't doubt that she was blessed with a multitude of talents. And yet she was wasting them all, travelling around in a camper van with her ukulele instead.

'How did you find being a waiter?'

'It was not as easy as I thought it would be.'

'No.'

His eyes narrowed. 'You *wanted* me to find it challenging.'

She frowned then too. 'If you understand the challenges your waitstaff face, it will make you a better maître d'.'

It was odd to discover that he wanted the playful, dancing, blue-eyed laughter back. He thrust out his chin. 'You do not think I will be a good maître d'?'

'I'm sure you'll be fabulous at it.'

'But?'

Her frown deepened. 'Have you ever done it before, Dante? Are you planning to be Lorenzo's full-time maître d'? It's clear that the restaurant means a lot to you, and it just makes me wonder why you haven't hired someone experienced for the position?'

'This is of no concern of yours!'

She blinked and took a step back. 'You're right, I'm sorry. That was out of line.'

Which left him feeling like an absolute heel. 'No, it is I who should apologise. You have, how do you say it, scraped me on my sore spot? For the summer, this is what I planned—to be Lorenzo's maître d'. I thought having me here as the face of the restaurant would add a touch that is personal and make the customers feel special and welcome and want to come back. I have a name that is recognised and I wanted to trade on that to bring in diners.'

'All very laudable.'

'But you were very busy behind the scenes, recognising potential problems and averting them. You have made me see that the job is not as straightforward as I thought it would be.'

On every step of this project, he'd allowed emotion to override reason. He needed to find a way to keep it in check. He'd never embark on a warehouse conversion or a housing development in such a fashion. He'd reprimand any of his project managers for doing so. Pulling out a chair, he sat heavily at the nearest table. Frankie hesitated, before sitting too.

'Dante, *you* are the boss. You have all the wealth and power in the world.'

That is not what it felt like to him. He had money, yes, and money meant security. It meant that he could ensure his mother and sisters would always be taken care of, that they would never have to suffer the hardships and indignities of the past again.

'*You* get to decide the role you want here at Lorenzo's. It's *your* restaurant.'

He lifted his head to meet that warm blue-eyed gaze. She wasn't laughing at him now. She was staring at him as if she could see into the very secret heart of him and liked what she saw. 'You can be the host without having to perform any of the other duties associated with maître d'.'

He straightened. She was right.

She sent him one of those carefree grins. 'You get to set

the tone and atmosphere, you get to choose the menus and the wine list, and you get to hire the right staff to make sure everything runs exactly how you want it to.'

She made it sound so simple.

It was that simple.

Somehow, he'd made it complicated.

Because emotion was complicated.

He forced himself to his feet. 'I will advertise for a new maître d' at once. But until then, you are still happy to perform the role?'

'Yes.'

'Did anything in today's session worry you or give you concerns.'

'Only the one.'

'What's that?'

'Me, Dante.'

He sat again. 'But you were superb.'

'Oh, I'm good with people. I enjoy the hustle and bustle of a restaurant. But...'

But what?

She dropped her head to her arms with a groan. 'I don't know wine.'

She didn't know...

'Nonna's restaurant was BYO.' She lifted her head. 'We had house red and house white and that was it.'

'*Dio.* This is sacrilege!'

She shrugged. 'It was a cheap and cheerful family restaurant. Good food and a casual atmosphere in an inner-city suburb. Nonna's had no pretensions of grandeur.'

He shot to his feet. 'This needs to be rectified immediately.'

CHAPTER THREE

A LIGHT FLARED in Dante's espresso-dark eyes, his body vibrating with…

Frankie frowned and studied his powerful frame. Not with feminine appreciation, but with a practised, clinical eye. Well, okay, she *almost* managed that. Even as a doctor, it was impossible not to admire such masculine perfection.

The tension, Frankie. You're supposed to be assessing stress levels.

She snapped back, doing her best to observe rather than appreciate. Dante crackled with an excess of energy, but it didn't draw all his muscles tight or darken his eyes as it had earlier when he'd stared at her and the rest of the waitstaff from the door of the kitchen.

That, at least, was something.

It was clear, though, that honouring his grandfather's memory meant a lot to him. Still, she doubted his grandfather would want it to adversely affect his grandson's health. And if Dante wasn't careful, his health would suffer.

This is none of your concern.

As he'd already told her. She ground her teeth together. *This* was why she wanted to be grape picking on a hillside somewhere. Then she wouldn't be worrying about stuff like this.

Brows lowered over those dark eyes. 'Why do you huff out such a loud sigh?'

Oh! She hadn't meant to. 'It's just I can't help thinking you should hire someone who has all the appropriate knowledge of the wines you offer here, rather...'

'Rather...?'

'Than a restless gadabout like me.' As she said the words, she couldn't stop her heart from dancing a delighted jig. What a joy that thought was.

'You promised me a month. Are you telling me your word is not to be trusted?'

The tension that now had him in its grip was of the jaw-clenching kind and she sobered. 'Of course not. I'll keep my promise.'

Restless gadabout lost a little of its glamour. It was fun to be thought of as a free spirit, but not if he thought it made her unreliable. She wanted to reduce her own stress levels, not add to anyone else's.

'Look, your restaurant clearly means a lot to you. I don't relish the thought of being the weak link in the chain.'

Her words had him shaking his head. 'You are not a weak link. You are...'

She found herself leaning forward as if hanging on his every word. She forced herself back in her seat, slouched and tried to channel laid-back and casual.

'You are an unexpected bonus,' he finally pronounced. 'You are at home in this world.' He gestured around the dining room. 'You are charming and fun and set a tone I want for my restaurant. The wine thing? *Pfft!*'

His pronouncement startled a laugh from her. 'I think this is where I remind you that Riposo is a winery. People will expect fine wines as part of the dining experience. They'll expect the staff to make knowledgeable recommendations.'

'I can teach you everything you need to know?'

Her heart leaped at the thought. And her pulse. *Be sensible.* She did what she could to channel visions of a Tuscan hillside and grapevines and the sun, but the vision kept slipping out of reach. She stretched her neck first one way then the other. Learning about wine could be fun.

'Come.'

Reaching down, he took her hand and pulled her to her feet. And just as it had yesterday, when they'd shaken hands for that brief moment, an electric charge skittered across the surface of her skin.

He, however, seemed utterly unaware of it as he led her through to the other end of the building and the wine tasting area, where polished cement floors, vaulted ceilings and a long wooden bar greeted them. Seating her on a stool, he moved behind the bar and pulled forth a selection of wines. At the other end of the bar a woman performed the same ritual for a group of six, and halfway along the bar a couple relaxed on stools, glasses of wine clasped in their hands.

It was clean, professional and... She searched for the appropriate description, but before she could she grew aware of the weight of Dante's stare. 'What?'

'I was trying to work out what you were thinking. The expression on your face...'

'Curiosity. This is the first winery I've ever been inside.'

'But Australia has some world-renowned wineries.'

They did. She just hadn't visited any of them. There were a lot of things she hadn't done. Pushing the thought aside, she stared around again. 'I was trying to find the right word to describe the atmosphere. I mean it's very clean, almost clinical.' At a pinch, she'd bet one could operate on a patient in here.

'If you think this is clean, you ought to see the room

where we ferment the wine in vats. It is a scientific business, this making of good wine.'

She didn't doubt that for a moment. 'And yet it's also relaxing too. One can walk through those doors and feel as if they're on holiday.'

He murmured a beautiful-sounding Italian curse. 'I did not think. This is your leisure time. I am once again impinging on—'

'I'll make a deal with you, Dante.'

'You are a big one for making deals.'

'I'll let you teach me what I need to know about wine in my leisure time, if you'll relax a bit more.'

He frowned. 'How do you wish me to do this? Does it involve a ukulele?'

'Now there's a thought!'

She grinned. He didn't grin back, but a ghost of a smile curved his lips. It gave her hope that she could actually get him to unwind a bit. Maybe it would be possible to delay that prospective ulcer yet.

'I'll show you what I mean.'

Reaching out, she unknotted his tie and undid his top button. The breath whistled between his teeth, the sound angling straight to her core. Something warm and sweet woke inside her, stretching and yearning. She gulped. Dear God, this had been a mistake. She hadn't meant to make this suggestive or seductive. Pulling back now, though, would mean betraying herself, making things even more awkward.

Swallowing, she slipped the tie from his collar. It seemed to take forever. Gritting her teeth, she kept going with dogged determination until she reached the end. Did Dante *have* to wear the longest ties known to man?

'Wrist please.' She used her doctor's voice, hoping it would help her find the equilibrium she desperately

needed. Instead, his instant response to the authority she
projected had her imagining a different scenario involving a bed, mood lighting and—

Don't go there.

All her years of training kept her fingers deft. As
quickly and efficiently as she could, she undid the button on the cuff of his business shirt and rolled the sleeve
halfway up his forearm, and then gestured for his other
arm. By the time she was finished her heart was racing
and perspiration prickled her nape and the secret space
between her breasts.

'There!' She clapped her hands. 'That's much better.'

'Better how?' he demanded, his voice full of gravel. He
looked as if he'd like to throttle her. She didn't blame him.
She'd like to throttle herself!

'Well, for a start,' she gestured at his throat, 'you now
look as if you can breathe.'

His fingers went to the column of his throat—tanned,
strong and inviting. She sent a silent message for him to
undo another button, but he clearly didn't hear it, because
that hand clenched and lowered back to the bar.

She dragged her gaze from his throat and folded her
arms. 'While the rolled-up shirtsleeves make you look
much more casual and approachable.'

He blinked as if the thought of being considered unap-
proachable had never occurred to him.

'We now look like two friends about to embark on an
adventure—a wine tasting adventure.' Except that he glow-
ered at her in a far from friendly fashion. 'Or if not friends,
then at least work colleagues having a friendly chat over a
glass or two of wine.' That was such a lie and if she were
Pinocchio, her nose would've just grown six inches.

He stared at her as if she was mad, and it took all her

strength to not reach up and touch her nose, just to make sure it was the same size and shape it always was.

She folded her arms tighter. 'At least this now feels like it could be a fun activity I'd do in my leisure time, rather than a work commitment.'

Liar, liar, pants on fire.

He adjusted his stance. 'And this,' he gestured to himself, 'is me keeping my side of the deal.'

Actually, he looked more wound up and tense than ever. She was clearly just as bad at this relaxation thing as he was. And if he didn't stop glaring at her like that, she had a feeling she might just catch fire on the spot! She glared back. 'Oh, yes, you look *so* relaxed, Dante. The epitome of light-hearted cheer.'

He leaned across the bar towards her and the sudden proximity made her breath catch. 'Then you should not have undressed me in public.' Dark eyes flashed. 'This is not the way to get a person to relax.'

She winced.

'If the tables were turned and I undid several of your buttons, it would be considered entirely inappropriate and sexually predatory. And—'

She reached out and touched her fingers to his mouth. 'I'm sorry,' she whispered.

She reefed her hand away because the touch of his lips against bare flesh burned. She rubbed her fingers against her leg. She'd gone too far and now she didn't know how to make things right again. So much for being carefree and happy-go-lucky! 'It was a ridiculous thing to do. I wasn't thinking. I didn't mean to make things…weird.'

He didn't say anything.

'You were looking so formal and perfect and I wanted to mess you up a little, make you look more human. But I should've asked you to take off your tie and roll up your own shirtsleeves. Will you please accept my apology?'

His frown didn't diminish and his jaw remained clenched.

She recalled his other words and straightened. 'I also want to assure you that I was not trying to make any kind of sexual move on you. You're a wealthy man, not to mention handsome, so you must be used to women throwing themselves at you, but that's not what I was doing.'

Heat flooded her face and she suspected she'd just turned scarlet, and no amount of medical training could help her counter that. 'I wish the floor would open up and swallow me,' she groaned.

Finally, there was a lightening in those eyes, a relaxation of the jaw. He looked as if he might even be trying to bite back a smile. 'It might have been a thought that did cross my mind,' he said, 'but the look on your face now tells me that it was not so.'

'If I was flirting with you, I hope I could manage it with a bit more finesse.' More heat flooded through her. Though she was so out of practise at flirting, it couldn't be guaranteed.

He nodded, and those dark eyes might've even been dancing. 'You look so uncomfortable now that I cannot help thinking you have been amply punished for your impulsiveness.'

Her heart did a funny little boom-boom at the sight of his lips curving upwards. Swallowing, she nodded towards the bottles lined up on the bar beside them. 'Am I correct in thinking you're not going to now allow me to slink away and have my wine lesson another time?'

'We made a deal.'

She couldn't help but laugh at the way he'd turned the tables on her. 'But you and me, we're okay?' she checked.

'And what just happened—my stupidity—we can pretend it never happened?'

He nodded.

Her entire body sagged. It was more than she deserved and they both knew it. Before he had time to rue his generosity, she gestured towards the wine bottles again. 'Okay, teach me everything I need to know. I want to do Lorenzo's proud.'

'What do you usually drink?'

'I don't really.'

He stared. 'You are a teetotaller?'

'No. And before you ask, I don't have a problem with alcohol. It's just that my parents rarely drank, so it wasn't something I learned about when I was growing up.'

Instead, she'd learned about things like vivisections, pulmonary structures and osteoclasis.

'What do you drink when you go to a bar with friends? What kind of wine do you take to dinner parties?'

She so rarely did either of those things. They belonged to a life she wanted, though. 'If I'm at a bar I usually have a shandy.'

He stared at her as if he had no idea what she was talking about.

'It's half beer, half lemonade.' He made a face so she rushed on. 'And if I'm going to a dinner party, I'll usually take along a bottle of Shiraz.'

'How do you choose this Shiraz?'

He would hate her answer.

'Come, come,' he said as if sensing her reluctance.

'I tell a shop assistant that I want a bottle of Shiraz for a dinner party and tell them how much money I want to spend.'

He threw his hands up. 'You are so brilliant with food and so clueless about wine.'

He thought her brilliant with food?

He leaned towards her, his eyes alive and determined. 'I am going to teach you how to appreciate wine, to understand how it can complement a meal, and how sharing something you love and appreciate with others—like a good bottle of wine—can make your soul sing.'

The breath left her lungs on a fast exhale, and she sagged against the back of her stool.

'What?' he demanded.

He'd given her a vision she wanted for her future. One where there was time and energy to not just share a meal, but to savour it as well. With people who mattered. She used to do that when she was younger—savoured such things—especially in Nonna's restaurant.

'Frankie?'

But how long had it been since she'd shared such a meal with her family? No wonder Nonna had left her that letter. Had Nonna felt—?

'Frankie?'

A warm hand clasped hers, making her jump.

'Where did you just go? What just happened.'

'When you were talking about wine you sounded like a poet. It made me think of my nonna.' Her throat ached, regrets burning in her belly. 'She would approve of this—of me learning to appreciate wine.'

His gaze raked her face. 'You miss her.'

'With all my heart.'

The expression in Frankie's eyes made Dante's chest burn. He suspected that, like him, she would give everything she owned just to spend another day with her beloved grandparent.

He dragged his gaze from her face. Fixating on luscious lips would be a mistake. As would becoming entranced with hair the colour of caramel that shone in the overhead lights and looked so soft he yearned to reach out and touch it. This woman made him *want* things.

He didn't *want* to want anything. All he wanted to do was keep his focus squarely on ensuring Lorenzo's was a success. The nonsense that had just happened between the two of them should be warning enough to keep him on his guard.

'So which wine are we going to start with?'

In answer, he poured sample-sized portions of prosecco into two glasses, and pushed one towards her.

'Bubbles!' Her smile was wide as she lifted her glass and held it to the light. She slanted him a mischievous glance. 'I've seen how this is done in movies.' She sobered and concentrated and he didn't know if it was a pretence or not. 'I believe this wine is very pale in colour while the bubble count must be in the hundreds of thousands.'

She was doing her best to make him laugh after what had just passed between them, and he should make an effort to play along, dispel the lingering tension, the threat of heat that remained in the air. But his gaze lowered to the fingers holding the wineglass and things inside him clenched as he recalled in precise detail how she'd slipped the tie from his collar, the pull as she'd tugged it free...the fierce and primitive desire that had burned through him, hard and fast and insistent.

He'd wanted to drag her across the bar and kiss her until she was boneless with want and need. The way she'd looked at him had told him that maybe she'd be more than happy for him to do that too.

What had started out as a joke had evolved into something else. Without warning. A deep burning betrayed by parted lips, quick intakes of breath, and hard swallowing. The pulse at the base of her throat had thrashed and fluttered like a wild thing, while deep inside him his blood had pounded too hard, too loud, too fast.

He'd wanted her, with a desperate fierceness he hadn't experienced since he was a teenager. But he was no longer a callow youth. His worry about the restaurant was skewing his judgment, had allowed barriers to fall. He needed to set them firmly in place again.

'I'm guessing that if someone has come to the restaurant to celebrate an anniversary or their birthday, I would suggest a bottle of Riposo's prosecco.'

He snapped back. 'That would be a very good option. If the celebration is an important one the diners wish to mark with something particularly special, our 2012 vintage, while more expensive, is like liquid gold.'

'2012. Liquid gold,' she repeated as if fixing it in her mind.

'Hold the glass to your nose and smell the wine.'

He demonstrated what he meant, but rather than the fruity accents of the prosecco, all he could smell was the warm amber notes of Frankie's scent. There was something else, a lighter note. He inhaled more deeply, searched his memory...*carnation*. Frankie smelled of amber and carnations. Warm, pretty...addictive.

'It smells fruity like peaches or plums.'

'That is the top note. You might also make out hints of honeysuckle and pear.'

He kept his gaze on his own glass as she lifted the glass to her nose again. He didn't want to note how alive her eyes were with interest. He didn't want to imagine those small hands on his body or—

'The way to best taste wine is to take a sip and let the wine coat your tongue, before swallowing. Then take a couple of smaller sips to try and identify the individual flavours.'

She did as he said, took a sip and held it in her mouth. She blinked as if…

His chest clenched. She looked as if she were coming awake.

'This is really lovely.'

'But of course.' He tried to make himself as haughty as he could, but her words warmed him too. 'We only make the best at Riposo. Tell me what you can taste.'

'It's sweeter than I thought it'd be, but not too sweet.'

'It pairs particularly well with cured meats and fruit-driven appetisers.'

She laughed. 'Thank you for the hint. I'm guessing this and the prosciutto-wrapped melon would be a match made in heaven.'

She was a quick study.

She set her glass back to the bar, glancing at it a little wistfully, as if she'd like to finish it, but then at the array of bottles she still had to try and clearly thinking the better of it.

He touched the spittoon beside them. 'You can spit it out if you wish.'

'No, thank you.'

She said it a little primly and he bit back a smile. She might act all carefree and casual, but the way she'd just said that made him think she considered spitting the height of bad manners.

Next they sampled the Vermintino, followed by a Pinot Grigio and then a rosé. He told her the kind of foods they would pair well with. Quick as a flash, she'd return with something that was on the menu.

He was impressed at how quickly she'd memorised the menu. She hadn't been bragging when she'd told him she had a good memory. 'Okay, let's see how good you really are? I will make up some new dishes for our menu and I want you to tell me what wine will pair well with them.'

'Game on!' She clapped her hands. 'I love a good challenge.'

Must this woman make a game of everything? Dismissing the thought, he focussed on dishes he would love to one day serve in the fantasy restaurant of his imagination— a restaurant where he was head chef for real rather than a temporary stand-in. He named dishes, describing their main ingredients, and she'd return a rapid-fire suggestion for an appropriate wine.

He stared at her afterwards. She'd had a ninety percent success rate. And she was only a beginner. She hadn't taken umbrage either when he made an alternate suggestion. Instead, he could practically see that good memory of hers filing it all away for future reference.

What a waste! This woman should be putting her significant talents to use, not frittering them away on some frivolous working holiday. She should be making a name for herself somewhere.

Her simple enjoyment of the wine, of learning all about it, though, had things inside of him unclenching. It had been a long time since he'd worked the cellar door. In summers past, he'd spent a lot of time in here, sharing his love of wine with visitors. But he hadn't done that for...

It had to be at least three years, though it was probably longer. The demands of his business had meant he'd grown increasingly busy. Maybe Frankie was right. Maybe one should take the time to remember these simple pleasures.

However, they should not be overtaken by them. One should not squander their time on only enjoying wine or creating a tempting menu or cooking good food. He pulled himself back into straight lines. He would remain practical, clear-eyed...dispassionate.

Frankie, though, was far from dispassionate. She beamed at him. When he noted the glitter in her eyes, he smothered a smile. 'I think perhaps we will save the red wines for another day.

Those lovely blue eyes danced. 'I think that's wise. I told you I'm not much of a drinker, and while I don't think I've drunk that much, I can feel it in my bloodstream.'

'And what would your nonna think of that?' he teased.

'Oh, she'd have loved all of this. She'd be so happy to know that I was experiencing it.' The dimples in her cheeks deepened. 'She would also approve of me stopping now too,' she added with a laugh. 'It would be very poor form if I was seen weaving among the grapevines trying to find my way back to Bertha.'

The image had him chuckling. 'That would not do at all.'

Her eyes widened and she stared, as if his amusement had caught her off guard. He rolled his shoulders and swallowed. 'Where in Italy was your grandmother from?'

She shook herself. 'Lucca.'

'But that is not forty minutes from here!'

'I know. I'm planning to visit.'

Is that what her holiday was about—to pay homage to her ancestors? 'Is this working holiday of yours about feeling closer to your grandmother?'

She leaned back on her stool, those cool eyes assessing him. Reaching out, she picked up her glass of Pinot Grigio and swirled the golden liquid. He wondered if she was noting the way it coated the glass, how the light reflected through it...or whether it was an absentminded movement and that she herself was far away, thinking of her grandmother.

'She left me a letter.'

He swallowed. He wished Lorenzo had left him a letter.

'She knew she was dying, you see, but she kept it from us right until the end. Said she hadn't wanted to worry us.' She grimaced. 'Cancer.'

He squeezed her hand. 'I'm sorry.' Reluctantly, he pulled his hand back to his side. Given the beast that stirred inside him at such a simple touch, he needed to be very careful around this woman.

'What about you? Did you know Lorenzo was dying?'

He shook his head. 'It was very quick and unexpected. A heart attack.'

'I'm sorry.' They stared at each other in the solidarity of their shared grief and then she shook herself. 'So, yes, she wrote letters to both me and Audrey, her granddaughters. In mine she told me she should like for me to spend a summer in Italy and provided me with a small legacy to do so.' She shrugged. 'So here I am.'

'Did she tell you why?'

She sucked her bottom lip into her mouth and worried at it with her teeth and a desperate hunger clawed through him. All he could think about was turning that mouth up to meet his and exploring every inch of those luscious lips with mouth, tongue and teeth until he'd had his fill, until he tasted her need and swallowed her moans and had them both burning for more. His groin went hard and tight and he cursed himself for such wayward thoughts.

He didn't have time for a woman in his life. He didn't need or want the distraction or the intrusion on his current time and resources. And if he did, he certainly wouldn't choose someone like Frankie.

Frankie released her lip, shiny and plump, to prop her chin on her hand. He ground his back molars together. 'She wants me to take stock of my life.'

He ground them even harder. Perhaps she'd given her granddaughter the luxury of one final holiday before exhorting her to knuckle down and make something of herself. One couldn't be carefree and irresponsible forever.

'Tell me something about your grandfather.'

He blinked.

'Fair's fair. I just told you about Nonna and why I'm here.'

'Is this another one of your deals?'

'Of course not. You're free to tell me you're a busy man with important things to do and walk away to do them.'

'I am a busy man and I do have many important things to do.'

Like going over the menu one more time before Lorenzo's opened on Saturday night, and checking the stock again, and...

'Thank you, Dante, for teaching me about wine. It was unexpectedly fun. This one,' she lifted the Pinot Grigio and took a final sip, 'is my favourite. And before I leave Tuscany, I'm going to eat in your gorgeous restaurant and pair this with the lemon garlic salmon.'

She smiled at him as she slid off her stool.

'I didn't meet Lorenzo until I was twelve years old.'

The words slipped from him without warning. If she'd harangued and hassled him for a story, he'd have clammed up. Instead, she'd been generous with her praise and had moved to not take up any more of his time. He might not approve of the way she was wasting her life, but frankly that was none of his business. Frankie was a lot of things he might not approve of, but he couldn't deny that she was gracious and charming. And generous.

And it was a surprise to discover that he wasn't yet ready to end their conversation.

CHAPTER FOUR

FRANKIE HAD TAKEN Dante's words about being *'a busy man with many important things to do'* as a dismissal. After her ill-advised attempt to make him look more relaxed, she'd been determined to retreat with dignity.

Questions clamoured through her now, though, as she struggled back onto her stool. She pulled the tiny portion of Pinot Grigio back towards her. She didn't have to drive anywhere today, had nowhere else she needed to be.

Besides, she suspected this heady, dizzy feeling had more to do with Dante than the amount of alcohol running through her bloodstream. Another couple of sips wouldn't hurt her. 'Why didn't you meet Lorenzo until you were twelve?'

He topped up her wine—just another quarter of a glass. It was an absentminded gesture, as if he'd noted the glass was close to empty. It was kind. And oddly nurturing.

Stay focussed.

'We didn't know about each other until then. My father was illegitimate and his mother had never told him who his father was.'

Wow.

'But when she died, her solicitor contacted Lorenzo and revealed the truth—that an affair they'd had when they were young had resulted in her becoming pregnant with my father.'

'Why didn't she tell him at the time?'

'He'd become engaged to someone else.'

Ouch.

'Was your father happy to meet his father?'

His face closed up and she immediately regretted asking the question.

'My father is an irresponsible gambler who, when he had spent all of our money, abandoned his wife and four children, and left us destitute.' The ice in his voice lifted all the fine hairs on her arms. 'I was seven when I last saw my father. I do not wish to see him again. To the best of my knowledge, Lorenzo never met him either.'

She rubbed a hand across her chest. 'I'm sorry, Dante.'

His chin came up at that haughty angle. 'It is not your fault. You have nothing to apologise for.'

She bit her tongue, but those dark eyes narrowed.

'You have a question?' he asked.

'I have several. But I probably shouldn't ask any of them.'

'I invite you to ask them.'

He sounded so formal and it made her frown. 'Why would you *invite me* to do that?' She didn't mean to sound challenging, but he didn't strike her as the kind of man who encouraged questions about his background.

'Because one can tell a lot about a person from the questions they ask.'

A test? 'Right, like there's no pressure now or anything.'

His lips twitched.

'Though, I also note, you don't promise to answer my questions.'

He laughed, and as the amusement rippled over his face, she again found herself hypnotised by the change in him. The hard lines of his face relaxed, making him look more…human. When guarded—and stressed—he looked like a statue of an angel—beautiful and perfect. But when he let down that guard, he looked like a man full of vitality and passion and the effect was ten times more powerful than the perfection.

'You have more talents than simply your good memory, Frankie.'

She pulled her mind back to their conversation. 'You were seven when your father left, but you said Lorenzo didn't learn about you—or you about him—until you were twelve. You said your father left you penniless. How did your mother make ends meet with four children to support?'

A deep, hard anger flared in his eyes, but she didn't recoil from it. It wasn't directed at her. 'My mother, my three sisters and I, lived in a three-room hovel in one of the poorest parts of Rome. My mother—' his hands clenched '—worked all the hours of the day, and many nights too, at menial jobs, to keep food in our bellies and a roof over our heads. It took a toll on her health and she developed pneumonia. If Lorenzo hadn't found us when he did, I do not know what we should have done.'

The shadows in his eyes had her throat thickening. 'But he did find you.' It took all her strength not to reach out and clasp his hand. She didn't think he'd welcome the touch.

He poured a little Pinot Grigio for himself, those broad shoulders unhitching a fraction. 'Yes, and I will be grateful for that till my dying day.'

'He loved you from the first?'

Stern lips curved into a smile. 'He was delighted to discover us. He mourned that he had not known about us until that time. His legitimate family, however, were not quite as enthused.'

She winced.

'They refused to meet us or to have anything to do with us.'

'What a shame. They should have been able to forgive him a youthful indiscretion. And it's certainly not as if any of you were to blame.'

One powerful shoulder lifted. 'Family can be complicated.'

She tapped her glass to his. 'Truer words,' she murmured. 'But despite what the rest of his family thought, he helped you leave Rome?'

'He brought us here to Riposo.'

The perfect retreat from a cruel world.

'He made to us a gift of this vineyard, and ensured that nobody could ever take it away from us.'

Nobody being the rest of Lorenzo's resentful family, she guessed. He had given the young Dante and his sisters, not to mention their mother, a priceless gift—a place to call home.

'It allowed my mother to recover her health and live a gentler life.'

The light in his eyes told her how much that had meant to him.

'He gave us four children the means to get a good education, while the profits from the vineyard ensured I could go to university and study business. We owe him *everything*.'

'So *that's* why Lorenzo's is so important to you. *That's* why you've lost so much perspective and have been so driven.'

His nostrils flared. 'I do not lose perspective, as you put it. But, yes, the restaurant is very important to me. I wish it to be a fitting tribute to a good man.'

Hadn't lost perspective? She folded her arms and quoted

verbatim one of his more colourful insults when he'd discovered that Eleanora Toussaint had let him down. 'It's usual then for you to lose your temper when setbacks happen—to utter insults while waving your arms about in the air and stomping about like a madman?'

He rubbed a hand over his face.

'It's why you hover in doorways when your staff are being trained, like some helicopter parent, glowering at all and sundry, making everyone worry they're not going to measure up?'

'That is not what I was doing today!'

She raised an eyebrow.

'I was merely interested in what was happening and how it was proceeding.'

She raised the other eyebrow.

With a groan he collapsed, elbows on the bar, head in hands. 'What is wrong with me? It is like a madness has gripped me and I can no longer think straight.'

She moved a couple of glasses that were in danger of being knocked over out of the way. 'So ordinarily you're not quite so…passionate?'

'How is it you say?' He lifted his head. 'Cool as a cucumber, that is me.'

'Tell me something lovely about Lorenzo.'

He eased back, the tightness slowly draining from his face. 'He was a man who worked hard, but played hard too. Not in ugly ways, you understand—he wasn't a drinker or a gambler or a womaniser. But he took great joy in good food and good wine and good company. He milked every moment for the joy it held.' He shook his head. 'I had never met anyone like that before.'

Her heart felt suspended between breaths at the warm affection alive in his face.

'But his kindness is the thing I most remember about

him. He was kind to my mother, my sisters and me. I believe he loved us. And although his other family refused to acknowledge us, and that hurt and disappointed him, he also understood their hurt and jealousy, and he did what he could to mitigate it. He never said harsh words about them, ever, in my hearing.'

'I imagine that must've been some pretty difficult terrain for him to negotiate.'

'*Si.* And yet he refused to allow them to browbeat him. He refused to turn his back on us, even though it would've made for far more harmony in his life. He did what he thought was right.'

Lorenzo sounded like a truly good man.

'He was good to the people who worked for him too— helped out on the sly when they were sick—made sure they saw doctors, had enough food…whatever they needed. It made them very loyal to him.'

'What did he do for a living?'

'He owned vineyards. Mostly in the Piedmont region, though he had several in Lombardy too. Riposo was an anomaly—the only vineyard he owned in Tuscany.'

Just as Dante and his family had been an anomaly. And by giving this one to Dante's family, Lorenzo had been able to provide them with a home far away from the rest of his family. He'd been able to shield them from the worst of the resentment and animosity. 'He sounds like a wonderful man. I think what you're doing here is wonderful, Dante.'

He straightened. 'Thank you.'

He said the words so gravely they pierced her heart. She leaned towards him. 'And I promise I'll help you make a success of Lorenzo's in every way I can.'

He leaned towards her too. 'You have already promised to give me your best work.'

'But now I promise you my best work from my heart and not because you're paying me.'

He sagged as if her words had punched the breath from his body. 'I do not know what to say.'

She waved that away, reminded herself to channel some chilled holiday attitude. 'It's no biggie.'

His brows shot up. 'It is indeed a *biggie*, as you put it.'

First thing on the Help Make Lorenzo's a Success agenda was getting Dante to somehow loosen the control freak grip he had on every area of the restaurant's day-to-day running and allow the staff to do their jobs.

He frowned. 'Now you do not say anything. This is not usual. I do not trust it.'

She barked out a laugh. 'Okay, okay, it's just…'

'Yes?'

He leaned towards her again and his lemon, sage and sunshine scent drifted all around, making her far too aware of him. Instead of fixing on those tempting lips or mesmerising eyes, she stared down at the bar and made circles in the condensation her wineglass had left behind.

He reached out and closed his hand over hers. 'I wish you to be candid with me, Frankie. I promise no more temper tantrums.'

She found herself turning her hand up to entwine with his. It was meant to be a sign of solidarity and friendship. And initially it was exactly that. They smiled at each other as if that was innate and understood.

But then something flared. Something delicious and dangerous. Something that had no place in their relationship and they both snatched their hands back.

Frankie gulped a mouthful of wine. It shouldn't be gulped, gulping it was a sin, but she needed something to burn sense back into her. 'You agreed that you've lost perspective where the restaurant is concerned, and it's easy to see why. Lorenzo meant so much to you, and you want to create a fitting tribute to the man you loved and respected. But your grandfather would want you to do this with a joyful heart, wouldn't he? He wouldn't want it causing you so much stress and heartache.'

He stared at her as if he'd not considered such a thing.

'I think you ought to be having fun and feeling joy at what you're doing. I know there's the inevitable stress and worry as well, but it shouldn't be negating the excitement.'

He didn't say anything.

She shifted on her seat. 'Maybe you don't agree with me and, obviously, that's fine too. I just… You wanted me to tell you what was on my mind.'

'I am not angry at what you have said.'

She let out a breath.

'You have given me a different perspective, which I appreciate.'

He didn't look appreciative.

'This attitude of mine, it is not one that is complimentary to my grandfather. You are right. He would want me to enjoy this process. Instead, I am treating it like a mountain I must climb or an obligation I need to see through to completion. I must do better.'

And just like that he'd gone and put even more pressure on himself. It was all Frankie could do not to drop her head to her arms. Instead, she asked a question she'd been burning to ask from the get-to. '*Are* you a good chef?'

He nodded. 'It is my passion. I learned from a very good chef in the village when we first moved here. He took me under his wing. I learned much. In my leisure time I cook to relax. When I can spare the time, I hire masters to teach me new techniques and dishes.'

She stared at him, recognised the sudden fire in his

eyes, and her mouth went dry. 'It makes you come alive, *feel* alive, when you're cooking?'

'*Si*, it is the best feeling in the world.'

Her heart thumped. She used to feel like that about medicine. She wished she could get it back. She wished—

She broke off with a frown. 'If you love cooking so much, why aren't you doing that instead of whatever it is you normally do?'

'Which would be running a multimillion-dollar construction business.'

Okay, so he really was super successful.

'I have a talent for business too.'

She reached across and poked him in the chest. 'Talent and passion are not the same thing. Which do you love more? If you were king of the world, and could choose to do anything, what would you choose?'

Dante's chest burned at Frankie's question. No one had ever asked him what he wanted before. His throat ached as he allowed himself to consider it.

Cooking filled his soul, made him feel complete in a way nothing else did, but not everyone was lucky enough to follow their dreams. Not everyone wanted to fritter away their life savings—*and their grandmother's*—on a life made up of holidays, ukuleles and grape picking.

'I have responsibilities, Frankie. Not everyone has the luxury of being able to follow their passions.'

The way she slid back in her seat away from him, made him realise how pointed that had sounded—the words shot at her as if from a gun.

Why? Because she didn't have the same responsibilities that he did? That wasn't fair. 'I greatly enjoy my business success,' he managed in a milder tone. 'I like what I have achieved.' It might not be his passion, but it didn't make those words any less true. 'What is your passion?'

She stared down into her wine. 'I don't know. I mean I thought I knew, once, but now I'm not so sure.' She shrugged, sent him a small smile. 'That's why I'm here in Tuscany.'

He had no right to judge her *or* to resent her freedom. Especially when she had just told him she would do everything she could to help him make Lorenzo's a success. When all she really wanted was a summer free of complications.

She was the only person so far brave enough to tell him where she thought he was going wrong, and to offer suggestions for how he could do better. He should be cherishing her, not rebuking her.

He straightened. He should be helping her. 'How is it you plan to discover your passion?'

'That's what this summer is all about—lots of relaxing in the sun, lots of time to ponder the future while noodling about doing things I enjoy, with no responsibilities impinging on my time. I'm hoping three months of that will help me consider the future with a clearer eye.'

Except now it wasn't going to be such a carefree time, was it? He'd bullied her into being maître d' and had somehow made her feel invested in Lorenzo's success. He opened his mouth to tell her that he would find another maître d'' immediately, but closed it again. He wasn't prepared to let her go. His instinct—the business instinct that rarely let him down—told him that Frankie had what it took, that indefinable X factor, that would help him make Lorenzo's a success.

His hands clenched and unclenched. He *had* to do Lorenzo proud. And if Lorenzo were watching from above—if such things were possible—he did not want his beloved grandfather to think that this restaurant was in any way a chore or burden. It was a joy.

At least, it *would* be a joy once it was a success.

'Maybe I don't have a passion. Maybe there are lots of things I like, but no one single thing that's a passion.'

'*Dio*, everyone has a passion!'

He wished the words back the moment they left him. As if aware of an altogether different kind of passion, her gaze lowered to his lips and her blue eyes darkened to sapphire.

He had not meant *that* kind of passion. He ground his teeth together. This heat circling through his veins, and hers if he were reading her correctly, had to be ignored.

Forcing steel to his backbone, he straightened. 'I apologise if working at Lorenzo's is playing havoc with your plans.'

She snapped away as if his words had released her from a spell. Reaching up, she pulled her hair into a makeshift ponytail, not meeting his eyes. 'Stop wracking yourself with guilt and feeling responsible for *all the things*, Dante. It wasn't part of the plan, but then I realised not being wedded to any particular plan is what this summer should be about. I've simply decided to go with the flow. Maybe this job comes with more responsibility than I'd envisaged, but it's only for a month.'

Would a month be long enough, though? He'd barely started making enquiries about a suitable chef. What if he—?

No. He could not ask more of her. 'You do me a great favour and I appreciate it. I do not want you thinking otherwise.'

She let her hair fall back down around her shoulders. 'You *are* paying me,' she pointed out.

She was worth twice the money. 'Maybe there will be

something I can do for you in return.' He would like to help her find a passion that would make her soul sing.

Those irrepressible eyes started to dance. 'Do you mean that? If so, then something immediately comes to mind.'

Unfortunately, several things came to his mind too, but none of them were fit to utter in polite company. All of them involved spreading her out on a large bed and—

Dio!

He rolled his shoulders, not meeting her eyes. 'Let me guess, it involves me playing a ukulele.'

A laugh gurgled out of her and she started humming 'You Are My Sunshine', and he couldn't explain why, but he found himself torn between laughter and exasperation.

'No, this is something much closer to home—*your* home, Dante. Come grape picking with me.'

He found himself placing a hand on his heart. 'The grapes aren't ready yet. In a few weeks' time, before you leave Riposo, Frankie, I will take you grape picking.'

On Lorenzo's opening night, Dante paced the length of the kitchen, past the long preparation bench, past the ovens and hot plates and then around the servery and back again. He was aware of the looks exchanged by his kitchen staff, of the way they tensed and fidgeted, but could do nothing to temper the tension that coiled him up tight—tension that felt strangely like panic.

This had been a bad idea. He should've delayed the opening when he'd discovered Eleanora's duplicity.

And allowed the general public to suspect Lorenzo's somehow lacking?

He slammed to a halt. *Never!* This was the lesser of two evils. But he should have moved heaven and earth to find a new chef.

In a week?

He ground his teeth together. He needed to find a chef with vision, a chef he could trust, a chef Lorenzo's deserved. Not someone who was simply available.

Stretching his neck first to the left and then to the right, he set to pacing again. He had the talent to fill in as head chef. He'd been offered positions in some of the finest restaurants in Italy. He knew food in the same way a musician knew the right notes to play on a piano, or the way an accomplished author knew what words to use to paint a vivid picture in a reader's mind. He knew what ingredients to put together to create a meal that would be long remembered in a diner's mind.

It was just…

He ought to be out there overseeing *everything*!

Frankie chose that moment to come waltzing into the kitchen, her eyes bright, a smile curving those luscious lips, everything about her exuding enthusiasm…and that indefinable something that had things inside of him shifting, tightening, *wanting*.

He tried to pinpoint exactly what it was she made him want. Because whatever she currently radiated, it wasn't sexual. He couldn't deny his stirring of sexual desire in reaction to just seeing her, but this was something different, something *more*.

Her gaze fixed on him, her eyes narrowed, and then she laughed. 'Oh, Dante, you really do have the soul of a chef, even if you manage to keep it trapped behind your cool-as-a-cucumber business demeanour most of the time.'

Behind him he was aware of his kitchen staff tensing even further. He glared at her.

'I mean look at you—all volatile and tempestuous.' She huffed out another laugh. 'You have your poor staff shaking in their boots.'

'Nonsense!' he snapped. 'I am not this mythical, unreasonable, tyrannical boss you wish to make me out to be.'

Her eyes danced. 'I'm sure they'll be glad to hear it.'

Was she deliberately trying to rile him?

'Okay, Dante, listen to me. All *you* need to focus on tonight is creating beautiful dishes to send out to our beautiful diners.'

But he wanted—*needed*—to know how the diners were reacting—

'You're the boss in here, but out there *I'm* the boss.'

He blinked.

She folded her arms and stuck her nose in the air. 'And I forbid you from coming out into the dining room.'

He clenched his hands so hard he started to shake. '*You* forbid *me*? You forget—'

'I won't have you frightening my diners.'

He gaped at her.

She moved in a step closer and her eyes gentled. 'I'm very good at my job, Dante. You know this. It's why you hired me.'

He closed his eyes and dragged in air scented with amber and carnations.

'You've hired the best waitstaff I've ever worked with.'

What she said was true. He *had* hired the best.

'My waitstaff and I are going to provide the best service tonight's diners have experienced in a long time. But good service will only take us so far. What's really going to put Lorenzo's on the map and make the dining experience extraordinary is the food, and you've put together a magnificent menu.'

He opened his eyes. 'This is a menu that cannot be beaten.' He planted his feet. 'I have hired the very best kitchen staff too.'

At his words, his staff all straightened.

'It is just this waiting for our first orders is hard.'

'Well, we'll be busy enough before you know it. Now, do I have your word that you'll focus on the food, rather than peering out the door every two minutes and checking on everything and upsetting everyone? Will you leave me to focus on the service?'

He knew she was right, but it felt precariously like giving control to someone else, and that was not something that came easily to him.

She stepped closer. 'You need to trust your staff,' she said softly. 'You know we're the best. Between us all, we can and will wow tonight's diners.'

He found his lips curving into an unexpected smile. Perhaps it was the picture her words created in his mind. Perhaps it was the confidence that shone from her eyes. 'How is it you put it, Frankie? You have yourself a deal.'

She laughed and he felt as if he'd done something magical.

She glanced at his kitchen staff. 'We're going to do Dante's late grandfather, Lorenzo, proud tonight, everyone. He was a very good man who made a big difference in a lot of people's lives. Our world would be a much better place if there were more people like Lorenzo in it.'

Her words made his eyes burn and his throat thicken.

'Also, for those who have the time to stay, we'll be having prosecco and nibbles in the dining room afterwards to celebrate tonight's opening, as a thank-you for giving your finest efforts.'

Dio. This was an excellent idea. Why had he not thought of it himself?

She rubbed her hands together and did a funny little happy dance on the spot. 'It's almost time for the doors to open. C'mon, Dante, test me on my knowledge. Give me a meal I need to pair with a good wine.'

'Veal scallopine.'

Her eyes widened in outrage. 'That's not on the menu!'

He folded his arms and tapped a foot, raising what he hoped was an infuriating eyebrow. He'd taught her reds on Thursday. She'd discovered a love of Brunello.

She tossed her head. 'I would suggest a Pinot Noir. It would give the palate a nice clean finish.'

'You are getting very good.'

'I keep telling you that.'

She turned on her heel and exited the room, and he realised she'd changed the entire dynamic in the kitchen. She had soothed the fear that had him in its grip. It was still there, but it no longer overshadowed his excitement or determination.

How had she done that? 'A most extraordinary woman,' he murmured.

Carlo, his second-in-command, nodded in hearty agreement.

He clapped his hands, that determination crystallising inside him. 'Very well, everyone, take your stations. Don't forget, if there is anything that you are unsure about, come and check with me. I will not bite off your head. And if I happen to yell at anyone, or yell in general, it is my excitement not because I am angry...and I will apologise at the end of the evening.'

Before they knew it, orders began pouring in, and the kitchen became a frenzy of activity. Dante found himself grinning and grimacing and feeling more alive than he had in an age. At one point he'd started absentmindedly humming 'You Are My Sunshine'. When he momentarily took stock, after sending one dish out into the dining room and before starting on the next, he realised his entire kitchen hummed the tune with him. It felt somehow right.

* * *

Dante glanced up from the desk in his office bright and early Monday morning when he heard Frankie calling out his name from the corridor outside. What on earth was she doing up so early? Her efforts over the last two nights definitely deserved a sleep in this morning. His opening weekend had gone better than he could've hoped, and that was in large part due to her. The next few days were hers to do with as she pleased. He'd told her as much last night when they'd closed up.

He rose and rounded his desk as she burst in brandishing a newspaper. 'Lorenzo's has received the most wonderful write-up, Dante! *Glowing!*'

Someone from the press had been here?

'Listen! Listen!' She bounced on the spot.

'If the opening weekend is anything to go by, Lorenzo's has proved itself to be the place to dine this summer. In a region known for its fine wines and fine dining, Lorenzo's is making a mark. As welcoming and charming as both the setting and the service were—and I assure you both exceeded expectations—it was the food that was the star of the evening. Lorenzo's boasts an innovative menu with new twists on Italian classics that had this foodie's heart beating faster. I have one word to describe it: *divine.* My meal was one of the best I have had in a long time. And, in a twist all its own, the chef proved to be none other than homegrown boy made good, successful businessmen Dante Alberici. I urge you to put Lorenzo's on your must-try list this summer. You will not be disappointed.'

Dante stared at Frankie in open-mouthed awe. She continued to dance on the spot, and then she flung her arms around him. 'You did it, Dante! You did it!'

Sensation flooded him as their bodies met in a full-length embrace. He had not been expecting an armful of warm woman. Especially not one as vibrant and full of life as Frankie. Especially not one that in the space of a heartbeat, fired his blood with a heat that threatened to turn into an inferno. His hand went around her waist and he closed his eyes to inhale her scent. To imprint the feel of her on his brain.

She leaned back to stare up him, those generous lips in a wide smile. 'Lorenzo's is on its way to being the best restaurant in all of Tuscany!'

And then, as if suddenly aware of the direction of his thoughts, as if the heat in his veins infected her too, her breath hitched and her gaze lowered to his mouth. Blue eyes darkened to the colour of sparkling sapphires, and her tongue flicked out to moisten plump lips, and every nerve ending he had flared and burned.

CHAPTER FIVE

FRANKIE FELL INTO the swirling heat of Dante's eyes, not ever wanting to leave the exciting warmth of his arms. As if in total agreement, his fingers dug into the flesh of her hips, and the urgency of it made her gasp. A fierce and intense wildness swept through her, had her gripping his arms to stay upright.

The muscles beneath her fingers flexed and she could've groaned out loud at the strength and potency pulsing from him. Dante was pure masculine power and beauty and she wanted to lose herself in him. Thoughtlessly, mindlessly. Completely.

One large hand lifted to push her hair from her face. 'Like silk,' he murmured, brushing the backs of his fingers along her cheek. Her skin tingled and she arched into his touch, silently begging for more. More touching, more whispering, more everything.

Oh, this was a bad idea. A bad, bad idea.

'Frankie.' Her name sounded like a caress and a curse, both at the same time. And she understood it. It was as if her name had been dragged from the depths of him without out his volition. This feeling building between them, it had taken him as off guard as her, and a man like Dante liked to be in control.

And she threatened that control. *Her.*

In that moment she didn't care if this was a bad idea or not. The fact she was shaking him to his foundations in the same way he did her shattered her restraint, filling her with satisfaction and joy. It made her bold; it made her soar.

His thumb brushed across her lower lip, pulling and dragging, building a need deep inside her that she'd never known before. Everything throbbed. She touched her tongue to his thumb, gently bit down on it, her eyes not leaving his.

She could reach up and drag his head down to hers, kiss him with all the fire building inside her, find relief and release in that mouth and all it could offer her.

Or she could do what he was doing now. Tantalise and tease, build the expectation until neither one of them could bear it.

Moving her hands to his chest, she tentatively explored the muscled contours hidden beneath his immaculately pressed business shirt. Slowly, deliberately, thoroughly. He sucked in a breath and tensed beneath her touch, those dark eyes flaring with hunger. Oh, how she wanted to see him ruffled and undone!

'This is madness,' he murmured. But he didn't move away. Instead, he wound his hand around her hair, pulled it back until her neck was exposed and he leaned down to graze the delicate skin there with his teeth. She couldn't contain her cry, couldn't prevent her hips from pressing against his where his erection throbbed against her. She wanted to wrap her entire body around his, guide him inside her and—

A low throaty moan sounded in the air. Hers? His arm tightened about her waist as if aware her legs were in danger of giving away.

He swore, but it sounded like a caress. *'Sei una tentatrice.'*

You are a temptress.

Nobody had ever called her a temptress before.

'Puzzi di paradiso.'

You smell like heaven.

His words built more heat, words whispering against her throat as he pressed hot drugging kisses there. This was divine madness and she couldn't get enough.

With palms and fingers, she teased flat male nipples into hard pointed arousal. 'You are perfection,' she murmured. She wanted to make him feel as beautiful and wanted as he did her.

A growl sounded from his throat, vibrating through her. Teeth closed around her earlobe and tugged gently. A tremor shook her entire body. Her breathing became jagged. Seizing her hips in firm hands, he pulled her more fully against him, and at the feel of him pressing at the very centre of her where she most wanted him, stars burst behind her eyelids.

They weren't even naked yet! He hadn't dipped his fingers beneath the hem of her T-shirt, she'd not pulled his shirt from the waistband of his beautifully tailored trousers, and yet she'd never felt more on fire in her life.

Her fingers immediately moved down that taut stomach to tug his shirt free.

'If I kiss you, Frankie, I do not think I will want to stop.'

He was asking her if this was what she wanted. He was asking her permission to continue.

Of course she wanted him to continue! If he should stop now, she might die. And yet her fingers stilled at his words.

And what of tomorrow? some inner voice demanded. *What of an hour from now when this is over?*

Shut up! she wanted to shout.

He dragged in a breath, rested his forehead against hers. 'You hesitate.'

And then he put her away from him and she missed the warmth and the magic, and had to reach out a hand to the desk to find her balance. Her body itched and burned, demanding more of his drugging kisses, more of his touch. She burned for release and pleasure—

At what cost?

He still stood near, as if waiting for her to reach out for him, but she snapped away from him so quickly he had to grab her arm and right her as she started to fall over the chair behind. As soon as she had her balance again, he moved back behind his desk.

'Oh, God, Dante, I'm sorry. I've gone and made things weird between us again. I just meant that hug to be a congratulations for Lorenzo's successful opening weekend. I didn't mean—'

She wanted to stamp a foot. She was seriously bad at the whole relaxed, carefree thing. But, worse than that, she was losing sight of why she was here, losing sight of what she owed her grandmother—wasting this opportunity that had been given to her.

She was a *bad* granddaughter. She was a *bad* daughter. She glanced at Dante. She was a bad person.

He shook his head. 'That was not your fault. I lost my head in the moment and—' lips twisted in self-disgust '—it was unforgivable. I apologise, Frankie. I'm a grown man, not some hormone-riddled youth. I should've known better and—'

'Stop it!' She fell down into the chair, not sure her trembling legs would keep her upright a moment longer. 'I'm not going to toss you for the blame. If we're being honest and adult—' two things she very much needed to be this summer '—we're both to blame.'

He sat too, rubbed a hand over his face. 'There is a heat

that exists between us. These things have no rhyme or reason. They just are. But we are not animals.'

'We can resist it if we choose.'

'We must.' He thrust out his jaw. 'You are my employee.'

She remembered what he thought of her and some devil made her say. 'Only temporarily.'

His nostrils flared; on the desk his hands clenched. 'You toy with me?'

Good Lord, what was she thinking? Swallowing, she shook her head. 'I'm sorry. I know you think me some careless flibbertigibbet—'

'This word, I do not know.'

'An irresponsible person.'

'Ah.' He leaned back.

'But I don't usually jump into a sexual relationship without giving it at least some thought first. That was why I hesitated. Things moved far more quickly than I expected them to, than I realised they had. I lost my head.' Her heart thumped. 'And if you hadn't slowed us down to ask the question, my head may have remained lost.'

They'd have made love and…

Her body dissolved at the thought. She did what she could to ignore the itching and prickling and yearning.

'And afterwards you would have regretted that?'

Would she? She dragged her hands through her hair. 'I don't know.'

Yes, you do.

His lips thinned. 'This is not what your face tells me.'

Dammit! How could he read her so easily? 'Okay, yes, I'd have regretted it. Not because I don't like you, because I like you just fine.'

He blinked.

'And not because I don't think it would've been pleasurable, because all the indications tell me it would be off the charts.'

'Off the charts? This is a good thing?'

It was a very good thing. Not that she needed to stress that any further. Or to even think about it. 'When did you learn English, Dante?' She folded her arms. Everything still felt shaky and needy and she wished she could just make it stop.

'Not until I was twelve.'

When Lorenzo had swept in to provide him with a home and a good education. It explained why he didn't recognise some of the more esoteric expressions she used.

'When did you learn Italian?' he asked in turn.

'I'm not completely fluent but my mother and grandmother taught me from the cradle. When I was growing up, on Mondays and Tuesdays we spoke Italian. The rest of the time we spoke English.' She shrugged. 'Or a mix.'

'That sounds nice.' Dark eyes throbbed into hers. 'So tell me why you'd have regretted making love?'

Why did he want to know? Did he hope to overcome her objections? The thought had heat circling in her bloodstream again, had her fingers clenching together in an effort to counter the heat and need.

'And then I will tell you why I would've regretted it, even though I'd have not stopped if you hadn't hesitated. It is my belief that if we are aware of the other person's reasons, we can doubly arm ourselves against future temptation.'

That made sense. Closing her eyes, she pulled in a breath. 'This summer is important to me. I have some big decisions to make. I don't want a man distracting me from making those decisions.' She hesitated. 'Or influencing them.'

She needed to work out the life *she* wanted. Not the life someone else dreamed for her.

'That sounds remarkably sensible.'

She laughed. She couldn't help it. It still delighted her that he thought her a free spirit. 'I guess it comes to all of us, eventually.' Shuffling upright, she clapped. 'Your turn.'

The pulse at his jaw jerked as if he clenched it too hard. It made her tired just watching it.

'First of all, you are in my employ. There is a power dynamic there that is problematic. I would not want a sexual relationship to threaten an important working relationship.'

The way he said the words made her realise that he wasn't worried so much about her feelings being exploited. He was worried about alienating her or distressing her in some way and her cutting short her tenure as his maître d' in a huff. Which meant he thought the power in their relationship rested with her.

And that was food for thought. But he was also right, she realised. She didn't need his money. She could find work elsewhere easily enough. She could get into Bertha whenever she liked and drive off into the sunset.

'In addition to that, like you, I do not want the distraction of a romance at this current moment in time. I want to exclusively focus on Lorenzo's.' He gestured to the newspaper lying on his desk. 'And we have started well. I would not want to do anything to jeopardise that.'

Dark eyes pinned her to the spot. 'Lorenzo the man, my grandfather, deserves my finest efforts. I want to do this for him—to honour him, to show my gratitude and my love for him.'

She understood that need in her bones. After all, if it wasn't for her grandmother she'd still be nose to the grindstone and living other people's dreams. In their different ways, they both wanted to pay homage to their grandparent.

'To become distracted with a frivolous affair… It feels disrespectful.'

Wow. Okay. She'd have not put it as strongly as that. Dante really needed to chill out.

Not with you.

She shot to her feet. 'Right. Well. It's good to know where each of us stands. We have far more important things to focus on this summer.'

'*Si.*'

'We agree to keep our relationship strictly professional.'

'*Si.* As you say—we have a deal.'

She nodded, but neither one of them offered to shake on it. From now on, there'd be as little touching as possible.

On Thursday night, they had a full house. The restaurant hummed with anticipation and a kind of low-key conviviality that straddled a perfect line between high spirits and relaxation. And Frankie was somehow the embodiment of it all. Dante did his best *not* to notice Frankie, however.

He started when a crash sounded from the dining room—*again*—breaking crockery shattering the warm hum. He turned and glared at the kitchen doors. That was the third time tonight. And each time it had sent a ripple of discord through the dining room's convivial atmosphere, threatening to overshadow the harmony.

A moment later, Frankie appeared and requested another *pollo alla cacciatore* and *ragu toscano* as fast as possible. One glance at her and he recalled that blistering near kiss in his office on Monday, and it made him burn with barely repressed need, which did nothing to improve his temper. Doing his best to ignore it, he fired instructions to his under chefs and whipped up a complimentary appetiser for her to take out to the couple whose dinner had obviously ended up on the dining room floor.

'Frankie—'

'It's under control, Dante, I promise.'

He knew he must have a face like thunder, and while to all appearances Frankie appeared as breezy and buoyant as ever, he sensed chagrin burning just beneath the surface. A quick glance around the kitchen, though, and he realised nobody else sensed it. Lorenzo's diners would not sense it either. Frankie would go out there and make all calm again.

But what if it happened a fourth time. He couldn't—

She lifted the appetisers, balancing both plates effortlessly on one arm. 'I'm afraid our new waitress isn't feeling well. I've sent her home.'

All of that havoc had been caused by one waitress?

'We'll have a small dry-cleaning bill, but it's nothing that can't be fixed.' She nodded at the complimentary appetisers and sent him a smile. 'And with these and a complimentary glass of Riposo's award-winning prosecco, our diners may even think the accident a blessing.'

And then she was gone and he knew grilling her for details now would be counterproductive. They were down a waitress and the dining room staff were going to be busy and Frankie would be picking up the slack. They'd have a debrief at the end of the night like they had last Saturday and Sunday nights.

He did what he could to put the incidents from his mind, to cook with a happy and grateful heart. He had only a short time to enjoy this stint as a head chef. He would take a leaf from Frankie's book and make the most of it. For his grandfather's sake, he would not cook with an anxious, unhappy heart. He would cook with gladness and appreciation.

'Tell me why you were so unhappy tonight?' Dante demanded later that evening when the last of the staff had said their farewells.

Frankie spun around, eyes wide. She opened her mouth

and then closed it. Folding her arms, she stuck out a hip. 'That waitress…'

'Yes?' He waited. 'Are you keeping something from me?' he demanded when she hesitated. 'I am not a child that needs protecting. Nor am I an unreasonable tyrant from whom the staff need protecting. You will tell me at once what this thing is!'

Her lips twitched. 'Not a tyrant, huh?'

He could feel his nose wrinkle.

'You really should take better care of your blood pressure, or you'll blow a blood vessel.'

His lips twisted too.

'I'm not keeping anything from you, Dante. I'm trying to find the words to give voice to something I'm not even sure of, that's all.'

Why did he always jump to the wrong conclusion where Frankie was concerned? He might think her a *flibberti-gibbet*, as she put it, but she hadn't been anything other than professional in his dining room. 'I apologise,' he said stiffly. 'Come,' he gestured to the bar, 'let us have a drink. What would you like?'

Frankie had pronounced the bar area as "small, but perfectly formed" when she'd first seen it. Four bar stools ran the length of the bar and four bucket seats arranged around a low table sat beside the hearth, which they would light in autumn when the weather turned cooler.

She settled into one of the bucket seats with a sigh. 'Surprise me.'

Remorse prickled through him. She'd been on her feet all evening. She'd not had a single break. Once she'd sent that waitress home, the rest of the evening had been smooth and trouble free. She didn't deserve his bellowing and bellyaching.

Seizing a bottle of red, he took her hand and tugged her

to her feet and towed her into the kitchen. He then went back into the dining room and carried in a table and two chairs and seated her at one. 'What would you like to eat?'

Her eyes widened. 'You don't need to cook for me.'

'I would like to.' He meant it. 'I love to cook. You know this of me.'

'Are you going to join me?'

'*Si.*' If it meant that she would eat too.

She chewed on her bottom lip. 'What I want isn't on the menu.'

His mind immediately slipped to tangled sheets, hot bodies and entwined limbs and his mind blanked.

As if suddenly realising how her words could be interpreted, she coughed and turned an alarming shade of scarlet. 'An omelette,' she croaked out. 'I would like an omelette.'

He dragged his mind back to food. *And only food.* 'You ask me for this because it is simple and you don't want to put me to any trouble.'

'I ask for it because it's light and will be kind to my digestion. In another hour, I hope to be asleep.'

In her silly, lovely camper van that she called Bertha. He refused to imagine himself tucked into that cosy bed beside her. 'An omelette with ham, mushrooms and shallots?'

'Perfect.'

A short while later he set the omelettes to the table, poured them both a glass of wine.

She touched her glass to his and nodded at her plate. 'Thank you for this.'

'My pleasure.'

They both sipped, and her lids fluttered in appreciation. 'This is lovely.'

He didn't quiz her on what it was. He simply wanted her to enjoy it. 'Try your omelette.'

She lifted a forkful of omelette to her mouth and ate it.

Her eyes closed and an expression of bliss raced across her face. 'How do you do that? How can you take a few ingredients and create something so wonderful?'

She forked more of the omelette into her mouth, and he smiled as she groaned her appreciation. *Dio!* She loved what he had cooked. The knowledge warmed him all the way through. He didn't try questioning her again about the events of the evening. He merely wanted her to enjoy her food and wine, and the peace and quiet. She'd earned it.

She eventually wiped her plate clean with the slice of sourdough he'd placed on the side of her plate, set her knife and fork neatly together and blotted her mouth with a napkin. He stared at that empty plate. She must've been starving! He should've taken better care of her. 'Can I get you more toast? Or perhaps you would like a dessert? A slice of *zuccotto*, perhaps, or—'

'I couldn't eat another thing, Dante. I ate more than I should've anyway, but it was too delicious and I couldn't stop.'

Was she telling him the truth? This woman, she was sometimes too carelessly happy-go-lucky. Was she skipping meals? Was she looking after herself?

'That's the best omelette I've ever eaten.'

She made him feel like a maestro. 'I am pleased you enjoyed it. I am sorry you did not get your break this evening.'

'I had a very hearty sandwich before my shift, full of cheese and cured meats and salad. It's wise in this business to be prepared for all eventualities, like having to miss one's break.'

He'd bet she'd made sure all of her waitstaff had their breaks, though.

'So about Carla, the waitress…'

His attention snapped back.

'She has me puzzled. Her qualifications were excellent.'

They'd hired her only this afternoon. 'One of the wait-staff had called in sick, and it had felt like serendipity when this new waitress had presented herself in person with a view to leaving her résumé in case Lorenzo's planned to hire more waitstaff in the future. '*Si.* She appeared personable and competent in her interview.'

Frankie nodded.

'But?' he prodded.

Clear blue eyes met his and without warning his heart started to pound. Clenching his hands, he tried to focus on what Frankie was trying to say, rather than the debilitating way his body ached and craved her. Frankie glanced at his fists, frowned, and then glanced up into his face before her gaze darted away again. She swallowed, and her fingers started to drum against her wineglass. Beneath the table her foot jigged. She was as aware of him as he was of her and it took all his strength to remain where he was.

'Accidents happened.' The words left her like bullets.

'Yes,' he bit out, vexed with himself. He needed to be more careful, more guarded.

'Carla…'

With a start, he realised she referred to the waitress, not what had happened between him and her on Monday morning. He forced himself back into straight lines. 'It is inevitable. Accidents will sometimes happen in both the dining room and the kitchen.' He tapped a finger against his mouth. 'But three in one night?'

'And all caused by the same person.'

Something in her tone had his senses sharpening. 'What are you saying?'

'I don't really know. I'd understand her being nervous on the first night, but she has had a lot of experience. One accident I could understand, but three…'

He leaned towards her, watching her face carefully.

'She didn't mention not feeling well, and she didn't look unwell.' Her gaze darted to his. 'It's something I pay attention to because we work with food, and it's not good practise to allow sick staff to work. Our diners deserve better.'

He tried to hide his surprise at her attention to detail. There was so much he didn't know about running a restaurant. Cooking—yes. But as for the rest of it… He understood in that moment why she hadn't wanted the maître d' role, and a dark grey mist rolled through his soul. It hadn't been fair of him to force her hand and make her take the job.

'And something Brianna said to me—she collided with Carla, which was incident number two.'

'What did she say?'

'That she didn't see Carla until the incident happened. That Carla had remained out of her line of sight, wasn't even in her peripheral vision until the very last minute.' Her frown deepened. 'When you're experienced—' those lovely eyes rolled '—when there's a collision or two lurking in your past, you learn to become hyperaware of the people around you.'

The way she said it made him think a couple such incidents rested in her past too.

'Normally you see something from the corner of your eye. And even if you can't avoid an accident, you can often mitigate it, but Brianna said it was as if Carla had snuck up on her.'

He stiffened. 'Did she accuse Carla of doing so deliberately?'

'Oh, no, it was nothing like that. More a throwaway comment.' Her lips pursed. 'But Carla had no business being on that side of the restaurant.'

'She may have just lost her bearings.'

'Yes.'

She didn't sound convinced. 'Are you accusing her of deliberately staging those accidents?'

She shook her head, frowning. 'Something feels off, that's all. I just can't put my finger on it. I asked her to wait for me in my office before she left so we could have a brief chat before she went home.'

He'd given Frankie the small office beside his. She might only be temporary, but she needed access to staff files and email while she was maître d'.

'I only kept her waiting five minutes while I settled things in the dining room, but when I got to my office, she wasn't there.'

'Why not?'

'I've no idea as she didn't answer her phone either.'

She stared at him with pursed lips, and he straightened. 'What?'

'You hadn't met her before, had you?'

'I do not believe so.'

'She's not a scorned woman from your past?'

'Absolutely not!'

'Are there any scorned women in your past who would want to do you a mischief?'

He went cold. 'That is…'

'Outrageous? None of my business? Ridiculous?' she supplied for him. 'I couldn't agree more. It's just, like I said, something about this doesn't feel right.'

His mind raced. She didn't think the events of this evening as accidental. Was there someone in his past who bore him a grudge? He dragged a hand down his face. He worked in the cutthroat world of big business. There would be many who'd like to see him humbled.

Frankie didn't have any evidence, though, only a gut feeling.

And experience, a voice whispered. He nodded. He

needed to be on his guard from now on and keep his eyes and ears open. 'Did you dismiss her?'

Startled blue eyes met his. 'Of course not. I wouldn't do such a thing without consulting you first.'

That wasn't necessary. He trusted her. The realisation made him blink.

'And it's not reasonable to fire someone just because they've had one bad night. But, Dante, I'm going with my instincts on this one and won't be rostering her on again. At least not until she contacts me and offers me an explanation.'

He nodded. '*Si*, I approve of this plan.'

The following morning, Dante read the emails that had just hit his inbox *three times* before exploding into a torrent of curses. The chair in the office next door scraped against the floor and a few seconds later Frankie appeared in his doorway.

She took one look at his face and her brows shot up. 'What's wrong?'

He stabbed a shaking finger at his computer screen and the offending emails, not trusting himself to speak. She moved across with a reassuring briskness to read them for herself—it was clear she could read Italian as well as she could speak it. Easing back, she cursed too. He couldn't explain why, but it made him want to laugh.

But then the import of those emails slammed into him again and he wanted to throw his head back and roar. His two main suppliers had just informed him that they wouldn't be able to supply him with the meat or poultry he'd ordered for the rest of the weekend, or the fruit and vegetables.

This... It was a disaster!

CHAPTER SIX

THINK, FRANKIE, THINK! Frankie wanted to find a solution and lower Dante's blood pressure *pronto*, help him bypass that prospective ulcer. Getting this worked up wasn't good for anyone. This man who was a self-proclaimed cucumber had no perspective when it came to Lorenzo's.

She knew what it was like to want to pay homage so badly it churned up your insides and robbed you of the ability to think straight or see clearly, though. 'They can't be the only suppliers.'

'Of course not, but look at the time! And I only source the *best* produce.'

And paid a pretty penny for it too, she'd bet.

'All that will be left now from the markets will be what others haven't deemed good enough, and those are not the standards for which I want Lorenzo's to be known.'

Her ears pricked. 'Quality is more important to you than price?'

'Yes.'

'And you're judging Lorenzo's success on the quality of its food and the experience it provides rather than it making a lot of money quickly.'

'*Si.*'

'And you're a wealthy man.'

'Why does this matter?'

'Because it means you can source produce from pretty much anywhere in Italy and have it helicoptered in, if you're prepared to pay through the nose to make such a thing happen.'

He raced around the desk, seized her shoulders in firm fingers. 'You are a genius!'

She found herself lifted onto her tiptoes as warm, firm lips smacked to hers in an exuberant kiss that sent ribbons of heat snaking through her bloodstream and had her breath jamming in her throat.

Startled eyes the colour of espresso coffee met hers and he immediately released her, cleared his throat. 'I'm sorry. That… I should not have done it.'

She tried to shrug the moment off. 'It was the equivalent of my hug on Monday.' But need and want jostled inside her, demanding she *do* something.

Absolutely not!

'A spur of the moment exuberance,' he choked out.

They both swallowed and looked away. She swiped damp palms down the sides of her sundress and wished she didn't like the way he put a sentence together so much.

They glanced back at each other again. 'Don't go all smouldery and seductive on me,' she snapped.

'Then don't give me that big limpid gaze begging me to—'

'*Limpid?*' she spluttered. 'Where did you learn a word like that?'

'This I cannot remember, and it is unimportant. I am simply pointing out—'

'Suppliers!' She clapped her hands together, *hard*, wanting their minds back on the task at hand.

He rubbed a hand over his face, moved back behind his desk. 'As I was saying, you are a genius. It is the perfect solution.

'And one you'd have thought of yourself soon enough.'
She pointed at him. 'Cool as a cucumber, remember?'

His lips pressed together, but he nodded. 'Thank you.
I will start to organise this immediately.' He jabbed the
intercom of his phone and barked orders into it.

'Do you need me to do anything?'

'No.' His gaze suddenly cleared. 'It is morning, Frankie.
What are you doing working?'

She edged towards the door. 'I was just checking to
make sure nobody had rung in sick for tonight. I'm done
now.'

He waved a hand at the window. 'Go and enjoy the sun,
play your ukulele, enjoy your leisure time.'

With a nod, she left. But her summer working holiday
suddenly seemed small and frivolous. She couldn't help
thinking that last night's incident with the waitress and
today's supply issues were somehow linked.

Even if she was right, though, she had no proof. Three
of Dante's assistants came rushing down the corridor towards his office. And now wasn't the right time to raise
the topic with him. She pressed herself against the wall to
let them pass, staring after them wistfully.

Stop being ridiculous. She had a valley to explore. And
a mind to de-stress, so she could get it to a place where
she could take stock and make the decisions she needed to.

The day darkened. What if she was no closer to knowing the answers at summer's end? What if this summer
didn't achieve any of the desired outcomes her grandmother had hoped for? What if—?

Dragging in air into lungs threatening to cramp, she
concentrated on her breathing. She had time. Lots of time.
Panicking about it wouldn't help. Panicking about Lorenzo's wouldn't help either.

Dante would be fine. He had an army of staff at his

fingertips. Both the man and the restaurant could function without her. Using them as a displacement activity was not the reason her grandmother had made this summer possible for her.

Go and do something fun.

'You are quiet,' Dante said as they finished up in the restaurant on Friday night. 'It is out of character.'

She didn't think it was. It was just out of character for the persona she'd adopted here at Riposo. Or was the persona she'd adopted at home the fake one? The thought had her swallowing.

'Is there something troubling you?'

She turned with hands on hips. 'Yes,' she said with sudden decision. She could be wrong, but if she wasn't...

He took her arm and led her to one of the bucket seats by the fire, took the one opposite and simply waited. She appreciated that about him—that he didn't rush or pressure her.

Pressing her hands together, she met his gaze. 'Do you think there's something going on—something iffy? First the waitress last night and then your suppliers this morning.'

His eyes throbbed. 'It's never wise to jump to conclusions.'

It wasn't an answer. 'I agree,' she said carefully. 'But nor is it wise to bury one's head in the sand.' She was proof positive of that.

'You think someone is sabotaging the restaurant?'

'I don't know. You use big name suppliers, right?'

He nodded.

'These are companies that have built a reputation based in part on their reliability.' She frowned. 'They do know who they're supplying, don't they?'

'Lorenzo's is a new customer.' One broad shoulder lifted. If there is a supply issue, they would perhaps prioritise their older customers first.'

That made her snort. 'They have to know that Lorenzo's and Dante Alberici are one and the same. Why would they let down someone with your clout? It makes no commercial sense.'

He remained silent.

She might not have any proof, but it would be foolhardy to ignore early warning signs of trouble. 'Dante, is there anyone who would want to hurt you?' Her mouth went dry at the thought.

He rubbed a hand over his face. When he pulled it away, he looked so exhausted her heart ached for him. It took all her strength to remain where she was, rather than to move across and hug him.

'It is something I have been pondering all day. I share your concerns that this could be more than a coincidence.' He let out a breath. 'Perhaps a business rival would wish me ill. There are companies who have lost contracts to me in the past. That kind of…disappointment can generate hostility. Maybe a disgruntled employee. It is inevitable, in a business the size of mine, that some people will feel aggrieved and resentful for any number of reasons.'

She grimaced. 'Has anyone tried to sabotage you in the past?'

Dark eyes met hers, and he gave the tiniest of nods. 'When I was first starting out and trying to attract investors.'

'Who?' she prompted when he remained silent.

'Lorenzo's legitimate family.'

Things inside her sagged.

'I never told him. But when I discovered the source of

the trouble, I hit back hard and fast. They did not try such a thing again.'

She didn't ask what they'd done or what he'd done in retaliation.

'But Lorenzo is dead. They know he would not wish for them to interfere in my life or business. I think they would have too much respect for his wishes to do so.'

She hesitated. She didn't want to ask, but... 'Would your father wish you ill?'

His hands clenched. 'He has no right to wish me ill. It is I who has cause to be aggrieved with him!'

She held her hands up. 'I agree wholeheartedly. I'm just—'

'You are trying to help.' He subsided back into his seat. 'And I appreciate it.' He met her gaze, and nodded. 'I will start enquiries.'

She left it at that.

'Frankie, I know you keep assuring me you're well, but your grandfather is worried too.'

Her grandfather?

Frankie leaped up and paced a path around Bertha, phone pressed to her ear, the sun no longer warm on her face. Her mother was bringing out the big guns. Grandfather was a *cannon*-sized big gun.

'We don't want you doing something you'll later regret. I know you would like to do your father proud, and we're proud of the path you've chosen, but—'

'There's more than one way to make someone proud,' she cut in, slamming to a halt. 'But it feels as if you'll only be proud of me if I go ahead and become a surgeon.'

'That's not true! But, Frankie, what of all your training and plans? You have such a bright future ahead of you.'

'What if I don't want that future?' She swallowed. 'What if it's making me miserable?'

There was a long pause.

'Or doesn't that matter to you?' she made herself ask, her eyes burning with tears she refused to shed.

'Frankie!'

She didn't know if it was shock or remonstrance in her mother's voice. 'I need some time, Mum. Can't you just please give it to me? I need to gain some perspective and gather my thoughts. Please don't ring me again.'

She turned the phone off and stared at the scene in front of her—grapevines under a summer sun—tried to drag its tranquillity and holiday vibe into her soul. *Happy-go-lucky and carefree*, she recited the words over and over in her mind.

Frankie started awake when someone thumped on the side of her van in the wee small hours of Monday morning. She sat up in bed, trying to blink the sleep from her eyes.

'Frankie?'

Dante?

'Frankie, wake up! We're going to be late.'

What on earth…? The weekend was over. Lorenzo's had surpassed itself as usual—there'd been no more supply problems and no more waitstaff incidents—and she now had three well-earned days off.

Scooting down the bed, she slid open the door, stifling a yawn. 'Late for what?'

He stared at her and she was suddenly aware that she was wearing nothing but a tank top and a pair of sleep shorts. She fought the urge to seize the sheet and wrap it around her. What she was wearing was perfectly respectable. 'Late for what?' she repeated, trying to smooth her hair down.

'Grape picking.'

He'd promised to take her grape picking today. She grabbed her watch from the bench. 'It's two-thirty in the morning. The grape picking shift starts at seven, Dante, so—'

'For the Sangiovese and cabernet grapes, yes. But today we're picking the chardonnay grapes. They must be picked at the time they are freshest and before the heat of the sun has touched them.'

Was he serious? Night-time grape picking? Behind him, the seasonal workers' staff quarters were brightly lit and the sound of people getting ready reached her. As she shared the staff bathroom, and as the workers also liked to sit out in the warmth of the afternoon, she'd made friends with several of them. No doubt the bus from the village would arrive soon with the rest of the grape picking staff.

Night-time grape picking? That could be fun! Seizing her toiletry bag and a bundle of clothes, she hopped out of the van. 'I'll be ready in ten.'

She was ready in eight and doing her best not to question the anticipation rising through her. 'You did that on purpose,' she said when she walked back to Bertha and found him settled on one of her camp chairs as if he belonged there.

He spread his hands, suspiciously innocent. 'Did what?'

'Chose night-time grape picking instead of the daytime version. You knew I thought we'd be starting at seven, not three o'clock *in the morning.*'

He shrugged. 'I did think it would be a fun joke. But...'

His frown had things inside of her crashing and protesting.

'Frankie, if you have your heart set on picking grapes in the sun, we can do that too. It is just that the night picking feels somehow special and I thought you might like to be a part of that. I know there will be no sun, but there'll be a moon. And a sunrise that will make you glad to be alive.'

'I *am* glad to be a part of it.' She gestured around. '*This* is what I meant when I said I wanted to have adventures this summer.' It'd be something she could to tell her friends and family about when she returned home. Learning new things and being part of something so totally foreign to her everyday world.

'We might not get sunlight,' she added, 'but we have moonlight.' She stared upwards. 'And stars. You have the most wonderful night skies here, Dante.'

'*Si.*'

But something in the way he said it made her think he'd not taken the trouble to notice them in recent times.

'Come.' He rose. 'The bus is ready.'

The bus drove them to a part of the vineyard she hadn't yet explored. Dante seemed at home here among the seasonal workers, and clearly knew some of them very well. Dressed in work clothes—cargo pants in a thick twill and a long-sleeved polo shirt—he looked like one of them too.

He looked at home in a designer suit as well, she reminded herself. But she liked him best in chef's whites, which contrasted with his olive skin and dark hair and brought the fire in his eyes to life.

Oh, stop it!

Clearly this early morning start was making her fanciful. What Dante wore was of absolutely no concern to her.

Arriving at their destination, she was given a pair of secateurs and a bucket, a brief demonstration of where she would find the grapes on the thick vines and how to snip the bunches of fruit, and then set to work along a row. While the moonlight was bright enough for them to cast shadows, floodlights had been set up at the end of the rows giving it all a festive atmosphere, like a carnival.

Dante worked the neighbouring row and something in her chest squeezed tight as she stared at him. He'd wanted to share this with her because it was special to him. In his own way, he was trying to thank her for taking on the role of maître d', and give her a little of what she'd wanted from her holiday in return. Most bosses wouldn't have bothered.

But then Dante wasn't most bosses.

It shouldn't turn her insides to mush.

No mush, she ordered silently.

He glanced up and caught her stare. She shook herself. 'Thank you, for all of this.' She gestured around. 'It's perfect.'

Those dark eyes danced. 'I will ask if you still feel the same way in an hour.'

Before long, his experience and fitness revealed itself and he had progressed much further down his row than she had hers. The night was cool, but when she finally made it down the end of her row, she had to swipe an arm across her perspiring brow. Her back had started to ache, protesting at all of the bending, and her arms felt like lead.

As if sensing her weariness, Dante appeared at her side with a water bottle. 'It is not as easy as one thinks at first, no?'

She drank long and deep. 'I think it's just as well you started me off on the night-time picking. It'd be so much hotter in the daytime. I'm sorry I'm not very fast. I'm probably the slowest worker you have.'

'Perhaps it is not so romantic as you thought it would be.'

She gulped. The moonlight and the stars, were ridiculously romantic and—

Stop!

He stiffened. 'What I meant is idealised. That perhaps you idealised it in your mind.'

'Absolutely.' She wished her pulse would stop doing that frenetic dance in her veins.

'Do you wish to stop?'

'Absolutely not! I've every intention of finishing my shift.' What did he think her? A giver-upper?

He blinked as if her answer surprised him.

He thinks you're an irresponsible flake.

She frowned. She'd channel less of the irresponsible, thank you very much. She'd given him no reason to consider her unreliable. A tad whimsical and happy-go-lucky, maybe, but not unreliable.

She straightened. 'However, if you've had enough, then by all means feel free to leave. I don't need a babysitter.'

'I am not babysitting you!'

A pained gasp and low cry behind her had her swinging around to find Greta holding her hand and biting her lip. She was beside her in an instant and gently peeling her finger away to see the deep gash Greta had somehow cut in her left hand.

'My hand slipped and—'

Blood gushed and Greta swayed, deathly pale. 'Let's sit you down,' Frankie said.

Dante helped eased Greta down to the ground into a sitting position. 'I'm sorry,' Greta murmured in a mixture of Italian and broken English. 'It is the blood. I cannot stand it.'

Pressing tightly against the wound, Frankie murmured assurances to Greta while searching for the water bottle. She finally saw it on the ground not too far from where she and Dante had been standing and gestured for him to get it.

Instead, he reached down to Greta's other side and pulled out the one she'd obviously been using.

'Greta, look at me,' she said.

The other woman did. 'What I'm going to do is to pour

water on the wound, and then smear it with some antiseptic cream, before binding it.'

Greta nodded.

'I'm afraid, though,' Frankie kept talking to distract her as she worked with swift fingers, 'that you're going to need stitches.'

Dante watched in amazement. Frankie worked with a deftness that made him blink as she cleaned and bound Greta's wound.

A small crowd had gathered and he ordered one of the nearest men to inform the driver of the bus that he'd be required to drive Greta back to the main complex, organised Greta's friend Stella to go with her, and arranged for a car to take them to the local hospital. He notified the hospital to expect them. He requested quietly that everyone else resume their work.

When Greta and Stella had left, and he and Frankie were alone, Frankie washed the blood from her hands with the water left in the bottle, and with a shrug in his general direction, moved as if to return to her duties.

'But you cannot just return to work.'

She turned back. 'Why not? Everyone else has.'

He moved across to her. 'You were amazing just then and…'

She raised an eyebrow.

He tried to find the words for what he felt, for what she'd done and how amazing he thought it. 'Are you not feeling shaky after that? You are allowed to take a moment to rest and regather.'

'The sight of blood has never bothered me.' She moved closer to peer into his face. The scent of amber and carnations rose up all around him. 'Do you feel shaky, Dante?'

'No. I do not like the sight of blood—it is the sight of

catastrophe—but it does not make me want to faint or be sick.'

She eased away again. But he noted the pulse at her throat skipped and jumped. The incident hadn't left her unmoved, whatever she claimed.

'I just thought maybe you would like a rest and a drink, that is all.'

'I'm fine. Honestly.'

She set back to work and there was nothing for it but for him to return to the other side of the row and set back to work too. He kept pace with her, however, reluctant to get too far ahead and let her out of his sight.

She eventually gave an exasperated huff. 'What are you watching and waiting for? For me to keel over and fall into a shaky heap because I saw some blood. Honestly! I'm not that feeble. It was no big thing, okay? I'm sorry Greta hurt herself. But I only did what anyone else would've done.'

'No, you were amazing.'

'Nonsense.'

He halted and straightened. 'I do not understand you at all.'

She glanced up and then straightened too.

'You who are such a free spirit and so blasé and find it difficult to be serious for ten minutes at a time.'

She stared.

'I understand how you can be a magician in my dining room, creating an atmosphere of warmth and welcome with your charm and your love of life. But that—' he gestured to where the incident with Greta had taken place '—feels at odds with who you are. How can someone like you be so efficient and brilliantly capable and...'

He wanted to tell her how splendid he thought her, but when he glanced back Frankie's expression had him taking a step away. 'What?' What had he said to put her in such a temper?

'In your world view, someone who happens to be happy-go-lucky and free-spirited is also unreliable, irresponsible, and incompetent?'

'No! This is not what I meant. I—'

'It's what you said!'

He stared. She was right. It *is* what he'd said.

A weight pressed down on his chest. All of this time he'd been badgering her to be what he wanted, while waiting for her to slip up. He'd pigeonholed her into this rigid idea of the kind of person he'd considered her to be, but it wasn't based on fact or truth.

His heart gave a sickening kick. He'd been waiting for her to let him down. In the same way his father had let him down.

Ignoring him, she resumed her work. Things inside of him ached and burned. He'd been spectacularly unfair. Frankie was not his father.

'Frankie—'

'I'm really tired of talking to you, Dante. I *don't* want to talk to you. Can't you go and work somewhere else?'

This expedition, this night-time picking, it was supposed to be a special memory for her, and he'd ruined it with his small-mindedness, with imagining disasters where none dwelled.

'I will move to a different location, but first let me apologise.'

She kept working, not looking at him. He didn't blame her, but it made him want to yell—not at her but himself.

'I am sorry for what I just said, for all that I insinuated about your character.'

She still refused to look at him.

He swallowed, his gut churning. 'My father was a very

charming man—*carefree* and *happy-go-lucky* were words often used to describe him.'

She stilled.

It took a superhuman effort to continue, but she deserved the truth. And he suspected the only way she'd forgive him was if he laid himself bare. And he wanted her to forgive him. Not for Lorenzo's, but for himself. He wanted her to like and respect him. He did not want to be the kind of person who let her down.

'My father was also rash, unpredictable, selfish and not to be relied upon. This is not you.'

Finally, she straightened and met his gaze.

'In my mind, though, I can see now how I have conflated being charming and carefree with all of these ugly negative traits.'

She pursed her lips. 'It's why you don't have much of a sense of humour.'

He stiffened. He had a sense of humour! He—

'Or, at least, why you don't laugh very much.'

Is that how she saw him? As humourless? It was true, though. He rarely laughed. He rarely let his hair down and *relaxed*.

He shook the thought off to consider later. At the moment he needed all of his focus for her. 'I have refused to see that charming and carefree can also be paired with traits like reliability, efficiency and competence. I do not know why I have continued to harbour doubt in my heart when everything you've said and done has indicated that you are all of those good things.'

She stared up at the sky. 'Your father hurt your family very badly. His betrayal has been etched on your heart since you were seven. It's natural for you to distrust anything that reminds you of him.'

He hated that his father and the past could have such an impact on his present.

'Also, even I have to admit that not everything I've done since arriving here has been what one could exactly describe as responsible.'

He recalled the playful way she had slid his tie from his throat—the slow seductiveness of it—and heat coiled in his belly. 'I have wanted to blame you for the desire I feel for you,' he rasped out, keeping his voice low, 'but that's not fair either.'

For several long moments, neither of them spoke. Then...

'You now acknowledge that I'm reliable and competent?'

'And generous and kind-hearted.'

Some of the tightness left her face. 'Now *you're* trying to charm *me*.'

'Not really.' But the hard things inside him started to unclench. 'Will you accept my apology and forgive me?'

'I accept your apology, Dante.'

He believed her, but he could also see that her earlier ease and delight had dimmed, and that was his fault. He wanted to make her laugh again, wanted her shoulders to lose their tightness. He pretended to search for a bunch of grapes on the vine. 'I know how much you like making deals. Is there some deal I can make to help you forgive me more quickly?'

His words startled a laugh from her. 'Absolutely,' she returned quick as a flash. 'You can cook me breakfast.'

A smile built inside of him. 'This is a deal I am delighted to make.'

'Oh, and Dante? You don't really have to move somewhere else. You can keep working where you are.'

His smile widened. She really had forgiven him.

* * *

The grape-picking shift was only for four hours, and when the sun rose, everyone paused to watch it. The eastern horizon lightened slowly until pinks and pale blues began to colour the sky. The air warmed with the fragrant scent of wild grasses, but not even the tiniest of breezes stirred. All felt still and calm and expectant…and then the birds began to wake with chirps and chirrups and singing, and gold exploded as the orange orb of the sun finally emerged over the horizon.

Beside him Frankie gave a quiet gasp. He wasn't sure if he imagined her moving closer to him or not. 'Magic,' she whispered.

He couldn't help but agree.

Afterwards, everyone piled on the bus for the short journey back.

'Come,' he said as the exited the bus, turning towards the main building.

She trotted beside him, and he shortened his stride to match hers, reminding himself that one did not need to walk as if they needed to be at their destination ten minutes ago.

Frankie rubbed her hands together. 'What are you going to make for breakfast?'

He smiled down at her. 'It is a surprise. I hope you are hungry?'

'Are you kidding? After all of that grape picking, I'm starving.'

He couldn't explain why he wanted so badly to cook for her, only that he did. When he'd been growing up, he'd revelled in feeding his mother and sisters, and his grandfather too when Lorenzo was at Riposo. It had given him satisfaction to prepare good food for them and to watch them eat it with enjoyment and pleasure.

He had experimented until he'd discovered his mother's and three sisters' favourite dishes. He cooked those dishes for them whenever they came to visit. And he wondered now what Frankie's favourite meal might be.

She halted when he left the path to head towards his car. He stopped two strides later, as soon as he'd realised he'd left her behind. 'Is something wrong?'

She pointed towards the restaurant. 'I thought…'

'The restaurant is closed today.'

'I know that, but… Then where are we going.'

He gestured at his car. 'To my villa.'

Her brows shot up. Small white teeth worried her bottom lip.

His gut clenched and he moved back to where she stood. 'Frankie, you have my word that you will be safe. This is not an attempt to get you alone or…' Was this inappropriate? 'All of the fresh ingredients that I had planned to use for breakfast are at my villa. Though if you prefer, I will return with them and cook for you here at the restaurant and—'

'No, no. That won't be necessary.' Her caramel-coloured hair floated around her face when she shook her head. 'I wasn't thinking, that's all.' One shoulder lifted. 'I'd like to see where you live.'

She would? Warmth spread through him. After handing her into the car, he drove back to the main road, turned right, and drove for three minutes before turning into his driveway. A well-maintained gravel drive took them up to the top of the hill, and then down a short slope to his villa.

Frankie leaned forward staring intently at everything. His stomach clenched. Did she like it? Leaping out of the car after he parked it, she skipped onto the lawn and clasped her hands beneath her chin.

Swallowing, he joined her. 'What do you think.'

'Oh, Dante, it's beautiful.'

He let out a breath he'd not been aware of holding. 'I am glad you approve.'

She glanced up as if suddenly worried that she might've said something that had vexed him. 'I thought—'

'What did you think?'

She coloured slightly and he leaned towards her, drew in that beautiful carnation scent deep into his lungs. 'Confess,' he ordered.

'Well, you're ridiculously wealthy, right?'

There was nothing ridiculous about money and security, but he knew what she meant. 'I have a great deal of money, this is true.'

'But this—' she gestured at his villa '—it's a home, not a showcase. I was frightened that you would show me into some impressive mansion that was all glass and marble and I'd be afraid of touching anything because I might mess it up.'

He thought of the villa he owned in Rome where his mother and sisters lived, the apartment he had in Florence, and grimaced inwardly. They were definitely showcases. It was expected of a man in his position.

But, yes, Frankie was right. *This* was home.

'Do you have staff?'

'I have a cleaning service that comes in a couple of times a week.'

'But no housekeeper? No butler?'

'I do not want staff when I come here to stay. Here I cook for myself, and tidy for myself. Here I am free to simply be myself, rather than the successful business tycoon.'

'Then I'm honoured you've invited me to your home, Dante. If you're ever in Australia, I hope you'll visit me in mine.'

His chest expanded. 'I would be honoured to.'

CHAPTER SEVEN

THEIR GAZES CAUGHT and clung. The breath jammed in Frankie's chest and her blood raced in her veins. Today Dante had revealed more of himself to her, had made himself more vulnerable, and it had touched her in ways she hadn't expected.

'Come,' he said, breaking the eye contact that was in danger of becoming *too much*.

Hauling in a breath, she followed him. It didn't mean anything had changed between them. He was still her boss.

Except he was starting to feel more like a friend.

Inside the villa, she forced herself to focus on her surroundings instead of the jumble of thoughts in her head. The cool slate floors of the foyer continued into a formal living room, which flowed into an open-plan kitchen, dining and family room at the back of the house. It was all warm wood, pale green tones and simple furnishings, and she just wanted to sink into it all.

The floor-to-ceiling plate glass windows that made up the entire back wall, overlooked a view even more spectacular than the one at Lorenzo's. Dante came to stand beside her and she gestured to the left. 'Are they Riposo vines?'

'*Si*. The villa is located on the western boundary of the vineyard.'

In front of them a gentle slope meandered down to a

river that sparkled in the sunlight. 'I bet you swam there as a child.'

'I still swim there. Especially on the days when I help bring in the harvest.'

Her mind flashed to him in a pair of swimming trunks, and she swallowed.

'Do you swim, Frankie?'

'I love to swim.' Not that she'd done much of it over the last few years.

'If you like, after breakfast we could go for a swim. If it is something you would find agreeable.'

Clasping her hands at her waist, she forced her gaze to remain on the view, while the surface of her skin skittered with an electrical charge. To have a chance to see Dante in a swimsuit…

She moistened suddenly parched lips. It'd be undoubtedly dangerous, but they'd agreed nothing could *happen* between them. And there was no harm in just looking. 'I didn't bring a swimsuit.'

'My sisters have swimsuits here.' He turned away with a shrug. 'You could borrow one of theirs if you like. Why don't you look at the rest of the house while I get breakfast started?' He gestured back the way they'd come. 'If you turn right at the hallway, you'll find the bedrooms— there are five of them. To the left is my office and the media room.'

When he turned back, those dark eyes took her in in one comprehensive glance that left her burning. 'You are a similar size to Maria, I think. Hers is the first room you will come to.'

Nodding, she shot down the hallway, needing a moment to compose herself.

Get a grip.

His gaze had been dispassionate. He was cooking her breakfast. That was all.

She found both Maria's room and a swimsuit without any trouble at all. She stared at the tiny bikini and then shoved it back into its drawer. Oh, Lord! She'd never worn anything like that in her life. A staid and comfortable one-piece was more her style.

And look where your usual style has got you.

Ha! That was true enough. A bikini could be…an adventure.

Not that she really expected they'd go swimming. He was only being polite. A man like Dante didn't take time off to go swimming during office hours.

The bedrooms were all of a generous size, and the bathroom was enormous with its double vanities, which would've come in very handy with three sisters in the house.

She moved to the door at the very end of the corridor. Holding her breath, she pushed it open. This had to be Dante's room. It smelled like him—all citrus sunshine with a touch of sage—but it also hinted at the side of the man she'd witnessed on the hillside this morning. A man who clearly felt things deeply. A man who admitted when he was wrong and did what he could to make amends. Dante might work too hard, but beneath that serious exterior beat a kind heart.

She frowned, trying to work out how a room could say so much. Perhaps it was in its sheer simplicity. There was no ostentation here, no pretension. This was a room designed for comfort. And rest—*riposo*.

An enormous bed covered in a comforter patterned in golds and browns looked out onto the same view she'd just admired from the living room. She could imagine sitting in that bed, sipping coffee, reading the paper, enjoying that view.

To have weekends where you could enjoy such things. What a life that would be.

Tension coiled through her as she continued staring at Dante's bed. It was huge. The comforter and piles of pillows promised softness and warmth. She fought the temptation to lie in the middle of it all to see if it was everything it promised. If Dante came looking for her and found her lying on his bed… She gulped. That'd be ten times worse than pulling his tie free from his collar or impulsively hugging him.

She jumped when a text pinged on her phone. She opened it to find a picture of Audrey bent over an embroidery frame. Beneath her fingers the most beautiful design in silver and blue was emerging. The text read:

Aunt Beatrice snapped this when I wasn't looking.

Which made Frankie laugh. Audrey wouldn't notice an earthquake when she was immersed in a project like that.

Nonna has given me such a gift. It's a joy to be studying under an expert like Madame De Luca.

Frankie pressed a hand to her heart. Audrey deserved every good thing, and the chance to follow *her* passion for a change.

Thank you for doing this for her, Nonna.

With one last glance at the bed, Frankie backed out of the room and closed the door.

Heading back to the kitchen, her nose twitched in appreciation. 'Something smells amazing,' she said, sliding onto a stool at the kitchen island.

Dante shot her a smile, though his gaze remained on the simmering contents of the pan in front of him.

'What are you making?'

'Baked eggs and sausage. It is nice and hearty after all of the hard work you have put in for the day. Should help to keep you going for the rest of the day too.'

Her mind immediately supplied her with multiple visions of what she could do with all of that extra energy. Gulping, she wrenched her mind back. 'What can I do to help?'

He sent her a swift glance and she tensed. Could he sense the vicarious thrill that seeing his bedroom had given her? Did he sense the guilt and temptation warring inside her?

She sagged when he turned his attention to cracking eggs into the skillet. 'There is nothing to do.' After placing the skillet into the oven, he cut thick slices from a crusty loaf and placed them under the grill to toast.

She gestured at the bread. 'Let me guess, homemade?'

'But of course.' Tiny gold flecks rested deep inside the dark irises of his eyes and for some reason they made things inside her unclench. She shook herself. Carefree and happy-go-lucky. She'd live in the moment and enjoy herself.

They ate on the terrace in the warm summer air, with the scents of grass and wildflowers drifting around them and that splendid view spread in front of them. And the food... After her first bite, Frankie was transported. Dante had a rare and wonderful gift, and she didn't know what lucky star had shone down on her to bestow on her such an experience, but she silently thanked it.

Closing her eyes, she tried to savour it the way he'd taught her to savour wine. The sausage was smoke and spice perfection, the tomato sauce tangy and flavoured

with garlic and basil and other things she couldn't identify and the eggs perfectly poached within it.

With a start, she recalled her manners. 'This is *so good*.'

'I am glad you think so.'

She reached for her toast, which in itself was every good
thing, and swirled it through the sauce.

'I thought you might like to know that I rang the hospital
and they told me Greta is fine. She needed four stitches.'

When had he done that? When she'd been snooping
around his bedroom? 'I'm glad she's okay.'

Maybe they should've gone to the hospital with Greta?
She'd have liked to have overseen Greta's care herself. She
swallowed. Except, for the next three months, she didn't
want to step a single foot inside a hospital. Still, it didn't
stop her from feeling a little wistful.

His gaze sharpened. 'They told me that the wound had
been remarkably clean and bound most professionally.'

Lifting her toast, she bit into it, pretended to concentrate on eating.

'Why?'

She did all she could to look baffled. 'Why what?'

He spread his hands. 'Why did you know what to do?
You reacted so quickly. Why did you have both antiseptic
cream and a bandage on your person?'

'Oh, that.' She waved the words off as if they were of
no consequence, but her chest started to clench. He wasn't
going to allow her to brush this off, was he? She didn't have
to tell him the whole truth, though. Maybe it was silly, but
she didn't want anyone here knowing what she really did,
didn't want them calling her Dr Weaver.

When people discovered she was a doctor they immediately thought she had all the answers, believed she had
her life together and mapped out and that the path at her

feet was clear and straight. They believed she had her vocation and that she would sacrifice all to it.

All of that felt like a lie.

This summer she just wanted to be herself, not Dr Weaver, straight-A student, serious and hard-working junior doctor.

'Frankie?'

'Before I left home, I did a first aid course. Seemed wise,' she added in answer to his raised eyebrow. 'It was one of those accredited ones.'

She tried not to wince. She was downplaying her skills not aggrandising them. The fib wasn't meant to furnish her with some kind of advantage. It wasn't a lie for gain.

Her conscience raised an eyebrow. She did what she could to ignore it. 'And, of course, I did my research about the equipment I would need for grape picking.'

He blinked. 'You did?'

He really thought her both reckless and feckless, didn't he?

'Before I left home, I packed a tube of cream and a couple of bandages as a precaution. A stitch in time and all that. I didn't want some little mishap ruining my holiday.'

'I see.'

He looked totally perplexed. Before he could ask her any further questions, she rushed in. 'So, if someone sprains an ankle or gets a tick, I'm your go-to girl.'

She held her breath, crossing her fingers and hoping he'd accept what she said and let the matter drop.

'It appears both I and Riposo were most fortunate that you decided to spend a portion of your summer here,' he finally said.

The tension in her shoulders eased. She tried to not let them sag too much, though. She didn't want to make him suspicious.

'Coffee?'

'Yes please!'

She helped him clear the table, and then they sat on the big comfy sofa as they waited for the coffee to brew. She rested her head back and stared at the view. 'You live in paradise, Dante.'

'*Si.* If only I could spend more of my time here.'

She meant to lift her head to look at him, there was something in his voice, but her head had grown too heavy. 'If you've given yourself the summer to establish Lorenzo's,' she stifled a yawn, 'then you need to make the most of it.'

And that was the last thing she remembered.

Two hours later she stirred and rolled to her side, blinked her eyes open to find herself staring into Dante's espresso dark ones. He had one of those L-shaped sofas and they'd both stretched out—her on the shorter side and him on the longer one—and had fallen asleep. Or, at least, she had.

That gaze didn't waver from hers, and then it lowered to her lips and his eyes grew darker, his nostrils flared and hunger raced across his face. Things low in her belly clenched and turned to warm honey. Those dark eyes moved back to hers and the air around them seemed to still as she hovered between breaths.

Dante wanted her. He wanted her with a fire and a hunger that made her pulse leap. And staring into those potent eyes, she knew he could see how much she wanted him. It would be so easy to reach across and—

'I'm sorry!' She shot into a sitting position—or tried to, getting tangled in the light throw he'd draped over her. Wrestling with it, she finally managed to wrest herself free. 'I didn't mean to fall asleep.' He'd said that there were *many* reasons he could not—why he would not—act upon the desire he felt for her.

She wanted adventure and fun this summer, but she didn't want to be anyone's regret.

'We were up at an early hour, Frankie. A nap did neither one of us any harm.'

But what about work? She might have Monday through Wednesday free, but he didn't.

Dark eyes smouldered. 'Would you like to go for that swim now?'

The smile he sent her was pure predatory challenge and, in the space of a heartbeat, she knew he'd changed his mind. He'd decided to give in to his desire. He now had every intention of pursuing her with every sensual weapon in his armoury.

Her heart started beating too hard and too fast. Was she going to allow him to catch her?

Very slowly, she smiled. 'A swim sounds perfect.'

Dante knew it was foolhardy. There were myriad reasons why he should resist what he felt for Frankie.

But something had changed between them on the hillside beneath the starlight. Something as fresh and promising as a new day. Resisting it felt more like an act of perversity than a sensible decision. He knew it made no sense. He made decisions with a cold and clear business head, but in this one instance, he decided to allow his instincts their head.

They rushed to don swimsuits, and he tried to hide his disappointment when Frankie appeared in his living room with her body covered in a full-length sarong. Still, it left those beautiful shoulders exposed and he could imagine running his hands along them, bending her back so he could press kisses against the soft flesh of her throat.

He went hard in an instant, recalling the way she'd pressed and arched against him that day in his office. His gaze fixed on her mouth. He wanted to know what she tasted like, he wanted—

'Swimming!' Frankie croaked and he slammed back to the present.

At this rate they wouldn't make it down to the river at all. Without another word, he ushered her through the glass sliding doors and gestured towards the path they should take.

'I wholly approve of this, Dante.'

He stumbled. She knew what he planned? What he wanted?

Dio! Of course she knew. She'd known the moment she'd opened her eyes and found him staring at her so hungrily.

'I think it's beyond time the boss started playing hooky.'

His brows beetled. 'Hooky?'

'It means to sneakily take a day off work.'

'And why do you approve of this.'

'Because you work too hard and your blood pressure is probably in danger of going through the roof. That's in my expert "I've done a first aid course" capacity, of course,' she added gaily.

'Of course.'

He smiled because he knew it was expected, but her words needled him. Had he misread her wholehearted approval of this swim, not as a prelude to something more sensually satisfying but as concern for his health?

His jaw clenched. He would do his utmost to correct this mistake as soon as they were in the water. He would leave her in no doubt of what he wanted. And if she wanted it too…? Things inside him throbbed and burned.

If she didn't.

He tried to quell the throbbing and burning. If she didn't, he would walk away.

When they reached the river, he dropped their towels

beneath the spreading shade of a large hazel tree, pulled his T-shirt over his head and dove straight into the water. The sudden shock of cold had his body tingling, helping to temper his rising need.

He turned back to watch Frankie unwind the sarong from around her body to reveal the bright blue bikini underneath. Long legs, gently flared hips, achingly generous breasts had his breath jamming. But it was the sparkle in those blue eyes that undid him—that made him hope; that had him noticing colours more vividly and scents more keenly, and the touch of the water against his skin.

He ought to dunk his head to try and cool off again, but he couldn't look away as she hip-swayed down to the water's edge, paused as her feet touched the water. Bending at the waist, she wet her hands, giving him a perfect view of the breasts he hungered to mould and curve against him, before she straightened again. Sending him a big smile, she dove into the water just as he had.

A moment later she emerged just in front of him, water streaming from her face. She opened her eyes and her gaze speared straight into his. As if she'd sensed him there. 'This was a most excellent idea, Dante.'

'Why? Because I am playing hooky?'

Her eyes never left his. 'Because it means I can do this.'

She reached out and slid her hands along his shoulders, and the breath hissed from his lungs. She wanted him! He had not misread her intentions. He—

A shock of cold encompassed him when her hands suddenly went to his head and she shoved him under the water in a playful dunk.

Laughing, he bobbed back up and reached out for her but she was too quick and his fingertips merely grazed her shoulder. Leaving his fingers hungry for more.

In two quick strokes he reached her. Grabbing her around

the waist he threw her into the air to splash into the deeper part of the river. Her laugh when she resurfaced sounded like summer and made things inside of him stretch and unfurl as if he were a grapevine and she were the sun.

They frolicked like children. He didn't know how they could have so much energy when they'd been up so early and had worked so hard, but the sight of her and the sound of her laughter filled him with a vigour he'd not experienced before.

'Pax!' she finally laughed, breathless with the exertion. 'Oh, that was the best fun. I can't remember the last time I went for a swim.'

For the first time it occurred to him that perhaps Frankie needed her holiday. That it wasn't just grief and an inability to settle down that was driving her, but something more.

He filed that away to consider another time, because all his mind could currently focus on was the way her body bumped gently against his. His hands had gone to her waist, and he tried to tell himself he was just steadying her, like a gentleman would. He could touch the sandy bottom of the river, while she could not.

In reality, though, it felt as if he would die if he could not touch her.

Her hands had gone to his shoulders and she made no move to push him away. He let his hands slide around her, his fingers moving across the skin of her waist to the small of her back.

Her breath hitched and her gaze flew to his. The ebb and flow of the water had her legs grazing his and he felt as if every atom of his body was alive and on fire.

'Dante.' His name whispered from her and he watched the rise and fall of her throat as she swallowed. 'You've gone all smouldery on me.'

But she didn't look alarmed or cross or as if she were berating him.

'And you are looking at me with big limpid eyes.'

Still she didn't move out of his arms.

'As if you like the fact I'm on fire for you.'

Her eyes went wide. 'You are?'

Very gently, he pulled her hips against his so she could feel the bulge straining in his swimming trunks.

A tremor shook through her, and the pulse at the base of her throat fluttered like a wild thing. 'Oh!' She swallowed. 'You said…' She swallowed again. 'You said there were many reasons you shouldn't give in to this temptation.'

'And now I think there is only one reason to continue resisting.'

'What's that?'

'If you are unwilling.'

Her eyes never left his.

'If you are unwilling, then we stop this now.'

A gleam appeared in her eyes and her hands trailed across his chest, as she leaned forward to press a light kiss to his jaw. 'What would I need to do to convince you that I am *most* willing, I wonder?'

He closed his eyes and revelled in the feel of her in his arms, the scent and rightness of her. The gratitude that she wanted him too.

'Maybe if I do this…' Her hands went around his neck to toy with the hair at his nape and it was all he could do not to drag her closer. As if reading his mind, she pressed herself full-length against him, the sweet curves of her breasts plastered to his chest.

Small teeth grazed his neck with a lingering relish and a growl ripped from his throat. Capturing her chin in his hand, he lifted her mouth to meet his—lips meeting in an open-mouthed kiss of such delicious abandon that before he knew it, he'd pulled her to him as close as it was possible for two still partially clothed people to get.

And she wrapped herself around him. Her arms around his shoulders and neck. Her legs wrapped around his waist as she moved against him with an abandon that had stars bursting behind his eyelids.

Dio! If he did not slow things down, he would disgrace himself. Swinging her up in his arms, he strode out of the water and onto the bank. Capturing her gaze in his, he set her feet to the ground, clenching his hands at his sides. 'I have never wanted a woman with the passion I want you, Frankie.'

A breath shuddered out of her. 'The feeling is mutual, Dante. And this feeling of losing control…it's not what I'd call comfortable.'

'Oh, I can ensure that it will be *very* satisfying, though.' He'd make her come so hard his name would be drawn from the very depths of her being.

Neither one of them moved. She glanced to where their towels were, and then around the clearing. 'It's very private here.'

'*Si.*'

'I've never made love outside before.'

Mio Dio!

She pressed a finger to his chest, the light in her eyes flaring. 'Please tell me you had the forethought to bring condoms down here with you.'

Her forthrightness disarmed him. 'It would not insult you?'

She shook her head. 'I was under the impression, from the moment I woke, that we were playing a game of kiss chase. You wanted to chase me, and I wanted to be caught.'

This woman, she was extraordinary. 'I did bring condoms. Not because I was confident, I was far from sure of you, but because I feared with you my control would be very thin. I needed to make sure I could protect you—protect both of us.'

'So...' She stuck out one delectable hip and his mouth went dry. 'We have this wonderfully peaceful spot where we won't be disturbed?'

He registered the question in her voice and without further hesitation, walked across to their towels and spread them in the low dip of land covered in grass and wild flowers beneath the hazel tree. The sun danced through the leaves of the tree, dappling everything golden and green.

Turning back, he raised an eyebrow.

She studied the bower he'd made for them. 'Even if somebody were to sail down the river, they'd not be able to see us.'

'No.'

'This—' she advanced upon him '—is totally private.'

His chest clenched at the expression in her eyes. Rather than drag her into his arms and ravish her, though, he waited for her to reach him.

'Are you comfortable with making love outside, Dante?'

He could see how much the idea intrigued her. He reached out to touch her cheek. 'It would be an honour for me to fulfil any fantasy of yours, Frankie. This—' he gestured around '—is one of my favourite places on earth and it would delight me to share it with you.'

He'd barely finished his words before she was in his arms again and kissing him fiercely, and he could not help but kiss her back with the same wildness. He'd been afraid that her need would not match his, afraid his hunger would overwhelm her. But her kisses were just as fervent as his, her hands on his body just as demanding and he'd never been more grateful for anything in his life.

She pulled away, her breathing ragged, to stare into his eyes. 'You are such a kind man.'

Kind? *Him?*

'You have no idea what a turn-on it is.'

He shook his head. 'You are...' He couldn't think of a word to amply sum up the way she startled and delighted him.

'A surprising woman, I know.'

'You are a delight.'

Her eyes grew suspiciously bright. 'I think that might be one of the nicest things anyone has ever said to me.'

He kissed her then, because he could not help it. But as he stripped that tiny bikini from her body, he told her how beautiful he found her, and how she was absolute perfection, and as he lay her down in their hidden bower, he trailed kisses down her body, making her writhe and moan as he catalogued all of the delights he found there.

'Enough with the talking, Dante,' she panted. 'I—'

He touched his mouth to the most private and sensitive part of her, and her cry of shocked pleasure filled the air. He stopped talking then and applied himself to giving her more of that same pleasure, slowly building the tension inside of her until she was incoherent and mindless with it, and only then did he send her rolling over the edge into that starburst of oblivion her body had been begging for.

He held her afterwards as she slowly drifted back, feeling like the luckiest man alive.

She had called him kind. He had been called many complimentary things before, but for some reason her simple compliment had pierced beneath his customary reserve to burrow into his chest and make a home there.

She thought him kind and it touched him in ways he couldn't begin to explain. But it made him feel taller, better and more worthy than anything in his life had ever done before.

And then she rolled over to meet his gaze and the sensual determination in those blue eyes had all coherent thought fleeing.

CHAPTER EIGHT

'THAT WAS AMAZING.'

As Frankie spoke, her hand trailed down Dante's stomach to his chest…and lower, her touch sparking across his skin like flame. When she palmed him through his swimming trunks, he couldn't stop from arching into her touch, couldn't prevent his quick intake of breath or the tremble that shook through him.

Heavy-lidded eyes gleamed, and a wicked smile curved her lips. 'You're wearing too many clothes.'

With that she shuffled down to slip her fingers into the waistband of his swim shorts and tug them down. He lifted his hips to help her, and her gaze darkened when she stared at him, standing proudly at attention as if he could not wait for her touch.

Because he *could not* wait for her touch. He gritted his teeth as she reached out and ran her fingers down the length of him. He bucked when her fingers wrapped around him and squeezed, and her eyes widened as if in surprise that she could have such an affect on him.

'You're beautiful,' she whispered, moving her hand experimentally up and down.

Sensation pounded through him threatening his control. Reaching behind for the canvas bag he'd filled with drinks, snacks…and condoms, he tugged it towards him just as her mouth closed over him in the most intimate of caresses.

He swore, he jerked, his hand clenched into the canvas of the bag as his gaze speared to her suspiciously innocent one. And then she ran her tongue down the length of him before taking him once more into her mouth and it was the most erotic thing he'd ever seen.

His body moved with a will of its own and it took a superhuman effort to rein in the wild abandon that wanted to overtake him.

'Frankie.' His breathing was ragged, his voice hoarse. 'My control is very thin.'

Her blue gaze burned into him. 'I can't believe I affect you in the same way that you affect me.'

'Believe it,' he growled, holding up the box of condoms.

He held it deliberately out of reach and as she reached for it, he took the opportunity to reach up and close his mouth over one rosy nipple and draw it deep in his mouth sucking and lathing and grazing it gently with his teeth. Her gasp of breath and soft, 'Oh!' had him smiling against her silken skin. His free hand drifted down to circle and tease and tempt the soft core of her. She was warm and soft and ready.

And then she pulled away, a condom in her hand. Trembling fingers sheathed him. As she lowered herself down onto him, his fingers dug into the hips of her flesh and hers did into his forearms and she stilled as if wanting to imprint this moment on her mind so as to remember it forever.

A sense of wonder filled her face and then she laughed, throwing her arms open wide, those dancing eyes meeting his. 'You said working holidays like mine should be filled with adventures, but never in my wildest dreams did I imagine an adventure like this. Dante, you make me feel like some kind of summer goddess!'

He didn't know how he could tell, but in that moment he realised the devil-may-care attitude she'd assumed this summer was all a pose—a disguise she'd donned to see how she liked it. Tenderness welled through him then, taking him off guard.

But then she moved with a deliberate sensuality, as if she were indeed a summer goddess, and the ability to think fled.

Frankie had never felt anything like this before. She'd intended to focus as fully on Dante as he'd focused on her. He'd sent her soaring into a dimension that she hadn't known existed. She wanted to give him that same kind of pleasure, the same kind of release. The same joy.

But as she moved against him, eyes locked to his, the pressure built inside her again—a sparkling shimmer moving towards her far more quickly than she meant it to. She wanted to resist it, but with a lazy smile Dante pressed a knowing thumb to where their bodies joined and, with a cry, she found herself falling.

As her climax broke over her, she was dimly aware of Dante's guttural cry and the pulsing of his body as the shock of his climax hit too and it spiralled her even higher, his name like a prayer on her lips.

She didn't know how long it took for her to come back to herself, but when she did, she found herself lying on top of him, spent.

She must be a dead weight. She made to roll away, but his arms tightened, and a beautiful flow of Italian rolled over her as he told her how desirable and beautiful and magnificent he thought her, those large hands moving over her with tenderness and warmth as if he wanted to imprint the feel of her on his memory.

They spent the rest of the day in decadent idleness. They

swam again before returning to the house and showering. Together. Which, of course, led to other things, one of them being Frankie's discovery that Dante's bed was every bit as welcoming as it had promised.

He made love to her as if he couldn't get enough of her. It was addictive and powerful and she felt as if she was an actor in some movie who'd stumbled onto the wrong set.

Not that it felt wrong. It felt very, *very* right. It felt righter than anything else in her life had ever felt before. It was just that this was as far from her usual reality as she could get. Her grandmother had been right. Frankie had been in dire need of a holiday.

Dante cooked a delicious late lunch while she raided his enormous walk-in wardrobe and borrowed a T-shirt that covered her to midthigh. He'd told her she was free to borrow anything from his sisters' wardrobes, but she preferred to wear something that smelled like lemons and sunshine.

As soon as she spotted the somewhat battered chess board, she challenged him to a game. When she soundly defeated him, he demanded another game. Which he won. They'd agreed to the best of three games, but somehow became distracted again. Lying side by side in his splendid bed, and watching the shadows lengthen outside, she couldn't recall a more perfect day.

Shifting her head on the pillow, she met his gaze. 'Should I be making a move to return to Bertha and leave you to your private space and time?'

'I would like you to stay the night. But if you wish to return to your campsite, I will return you whenever you wish it.'

It was an effort to hide the delight his words gave her. 'I'm not ready for the day to end yet either.' She studied him. 'And you look all the better for having had a day off, Dante. You looked relaxed, your colour is good, and you don't have all of that horrible tension in your neck and shoulders. You should take days off more often. You might work weekends, but that doesn't mean you can't take a couple of days off through the week for rest and relaxation.'

He shifted up on the bed. 'You look and sound like a doctor making an assessment and giving me a prescription.'

Her chest immediately clenched, but she kept her voice light. 'How depressing. I much prefer to look and sound like a summer goddess.'

He grinned and it eased all of the tightness inside of her. 'The summer goddess has worked her magic. I have so many feel-good hormones flooding my system it does not know what to do with them.'

'And this summer goddess is trying to tempt you to take tomorrow off as well. I haven't been to Lucca yet and it would be lovely to play tourist with you.'

He rolled her onto her back, his body pressing against hers, making her come alive again in a heartbeat. 'You, my goddess, are a temptress.'

When they woke the next morning, Frankie fully expected Dante to dress for work and head into his office, but over a leisurely breakfast he said, 'And what is your plan when we arrive at Lucca?'

Her pulsed leaped at that *we*, though she ordered herself to be cool and laid-back. 'My guidebook tells me Lucca is very beautiful. I'd like to walk around and see that beauty for myself—see the cathedral and the palace, and maybe walk the ancient walls. But my real aim is to find the house my great-grandparents once lived in.'

'And you have not changed your mind? You would still like to share this experience with me?'

The assumed nonchalance fell away. 'More than any-thing.'

Something in his gaze softened and he nodded. 'You were right in your advice to me, I think. I will be more use to Lorenzo's if I am well rested. It will help me make better decisions and it will help me be a better chef.' He glanced at the shirt she wore—his—and his lips lifted. 'I am guessing you would like to return to Bertha for a change of clothes first before we embark on our adventure to Lucca?'

She leaned across and kissed him. 'Thank you, Dante.'

The drive to Lucca was exquisitely beautiful with the roll-ing golden hills and avenues of magnificent cypresses that the area was known for. Dante parked the car outside the walls of the old city, and excitement shifted through her.

He turned to her. 'Why have you waited so long to come here?'

'I guess I've just been waiting for the right moment. Something in Nonna's letter…' She shrugged. 'It's just a feeling I have, but I think she wanted me to find out about my forbears.' Though she had no idea what Nonna wanted her to discover. 'I didn't want to rush it.'

He stared at her and waited, as if he knew there was more. 'And I guess I wanted to feel at home or at least ac-climatised to Tuscany, before imagining another life— one in which my grandparents had never left Lucca, one in which Lucca was my home.'

'Do you wish they had never left?'

'Oh, no! I love Australia too. But I wonder if there is a part of me that will feel an affinity here.' Was that what Nonna wanted her to experience? 'As if I belong. It seems a comforting thought to have.'

'And what if you are disappointed?'

She reached out and touched his arm. 'It's going to be an amazing day either way. It couldn't be a disappointment.'

He pushed his shoulders back. 'I suggest then that we go and explore the old city first, starting with the walls, and then walk the streets your ancestors would have walked. After lunch we will find this address of your grandparents.'

'Perfect!'

The walls of Lucca dated back over two thousand years, and over the centuries had been added to and updated. As they were over four kilometres long, they hired bikes. She delighted in the tree-lined promenades and the grassy areas around the bastions where children played and people picnicked beneath plane and chestnut trees.

The lazy cycling, the warm sun and the light breeze on her face made her feel alive, and one glance at Dante told her he felt the same. It made her want to fling her arms out and sing.

There was so much to see. To one side stretched a lovely view of the countryside. To the other sprawled the preserved medieval city with its winding cobbled streets, narrow stone houses that had stood for centuries—the cream and grey stone glowing warm in the late summer sun.

A smile curved Dante lips at whatever he saw in her face. 'You love it.'

'There so much I want to see and do. More than I can fit into one day. I'm going to have to come back.' Probably several times. 'I want to explore the cathedral.' She pointed. 'And I want to climb Guinigi Tower.' She wanted to see for herself the holm oak trees that grew at the top. 'But today I think I just want to get lost in the streets of the old town.'

And that's exactly what they did. Hand in hand, they walked along winding promenades, stumbling across beautiful architecture like the Romanesque Basilica of San Frediano with its extraordinary mosaic, and the ducal palace. There were gorgeous boutiques that looked as if they'd always been there and markets selling the olive oil, cured meats and honey that Lucca was renowned for.

When they became ravenous and foot sore, Dante, with his uncanny nose for hunting out exquisite cuisine, found them an outdoor restaurant in a beautiful square with a tiny fountain where they ate the best pizza she'd ever had and sipped a deliciously fruity red wine.

Staring around, she stilled. *This.* She wanted a life that made room for *this.* A life where she was free to enjoy good food and wine; one that made time for friendship, and more, with a handsome man; a life that made time to explore the world and marvel at its splendours. A life where she could have an adventure every now and again. A life where one breathed in the summer air, enjoyed the warmth of the sun on one's face, and understood the importance of stillness and gratitude.

It was not the kind of life her father or grandfather lived, and theirs was the one she was in danger of binding herself too.

This was the life her grandmother had lived. It was the life Nonna wished for her.

When her father had died, it had knocked her off balance, had sent her reeling. It had all felt so *wrong.* It was Nonna's death, though, that had brought home to Frankie the meaning of family. It wasn't until Nonna was no longer there that what family meant—*really* meant—had become violently and blindingly clear to her.

Frankie wanted family, she wanted to create a family, she wanted to love, nurture and celebrate *her* family. She wanted to follow in her grandmother's footsteps, not her father's.

'Where did you just go in your mind?'

She turned to find Dante staring at her. 'I was think-ing of my grandmother, and realised something. It's not a place that can make you feel happy or as if you belong.'

'No?'

'It is how you feel in your own mind about yourself and what you are doing with your life. It's in those things, I think, where our spirits truly reside.'

Dante blinked at the profundity of Frankie's words. If asked, he'd say that it was at Riposo where he felt most at home. But maybe it was that he simply felt most himself when he was at Riposo. He allowed himself to be free there.

He stared at her for a long moment, tempted to ask her what it was she really did because he no longer believed her to be a mindless wanderer, but he bit the question back. He would wait until she was ready to tell him her-self, unprompted.

An hour later, they stood in front of a modest house to the northeast of the medieval walls. It was very similar to the other houses in the neighbourhood—built of grey stone with a red-tiled roof, and pink shutters at the windows. Frankie gazed at it with wide eyes, her hands clasped be-neath her chin. He recalled how those hands had moved over his body—a curious but compelling combination of shyness and confidence, and wondered if he could hurry her back to his villa and—

No. He'd give Frankie all the time she needed here in Lucca. He'd not rush her in any way. He pushed his shoul-ders back. 'Would you like to look inside?'

She hesitated and then shook her head. 'My great-grand-parents have been long gone. And I've no desire to in-vade somebody else's privacy. It's just been lovely to have seen it, and to walk the same streets that they'd have once walked, to see the house where my nonna grew up.'

'I have something I'd like to show you.'

Her eyes brightened. 'You do?'

'It's a surprise.'

Tucking her arm through his, she grinned up at him as he led them along the narrow street. 'I like surprises.' She nudged him. 'You, though, I think, don't.'

'Surprises in business, are generally not a good thing.' He liked to have all his bases covered—to be fully informed and fully prepared for all eventualities.'

'I was a surprise,' she pointed out.

'I didn't say I thought surprises were bad.' He smiled down at her. 'You have been a delightful surprise.'

Her answering smile was the only reward he needed. Frankie had indeed been a surprise, and as a rule he didn't like being taken off guard. But she'd taken him off guard in the most delicious way. He did not regret a moment of it.

They walked in companionable silence for fifteen minutes, Frankie taking in the sights and sounds. She'd often point to something she found interesting or eye-catching—a hanging basket of flowers, a tiny deli tucked away, a bright red post box. Ordinary things. But seeing them through her eyes, made them extraordinary. He found himself drawn to the way she saw the world.

He halted outside of a large building. 'Here we are.'

'A hospital?' She frowned. 'Why would you bring me to a hospital?'

He'd expected curiosity, not consternation. His heart kicked against his ribs. How long had it been since her grandmother's passing? Had she spent a long time in hospital? He hadn't considered that. 'We're only going into the foyer. There's a plaque I think you should see.'

Entwining his fingers with hers, he led her inside, scanning the walls for the plaque he'd found on his earlier internet search. 'There!' He dragged her across to it. He read it out in Italian, and then translated it into English, even though he suspected she'd understood every word the first time. *'"In loving memory of Gaetano and Adelina Mazzini for their service and largesse."'*

Her fingers tightened in his. 'Mazzini? That was Nonna's maiden name.'

'I did a little digging.'

'When?'

'While you were getting ready for today's excursion.' Did she mind that he'd researched her family? 'Gaetano and Adelina are your great-grandparents.'

She glanced at the plaque again and then back to him. 'Did you happen to find out what the service and largesse mentioned there was?'

'Gaetano and Adelina were both doctors.'

Her jaw dropped. 'No way.'

'Yes way,' he said with a smile.

She gave a little huff of laughter. 'Surely this is something I ought to have known.' She reached up to trace their names with a finger. 'What kind of doctors?'

'General physicians. They lobbied hard for improvements to the hospital and provided several generous donations to help fund the improvements. According to the history of the hospital, they were central in providing a teaching centre to help train young doctors.'

'But that's…'

'It's?'

'Extraordinary.'

And yet he couldn't tell if she was pleased or not. He shifted his weight to his heels. Should he have told her about Adelina and Gaetano before coming here? Maybe she was more like him than she thought, and did not like surprises either.

But surely this was a good surprise? 'Is this not something to be proud of?'

'Yes!' She straightened, and sent him a smile that didn't reach her eyes. 'It's something to be *very* proud of. To leave such a legacy is something that should inspire admiration and...'

'Then why are you not filled with admiration?'

She wrinkled her nose. 'I am, actually. I think both Gaetano and Adelina must have been amazing people. I just don't know why my grandmother never spoke of them to me. And now I can never ask her.'

Families could be complicated. He should have considered that.

'But,' she said slowly, 'in sending me here to Tuscany Nonna had to know I'd find out about Adelina and Gaetano.'

Perhaps Frankie's nonna hoped that discovering two such admirable people in her background, would give her granddaughter a sense of direction and purpose.

A warm hand on his arm, brought him back from his musings. Frankie smiled up at him. 'Thank you, Dante, for finding this out for me. It was very kind of you.'

He could see that she was touched at the trouble he'd taken. 'It was my pleasure.' It had been no trouble at all. He'd exert himself in any number of ways to give her pleasure.

He immediately thought of all the illicit ways he could give her pleasure and his pulse began to pound. As if she could read his mind, her blue eyes turned the colour of sapphires. 'You're looking all smouldery, Dante.'

'And your eyes are limpid,' he murmured, aching to kiss her but resisting because if he did kiss her, he was afraid he would not be able to keep it within the realms of propriety.

'I think it's time to go home.'

Without a word, he took her hand and led her back the way they'd come.

He played hooky on Wednesday too. Not that Frankie urged him to, but she did ask him how he felt for having taken two whole days off. He hadn't known how to answer, other than to tell her that he felt rested and refreshed.

It occurred to him that he felt more rested than he had in a several years.

She'd folded her arms, a challenge in her eyes. The sight had heated the blood in his veins. Or maybe that was simply the fact that she was naked in his bed at the time. He'd wanted to ravish her, again, but she'd held a finger up and shook her head. 'Hold that thought, though,' she said with a cheeky smile as she slipped out of bed and tossed one of his shirts on over her head. 'We need coffee.'

He made her the strong Italian coffee that they both favoured and when he brought it to the table, he found her with writing pad in her hand.

'If you thought I'd not noticed the way you checked out the food markets and that lovely deli we wandered into yesterday, then you're very much mistaken.'

What did that have to do with anything?

'Your mind is brimming with new menu ideas, isn't it?'

How could she tell?

'Describe them to me,' she ordered.

With a shrug, he did, and she wrote each of them down. She asked sensible questions that had him explaining each dish in greater detail. She idly pondered which wines she'd pair with each new dish he created; he weighed in with suggestions as well. And the longer they talked, the more and more animated he became.

He told her about a recipe he'd been wrestling with for

years, but still didn't have quite right—that he continued to search for an elusive ingredient that would help pull it all together and make it amazing. He was no closer to solving that puzzle when they were finished, but having a chance to talk about it reinvigorated his passion.

She was right. Taking a little time off from the daily grind could provide unforeseen benefits—benefits that Lorenzo's would reap.

They spent Wednesday playing with new menu ideas and considering all of his plans for Lorenzo's. It left him both relaxed *and* invigorated. It felt wonderful.

And he had Frankie to thank for it.

She met his gaze. 'How do you feel when you're cooking, Dante? Describe it to me.'

He recognised at once that it wasn't an idle question. He shifted, eased back, considered how to best explain it. 'It is as if all of my instincts and expertise come together in a kind of dance. They fall perfectly in tune with each other and, somehow, they make of me their vehicle. It is as if, when I am cooking, I can do no wrong.' He shrugged, half laughed. 'It will sound odd, but when I'm cooking, it feels as if I could right all the wrongs with the world.'

She leaned her chin on her hands. 'That's sounds amazing.'

He reached out and took her hand, squeezed it. 'You will find your passion too, Frankie. I'm sure of it.'

'What makes you so sure?'

'Because you are smart and generous. You will work it out. Take this time your grandmother has given you, savour it. And then you will see.'

Her answer was to kiss him. Which, of course, was the perfect answer.

On Thursday, Dante woke with a slow stretch and unfamiliar sense of wellbeing. Turning his head on the pillow, he found Frankie already awake, and propped up on one elbow surveying him.

Her eyes filled with warmth and she leaned over to give him a quick kiss. 'Good morning.'

He pulled her back down for a more thorough kiss before releasing her. 'Good morning.'

She gave an unsteady laugh. 'You kiss like an angel, Dante.'

Holding her lovely body fully against his, he grazed her ear lightly with his teeth. 'Shall I show you what else I can do like an angel?' he murmured, moulding her curves to his.

He felt her quick intake of breath and the way her body melted against him. Pressing a kiss to his collarbone, she drew back a fraction. 'Before…' She swallowed and he revelled in the effect he had on her. 'Before you start something neither one of us wants to stop, you might want to look at the time.'

He glanced at the clock on the bedside table and immediately stiffened. '*Dio!* It is after nine!' He *never* slept in.

But then he recalled the exertions of the night before and that explained why he'd slept so deeply this morning.

'As much as I want to stay here,' she said, 'I know you wanted to get into the office at a reasonable hour today.'

'*Si.*' It didn't stop him from considering going in later, though. They could have a slow lazy start to the day and then—

They couldn't. He needed to check in with Michael and then triple-check with all of his new suppliers to make sure today's deliveries would arrive as planned, and that everything else was ready for tonight.

They were fully booked for the next four nights. There was much to be optimistic about where the restaurant was concerned and much to celebrate, but it was too soon to rest on their laurels.

As if sensing the conclusion he was coming to, Frankie pressed another kiss to his chest—her lips lingering and warming him to the soles of his feet. As she made to push out of his bed, he wrapped an arm around her waist and tugged her back, covering her body with his. Her gasp and the way she arched into him sent satisfaction coursing through him.

Lowering his lips to hers, he kissed her with a ruthlessness thoroughness that had her moving against him restlessly, those clever questing fingers pushing him to the edge, until their bodies surged together and their cries of pleasure rang around the room.

Eventually, he dropped her off in the staff car park on the way to his own dedicated parking spot. She hopped out with a smile. 'I'll see you soon.'

She planned to come into the office for a couple of hours to check her email and any messages the staff might have left for her. The knowledge he'd be working so close to her for the next few hours lifted something inside of him. Reaching for her hand, he pressed a kiss to her palm. 'I am missing you already.' And then he released her before he changed his mind and tugged her back inside the car to spend the day ravaging her.

He set the coffee to percolate before switching on his computer. And then he moved to the first item on the day's agenda—rang all of his suppliers to ensure that nothing untoward had happened with the day's orders. The fishmonger told him that he didn't think the day's catch of octopus would fill Dante with much enthusiasm, but that he had some most excellent crabs. Dante began rearranging the menu in his mind to suit as he agreed to the fishmonger's suggestions.

In the office next door, he could hear Frankie moving about. He would take her coffee soon. Ringing off from the last of his suppliers, he watched as his morning's emails loaded, and as he read them the smile slipped from his face, his every muscle clenching.

Dio! This was a disaster!

Before he could move, a white-faced Frankie appeared in the doorway. 'Oh, God, Dante you're not going to be-lieve this, but ninety percent of the waitstaff are claiming they can't come in this evening.'

He shot to his feet.

'And it's the same for tomorrow night.'

His hands clenched so hard he started to shake. 'This is also the case with the kitchen staff.'

She moved into the room, her eyes narrowing. 'This can't be an accident.'

He stabbed a finger at her, fury exploding inside him. 'This is what happens when I take my eye off the ball for a moment and allow myself to be distracted! How could I have been so stupid?' He whirled away, registering in some small part of his brain that Frankie had gone white, but unable to quell the self-condemnation rolling through him. He'd known someone could be trying to undermine him and the restaurant and yet he'd still—

He'd let Lorenzo down!

How could he have been so careless, so negligent? His grandfather deserved better from him.

'I have been selfishly satisfying my own desires with-out a thought for my responsibilities or what I owe to my family. I—'

'That's not true.' Warm fingers closed around his arm. 'You've been making room in your mind for your plans for Lorenzo's, letting them evolve, consolidating them. That's not selfish.'

'I knew someone might be making mischief for the res-taurant. *That's* what I should've been focussing on.'

'You have been! You've been checking your emails and texts religiously in case of an emergency. Checking in daily with Michael.'

Maybe so, but all the while his mind had been else-where. It had been focussed squarely on Frankie. The res-taurant had played second fiddle.

'Dante, it's not unreasonable for you to take time off.'

'Says a woman who has no responsibilities and noth-ing else to care about except to follow an agenda of plea-sure and distraction.'

Her hand dropped and she took a step away. 'I would never do anything to harm Lorenzo's. You must know that.'

'Must I?' he shot back. 'You don't seem to care what you do with your own life, so why should I believe that you care about other people's lives?'

She stared at him with eyes full of betrayal and he had to wheel away. In a far-off corner of his mind, he knew he wasn't being fair, but had he learned nothing? How had he had allowed this careless, happy-go-lucky charmer, who didn't have a care in the world, to turn his head like this and distract him from what was really important? He who had witnessed the devastation his father had wrought.

Just as his mother had done, he'd allowed emotion to govern his actions when he should've been focusing on duty and maintaining a clear-eyed objectivity. His mother had lost everything. And now he was in danger of losing Lorenzo's.

The thought was like a cold knife between his ribs. He needed to excise all emotion from his heart and mind if he wanted to save Lorenzo's. His hands clenched. He *had* to save Lorenzo's.

Pulling himself up to his full height, he turned back to

face her. 'If I had not wasted all of that time with you in bed this morning, I would have learned about this sooner.' His voice shook, but he kept a strong rein on the roar that had started up at the centre of him. 'I have lost valuable time because I was hell-bent on pleasure.' He thumped an open-palmed hand to his desk. 'Well, no more! This will not happen again.'

CHAPTER NINE

WASTED?

The air punched from Frankie's lungs, making it impossible to speak. Dante considered the time they'd spent together these last few days *a waste*? An unfamiliar and shocking sense of betrayal held her frozen.

Very slowly, she shook her head. No, he considered them something far worse. He considered them a deliberate undermining of his mission to make Lorenzo's a success.

And he thought her a woman of absolutely no substance. While she—

She swallowed. While she thought the last three days some of the most wonderful she'd ever spent.

As she watched him pace, she had one of those epiphanies she suspected her grandmother had hoped for her this summer—Dante's single-minded drive wasn't only harmful to him, but to those close to him. And Frankie *didn't* want to be like that.

She who'd always considered herself a failure if she wasn't top of her class, who'd refused to submit work that wasn't her best. She stared at Dante and realised that if she continued on the path she'd set for herself, she'd become exactly like the man in front of her—a tyrant to duty.

She knew something else too—a summer adventure shouldn't leave her so soul-crushingly shattered. It didn't matter how much Dante's body could make hers sing. She didn't want to be with a man—not even temporarily—who could turn into a humourless robot and make her feel like she was...*nothing*.

He was busy barking orders into his phone, having clearly dismissed her, so she turned and left.

She didn't return to her office but made her way down to the staff quarters. 'Greta, I'm glad you're here. I was hoping to have a word with you and Stella.'

An hour later she returned to her office, cornered Michael, and bullied Dante's mother's phone number out of him.

Twenty minutes later, she knocked on Dante's office door and strode in without an invitation. He opened his mouth, but she spoke before he said something that would tempt her to stalk off and leave him in the lurch. 'I have a list of staff I've arranged to work in the dining room tonight.'

He blinked and straightened.

She held up a sheet of paper. 'This is only a temporary measure. You'll need to hire new staff next week. I also have names of those with kitchen experience if you haven't found replacements there yet.'

He took the sheet of paper as if in a dream. 'How have you—'

'You had the resources at your fingertips this entire time. Seasonal staff often have other skills. All I did was go down to the staff quarters and ask who had waiting and kitchen experience and if they'd be prepared to work in the restaurant this weekend.'

He stared at the sheet of paper and then at her. 'This is a very good solution.'

She remained silent.

He moistened his lips. 'Frankie, what I said earlier...'

She didn't want to hear it. 'Your mother and sisters are also on their way to help in whatever capacity they can.'

'They're *what*?' he roared, jumping to his feet.

Wow. Okay. Not the reaction she was expecting. But the thought felt somehow academic. She felt as if she were in a bubble where his outrage couldn't reach her.

Planting his hands on his desk, he leaned across it, his face twisting. 'They are *not* to be bothered with any of this! What gave you the right to do such a thing? How did you even get the number?'

Her assumed calm shattered. Planting her hands on his desk, she leaned towards him too. 'Well, as I'm nothing more than an irresponsible charmer, getting a phone number is a piece of cake for someone like me!'

He had the grace to look momentarily discomfited. 'Perhaps I was hasty when I said that, but—'

'Perhaps?' She raised a mocking eyebrow.

'But you had no right—' he thumped his desk '—to drag my mother and sisters into this.'

She eased back and folded her arms to try and hide the way her hands shook. 'Why not? Because they must always be protected and kept safe? Has it never occurred to you that they might chafe against the constriction of the ivory tower you've put them in?'

'They want for nothing!'

'Except an occupation to give some meaning to their lives.'

He blinked.

'Except the knowledge that if you should lose everything, they don't have the skills to make their own way.'

He went hard as granite. 'I will *not* lose everything. I am not my father.'

A harsh laugh scraped from her throat. 'No! Heaven forbid you should enjoy even a moment of carefree fun without beating yourself up about it.'

They stared at each other breathing hard.

'Has it not occurred to you that they loved Lorenzo every bit as much as you did, and would love be involved in a restaurant created to honour his memory?'

'My mother deserves a life free from stress, worry and work.'

She stabbed a finger at him. 'Your mother deserves a life where she gets to decide her own destiny!' So did she, she realised in that moment. *So did she.*

'You make me sound like a jailer or a tyrant!'

'If the cap fits...' She gave a careless shrug, one designed to irritate him, but his quick intake of breath gave her no satisfaction. She hitched up her chin. 'If you want Lorenzo's to be a success, you're going to have to surround yourself with people who you trust, because I've found out why so many of the staff have walked out.'

His head rocked back. 'What are you talking about?'

'They were offered bribes. Or threatened.'

The pulse at the base of his neck pounded. 'How do you know this?'

'Because I received one such phone call not an hour ago.'

'From whom?'

'The man didn't give a name, though he was certainly happy enough to pay me a pretty penny to jump into my camper van and drive off into the sunset.'

He turned grey. Though she wasn't stupid enough to think he cared if that's what she did. Except he'd then need to find another maître d'.

'When I refused, I was told to take care on dark lonely roads.'

Dante was in front of her in two steps, his hands curving around her shoulders, his body vibrating with barely contained emotion. 'He threatened you?' That strong jaw clenched though his hands remained gentle. 'We must go to the police.'

'I believe the threat was empty.'

'We are not taking risks with your safety, Frankie. You will move into my villa at once and—'

'I'll be doing nothing of the sort!' She stepped out of his grasp. 'By all means alert the police to the threats. And if you're truly worried about your staff's safety, then hire security guards to patrol the grounds and keep an eye on things.'

He stared at her, his hands clasped, and for a moment she had an image of him tossing her over his shoulder and locking her up in a tower where she'd be safe. To her eternal shame something in her stomach softened at the thought.

She shook herself upright, steeled her spine. 'Has your research turned up anything?'

The pulse at his jaw pounded. 'It is not my father who is trying to sabotage me or the restaurant. My sources tell me he is living in South America with wife number five. The children of her first marriage are apparently keeping him in check by maintaining a very tight rein on the finances. He is basically living in a gilded cage. I do not believe he has had a second thought for the first family he left behind.'

She rubbed a hand across her chest. 'I'm sorry, Dante.' It had to be the bitterest kind of knowledge.

His only reply was a casual shrug that didn't fool her for a moment.

It wouldn't do either of them any good to wallow, though. She pushed her shoulders back. 'I don't believe this is a business grudge either. It feels too personal for that.'

Those dark eyes met hers again.

'Tell me, Dante, who would want to see you brought low?'

He braced his hands on his knees for several seconds,

before straightening again. 'Lorenzo's other family—the children and grandchildren from his marriage.'

Exactly.

'Do you think any of them would physically harm your staff?'

He hesitated and then shook his head.

'Or you and your family?'

Dragging a hand through his hair, he strode across to stare out the window. 'They resent us, yes. They are perhaps jealous of us, but I do not believe that they are wicked at heart. It always grieved Lorenzo that they would not accept us, but he loved and respected them. I trust his judgment.'

'Seems to me the best way for you all to pay homage to Lorenzo is by burying the hatchet.'

He swung around, his eyes flashing. 'Oh, and you make that sound as easy as ABC.'

'Of course, it's not easy! Few things of worth are.'

She gestured to the chair on her side of his desk and he nodded. 'Yes, please sit.'

She collapsed into it, suddenly exhausted.

'Thank you for finding staff for this evening, Frankie. I have an agency working overtime to organise staff to cover our shortfall but—'

'Why didn't you hire staff from the village?'

His head rocked back at the accusation implicit in her voice. 'Because I wanted the best. I wanted staff who were experienced and had worked in the kind of restaurants with reputations that Lorenzo's would also acquire.'

'And look where that got you. If you'd hired staff from the village, they'd have been loyal to you.'

As far as she was concerned, he'd been focussing on all the wrong things. But she doubted he'd appreciate her pointing that out. And as she knew she'd stepped out of line in speaking to his mother, she kept her mouth shut.

He sat, rubbing a hand over his face. 'I believe I owe you an apology.'

Something too bitter to be a laugh rasped from her throat. 'You certainly do.'

Shadowed eyes met hers. 'I apologise for ranting and raving at you this morning. This situation I now find myself in is not one of your making. I should not have blamed you for it or taken it out on you. I am truly sorry. I hope you will forgive me.'

She wanted to cry then because she knew he meant what he said, but she also saw what he wasn't saying. 'I accept your apology, Dante.'

And she did forgive him because she knew what it was like to be single-minded to the point of obsession.

'Thank you.'

She swallowed and took a punt because...well, because it was what this summer was all about. 'It wasn't one of *your* making either, Dante.'

That autocratic chin lifted, and dark eyes hardened. 'I have been much at fault. I should have been paying more attention. If I had, I'd have had a Plan B in place for an eventuality such as today's. I cannot allow myself to become distracted again.'

She pressed her hands together, her eyes burning. 'By, for example, having a holiday fling with your maître d'?'

'Exactly.'

She couldn't explain the darkness that wanted to descend over her, only that it took an effort to appear unmoved. Her eyes ached, her temples pounded, her body felt as if it belonged to someone else.

'You are a very special woman, Frankie, and I have enjoyed our time together. But now it must end. I need all of my concentration for Lorenzo's. It must be my focus.'

She found herself nodding, but it wasn't in agreement—

just that he'd uttered the words she'd expected. 'It's funny. The shoe is usually on the other foot.'

He stared at her as if he had no idea what she meant.

'Usually it's me who gives the "it was lovely while it lasted" and "it's not you it's me" speech.' Usually to fun-loving guys who wanted her to let her hair down and have some fun. Not that she'd dated much these last couple of years. She'd become as single-minded and blinkered as Dante. No wonder her grandmother had become so worried about her. 'I'm not usually the recipient of *the speech*.'

He frowned. 'I do not say it to make you feel bad or—'

'I know. Which only makes it all the more mortifying.' She rose. She didn't have the heart for any more. 'Time to get back to work. There's a lot to organise before tonight.'

She turned and left—her chest aching, her head throbbing. She wouldn't think about any of that either—the aching, the emptiness, the desire to cry. For heaven's sake, it was just a holiday fling, nothing more. It was always going to end.

Shoulders back. Chin up. Deep breaths. *Carefree and happy-go-lucky.*

'Frankie, I can't thank you enough for contacting me.' Ginevra Alberici reached out to take Frankie's hands. 'It is a delight to be of service to Dante and be involved in his plans for Lorenzo's. Maria, Sofia and Giorgia are beside themselves with happiness.'

Frankie squeezed Dante's mother's hands. 'I'm so pleased it's all working out. But you must stop thanking me.' Ginevra had thanked her every day so far this week. And as it was Tuesday that was at least three more *thank-yous* than necessary. 'It's you, Dante and his sisters who are making this work. Not me.'

'But it was you who brought us together and it is something I will always be grateful for. I should have insisted on this earlier, but Dante was so proud to look after us all. It was as if it was something he needed to do, and God forgive me, but I let him.'

'Nobody needs to forgive anyone. What you need to do is turn your faces to the future and not the past.'

'You speak very wisely. Come and see how Maria is doing with the tastings.'

Maria, it appeared, had an aptitude for wine. She'd not been there a full day before confiding that she'd been secretly studying to become a vintner. Dante had been speechless, before glancing at Frankie who'd been setting the tables in the restaurant at the time. She'd merely lifted a hopefully speaking eyebrow.

He was arranging for Maria to now be involved in every aspect of the winemaking process at Riposo.

Ginevra was going to take over as maître d' when Frankie's tenure ended, while Sofia was working towards a business degree. Maybe she'd one day work in Dante's business empire. Giorgia, the youngest, had no idea what she wanted to do, but her delight at being back at the vineyard was certainly genuine. They were all of them lovely, and had embraced Frankie as one of their own. She'd miss them when she left.

When she left... A familiar darkness began to descend and—

'Was there something you needed, Frankie?'

She started at Dante's voice. Forced a smile. 'Greta, Stella and I are going on a picnic and I was hoping to buy a bottle of prosecco.'

'You need *never* buy wine from Riposo, Frankie. You have earned as many bottles of wine as you can drink.'

He looked so happy to have his family around him. It made no sense that her heart should ache so. If she could just extinguish the burning that took hold of her whenever he was near…the burning to be in his arms and—

Stop it!

'That's very kind of you, Dante, but—'

'Frankie?'

The familiar voice, so out of place here, had her freezing. Surely not… Surely she was mistaken… She turned. *Oh, God.* 'Grandfather!'

Dante had only a glimpse of Frankie's horrified expression, but it had him vaulting over the bar and landing beside her. This man might be her grandfather, but she seemed far from happy to see him, and he had no intention of allowing anyone to hurt or bully her.

No, that's a right you reserve only for yourself.

The thought had acid churning in his stomach. Holding out his hand, hoping to buy Frankie time to gather her composure, he said, 'I'm Dante Alberici. My family and I own Vigna di Riposo.'

'Franklin Weaver,' the older man said, shaking it. 'I'm Frankie's grandfather.'

As if coming to her senses, Frankie stretched up to kiss the older man's cheek. 'It's lovely to see you, Grandfather, but why didn't you warn me you were coming?'

'Your mother has been worried, Frankie. We all have been and—'

A crash on the other side of the room had them all swinging towards it. A man who looked to be in his sixties had knocked his glass to the floor and stood there swaying, one hand scrunched in the front of his shirt, before falling to his knees.

Frankie leaped towards him, catching him as he fell and Dante moved with her to help ease him to the ground. She loosened the man's collar and felt for a pulse. He was the colour of loose cement and—

'No, no, no,' she murmured under her breath. Straddling him, she started chest compressions. 'Defibrillator?' she shot at Dante, not taking her eyes off the man.

Dante leaped up and seized the defibrillator from the wall and returned with it, calling to his mother to ring for an ambulance.

Frankie took the machine and, without even reading the instructions, positioned it with the ease of an expert.

Dear god, he hoped she knew what she was doing and—

A firm hand wrapped around his arm—Frankie's grandfather. 'Give her room. She knows what she's doing.'

Dante held back, but remained alert for any indication that she might need assistance. He couldn't help flinching when the man's still body jerked as she shocked him.

She did things, checked the man's vital signs. Dante made a silent vow then and there to do an accredited first aid course just as Frankie had done.

'His heart has started,' she finally said, but she didn't lower her guard or sag or any of the things Dante felt like doing. Instead, she rolled the man to his side and tilted his head back and kept her fingers on his pulse and looked as if she was counting.

None of them dared disturb her. She looked utterly and completely in control. If she'd told him to get her a sharp knife, that she needed to perform emergency surgery on the man, he'd have done her bidding without question.

It felt like an age before two paramedics raced into the room and took over. She spoke to them in a language he didn't fully understand. Oh, it was Italian but filled with unfamiliar medical jargon.

He knew in that moment. Knew that Frankie was far

more qualified than she'd let on. And for the man's sake, he was glad.

But why had she not told him? He rubbed a hand over his face. Had he really accused her of being an irresponsible gadabout? And why should such an accusation so delight her?

When the ambulance drove away, Frankie swung to her grandfather with a glare. 'Thanks for the help.'

'You had it all under control. You didn't need me. Besides, your training in such things is more up-to-date than mine. Come, come, Frankie, stop being so childish. Surely this incident has proved to you where your future lies. Go pack your bags and let's take you home where you belong.'

Frankie folded her arms and straightened to her full height. Dante had started to recognise it as her fighting stance. He ought to. She'd used it often enough on him.

'I have earned a summer off, Grandfather.'

'Don't be ridiculous! Don't throw all of your hard work away on a whim. You have a bright future ahead of you and—'

'I will return home at summer's end as planned, not before. You've had a wasted trip, and I'm sorry for it. Goodbye, Grandfather.' She kissed his cheek before turning on her heel and striding towards the door.

'You owe it to your family,' Franklin called after her. 'You owe it to your *father*!'

Frankie halted, but then continued on without turning around. Things inside of Dante throbbed and ached. What did her father have to do with anything? What difficulties had she been dealing with all on her own? Why hadn't she confided in him?

His stomach gave a sickening roll. Because she knew how focussed he'd been on making Lorenzo's a success. Because he'd told her again and again how he had no room in his life for anything other than Lorenzo's.

She'd been a good friend—had helped him gain perspective more than once; helped him find solutions to all the problems that had arisen. She'd gone above and beyond in her role of maître d'.

What had he given her in return? A load of grief and castigation that she hadn't deserved. He'd been selfish, self-involved and inconsiderate. His grandfather would be ashamed of him.

He swallowed. He was ashamed of himself.

His mother's touch had him crashing back. 'You should go after her and make sure she's okay.'

He glanced at Frankie's grandfather.

'I'll deal with him.'

He didn't need any further urging.

He found Frankie slumped on one of her camp chairs, her head in her hands. All he wanted was to wrap her in his arms and try to make the bad stuff go away for her.

But this wasn't about what he wanted. It was about what she wanted. He was through with being selfish.

He took the seat beside her. 'Frankie?'

She immediately straightened, her lips twisting. 'Have you come to demand an explanation?'

He deserved her bitterness. Swallowing, he shook his head. 'I came only to make sure you were okay.'

She looked suddenly shamefaced.

'No!' The word shot from him. 'You have nothing to feel bad about. Also, my words weren't meant to imply I'm not interested. I am, but I have treated you badly enough. I've no intention of forcing a confidence you don't wish to give.'

Closing her eyes, a long breath eased out of her. She looked exhausted, and a bad taste stretched through his mouth. How could he have treated her so cavalierly. This woman, she was everything that was kind and generous and he'd stomped all over her.

Those eyes opened. 'I'm guessing you've worked out I'm a doctor.'

Why had she wanted to hide it? 'You might not believe this, but I realised some time ago that your devil-may-care attitude was a pose.'

'You did? When?'

His skin drew tight. 'The exact moment?'

Her brows lifted at whatever she saw in his face. 'Yes, please.'

'That afternoon down at the river.' He moistened his lips. 'You were so delighted to be making love in the sun and playing the sensual goddess. Which you did to perfection, I must admit.'

She pressed her hands to cheeks that had turned pink.

'I'm not sure how I knew. It was just…' He thought back. 'It was as if in that moment you had fallen in love with life again.'

She pulled her hands away. 'That's exactly how I felt.'

Why had he not trusted his instincts? Why hadn't he pursued that line of thought and dug deeper instead of allowing himself to become consumed with Lorenzo's again?

She searched his face, her brow pleating. 'Do you believe in soulmates, Dante?

'No.'

The word dropped from him. He had seen no evidence of such a thing. It was a myth designed to sell Valentine's Day cards and encourage couples to spend far too much on weddings. His mother and father certainly hadn't been soulmates. Nor, he suspected, had Lorenzo and his wife.

Something in Frankie's eyes dimmed and she turned to stare at the grapevines. He stared at her profile and his heart crashed about in his chest. Surely she wasn't saying she thought he and she were soulmates? That'd be *ri-*

diculous. And yet his mouth went dry at the thought and a giant ache opened inside of him.

He pushed all of it away and lifted his chin. 'What you did for that man... I am in awe.'

'When you've had as many years of medical training as I have...'

'Do not downplay it. You've had an impact on that man's life and his family's in a way they will be grateful for forever. You should be proud of what you have done.'

She frowned and blinked. 'I am.' Her frown deepened. 'I am glad I was able to help.' She shook herself upright. 'It's kind of you to check on me, Dante.' That gaze sharpened. 'How are you, though? It can often be a shock to be a bystander and—'

'I am fine. You do not need to worry about anyone except yourself.'

'My grandfather...?'

'My mother is taking care of him. Which I suspect means she will see him off the premises.'

'He won't enjoy that.' She stared down at her hands for a long moment. 'Franklin is my paternal grandfather.'

That explained why the older man had invoked Frankie's father. His heart beat hard. He didn't know why, but he sensed the mention of her father mattered. That it mattered a lot.

'Franklin is a surgeon—very well respected.'

It explained the man's aura of authority.

'His father was a surgeon.' She expelled a long breath from her lungs. 'And so was mine.'

When the import of her words hit him, a vice tightened about his chest. 'It is expected you will follow in their footsteps?'

She nodded.

He studied her downcast expression and his heart burned. 'But that is not what you want?'

'I always thought it was.' She sent him a smile that made his chest ache. 'My father died when I was seventeen. A car accident. You can imagine… It was awful.'

He reached out and took her hand. 'I am sorry.'

She nodded, but her hand gripped his as if it were a lifeline. 'I made a vow to follow in his footsteps. I wanted to do something that would've made him proud of me.' She swallowed. 'And I wanted to mitigate my mother's and grandfather's grief. I wanted to give them something to hold on to.'

'Oh, Frankie.' He fought the urge to pull her into his lap and hold her close. He was through with imposing what he wanted onto her, though. From now on, he would take his cues from her. 'You were trying to look after everyone.' It is what this woman did—she cared for people. 'But you were barely more than a child. And grieving yourself.'

She nodded, but it was absently as if her mind were elsewhere. 'Nonna asked me to take this summer off, before I made a final decision.'

'Final decision?'

'When I return to Australia, I have to choose my medical specialty.' She stared up at the sky, though he suspected she didn't see how blue it was or notice the white clouds drifting past. 'I have to decide if I'm going to become a surgeon. Or not.'

He saw then what a gift her grandmother had given her—three months of rest and relaxation to clear her head before having to make such a momentous commitment.

'When I arrived here, Dante, I didn't even know if I wanted to be a doctor anymore. My entire life from the time I was seventeen onward has been focussed on study, on learning all I needed to know, and being top of my class.' Her lips twisted. 'Because, of course, nothing but the best would do.'

She'd burned herself out. 'Have you come any closer to a decision?'

'Not yet,' she whispered.

His heart ached for her. 'Frankie, that vow you made, it is not one you should hold yourself to. It is not one anyone should hold you to. You were young. It was a promise made in grief. You deserve a life that brings you satisfaction and happiness, not to yoke yourself to one that doesn't.'

'I keep telling myself the same thing, but that doesn't stop it feeling dishonourable to break my word. And you want to know why?'

'Tell me.' If he could, he would fix it for her.

'Because in my heart, I know my father would want me to follow in his footsteps.'

Her words cracked his chest open. 'You are not dishonourable. You are the most honourable woman I have ever met!'

She rocked back in her seat.

He dragged in a breath, tried to temper his vehemence. 'Your father, was he a good father?'

It took a moment before she answered. 'He was a good provider—we never wanted for anything. But I sometimes wonder if I really knew him. He spent so much time at work, and rarely made it to any of my school events. Even our holidays were interrupted because of some emergency or other. And when someone's life is hanging in the balance, how can you begrudge it?'

Would it really have been so difficult, though, for him to have shown her a little more love and attention?

'I don't want my children ever feeling that way about me. I don't want to be that kind of parent, Dante. Do you?'

The question had his head jerking up. 'It is not a question I have ever considered.'

CHAPTER TEN

FRANKIE STARED INTO the dark pools of Dante's eyes and her heart burned. Her hand still rested in his and she tugged it free. 'Why not?' Why hadn't he considered what kind of parent he'd like to be?

'It is not a life I have considered for myself.'

She spread her hands. 'And again… Why not?'

She could tell he didn't want to talk about it. And if she was kind and considerate and sensitive, she'd let the matter drop. But she and Dante were beyond such things. Whatever it was that lay between them, it was raw and emotional. And honest.

She hadn't always appreciated that honesty and she suspected he hadn't either, but it was like the wind and the weather and the turning of the earth—not something they had any control over.

'Well?' she prompted.

Those dark eyes flashed, and she suspected that if she hadn't just saved a man's life, he'd have walked away. That strong jaw firmed. 'I saw how badly my mother suffered when my father left. I will never allow a woman to reduce me to those same kinds of circumstances.'

She gaped. *Seriously?* 'For such a successful man, you can be incredibly stupid sometimes.'

His head snapped back as if she'd slapped him.

'First of all, no woman is ever going to leave you in abject poverty with four children to raise. Even if you gave all of your money away to this hypothetical Wicked Witch of the West, you'd still have the resources, experience, and connections to draw a good wage and support yourself and said children.'

'But—'

'You'd still have Riposo and your family.'

He shot to his feet. 'It is not my family's job to support me financially!'

'Oh, that right only belongs to you does it?' She stood too, clenching her hands as heat rose in her face. 'What kind of paternalistic patronising crap is that, Dante? *Seriously?* You want to keep them as pampered pets who look up to you adoringly, rather than women capable of determining their own destiny?'

'I— This is— You have no idea what you're talking about!'

'Then ask yourself why Maria and Sofia have been keeping their studies a secret from you.'

He starred at her with throbbing eyes. 'I am not this dragon you accuse me of being.'

Unbidden, tenderness threatened to drown her then. 'No one thinks you a dragon. But your mother and sisters are aware of this deep-seated need of yours to take care of them, and because they don't want to make you feel lesser or somehow inferior to this idea you have, or want to have, of yourself, they've kept their qualms to themselves. It has been their way of looking after you.'

He collapsed back in the chair as if her words had robbed his legs of strength.

'They want to help you as much as you want to help them.' She sat again too. 'But, Dante, they want to empower themselves as well. So they never find themselves in that situation again either. But even if they do, they know they can count on you. That's what having a family is or should be about. Your mother had no one except your father and the four of you children. When he left, she lost the one other person in this world she was supposed to be able to rely on. And having no formal qualifications made getting work that paid a halfway decent wage very difficult for her.'

He rubbed a hand over his face. 'She should never have had to deal with all of that on her own.'

'I agree. But it's not a situation you or your sisters or your mother herself will find yourselves in ever again. So let it go. All of you are safe from that fate now.'

Those dark eyes lifted. 'When Lorenzo came, it was wonderful. But even after he had legally ensured we would always have Riposo, it still felt as if it could all be taken away. It was very important to me to become financially independent very quickly. So that if it was, I could make sure we were all safe.' He nodded slowly. 'But you are right. I have achieved that now.'

'Lorenzo knew the power and worth of family.' She gestured around, drinking in the view, knowing she wouldn't be here for much longer to appreciate it. A chasm yawned open in her chest. She swallowed and ploughed on. 'He made sure this was a *family* vineyard—*your* family's vineyard. Don't you think it would make him happy to know all of you were here working together to make the restaurant a success?'

He blinked. '*Si*, he would like that very much.'

'I know you think you and your sisters were a complication in his life—'

'We were.'

'But you clearly weren't an unwelcome one. Maybe to

his other family,' she rushed on when he opened his mouth, 'but not to him.'

Eventually he nodded. 'He loved us.'

'So why would you continue to deny yourself the love and joy that having your own children would bring?'

'It is perhaps something I need to think upon.'

He said it gravely, and she couldn't tell if he meant the words or was just trying to humour her. 'One day you'll meet a woman who'll change your mind.' And she could no longer deny that it broke her heart that she wasn't that woman.

What a foolish thing it had been to do, to fall in love with Dante. But an inevitable one, she now saw. Despite his drive to succeed, his obsession with it, he had a generous heart and an honourable spirit. And something in him spoke to something in her. He'd given her the confidence to explore aspects of herself she'd never dared to before. He hadn't mocked her when she'd made mistakes or made her feel lesser about herself. She swallowed. He'd allowed her the freedom to simply be herself.

'*Dio*, enough about me! I came to talk about you, Frankie. And yet even now you continue to give—to get involved in other people's lives and do what you can to make them better.' He glared at her, but there was no real heat behind it. 'You would be wasted as a surgeon.'

It was her turn to gape. Her grandfather would have a dozen fits if he could hear Dante now. 'How so?' she choked out.

'You are so good with people. You should be doing a specialty where you are face-to-face with conscious people, not unconscious ones. Like a…' He tried to grasp the air. 'Like a psychiatrist.'

Did that mean he agreed with the advice she'd doled out so relentlessly to him over the course of the last few weeks? Maybe he'd stop working so hard. Maybe he'd let his family help him more. Maybe he'd follow his dream and remain the chef here at Lorenzo's. She crossed everything she had that it'd be the case. She wanted Dante to be happy, even if she had no part in the life he meant to live.

His face lit up. 'Or a doctor in the emergency department of a hospital. You would put your patients at ease and they would have confidence in you. Or how about a paediatrician? Children would love you! You would be brilliant at all of those things.'

She laughed. Partly at his enthusiasm, but also at this new vision he provided her. He clearly thought her capable of anything. He made her feel she could be whatever she wanted to be.

He sobered again. 'You have the right to fulfil your own destiny, Frankie. You were only a child when you made that promise to your mother and grandfather.'

She'd give the same advice to someone in her shoes too. She knew she would. But it didn't stop it from feeling dishonourable to break that promise.

'You have given me all of this lecture about family and what it should mean and how it should work. Why do you not demand the same from your family—from your mother and grandfather? Why do you not tell them what will make you happy and demand their loyalty and support for what you wish to do and become?'

Everything inside of her snapped to attention. If she went to them with a plan for her future—one that would make her happy... They might be disappointed that she wasn't going to be a surgeon, but surely they'd support her decision? They weren't ogres. They *wanted* to see her happy. They just didn't want her to throw her future away.

'Frankie?'

She shook herself. 'That is some of the best advice I've ever received!'

His shoulders went back. 'I would like to help you in any way I can. If there's anything I can do to help, I beg you will ask it of me.'

She ached to ask him why—wanted to wrest a declaration of love from him. But she already knew that wasn't why he wanted to help. He was merely grateful to her for her help with Lorenzo's, and guilty about how abruptly he'd ended their affair.

'What are you going to do? Do you want to walk away from medicine?'

He'd said cooking made him feel alive, that when he cooked he felt as if he could right all the wrongs of the world. Practising medicine didn't make her feel like that, but her knowledge and skills worked in tandem in a way that made her feel...'

True.

As soon as the word whispered through her, she sagged as the weight she'd been carrying for the last nine years lifted. Practising medicine made her feel like she was being true to herself, being who she was meant to be.

Practising medicine and being a doctor, yes.

Practising surgery and being a surgeon, no.

She didn't want to be a surgeon and pretending otherwise, forcing her feet to follow that path, would be a perversion of her truth and a betrayal of who she was.

Nonna had sent her to Tuscany to find out about her family. What had she discovered? That medicine ran in both sides of her family—her father's *and* her mother's. It was no surprise to find she had an affinity for medicine. It was no surprise to find herself attracted to other branches of medicine either.

'Frankie?'

She started when Dante's voice broke into her ruminations. She glanced up. 'Binding Greta's wound, providing the occasional bit of advice to the other workers—both the grape pickers and the waitstaff when conversation has strayed to such topics—and getting that poor man's heart working again, has all felt so natural.' She shrugged. 'I like that I can do those things. I want to keep doing those things.'

As she spoke, she could see the future she wanted opening up before her. She stared at Dante with what she suspected was sparkling eyes and a goofy grin. He grinned back as if he couldn't help it. It made her breath catch.

'I know exactly what I want Dante! I want to be a GP. A general practitioner who has her own practise.' She leaped up, clapping her hands. 'I want to be a *family* doctor.'

With a whoop, he jumped up and swung her around. 'But this is perfect for you.' He set her back on her feet.

'I can be a family doctor *and* have a family of my own. I don't have to choose one or the other.' She closed her eyes in momentary thanks. 'I can be both the mother I want to be *and* the doctor I want to be.'

She realised then that he still held her hands. Her breath hitched and her pulsed raced. She wanted him with a ferocity that frightened her. It would be so easy to stay here, to resume their fling because she could see that Dante still wanted her—it was in the way his eyes darkened and his jaw clenched. All she'd have to do was make the first move and—

No.

She wanted more. So much more. To settle for less would make the pain all the greater when she left.

She stepped away, reclaimed her hands, ignored the protest sounding through her. 'I still mean to take three whole months off as Nonna urged me to. I've earned it.'

His gaze sharpened as if he'd sensed the change in her.

She ordered herself to remain strong, forced a smile. 'You do realise my six weeks here is up at the end of next week?'

He stiffened. 'You still wish to leave?'

She did what she could to make her shrug casual. 'It was always the plan. I have the rest of Tuscany to explore.'

'But you could do that while based here. *Cavolo!* It is why you agreed to work so hard for me and Lorenzo's. So you didn't have to work for the rest of your holiday.'

It took an effort not to hug him, for in that moment he'd put her first before Lorenzo's and she loved him for it.

Stay strong.

'I think it will be better this way, Dante.'

'You will come back and see us before you leave Italy altogether?'

She shook her head. 'I'm not making any promises.'

Dante beat the schnitzels with a ferocity that had Carlo, his second-in-command, eyeing him warily.

Ignoring him, he crumbed the steaks and dropped them into the pan of oil. 'Keep an eye on those,' he ordered, stalking to the door and peering into the dining room. His mother ably manned the maître d' stand, welcoming the diners with a warmth he could not fault, but it was not the same as having Frankie there.

Frankie was still out there, of course, though tonight she was acting more as a waitress along with all three of his sisters. She was the presence that smoothed everything— the one all the others turned to for advice and guidance.

The bell to alert the waitstaff that a meal was ready pinged nearby and Frankie turned with a fluid step, only faltering momentarily when her gaze connected with his. Her eyebrows rose, but she righted her step and moved towards the kitchen. 'Is there an issue?' she asked him, reaching for the dishes waiting for her.

'Yes.' Taking her arm, he began towing her through the kitchen.

She tried to dig her heels in. 'Dante, we have a restaurant full of diners!'

'They'll have to wait.' His temples pounded. Not with pain, but with something he couldn't identify. 'I need to talk to you.' He needed to talk to her *now*.

'Inform Ginevra,' Frankie shot at Carlo. 'Hopefully this won't take long. And don't drop any balls,' she managed to toss over her shoulder before the door closed behind her.

'What on earth can be so important you'd abandon your post in the kitchen and drag me out of the dining room, Dante?' she demanded as he towed her into his office.

'This!'

Pulling her into his arms, he lowered his mouth to hers, claiming her lips in a kiss of heat and passion. The taste of her, the scent... He kept his mouth gentle, his hands cradling her face as he focussed on trying to tell her with his kiss all that she'd come to mean to him. She melted against him, her arms going around his neck, and she kissed him back with what felt like all of herself. The things inside him that had felt wrong became right again.

Kissing this woman was as necessary to him as breathing air. Having her near was like his lifeblood. He was not ready to part with her yet. He had to find a way to convince her to stay at Riposo for a little longer.

Eventually the kiss ended. She touched trembling fingers to her lips. 'Why did you do that?'

'I do not want you to leave.' He swallowed. 'Frankie, please do not leave.'

For a moment he could've sworn that something in her eyes lightened, but if it did, turbulence reclaimed it almost immediately. 'You want me to remain for what's left of my holiday?'

He nodded. 'You did not promise your grandmother that you would continually be on the move. You just said you would spend the summer in Tuscany. Why not spend it here where you have friends? I will not ask you to work in the restaurant again. You have amply fulfilled the promises you made me. But you can stay here—'

'And when my holiday is over?'

He blinked. He'd refused to think that far. But… He swallowed. This summer was one magical season out of time, nothing more. 'And then you will return to Australia and become a GP and I will return to Rome and once again take up the reins of my business.'

She turned to stare out the window. 'You don't see any future for us beyond this summer.'

It was a statement, not a question, but the import of what she suggested had his chest clenching. Maybe it could be possible. Maybe…

He shook himself. The notion was preposterous. As he'd already told her, he was not the kind of man interested in long-term commitment or having a family of his own.

Frankie gave a soft laugh. 'Well, the answer to that question is written all over your face.'

'I have already told you—'

'You don't need to explain, Dante.'

He did not like the expression on her face, although it held not an ounce of remonstrance. She moved towards him and things inside him electrified. He wanted that beautiful warm body pressed against his. He wanted to hear her soft cries in his ears. He wanted to hear his name on her lips as she shattered in pleasure.

She stared up into his face. 'Are you really going to return to Rome?'

'Of course.'

She flung her arm in the direction of the kitchen, her face darkening. 'Have you learned nothing this summer?' 'You come alive when you're in there, Dante! Creating delicious meals is what you were born to do. Being a chef is your vocation in the same way being a doctor is mine. Why would you exile yourself to the city and a job that means nothing to you when you could be doing this.'

'Means nothing to me? My business saved me!' His head rocked back when he realised what he was doing. He was in danger of allowing emotion to rule him. 'It is my business that makes the real money, not Lorenzo's.' He *would* be practical.

'Life is about more than making money.'

'It is clear then that you have never had to live without it.'

Her lips pursed. 'That doesn't change the truth of my words. You're ridiculously wealthy and yet—'

She broke off, hauling in a breath. 'When will you have made enough money, Dante, that you can finally allow yourself to be happy?'

He thrust out his jaw. 'I am happy.'

Those lips pressed together as if to stop more words from spilling out. Eventually she said, 'We've both been away from our posts for too long.'

He hauled in a breath. 'You will leave Riposo as planned?'

'Yes.'

'It is perhaps for the best then.' If he did not want emotion and desire in constant conflict with rationality and practicality, it would be best if they parted ways.

She turned and left.

He had to lean on his desk and wait for the breath to return to a body that felt suddenly and inordinately heavy.

* * *

They all of them gathered to farewell Frankie. Not just Dante and his family, but the seasonal workers and Lorenzo's staff. The crowd made him chafe. He wanted to sweep her up into his arms and kiss her one last time, but with everyone there, he couldn't.

Even if they hadn't been there, he couldn't. He scuffed the toe of his shoe against the ground. Frankie had armoured herself with a don't-touch-me air whenever he was near, and no man of honour could ignore such a warning.

It was his own fault. If he hadn't ended their summer fling with such vehemence—all but accusing her of undermining him and Lorenzo's—then she might not be leaving now. But that knowledge gave him no comfort.

Frankie moved around the group, hugging and farewelling everyone, promising to keep in touch. When she reached him, she hesitated for a second before reaching up and kissing his cheek. He held her for the briefest of moments, but then she was out of his arms again. It passed too quickly. He had not even had a chance to imprint the kiss on his memory!

'Dante, it's been an adventure.' Her eyes danced for a moment before sobering. 'You've given me so much. And I'm not talking about the opportunity to make enough money for the summer,' she added with a roll of her eyes. 'I'm very grateful. I'll never forget you.'

Before he could make any kind of answer, she'd leaped into Bertha and started the engine. He swore she swiped a hand across her eyes. It took all of his strength not to pull her back out again and demand she stay.

Her lips curved into a smile, but her eyes remained suspiciously bright. 'I left a present for you on your desk.'

A present? For him? But why?

And why on earth hadn't he given her something to remember him by? He wanted to turn back time and—

But then she was gone and his entire body turned to stone and he didn't have the strength to even lift his hand in farewell.

His mother's hand on his arm drew him back. 'Dante—'

'Not now, Mamma.'

Turning on his heel, he strode off towards his office. He would bury himself in work.

It was work that was important. Not holiday flings.

Work would drive all of this nonsense from his mind.

Several hours later he glanced up at a tap on his door. Ginevra stood there with a plate of cured meats, cheese and olives in one hand and a basket of bread in the other. 'It's well after lunchtime, Dante. You need to stop and eat.'

He wasn't hungry, but something in his mother's voice told him she wouldn't accept such an excuse. He waved her in, made room for the food.

She didn't leave, but took the seat opposite, helping herself to a piece of cheese. He ground down a sigh. He should have known she'd stay to make sure he would eat. Seizing two slices of sourdough, he made a sandwich of cheese and salami and took a bite, barely noticing the taste or textures like he normally would.

Normal was nowhere to be found today. He had multiple files open on both his desk and his computer, but none of them had managed to hold his attention. Sweeping the physical files into a pile, he tossed them onto the bench behind him. Taking another bite, he set his computer to sleep mode.

Ginevra gestured to the brightly wrapped present on top of his filing cabinet. 'You haven't opened Frankie's gift yet.'

He did his best not to scowl. 'I'm saving it as a reward for when I have finished my work.'

'There's more to life than work, Dante.'

Her words were reminiscent of the ones Frankie had spoken. 'Work is important.'

'Not more important than family or love, though.'

'I agree. It is why I have taken this time off to create a restaurant to celebrate Nonno.'

She was silent for so long he shifted on his seat. 'You wish to say something?'

Shadowed eyes met his. 'I know what happened between your father and me marked you dreadfully.'

'*Mamma*—'

'No, let me finish, Dante. Just because things didn't work out between your father and me, does not mean that love isn't worth fighting for.'

'He broke your heart. He abandoned you and—'

'And I have found love again.'

Her words punched the breath from his body.

'His name is Roberto and you will meet him next week when he arrives for a visit.' His heart kicked at her sudden smile. It transformed her face in a way he'd never seen before. 'He makes me happy, Dante.'

'I am very happy for you, Mamma.' He came around from behind the desk to embrace her. 'I look forward to meeting him.'

His mother drew back, gripping his hands. 'Why did you let your Frankie go when you love her so?'

Love her? He didn't—

It was suddenly hard to get air into his lungs. He loved Frankie? But—

He loved Frankie!

It explained this darkness in his soul, explained why nothing made sense now that she was gone.

Whirling away, he paced, hands clenching and un-clenching. 'How did you find the courage to love again when it ended so badly the first time?' he demanded of his mother.

'Love, when you find it, makes your whole life better, Dante. In every respect. I fought it for a long time. But some people are worth risking your heart for.'

Some people are worth risking your heart for.

He lowered himself to his chair, his mother's words going around and around in his mind.

'Dante.'

He glanced up.

'Do you really think Frankie would treat your heart with cruelty and trample all over it? Do you think she is selfish and without compassion?'

He shot to his feet. 'She is everything that is kind and generous!'

And he'd driven her away.

Ginevra said nothing more. Simply glanced at the gift Frankie had left, before pulling a folded sheet of paper from her pocket and placing it on the table beside the plate of food. Then she left.

He stared at the note. He stared at Frankie's gift. With a smothered oath, he seized the gift and unwrapped it, his heart clenching when he unwrapped the object from its protective blanket. She'd given him Leilani. Her beautiful Hawaiian ukulele. The ukulele she'd said she'd aspired to play well. The ukulele of her dreams.

His throat thickened.

She'd left no card, but she had printed out the music and the finger chart for 'You Are My Sunshine'. Scrawled across the bottom of it in her messy handwriting, she'd written:

To play whenever you need to relax or are feeling blue.

He immediately began strumming the chords she'd taught him. And while his heart remained just as heavy, playing and singing helped to push back some of the darkness that engulfed him.

He played it twice before reaching for his mother's note and unfolding it. Everything inside of him stiffened when he realised what she'd given him—Frankie's projected itinerary for the next month.

Some people are worth risking your heart for.

He played the song one more time, staring at Frankie's itinerary. By the time he reached the end he knew exactly what he had to do.

CHAPTER ELEVEN

CAREFREE AND HAPPY-GO-LUCKY.

Frankie wanted to throw her head back and laugh—harsh ugly laughter. It didn't matter how many times she repeated the words, she couldn't make herself feel anything but heavy, sad…heartbroken.

'This wasn't part of the plan, Nonna,' she whispered.

Not that she'd stuck to the plan. When she'd left Riposo and Dante seven days ago, she'd been planning to spend the night in Lucca—to further explore the town of her forbears. But when she'd arrived, all she'd been able to think about was the day she'd spent there with Dante.

She hadn't even switched off Bertha's engine. Instead, she'd slammed her foot to the accelerator and raced out of town. She'd driven to Pisa, but that hadn't felt far enough away from the memories that plagued her, so she'd continued on until her eyes were too gritty to keep driving any longer. She'd stayed overnight in a tiny hotel in a town whose name she couldn't pronounce.

And now, today, she'd driven through ridiculously scenic Val d'Orcia with its rolling golden hills and cypress trees, and so much beauty it should fill her soul. The photo opportunities had been plentiful, and she'd dutifully stopped to take said photographs because it was expected. She'd sent various photos to her mother and Audrey. She didn't want anyone worrying about her. She wanted them all thinking she was having the time of her life.

She hadn't stayed in one place for longer than a night, though. Some nights she'd stayed in camping grounds sleeping in Bertha. Others she'd spent in a hotel. For the last two nights, though, she'd stayed in a tiny room at a Renaissance inn with breathtaking views.

Her phone rang as she walked into her room now. Glancing at the caller ID, she dragged in a breath, and donned a happy voice. 'Audrey! How are things? Did you get the picture I sent earlier?'

'I did. Thank you. Oh, Frankie, you're travelling through the most beautiful countryside!'

She stiffened. 'What's wrong?'

'Nothing! I just...'

'Audrey...' She used her bossy doctor voice. She knew Audrey too well. Something was up.

'Oh, heavens, Frankie, I hardly know where to start! You know the package Nonna wanted me to deliver to Aunt Beatrice?'

Aunt Beatrice had been Nonna's best friend. She'd visited them in Australia several times. Nonna had tasked Audrey with hand delivering a *'very special package'* to Beatrice. They'd thought it was simply an excuse to ensure Audrey had a holiday.

'Well apparently that package included all the details of my mother's family.'

Frankie straightened. 'No way!'

'And, Frankie, you won't believe it but they're an old aristocratic family that goes back centuries.'

Her heart beat hard. This was such momentous news. 'Are you okay?'

'I...think so.'

She let out a breath. Audrey sounded shell-shocked, but not upset. 'What are they like?'

'They're so different to our family, Frankie.'

'Do you want me to come to Lake Como?' If Audrey needed her support, she'd be there in a heartbeat.

'Thanks, Frankie, but I think this is something I have to do myself.'

She understood that. 'Okay, but don't forget I'm only a phone call away.'

'I know.'

'If you need the cavalry to ride in, Bertha and I can be in Lake Como in under five hours.'

'That won't be necessary.'

Audrey's laugh helped allay some of Frankie's worry.

'They're going to love you, Audrey. I promise you.'

'Thanks, Frankie,' she whispered. 'Love you.'

'Love you too.'

Frankie stared at her phone when they rang off, hoping with all her heart that things worked out for Audrey. Her cousin deserved everything good that life had to offer—including a family who appreciated her.

She glanced around her room, sat on the bed, but the walls felt as if they were pressing in on her. Muttering a curse, she grabbed Saffy and headed back outside.

Carefree and happy-go-lucky.

Not knowing what to do, she wound down whimsical cobbled alleyways until she eventually found herself in a square with a glorious view of the early evening sunset. Planting herself at a wrought iron table beneath a lime tree, she ordered a glass of white wine and forced herself to do a meditation exercise.

It had been seven days. It was time to stop indulging in self-pity and wallowing in such sadness. She might miss

Dante with the same fierceness she'd miss a limb, but that didn't change the fact that he didn't love her.

Nor was she silly enough to believe that she could recover from a broken heart in seven days. It would take a long time for her heart to stop pining for him. But that didn't mean she couldn't turn her face to the future. It didn't mean she couldn't still enjoy things.

She was going to be a GP—a family doctor—and the realisation that it was the perfect path for her made her thankful. She focussed on that feeling for a little while— the freedom, the cessation of the constant, chafing stress. When her wine came, she silently toasted the sunset and Nonna. She'd accomplished what she'd set out to do on this trip—to decide her future. And that future looked and felt bright and right.

But Dante...

She resolutely pushed all thoughts of him from her head, picked up Saffy and idly started strumming. It was time to make way for fun and frivolity and simple pleasures again. They might not mend a broken heart, but they'd help it become easier to bear.

She sang 'Over the Rainbow', because, of course, it was *the* iconic ukulele song. She stared at the view and sipped her wine and tried to not compare it to Riposo's Pinot Grigio. Unable to stop herself, even though the song held too many memories of Dante, she played 'You Are My Sunshine'.

Eventually she became aware of someone to her left singing too in a lovely deep baritone.

When the song ended, a shadow fell over the table and a deep, rich voice asked, 'May I take a seat?'

Her breath caught in her throat. All she could do was stare. *Dante!*

What on earth was he doing here? Was it a coincidence

or had he come looking for her? If he'd come looking for her then why—

Of course it's a coincidence.

He sat and nodded towards her glass. 'How is the wine?'

'Nothing to write home about.' She couldn't believe her voice actually worked.

'That is an expression I do not know, but I can guess it's meaning.'

He took her glass and sniffed the contents before setting it back down with a shake of his head. Calling the waiter over, he ordered two glasses of a wine she'd never heard of before.

'Try this,' he ordered when it arrived.

She did and it was perfection. It tasted like moonlight and the stars and happy thoughts. 'Delicious,' she agreed, fighting the urge to cry.

'Have you tried the Pecorino yet? It is what this town is known for.'

He was here to buy Pecorino? She should've known. Pushing her shoulders back, she kept her chin high. 'I hope everyone at Riposo is well?'

'*Si.* Very well.'

'And you're here to buy Pecorino?'

'I'm here to find you.'

She blinked.

'You have been very hard to find.' His brow furrowed and he pulled a piece of paper from his pocket and set it on the table, stabbed a finger at it. 'You were supposed to follow this!'

She glanced at it. Her itinerary!

She glanced back at him. He looked enraged and baffled. She noted the tired lines fanning from his eyes and the deep grooves bracketing his mouth. Before she could stop herself, she covered his hand with hers. 'Are you all right, Dante?'

'No, I am not all right,' he shot back, glaring at her. 'I have been half out of my mind with worry for you. I have been searching for you all this time.'

All this time? 'Who has been cooking at Lorenzo's?'

'Carlo. He is very good.'

Dante had left his second-in-command *in charge* of Lorenzo's kitchen?

'Finding you was more important.'

The set of his mouth had her blood pounding. 'Why did you need to find me?'

She went to move her hand, but he caught it in both of his. 'Because you are my sunshine, Frankie. I was afraid I would never be able to find you so I could tell you that.'

He...

Was...

What?

'I love you, *cara*, heart and soul. It is just that I did not realise until you were gone. And I know you have no reason to trust me, but the words I speak are true. My mother called me an idiot for letting you go.'

Ginevra had...?

'She made me see that there are some people worth risking your heart for. And I do not have any expectations that you feel the same way about me, Frankie. But I think, if given a chance, I could eventually win you over.'

He had her heart, but her throat had closed over and she couldn't push a single sound out.

'All my life I have considered *happy-go-lucky* and *charming* synonyms for irresponsibility and recklessness, but you proved to me otherwise. In this same way, I have always considered emotion a bad thing—something that is misleading and not to be trusted. Hence the reason I have always focussed on work and practical things. But again, I have been wrong. The right kind of emotion is—' His face lit up. 'It is nourishment for the soul in the way a delicious meal is nourishment for the body.'

Her mouth fell open.

His hands tightened about hers. 'I have considered very closely the kind of life that will make you happy. I have researched how you can practise medicine in Italy. It is not straightforward…there are exams—'

There were always exams.

'Or you can complete your specialisation in Australia and then register to have your qualification recognised. This of course means conducting a long-distance love affair for a year, but I will do anything to make you happy.'

The lump in her throat grew.

'Once those things are done, however, it would be possible to establish a practise wherever you would like in Italy. And I will be your sponsor in every way I can to help ensure all goes smoothly.'

'I…'

'That leads us to where we would live. And I think that, if you are agreeable, we would live at Riposo.'

She tried not to gape. 'What about Rome?'

'Rome would not make you happy.' His eyes gentled. 'And you were right. I am not living the life that would make me happy. Not deep down in my heart. I will work on handing over the reins of my business concerns to my executive team. And then I mean to take over as head chef at Lorenzo's for good.'

Dante was choosing happiness over duty and security? The thought stole her breath.

'I have also considered the possibility that you would like to reside in Australia.' He gave a careless shrug. 'In which case I will relocate to Melbourne or wherever it is you decide to live.'

'You can't— Your family!'

'I love them, *cara*, but it is you who are my sunshine. Without you, there is no joy in anything I do and no meaning in my life.'

She pressed her free hand over her madly beating heart to stop it from pounding out of her chest.

Those dark eyes speared hers, holding her captive. 'You know what my greatest fear is, Frankie.'

She swallowed. 'To lose all your money and be left destitute once again.'

Those eyes smiled at her. 'The thought of losing you is ten times worse. If it would help to win your heart. I will freely give you my entire fortune.'

She shot back in her chair. 'You can't do that!'

One careless shoulder lifted. 'I know you would not wield it against me with cruelty or fritter it away in gambling or some other vice. You are an honourable woman. And if it would give you a sense of security to be the one controlling the purse strings then I would hand them to you without a moment's hesitation. I want you to know that I not only respect you, but that I trust you.'

The words he was saying, they were too much. Her mind blanked, but her body burned and fluttered.

'And maybe one day, if you decide you love me too, we could have children.'

Her eyes filled.

He gripped both her hands, suddenly urgent. 'Please, Frankie, tell me that I at least have a chance of winning your heart? I will do—'

Reaching across she pressed her fingers to his lips. 'Dante, you cannot win what is already yours. I love you with every part of myself, and I want the life you describe to me with all of my being.'

He stared at her in incomprehension, clearly not expecting such an answer, and then his face lit up with such delight it heated her blood. And then she was in his arms and he was kissing her with such fervent gratitude her head spun. She didn't know how long it was before he lifted his head, but her entire body fizzed with desire and happiness.

'You will come home with me tonight to Riposo?'

She sent him a slow smile. 'My hotel room is closer.'

His eyes twinkled in a way she'd never seen before. 'But I did not bring pyjamas or a toothbrush.'

'We can buy you a toothbrush, and you won't need pyjamas. We can go home tomorrow.'

He sobered. 'Will you be happy to live at Riposo? My family is all there and maybe you will find it too much.'

'Never,' she vowed. 'I love your family.'

He smiled. 'I do too, but I would sometimes like to have you all to myself.'

'We can always camp out in Bertha.'

'*Si*, that is perfect! Though I do not expect my family will remain at the villa for much longer. Mamma is in love, and I suspect she will soon want a place of her own. Sofia is talking about returning to Rome and taking up an internship in my company, while Maria and Giorgia say it is too much to live with their brother and want to rent a place in the town so they can go out at night and *"have more freedom"*.' He frowned. 'Should I be worried?'

'No, you should not,' she told him with a laugh. 'And speaking of families, I took your advice and have spoken to both my mother and grandfather and told them of my plans. They were disappointed, but when I told them how happy this would make me, they accepted it. They even said they were happy for me.'

'But that is excellent news!'

He grinned at her and she couldn't help but grin back.

'I have more family news too,' he said. 'You will not know the name, Antonio, but you will remember the man whose life you saved.'

'The man who had a heart attack? Is he doing well?'

'He is making a good recovery, but here is the thing—he was a spy, sent by my aunt. He is her lover. They were looking for ways to undermine the restaurant.'

Her hand flew to her mouth.

'They were jealous that I had thought of creating a restaurant to honour Lorenzo. They wished they'd thought of it first. They wanted to put the restaurant out of business.'

She folded her arms. 'Which is ridiculously childish!'

'But she was so grateful that we saved her lover's life that she has given up her grudge and apologised. When I asked her, wasn't it time we were friends? she agreed.'

She leaned towards him. 'Really?'

'*Si.* It is a start.'

She pressed a hand to cheek. 'It would've made Lorenzo very happy.'

'*Si.*' His eyes darkened. 'But not as happy as you make me, Frankie. I thought I had lost you, and they were the darkest days of my life.'

'I know. This last week has been one of the worst of my life too. But now we've found one another, we won't ever lose each other again. I'll take care of your heart and you'll take care of mine.'

'This is something I solemnly vow to you.' His eyes never left hers. 'I will love you and take care of you forever.'

'Forever,' she agreed. 'And tomorrow we'll return home to Riposo.' Her home of rest. Who knew six weeks ago, all she would find there? 'And we'll work out the logistics of our future then.' The important thing was that they had a future. *Together.* 'In the meantime, Dante, I think you better kiss me again.'

He did, and then reached for her ukulele and played 'You Are My Sunshine' with all of his love for her shining from his eyes, and without making a single mistake. Which meant she then had to kiss him again. And again.

* * * * *

COMING SOON!

We really hope you enjoyed reading this book. If you're looking for more romance, be sure to head to the shops when new books are available on

Thursday 2nd March

To see which titles are coming soon, please visit
millsandboon.co.uk/nextmonth

MILLS & BOON

MILLS & BOON®

Coming next month

BILLIONAIRE'S ISLAND TEMPTATION
Rachael Stewart

"I'm sorry, Jessie." He squeezed his eyes shut to her appeal, pressed his forehead to hers as he dragged in a breath. "We shouldn't be—I shouldn't be doing this."

"Why? What did I say? Is it the job?"

He backed away as though stung, shaking his head.

"Joel?" She pushed off the side, closing the distance he'd created, trying to get into his line of sight but he wouldn't let her.

"I don't work here!" he rushed out before anything could get in the way again.

"I don't—you what?" He could hear the confusion in her tone, sense her frown. "But you were working, today, earlier…? I thought…"

His eyes found hers on impulse, guilt chewing him up inside. But this hadn't been his fault. He hadn't intended to mislead her. And he'd certainly never told her anything of the sort. She'd assumed and he hadn't corrected her.

Which was hardly any better…

"Hang on…" She raised a hand to cut him off. "Just back up a step."

Propping a hand on her hip, she pinned him with her stare, the fire behind her eyes morphing into something else. "If you don't work here and yet, you are here, just who exactly are you?"

He raked his teeth over his lower lip, held her eye without wavering. "A guest." Her brows nudged up, her eyes widening. "Or I was until your arrival…at which point I was supposed to leave to make way for you, but then we had a blow out in the jeep which took us down a ditch and by the time we got back on the road, it was too late for the plane to depart so Paolo and I went to Basil's for a drink and something to eat and I intended to explain myself tomorrow morning but then I came in here and…"

And breathe.

He gestured to her, his smile half-cocked. "Need I say more?"

She was staring at him, her eyes racing with thoughts that only she was privy to. In all honesty, he thought he'd done a pretty good job of explaining himself, even if it was a bit of a ramble, so maybe—

"Are you for real?"

Okay, so maybe not.

Continue reading
BILLIONAIRE'S ISLAND TEMPTATION
Rachael Stewart

Available next month
www.millsandboon.co.uk